Unbound

Peyton Corinne is a *USA Today* bestselling author of romantic fiction with high emotional vulnerability, angst, and heart. She has been telling stories since before she could read, and has never stopped pursuing a life in writing and authorship. If she's not currently dreaming up new worlds and characters, Peyton is at home making another cup of coffee, listening to new music, or reading every type of romance she can get her hands on.

Visit PeytonCorinne.com and follow @PeytonCorinneAuthor on Instagram and TikTok for more.

Unbound

PEYTON CORINNE

HODDER &
STOUGHTON

First published in Great Britain in 2026 by Hodder & Stoughton Limited
An Hachette UK company

The authorised representative in the EEA is Hachette Ireland,
8 Castlecourt Centre, Dublin 15, D15 XTP3, Ireland (email: info@hbgi.ie)

3

Copyright © Peyton Corinne Satterfield 2026

The right of Peyton Corinne to be identified as the Author of the
Work has been asserted by her in accordance with
the Copyright, Designs and Patents Act 1988.

Internal design © Atria 2026

All rights reserved. No part of this publication may be reproduced, stored
in a retrieval system, or transmitted, in any form or by any means without
the prior written permission of the publisher, nor be otherwise circulated
in any form of binding or cover other than that in which it is published and
without a similar condition being imposed on the subsequent purchaser.

All characters in this publication are fictitious and any resemblance to real
persons, living or dead, is purely coincidental.

A CIP catalogue record for this title is available from the British Library

Paperback ISBN 978 1 399 75626 6
ebook ISBN 978 1 399 75627 3

Typeset in Minion Pro

Printed and bound in Great Britain by Clays Ltd, Elcograf S.p.A.

Hodder & Stoughton policy is to use papers that are natural, renewable
and recyclable products and made from wood grown in sustainable forests.
The logging and manufacturing processes are expected to conform
to the environmental regulations of the country of origin.

Hodder & Stoughton Limited
Carmelite House
50 Victoria Embankment
London EC4Y 0DZ

www.hodder.co.uk

*To the ones who had to put on armor every day,
no matter how heavy it was or how much it hurt—
this one is for you.*

AUTHOR'S NOTE

This book is very special, near and dear to my heart. In these pages you will find a beautiful romance between two people who deserve the world. You will also find a few serious topics discussed.

Bennett Reiner, one of the main characters in *Unbound*, is autistic and deals with diagnosed obsessive-compulsive disorder. He has been in therapy since he was a child for both. During the formation of his character and throughout every draft of this book, I was able to work with Monica Rush, PsyD, on every facet of him as well as the on-page therapy scenes, in hopes to give the most accurate depiction I could. I am incredibly grateful to Dr. Rush for her guidance in every little piece. My hope is that the grace with which I approached this character allows many of you to see yourselves reflected in him. For any reader to see themselves in one of my characters is so often my greatest hope in writing.

And while my books are always romantic, there may be some themes that are triggering for some readers. If you feel trigger warnings are spoilers or do not need them, please skip the next paragraph.

This book contains on-page depictions of obsessive thought spirals, compulsive acts, and panic attacks. There are mentions and discussions of childhood trauma, child neglect, sexual abuse, and grooming of a minor.

Be kind to your brain, friends.

PLAYLIST

Love Letter from the Sea to the Shore • *Delaney Bailey*
World Spins Madly On • *The Weepies*
Doing Fine • *Eliza McLamb*
Like Real People Do • *Hozier*
Garden Song • *Phoebe Bridgers*
Picking Flowers • *Boy In Space*
The Prophecy • *Taylor Swift*
Cutting My Fingers Off • *Turnover*
Flight Risk • *Tommy Lefroy*
the lakes • *Taylor Swift*
I Don't Like My Mind • *Mitski*
Fuck Me Eyes • *Ethel Cain*
We Hug Now • *Sydney Rose*
Satellite • *Harry Styles*
Hold My Name • *Ocie Elliott*
Big Black Car • *Gregory Alan Isakov*
Cinnamon Girl • *Lana Del Rey*
Funeral • *Phoebe Bridgers*
when the party's over • *Billie Eilish*
Feels Like • *Gracie Abrams*
Sailor Song • *Gigi Perez*
Beach Baby • *Bon Iver*
Tonight You Are Mine • *The Technicolors*
Rosyln • *Bon Iver, St. Vincent*
If U Love Me Now • *MUNA*

Crystal • *Stevie Nicks*
Rockland • *Gracie Abrams*
back to friends • *sombr*
Hearing Damage • *Thom Yorke*
Words • *Gregory Alan Isakov*
You're the Only Good Thing in My Life • *Cigarettes After Sex*
With Or Without You • *U2*
Sullen Girl • *Fiona Apple*
Unknown/Nth • *Hozier*
Lust for Life • *Lana Del Rey ft. The Weeknd*
S P E Y S I D E • *Bon Iver*
We'll Never Have Sex • *Leith Ross*
Each Coming Night • *Iron & Wine*
Decimal • *Novo Amor*
anything • *Adrianne Lenker*
At The Beach, In Every Life • *Gigi Perez*
Sky Blue and Black • *Jackson Browne*
would've been you • *sombr*
Alright • *Keaton Henson*
Rivers In Your Mouth • *Ben Howard*
Let's Talk About Your Hair • *Have Mercy*
Silver Spoon • *Erin LeCount*
What Was I Made For? • *Billie Eilish*
champagne problems • *Taylor Swift*
lover's grip • *Them & I*
Can't Deny My Love • *Brandon Flowers*
Gibson Girl • *Ethel Cain*
How to Disappear Completely • *Radiohead*

Bones • *Ben Howard*
Little Freak • *Harry Styles*
Cherry • *Lana Del Rey*
Paris • *Taylor Swift*
Old Pine • *Ben Howard*
Strangers • *Ethel Cain*
not a lot, just forever • *Adrianne Lenker*
runnning in place at the edge of the map • *Runnner*
Movement • *Hozier*
Me & My Dog • *boygenius*
Let Down • *Radiohead*
True Blue • *boygenius*
The City and the River • *The Rescues*
You Are in Love • *Taylor Swift*

PROLOGUE

THREE MONTHS AGO: Senior Year, October

Bennett

It's late and the party is a little overwhelming, but the beer I've had is slowly taking the edge off.

We won our game—hard fought, but a great win. Rhys, my best friend and our captain, has already disappeared with Sadie, his new girlfriend, up the stairs, while I meander through the irritatingly messy kitchen for another one of my carefully stashed IPAs.

"She's so far gone," someone mutters, stepping up beside me in the mostly empty kitchen. "But that's usual for Paloma."

The name works down my body like an ice cube slipping across my spine.

Paloma.

I clench my fist tight, putting the beer back in the fridge and closing the door with a stiff shake of my head. I don't hear another word before I'm answering a call for help that she didn't make, shoving through sweat-damp bodies and out the back door.

"Hey, Ben—"

I ignore Holden, a kindhearted defenseman from the first line, and edge around him until I spot her. Her head is lulling into her hands. Bright blond curls cascade in a tangle to cover her face.

We don't usually do this, both accustomed to hiding our history from those around us, but there will never be a day I'll let her hurt or suffer. The way I feel about Paloma Blake is both a leash around my heart and a noose around my throat, threatening me in every capacity.

"Hey, P," I try, dropping to my knees in front of her. "You okay?"

Brushing back tendrils of blond, I meet her half-lidded brown eyes, my stomach in knots.

"Bennett," she breathes, almost in wonder. Like seeing me before her is something divine.

"Let me take you home," I whisper, body hunched to not frighten her, but shoulders hiked to block her from view as much as I can manage.

She shakes her head slowly, her plump bottom lip sticking out in a pout.

"I don't want to go."

A sigh works from my mouth, and I start to stand back up. Paloma's hand reaches for me, scrambling fingers latching onto my belt loop.

"Don't go," she whispers, her hand flat against the fabric of my pants. Heat emanates from my face, but I bend back down to her level in the chair.

"Then let me take you upstairs."

"I thought you said I couldn't sleep with you anymore." She hiccups, eyes watery, pupils blown. Her fingers move gently, grasping at my waistband.

"I changed my mind. C'mon, P." I scoop her up and carry her inside. Halfway up the stairs, she grasps my shirt.

"Wait," she says, so quiet I almost don't hear her. "I don't wanna sleep yet."

My brow furrows. "Why not?" She shakes her head, eyes dropping. "Nightmares again?"

"Yeah." Her soft admission brushes over my skin. I seat us on the stairs, far enough up that we're mostly covered in the shadowed lighting of the second floor.

"We can just sit for a little then. People watch." Paloma smiles gently at me, and I can't help the matching grin that slips out. "Lay down if you want, P."

She slips her head onto my lap, and my hand combs the tangles from her difficult, hair-sprayed style. Slow and attentive, I smooth the strands.

It's much later, the party finally dwindling to nothing, when I finally maneuver her up into my arms, carrying her bridal-style up the rest of the stairs and into my room. Mere seconds after I've laid her down on the bed, my black lab, Seven, is whining and pressing his nose into her hair, her shoulder, anything he can reach from his patient position on the floor.

"Shh." I bat him away slightly, but Paloma's lips move into a gentle grin as she reaches blindly for him.

"My baby," she mutters, and my mouth hitches into a bright smile. "C'mere, Seven."

He doesn't wait for my permission before hopping up into her arms to loll his head next to hers.

My dog is loyal to a fault, has protected her from the first day he met her. When I first started coming home without her, Seven whimpered and whined, echoing my own grief of it all. He still whines at least once when I show up at home without her.

Now, his tail wags happily as he snuggles into her on the bed.

"Did you want a shower, P?"

She shakes her head, eyes half lidded as she gazes up at me. "Too tired."

I comb back a few strands of her hair, pressing a kiss to her forehead. Her fingers lazily graze the sides of my jaw where I've recently shaved.

"Sometimes I think you're not real," she murmurs, soft and

sleepy. "That I dreamed you up." Her brown eyes are burning, almost distraught as she takes me in. I feel like I'm losing her in real time, so I sink into the mattress and tighten my arms around her.

As if that might keep her here.

As if that might make her *mine* again. How it's supposed to be.

The soft glow of the lamp dances over Paloma's face as she drifts to sleep.

Once, she'd told me she didn't like total darkness. "*I don't like finding my way in the dark,*" she'd admitted softly, shrinking in on herself. "*Like when I turn off the light and it's too dark and my eyes haven't adjusted. I just . . . I don't like not being able to tell where I am.*"

Now, I always keep it on for her, an amber hue to everything in my simple room. It won't be long before she rouses, usually frightened at first, and then hungry when she realizes she's here, safe with me.

It's our routine now. It hurts, but I worry it would hurt infinitely worse to not know if she was okay.

To always be wondering.

So, for now, this is enough. I'll take whatever she's willing to give—even if it's only this, forever.

CHAPTER 1

NOW: Senior Year, January

Bennett

"Sometimes I think you're not real," she whispers, her hands tracing my jaw lightly, brown eyes burning enough that my throat catches. "That I dreamed you up."

Then she opens her mouth again. She's asking me something—begging me—but her words are silent screams and no matter how much I plead, I can't hear her.

I feel a little like I want to cry, enough that my hand reaches up to rub at my eyes.

Water—not tears.

The harsh spray of the shower turns painful. My focus shifts to the soap suds sliding down my body to swirl into the drain, shaking me from the memory.

She's not here. I'm alone. Again, I remind myself, a harsh but necessary mantra.

I'm in the shower. She's not here.

I'm in the shower and she is gone. Remember.

I press my hands to the tile, breathing harshly as I try to center myself. I count the scattered black squares amongst the gray tiles again, then reach for my body wash *again*—despite how inflamed my skin is from the steaming hot shower I've been standing in too long already.

It's the only way to make the vision of her disappear.

Today is a game day, which means I need to get back into my routines before something completely derails my focus.

I pull on gray sweats and a Waterfell athletic tee, then let Seven meander to the door as I fold down my sheets and set my hockey bag by my desk, my lucky sweatshirt folded perfectly atop it, the chewed edge of the sleeve tucked away.

As I go to turn off the lamp, a small rush of anxiety threatens, and I decide to keep it on.

Don't be ridiculous. Turn it off. No one needs the nightlight. She doesn't need it anymore, just like she doesn't need you—

I leave, the lamplight still casting an amber glow over my room.

Impulsively, I check my phone again—no new notifications. It's not surprising, but it doesn't hurt any less. I haven't heard from her, or even *seen* her, since October.

Seven nudges my leg when he realizes I've frozen—just a check, to make sure I'm okay.

My hand taps his head and I start toward the kitchen, attempting to leave the memory of her behind, safe in my room. To pretend I didn't wake up to empty, cold sheets the next morning. That I didn't worry about her so much over the months after that I started driving through downtown Waterfell over Christmas break to make sure she was okay. That she was safe.

Checking the group chat to see if anyone is up yet, I send a quick text to Holden inviting him to our "family breakfast," as Freddy has taken to calling it. His response irks me: *Is Toren invited?*

I can say yes, knowing the well-hated defenseman on our line won't show. But the word still feels like some sort of betrayal.

Toren Kane hit Rhys on the ice during our Frozen Four game last year, ending his season as he was stretchered off. My best friend, broken and bleeding and terrified—and I couldn't do anything to help him.

Then, our coach decided to recruit Toren—despite his history with our team and his reputation on the ice.

I was fully prepared to hate the guy when he was announced, to follow my captain and best friend's lead and do what needed to be done to get him off Rhys's line.

But since then, Toren has started making my job easier. He is easily the *best* defenseman that I've ever played with. That was hard to ignore, but I did, because my loyalty will always be to Rhys.

But then I saw him defend Ro—Freddy's tutor-turned-girlfriend and Sadie's best friend. He didn't know the girl, didn't care about anything other than stopping an asshole from hurting a defenseless person. After that, it became harder *not* to like him.

But I'm a good secret keeper, even if I don't have many myself.

Though, I have one secret I keep above all else. The most important one.

"You're the only thing I've ever cared about. Ever. And I—"

Shaking away the sound of her voice—though it's far away and swimming in a sea of painful memories—I start to work on our usual pregame breakfast, turning my music on and letting "World Spins Madly On" by the Weepies play through our speakers in the kitchen. I check the group thread again—no one has answered Holden's question, so I don't either. When it comes to Toren Kane, I'll follow Rhys's lead.

I gather eggs for omelets, mix and buttermilk for pancakes. Plenty of meat and carbs for a late-afternoon game. A full menu spread for our very full house. It's warm and loud with love, but it doesn't do much to stop the constant hollow ache in my chest. A permanent scar of something missing.

A high-pitched giggle signals the end of my slower morning ritual; Liam appears first, followed by Rhys dressed only in his boxers as he scoops the seven-year-old up off the hardwood and over his shoulder.

"Morning, Bennett," my best friend says with a smirk, speaking over the loudly screeching child. "Sorry about that."

Rhys's girlfriend Sadie, a figure skater at our school, rounds the corner after them, face burning red. Last summer the two struck up a secret friendship that inevitably turned into more. She was able to fix the things that were broken in my best friend more than I ever had—for that, she has my unending loyalty. She and her little brothers—both of whom stay with us now and again. Usually, they stay with Rhys's parents—Max and Anna Koteskiy—but when they miss their sister and the timing works out, they stay in our spare room.

"All good. I'm making breakfast. For everyone."

Rhys nods. "I'll inform the lazy ones."

"Put me down—"

"I told you, Liam, no more coming into our room without knocking or we'll have to lock the door," Sadie grumbles, eyes wide awake at an earlier hour for her than I'm used to.

"Oh? Did the little man see more of my captain than he should?" Freddy yawns through his joke, smacking a shoulder into the doorframe as he stumbles into the kitchen in only a pair of boxer briefs.

"He's currently seeing more of *you* than anyone ever should," Sadie snaps. "Put some fucking clothes on."

Liam laughs louder now, face red from lack of breath because he's so tickled. "You said a bad word, Sissy."

"Yeah, *Sissy*," Freddy laughs, hip checking the much smaller girl as he passes her. "Besides, I'm literally wearing the exact same thing as your boyfriend!"

"It's different." Sadie fakes a gag and covers her eyes.

"If Ro were here, she'd be very mad at you."

Rosalie Shariff has been dating our left winger Freddy for who knows how long—though my suspicions are for far longer than they'll admit to. She tutored him last semester, came to nearly every one of our games as his *friend*—since then, they've been inseparable. And unbearable to be around with their intense flirting and never-quite-hidden intimacy all over our house.

"Where exactly is my roommate?" Sadie asks.

It is strange. Ro is usually the first one up with me.

Freddy is beaming ear to ear as he starts to open his mouth—leaving both Rhys and me to groan before he's said anything.

"Let's just say it's a good thing we lock our door. Your roommate is a menace, Brown. She kept me up all night—I'm exhausted—"

"All right." Rhys cuts him off. Liam is repositioned onto his hip now, *Star Wars* pajama shirt stretched out nearly off his shoulder. Both of them have bedhead, messy locks brushing each other as Liam leans to rest his head on Rhys's shoulder, like it might soften him out of trouble with his sister. "Everyone get dressed for family breakfast. Freddy—boxers do not count. You need a shirt. Liam—"

"Please don't lock the door. How do I come in if I have a nightmare?"

The puppy eyes Liam is sending Rhys are practiced, but my captain is soft as butter when it comes to the entire Brown family. Sadie has always played parent to her brothers when she needs to, but Rhys isn't used to being anything but a gentle friend.

"You *have* to knock," he finally says, but the words are accompanied by a tight hug before he sweeps Liam up onto his shoulder.

"He must've walked in on something *good*," Freddy murmurs beneath his breath, tapping me on the shoulder as he passes to go back upstairs.

Rhys blushed again at Freddy's words and a chuckle works its way through my lips.

"Do I want to know?" I ask Sadie quietly, arms crossed. She looks up at me and shakes her head.

"Nope."

They all exit to properly dress while I start on pancakes, waffles, eggs, and everything any of them has ever requested for breakfast. Once the table is full with both food and my friends, we all settle in.

Mornings are loud now, where they used to be quiet. I wouldn't trade it for anything.

But that doesn't mean it isn't hard. It's hard not to notice where I sit: at the head of the table, alone. That while Rhys watches over Sadie at his side, and Ro watches over Freddy, the one person I want to take care of most isn't here, letting me watch over her. I worry she never will be.

It's easy to imagine Paloma here, sitting at a chair pulled up beside me. Eating the food I made for her, warm feet tucked under my thigh, bundled up in a sweatshirt with a messy braid. Maybe she'd let me feed her. Maybe she'd talk with everyone—or she'd be like me. Quiet, just taking it all in.

But she's not here.

"Sometimes I think you're not real. That I dreamed you—"

I shake my head, shoulder twitching to my ear.

Everyone thinks Paloma is the party girl. A good time, fun and drunk and smiling. They think she thrives under burning strobes and a moshing sea of bodies.

But I know her.

I know she likes quiet most, or an early morning when only the distant noise of birds chirping fills the space. I know she plays ocean sounds to fall asleep, that she's at peace when she's in the water. I know that she would rather sit in complete silence, in my clothes, in my room, than attend another party.

But I also know she'd willingly choose to cause herself more pain than ever allow herself to have those things.

I really know her. I might be the only one who does.

My Paloma Blake is a secret I will always keep safe, closest to my heart.

CHAPTER 2

NOW

Paloma

The cold night air bites at my cheeks harshly instead of relieving my overheated skin like I'd hoped it might.

"You sure you don't need a ride?"

I'd rather gouge my eyes out with my dull kitten heels.

"I'm fine, thanks," I say, pretending to search for my keys while keeping a close eye on the man just feet away. Saying I'm scared wouldn't be correct. I'm just cautious. Aware. I've seen enough of the malice of ordinary men that I don't underestimate any of them.

"You did well, Ms. Blake," he praises me. I let it bounce off me easily. He might as well have said, *You didn't scream when I put my hand on your thigh beneath the table.* This was supposed to be a job interview, not an hour for him to openly leer at me. "We'll be in touch."

"Great."

I hope I never see him again.

Frustrated and still a bit shaken up by the whole thing, I pretend to text on my phone and walk into the still-open Thai place next door, just to wait for my rideshare away from him.

The low ambient lighting of the modern interior is warm and comforting. The place is mostly empty this late—except for one booth near the back filled with two couples I recognize.

Sadie Brown and Rhys Koteskiy, across from Ro Shariff and Matt Freddric.

You have got to be kidding me.

I don't chance asking myself if this night could get worse—there's always room enough for that to happen—but instead duck down a little ridiculously, hoping they haven't seen me as I squeeze back out into the frigid air.

My stomach rolls. Maybe from the constant tossing as I tried to nibble on bread through the interview, desperate to get out of there. The meeting was supposed to be a dinner with *several* of the hiring committee, but that didn't happen; now I'm starving and cold.

But it's most likely the sight of the two happy couples sharing warm food and laughing without a care in the world.

Why does she get to move on? Why can't that be me?

I attempt to shut down the ridiculous whiny train of thought before it can devour me or send me spiraling out of the controlled existence I've been working toward.

Sadie was the other half to my bad decisions junior year. I'd seen her before, at parties or in passing: a figure skater by day and a girl with a bit of a reputation by night. She had a penchant for athletes as much as I did, which meant we often ran in the same circles on accident. It wasn't hard to switch to on purpose.

It was less lonely, for both of us.

I heard what people called us. Cleat or jersey chasers, puck bunnies . . . endless names for both Sadie and me. We didn't let it bother us.

Though I did punch someone once for calling her a whore.

Once upon a time, we'd been close, thick as thieves, flouncing through frat house parties side by side. Sadie had my back, even if we'd never been actual friends.

But then, last semester, she and Rhys Koteskiy found each other. I figured it would be brief—the girl never did much beyond quick hookups or friends with benefits—but . . . they just stayed. Together. Happy. And despite all her usual hang-ups concerning relationships, she seems content.

There's a flash then, of tangled wet hair, of calloused hands carefully scrubbing every piece of sand off my skin. A big, warm sweatshirt and a handful of cheese crackers pressed to my lips as I doze off slowly on a soft chest.

Stop it. I shake my head, refocusing on the couples in the window.

Rhys tucks an arm around Sadie's shoulders and brings her closer, pressing a soft kiss to her temple before grasping her chin to direct her eyes to his. She softens for him, the angry figure skater I'm so used to gone beneath the care of the campus golden boy.

Jealousy wriggles in my gut like a fish out of water.

Sadie was stressed. She just needed help. You can't be fixed.

The reminder strikes between my ribs, but I find my balance and force myself to the car now waiting for me outside in the cold, alone.

CHAPTER 3

THEN: Freshman Year, August

Paloma

Most people have difficulty sleeping in new places. I struggle with familiar places—a mattress in the corner of a princess-themed room, a stained floral sofa, a crowded queen bed—which might explain why sleeping in my new, empty dorm room was so peaceful.

I didn't even set an alarm, ready to take advantage of the early move-in silence in the otherwise empty dorm.

Waterfell University. My new home.

I'd applied for other schools that were farther away from my hometown, but this was the only one that offered me a full ride, room and board, and a stipend for textbooks. Which meant it was the one I could afford.

It helps that I'm already half in love with it. The lush trees and well-kept landscape of campus, the ivy-covered red brick buildings, the quaint feel of the entire place, as if they dropped a big university into the middle of a small town. Only three hours away from where I grew up, and it feels like I've entered a new planet.

Which is exactly what I wanted.

I can do this.

Renewed energy courses through my veins as I toss on shoes and head out—still in my boxer shorts and oversized tee—to my car in the slightly-too-far dorm parking lot. The sun is hot on my skin, vibrant despite the early hour, and I drive around the empty campus with the windows down.

It feels like a movie.

A little too good to be true, huh, Polly? A darker voice threatens.

I shiver, closing my eyes and tossing my hair into a messy ponytail after parking in front of the school athletics complex. Once I've signed in and scanned my brand new Waterfell ID, smiling at the chipper girl who greets me, I turn toward the nearly empty lap pool.

My stomach bubbles with happiness.

I'm used to sneaking in in the middle of the night, to swim in the light of the moon. I didn't have money for a membership to any local pools and my dingy public school didn't have anything like this.

Taking a moment in the locker room to change into my swimsuit, I put on my new swim cap, careful to tuck all my recently dyed hair under the tight blue latex. Dyeing my hair over a bathroom sink on my own was hard, and it's not perfect, but I'm trying to make it last as long as I can.

Before I jump in, I shoot a picture and text it to Alessia, the woman who made this all happen. Six months ago, she'd become my lifeline, my way out of the darkness that still tried to haunt me.

PALOMA
Off to a good start!

I wait for her excited, approving text back before hiding my phone in my bag and diving in.

The water is an arctic blast against my heated skin, all at once refreshing and soothing.

Swimming has always been soothing to me. I learned on my own, accidentally, when a few older kids pushed me into someone's backyard pool. It was a birthday party, I think; my mom was there, but too drunk or high to keep an eye on me. I'd guess that most of the adults there were the same, but I can't truly recall.

The memory is hazy. But the water didn't kill me.

So, I kept finding new places that were easier to sneak into. Family pools in the nicer neighborhoods that sat abandoned during far-away summer vacations. Community spaces that assumed I was the daughter of the adults I entered beside.

It didn't matter. I made it work. I needed the water.

Now, I swim until my limbs throb and my breath is wearied, huffing through a smile that makes my cheeks ache.

This is the beginning of something new. Something better. It's the same promise I made myself while packing up my car with my handful of belongings and driving away from the darkness that made me.

My mother is standing on the threshold of my room. Her dull eyes—brown but faded—well with tears of rage or loss, I'll never know. They scan over me again.

"What did I ever do to deserve a daughter like you?" She sneers.

I can almost reshape her words in my head. Pretend she said it differently. Pretend, for a moment, that I'm still six years old and she's braiding my hair before school.

But that never happened again.

"Things *will* be different," I vow, toweling off and redressing. My clothes stick to the wet outline of my swimsuit, but the sun is bright and warm on my skin as I head back to my car. I turn my face toward the golden light through my window and crank my music louder.

I breathe in deep.

CHAPTER 4

THEN: Freshman Year, August

Bennett

"It's a little small, right?"

Max Koteskiy's laugh is as booming loud and animated as the smile on his face. I can't stop my slight flinch at the sudden sound, only settling when my dad sets a heavy hand on my shoulder.

"Of course it's small. It's a dorm."

"It's an athletics dorm, Max," my dad snips back, but his tone stays quiet and calm. "I just feel like it's too small."

For me, he means, because I need the space. This is where I should say that it's fine. *"It's only a year before we move into the house."* But it's not really fine for me. I can't force the words out, even to help my dad.

Rhys opens the door again, his arms full of boxes and his smile wide and identical to his father's, dimples gleaming. I relax slightly.

Rhys Koteskiy has been my best friend since literal birth—the proof lives on my dad's desk in a photo of him and Max holding each of us as babies in the hospital, with Anna Koteskiy in the background giving a thumbs-up and a cheery, tearful smile from her hospital bed. Since then, we've been inseparable. Even through the more difficult years for me and my family, Rhys never faltered in our friendship. Just like his dad never gave up on mine.

Our dads might've masterminded the origins of our friendship, but what we built beyond that was just ours. If we were always going to be a package deal, I am thankful to call the other half my best friend.

"Bennett?"

No one can help if you don't verbalize what's wrong.

I shake my head. "It's—the bathroom thing. Sorry, Rhys."

My best friend only smiles and shakes his head. "Not a big deal, Ben. Just want you to feel comfortable." He sets his load of cardboard onto the floor in front of him, looking toward my dad. "They've got six townhouse-style dorms that are technically on campus. So, we wouldn't be breaking Coach's rules. Think you can work your 'I'm a Reiner' magic?"

Dad laughs and nods, slipping his phone out of his pocket and squeezing my shoulder hard as he walks back outside the dorm, followed by Rhys's dad.

Our new roommate stumbles in right after, blond hair sweat damp and breath heaving as he slams down what looks to be everything he owns. My anxiety skyrockets and I want to demand he grab it and take it back outside or into the room that I know we aren't staying in. Matt Fredderic and I haven't known each other long, but it's clear mess and chaos follow wherever he goes, which would be hard enough on its own. However, he and Rhys are already becoming fast friends.

You knew this was coming. Rhys has always been the easy friend, the one everyone wants to be or be friends with. He will outgrow you.

Rhys shakes his head at the messy left winger, but there's a smile on his face. "Don't get settled. We're getting an upgrade."

"Upgrade?" Freddy's brow crinkles. He wanted to be called Matty, and I would've obliged, but Rhys called him Freddy just like the upperclassmen all summer at our training camp. And when in doubt, it's easier to follow Rhys's lead.

"Yeah." Rhys slaps a hand on Freddy's shoulder with friendly ease. "Pays to be a Koteskiy sometimes."

And just like that, my best friend deflects the attention off me, like always.

"All good," my dad says as he re-enters the room with Max close on his heels. They're like two pillars of constant strength. "Ready, Ben?"

"Yeah," I nod, grabbing my bag and two boxes—both heavy and filled with too many books—before following him out and back down the stairs, shoulders tight.

He waits until we're in the car again before turning to me. "If it's not okay, you have to tell me."

People say we look alike; they always have. Same brown hair with a few honeyed strands dancing and weaving, all soft gentle curls. Same blue eyes, same startling height and build, same dark furrowing brows that made us a little more unapproachable when standing next to the Koteskiy men. But besides the looks, we aren't the same.

Even with as much as he tries, he doesn't really understand.

He runs a hand over his mouth and slides his sunglasses back into place. I mimic the movement.

"I really fucking hate this," he huffs. "I know you're not far—I'm in Boston and Max and Anna are here now. I just . . . Bennett, you *have* to call me if you need me."

A nod is all I can manage, because my throat feels a little tight.

"Promise me."

"I promise."

"And every Tuesday, five p.m., I can drive you to therapy, and we can have dinner after."

"Okay." He pulls into a small cul-de-sac, catty-corner to the rest of campus, facing out toward a row of older neighborhood houses that have mostly been taken over by students, rented and passed down to friends.

The townhouse is attached to the dorms, still in that same Ivy League–inspired style, red brick and beautiful, that's part of the draw of Waterfell University.

The inside is much more spacious, with a vaulted ceiling in the living room because of the secondary common space upstairs, and non-carpeted floors on the first story. I inspect the kitchen first—it's clean, with a good enough stove to work on and a spacious fridge. Rhys and his father saunter in, laughing and smiling. Freddy follows behind, a strange, hesitant, lopsided grin on his face.

"How much more expensive is this, exactly?" Freddy asks, but Mr. Koteskiy shakes his head.

"Nothing that your scholarship won't cover—you're fine."

The words settle his anxiety almost immediately. A niggle of regret tugs in my stomach for being so selfish, but I can't figure out how to apologize or offer anything to him.

"It's a four bedroom, so you'll end up with another roommate. No guarantees he'll be from the hockey team," my dad adds, crossing his arms. Both Max and my dad are usually in suits if we're not at the rink together, but today they look younger, clad in shorts and T-shirts. Rhys's father even sports a backward baseball cap, like *he's* the one moving into his college dorm.

"We'll make it work," Rhys interjects, settling everyone, me included. "Bottom floor? I think the right-side bedroom and bathroom are farthest from the noise."

I follow Rhys, like I have since day one.

• • •

First days, hell, *months*, in new facilities are tough—new anything is tough for me, really.

I was at Berkshire for the last four years; I adjusted there. I had my routines, my classrooms, my friends. To start over, with how much groundwork it takes me to become "adjusted," is like watching the formation of mountains in real time.

So, between the unavoidable disruption to my routines and the embarrassing explanation that despite how state-of-the-art the facilities are, how top-of-the-line the staff is, I don't want anyone to touch my fucking things, my anxiety has skyrocketed.

The first week, Rhys would step in for me. I didn't have to ask; he would just stop the man who was reaching for my pads and tell him my preference with the smile that I've seen Rhys and his father use to soothe everyone in the room. Like a goddamn superpower.

On my own, it's harder.

I'm last off the ice today, doing a final drill and chatting with the senior goalie. He heads to the showers, leaving his pads and practice uniform in a heap on the floor that makes me sneer a little in disgust as I step over it and start to strip off my entire uniform, gently stacking my leg pads in a pile.

I take a minute to breathe, tilting my head down and side to side three times. I roll my shoulders, left then right then both, three times over, before—

"Oh, sorry," a gentle voice echoes in the cavernous room. "I didn't know anyone was in here."

I look up, breath still a little choppy midway through my cooldown. A girl, dressed in a Waterfell University long sleeve and leggings, murky brown hair high in a swinging ponytail, stands just inside the room looking toward me a little apologetically.

Her gaze drops for a second over my body—shirtless, in nothing but my black jock pants—before coming back to my eyes as pink tinges her cheeks. Mine accidentally do the same, a flush matching hers making me feel warmer in my already overheated state.

Wonderful. Now we're both embarrassed.

It would be easy to snap at her, my usual default setting dialed up to a thousand after being interrupted mid-routine, but I swallow the verbal assault and freeze instead.

"I'm—I just need to grab the . . ." She gestures widely to the left behind scattered clothes and goalie pads.

My brow furrows as she drags one pad in and, holding her breath, tosses the dirty laundry into the chute.

"You always do that for him?" I ask. Before she can answer, I add, "I haven't seen you in here before."

"Oh." She pauses, biting down on a plump pink bottom lip. "Um, no, actually. I'm new, just started. I'm a freshman, I mean, but I'm an equipment manager—trainee, for now."

"Me too." I nod before realizing how ridiculous that sounds and shaking my head, skin growing warmer with the familiar heat of embarrassment. "I mean, I'm a freshman, too. Not an equipment manager."

"Clearly." She laughs, all low and smoky, and it makes me freeze further. "I'm Paloma."

"Bennett." I nod at her instead of reaching out to shake her hand.

"Nice to meet you." She pauses, eyes wandering to my pile of pads and discarded clothing. "I can take those—"

"No," I bite out, a little too harshly based on how quickly she shifts away from me. She almost trips over her own thick tennis shoes before nodding rapidly.

"Sorry."

Heaving a sigh, I tuck my head into my hands. Why is everything this simple so fucking hard for me?

"No, I'm sorry. I'm just—" I cut myself off, standing and collecting all my pads like I'm protecting the sweat-wet equipment from her. Feeling as ridiculous as I look, I keep my back turned to her as I pray and hope she just leaves quietly and lets me do what I *need* to do.

My hands tremble as I stack them again, in the order I always do.

"Bennett?" My name rolls off her tongue, gentle and soothing against the heart-pounding anxiety growing louder and louder.

I shift, realizing she's closer now; close enough that I could reach out and touch her, but far enough away not to crowd me. Her arms are crossed, not defiantly but more . . . self-consciously. Her hand rubs against the soft sleeve of her shirt in a rhythm my brain starts to follow.

"You like to do it yourself?"

The question is genuine, curious if anything, so I nod.

"Yes, but Coach doesn't like it. He'd prefer I leave it. But they just . . . It's—"

"Okay," Paloma says, not pressing me for more. We stand side by side, surveying my neat pile of blockers and pads, my glove and stick carefully laid inside my cubby.

She's about average height, but like most people she has to look up at me because of my height. Her skin is tanned, cheeks and nose reddened like she got a little too much sun this summer. No makeup to be seen, except black lashes that have smudged lightly under her dark brown eyes.

"What if you showed me how to do it right? Cleaning and care—exactly how you do it. And I'll just watch you." She chews on her lip and looks away, like my stare is a little too intense for her to gaze directly into. "Then you can watch me do it—make sure I do it right, and if I don't, I won't bother you again. But . . . if I get it perfect, then you let me handle your equipment from now on?"

She's patient in the silence that follows her offer. She seems serious, no mark of teasing or innuendo. No annoyance, just acceptance. And . . . and a solution, one that has never been offered to me.

If I can watch her, see that it's cleaned *right*, then maybe I can trust her to do it when I'm not watching. Maybe she'll let me watch a few times first, just to make sure . . .

My continuous thread of anxiety and embarrassment seems to

evaporate, leaving me a little empty and exhausted without something dire to focus on. So, I focus on her.

"Just you?" It slips out.

"Just me," she swears, meeting my gaze with a bright-eyed smile that seems to glow even in the fluorescence of the room. "Deal?"

Paloma reaches her hand out, and I stare at it hard but don't move to take it. Eventually, she lowers it. Something tugs at my chest.

"Deal."

CHAPTER 5

NOW

Paloma

"You're the only one I haven't placed for your practicum."

Biting down on my lip, I nod. "I know."

It's warm inside the old wood-paneled office of the College of Business. My department head sighs, like he's as irritated with me as I am with *myself*. I put this off for long enough, making spring semester almost ridiculously difficult.

"Paloma, I can't just toss you anywhere. Most of the class has already chosen—even some juniors. Now, I'll give you priority over their choices, but it has to be done now. Today."

"Can't you just count my freshman year experience? With the hockey team?"

"You were an equipment manager."

I raise an eyebrow and shrug my shoulders. "Fine—then let me do an off-campus internship to replace it."

"We tried that, remember?" he says, hands threading through his hair. "They rejected your application."

After it became clear at the dinner that I wouldn't be putting out in the office, which was the only reason they interviewed me at all.

"Football is taken—they barely took two people considering it's off season. Figure skating has an opening, and hockey has a junior in there so if you want that—"

"No hockey."

He shakes his head again. "You don't have too much of a choice. I was hoping you'd just say yes to figure skating. You'll have to split shifts. There's a new coach, so they'll only let you practice with one of them. Besides, your sport of choice when you applied was left blank, but I'm gonna take a wild guess based on your work experience and say you might love hockey."

I don't say a word about his guess, only asking, "What about an event team?"

"You specifically entered the coaching track."

"Fine. Swimming?"

A deep sigh comes from his chest. "Off season."

"They go 'til April—"

"No. They already filled the *one* spot they allow for. Try again."

My stomach churns.

"Paloma, I've seen your résumé. You've excelled in all your classes. You've worked summers and part time for local hockey clubs—even the Providence Bruins last year. And they all have beautiful things to say about you. Why are you so adamant about not working with the hockey team here?"

His voice is still soft, kind, as he dips it even lower to ask, "Did something happen? Are you—"

"I'm fine," I quickly cut him off. "Nothing happened."

He breathes out quickly, a rush telling me he's relieved. But his eyes scan me again, like they're looking for deception.

"Okay. Fine," I agree, head ducked.

"Wonderful. You'll slot on and off as the 'ice sports' mentee. So, with—" He pauses to glance down at a few papers in front of him, searching. "Coach Moreau for pairs skating on Mondays. And Coach Harris for hockey on Thursdays. He can move you to shadow an assistant coach if he wants, but you'll report to him as your supervisor."

I nod, fists tightening on my thighs. "Anything else?"

He sighs deeply. "No. That's all."

I excuse myself with a sarcastic salute to cover the nausea, opening the door and striding out into the ornate dark hallway, only to slam right into a girl trying to sprint through me.

She stumbles but stays upright. She's short, her pale face red enough to match her auburn hair. Her attire almost looks like a movie-worthy prep academy uniform—nylon tights, a pleated navy skirt and a frilly blouse, complete with a thick headband that she fixes back into place.

"You, okay?" I ask, because she seems almost out of it.

"Mmhmm," she says, while staring unabashedly at my cleavage. I almost laugh, but manage to hold it in. It doesn't seem like she's trying to blatantly check me out, but her gaze is *focused*.

"All right." I eye her again. As I move away her gaze stays pinned to the wall behind where I once stood. So maybe she's just a little weirdo and not a pervert. She's so still that it makes me pause, watching to make sure she's okay.

A man in a crisp navy suit steps past me toward her, arms crossed as he hovers over her small frame. She's much shorter than me, and I'm a solid five-foot-five.

"Are you finished?"

She responds with the same humming sound she made at me and shakes her head a little, like drawing herself out of a daydream. He sighs, a frustrated, exhausted noise.

"And where is everything? Your schedule? Papers? Did he not give you anything?"

"Oh—" She sprints back to the door she busted out of earlier.

I turn and head out, tucking my own papers into my backpack as I walk the mostly empty hallway.

• • •

My first day with the pair skating team is easy enough. Coach Moreau is a nice, albeit loud, French coach who mostly has me observe. I take notes when she speaks to me, but mostly I watch Luc Laroux with his new partner.

He's the only one on the pairs team I know, because when Sadie and I were friends, we often partied with him. He'd blow insane money on overly expensive alcohol, hook up with some girl, and then cry in the bathroom or disassociate in the rideshare back to the dorms with us.

We got along great.

As they finish up, Luc skates right over to me with a wink.

"Since when did we get a hot new coach?" he asks with the same infuriatingly handsome smirk. People call him the Ice King, and he's got the jet-black hair, pale skin, and icy blue eyes to make the nickname fit. And the annoyingly arrogant attitude to match.

Just as I open my mouth to respond, my eyes snag on a different vignette.

"Ah yes, the lovers," Luc sighs beneath his breath, sitting on the bench next to me as we watch Rhys Koteskiy in his practice uniform, sans skates, lean over the other bench and kiss his little figure skater girlfriend.

Sadie smiles softly—something I've rarely seen from her—and lets him tuck a strand of hair back from her face. They're intimate and warm in their bubble of bliss.

"Nauseating," I sneer to Luc. He laughs and continues sliding on his guards before bidding me a quick goodbye on his way back to the locker rooms.

Sadie finally leaves the bench and heads over to our side to exit the ice. She stops by me, grabbing her own sparkly black guards and cloth, drying the blades carefully before sliding each one on.

"Got something to say?" She finally cracks, eyebrow arched.

"Seems like you're doing great," I say, my sarcasm a little heavy-handed. Sadie smiles, like I've told her I missed her and not tossed a sarcastic comment her way.

"Great to see you as always, Paloma." She rolls her gray cat-like eyes. But then looks me over again more intentionally, and my stomach rolls with nausea. "How are you?"

Her question is genuine. I feel like a frayed nerve.

"I'd be doing better if you stayed out of my business."

She smirks and shakes her head, standing next to where I'm still sitting on the bench—her only chance to be taller than me.

"Got it. Excuse me for even attempting to be nice to you," she snips. There's a niggle of regret clawing at my throat, but I manage to suffocate it back down into my usual numbness and anger.

. . .

"You can't be serious."

"She is," my roommate smarts off, crossing her arms and leaning against the doorframe by her side of the apartment-style dorms. They're the smallest ones on campus: a tiny room each with a shared bathroom and tiny living space. I've gone the random roommate route every year—and this year turned out worse than usual.

Taylor is about my height, but thin and objectively beautiful. She's active on campus and nice to everyone, usually. But her annoying boyfriend has "accidentally" walked in on me in the bathroom multiple times. Enough that I keep my showers short and at odd hours.

"Felicity—"

Our RA holds her hand up, biting her lip as she avoids my eyes and hands me a paper that explicitly says I'm not allowed to live here anymore. The reasons barely make sense, nor are any of them true: partying at all hours, presence of drugs and alcohol; anything it seems Taylor could think of. I don't try to argue, very aware of her connection with our RA.

"It's January," I snip. "The semester has already started. Where am I supposed to go?"

"Not our problem," Taylor says, butting in again.

I head to my room before either of them can see the burning redness of my eyes. It only takes me a minute to pack everything into my large duffel bag.

Most of what I own in one bag. How pathetic.

Still, I'm careful to tuck my well-worn velveteen rabbit plush into my faded blue backpack.

The RA tries to stop me again as I step back into the common area.

"Paloma, you have until the end of the week—"

"Consider me moved out," I growl, shoving past her and clipping her with my shoulder. It's petty and rude, but I'm livid.

There's no way I can find an apartment fast enough. I'll be sleeping in my car tonight. I'm too poor to grab a hotel but too prideful to stay in that dorm room any longer than I have to. Another batch of angry tears threaten, but I smother them before they can fall.

I reach for my phone, tempted to no end to call him, the one person I know who will swoop in and save me—but stop myself immediately, banging my head on the steering wheel as I attempt to get my breathing under control amidst the torrent of anger and fear.

Three steps forward, one thousand steps back. The same path for me since I was six years old.

• • •

" . . . easy, Freddy."

"Relax, I can . . ."

The voices blur in and out of my consciousness. I try to open my eyes, but my eyelids are too heavy. So is my head—am I resting on something?

"Was she alone?" The girl's voice is low, recognizable. A little smile pulls at my lips. *Sadie fucking Brown.* This has to be a dream.

" . . . you've been here before?" Sadie asks, voice quiet as she approaches me.

"Yeah. Not my proudest moment," a male voice says, irritated and jumpy. I don't recognize it. *Is this a memory?* I don't know it, at least not enough to place it. "But you're welcome."

"Right," Sadie sneers.

I finally blink my eyes open. This time, I do laugh—I have to be dreaming.

Sadie Brown and Matt Fredderic are standing over my corner barstool. There's no way this is real.

My eyes flutter again, body slumping before someone catches me.

"All right, guess I'm carrying you," Freddy says, lifting me into his arms in a bridal carry.

"Did someone bother her?" Sadie asks. She must be talking to the bartender, but I'm close enough to hear her. "How did you even find my number?"

"She gave it to me," the man says, his voice calm and quiet. "I asked if there was anyone I could call to help her when I realized she wasn't okay. I don't know who was serving her, but clearly someone was sneaking her more to drink than I would have allowed."

"And she asked you to call . . . me?" I blink my eyes open. Sadie looks over her delicate shoulder at me. "Damn, Paloma, you must've been desperate."

It's a joke, but I can almost see the worry present in her eyes. An emotion I've never seen there before. She always kept things locked down tightly.

Eyes closing again, I relax at the fact that reluctantly, I trust the two people around me to have my back. At least enough that I know they won't hurt me.

I blink, losing time, and we're in the car in front of the dorms. My head is pressed to the cold window, a relief to my overheated skin.

"I'm gonna get out and help you in, okay?" Sadie says, turned toward me in the passenger seat. Freddy's driving her car.

"I . . . I'm not allowed," I whisper, the words difficult to push through my tired lips. "I don't live there anymore. I'm—" Embarrassment clogs my throat even with the alcohol running through my system. "Was gonna just sleep in my car. I don't have anywhere else. I'm sorry."

Sadie looks at Freddy and says something quietly to him. He nods and starts driving again, slow enough not to jostle me. I fall easily back to sleep with the movement.

CHAPTER 6

NOW

Bennett

"I said I can't today."

"Ben—"

"I have to go," I snap, hanging up and tossing my phone into my bag as Rhys exits from the showers, towel tucked around his waist. He pauses, examining my face before sitting down next to me.

"All good?"

"Mmhmm."

"That your dad?" he asks. I can hear the reluctance in his voice. Rhys and I don't talk about Adam anymore. He still has dinners with Max and Anna—they're his best friends, though I'm convinced there's much more to their relationship. Sometimes I go to dinner at the Koteskiys', sometimes I don't. But Max Koteskiy's relationship with his son is different than my father's relationship with me.

I just . . . don't trust my dad right now. And part of me hates that Rhys still does.

Trying to talk it out with my therapist didn't help. And then I'd tried to talk about it with my dad—resulting in the stalemate we currently find ourselves in. It hurts to feel so distant from him. It's never been like this between us. Adam Reiner had always been the soothing lullaby in my brain. He was my defender and protector;

the only person who managed to make me laugh as a kid—before Rhys—and the only person in the world who hugged me the exact right way.

And now . . . now all that is left between us is a tangled knot of blame and anger and frustration and sadness, tightening around us both like collars of iron until I can't breathe from the strain.

"And your dad?"

"I don't want to talk about it."

"Why not?"

"He never loved my mom. He left her. Same as he always does with everyone." A pause. And then, *"I don't want to talk about it."*

My therapist moved on after that, but I knew I hadn't escaped the conversation entirely. I just wasn't ready to discuss any of it—to her or him or anyone.

Today was a two-a-day practice and it's late as I make my way to my truck. I idle in the parking lot while I collect myself.

I check my phone. And then again, impulsively. I clench my teeth when I realize I've grabbed for it a third time. The compulsion has become bad enough that my therapist brought it up last year.

Paloma soothed your anxiety, and now that she's gone, your brain is trying to find other outlets. What else could we do when you worry like that?

I turn on my music, the soft guitar of Ben Howard comforting me as I close my eyes, lean my head back against the headrest, and massage the bridge of my nose.

She's fine.

She's fine. She's fine.

But what if she isn't?

My thoughts start to scramble away from me, a losing battle as I try to collect myself.

"Check the facts," I mutter beneath my breath, tapping my knee and blowing out a breath.

1. It's a Monday night. There are no parties, and nearly all the Waterfell University bars are closed.
2. Paloma has always called me when she needed help.

"Which means she's fine," I grit out, grabbing for the steering wheel as I finally reverse out and force myself to drive home.

Sometimes, when my anxiety is bad enough, I drive down Greek row and through the downtown strip just to make sure she isn't there. Cold. Waiting for me.

Maybe things are good. Maybe she doesn't need me as her crutch and comfort anymore.

Just like Rhys. Just like everyone in your life who moves on without you and leaves you behind.

I shake the thought from my brain as I head in from the garage, upstairs, and into my bathroom. I take a moment to breathe, turning on the shower and stepping under the hot spray.

Afterward, I make my way to the quiet kitchen once everyone has settled into their rooms for the night. I turn on my music and start to prepare our meals for the week ahead. I've already washed and dried the blue and green containers—for Rhys and Freddy, respectively—so that I can label and stack their food. It helps to follow the familiar routine.

I let it soothe me.

Once everything is prepped, stored, cleaned, and put away, I make my way to bed, praying that the quiet stillness will allow me some rest.

I turn on soft music and grab one of my notebooks, but as usual the words aren't there. I can't write anything. I can barely stand to read poetry now that—

Seven raises his head at the sound of the front door closing. He pushes up off the bed and pads toward my bedroom door with a whine.

"Shh," I say, clicking my tongue and patting the space beside me on the bed. "It's fine—it's just Sadie and Rhys coming home late or something. Calm down."

But he doesn't. His paw comes to scrape at the wood on the door, making my brow furrow further. It's not as if whoever came in so late is making a lot of noise—if anything they're too quiet. I stand and push my ear to the door, listening intently.

I only hear Freddy's voice, but too low for me to make out his words, before I tug at Seven's collar to come to bed.

"Everything's fine, Sev. Come here."

He doesn't and it makes my chest ache a little. What is wrong?

Everyone is home and safe. Everyone is okay.

Except one, my mind threatens, preying easily on the slip of my focus. *She's alone and in the dark and hungry—*

Stop. I turn off the lamp before Seven whines louder and I click it back on, rolling over to try to sleep.

Seven doesn't sleep much, staying curled up by the door, refusing to come back to the bed. I don't sleep much either.

CHAPTER 7

NOW

Paloma

"Good morning, sleepyhead."

The words are low, but loud enough to have woken me if I wasn't already awake and staring up at the ceiling.

I press up on my elbows in the bed. My chest squeezes at the sight of the disheveled bedding on the opposite twin bed, knowing full well she stayed by me all night.

"Morning," I mutter quietly, rubbing at the bridge of my nose.

Sadie slumps against the doorframe, the gray T-shirt she's swimming in a near-perfect match to her eyes. "Drinking yourself under the table this time, huh, Blake?"

There's a sarcastic, equally snarky retort on the tip of my tongue—but that's not what comes out.

I shake my head and duck my chin. "Not really doing great right now, Brown."

Her brow furrows, teeth biting down on her lip. There's a slip of understanding in her impenetrable gaze. "Do you want to talk about it?"

My shoulders lift almost imperceptibly. Sadie turns and closes the door. It's hard to miss the giant letters spelling out KOTESKIY across her shoulders.

There's a piece of me that will always envy her—that sees her relationship with Rhys and her genuine happiness as some achievement she doesn't deserve. And maybe that's cruel, but knowing I can't have that, that I tried and still messed it up, haunts me. Sadie Brown was my friend, once upon a time. Now she's a walking taunt about everything I wished for.

"Things have been rough," I try, eyes ducked down as Sadie sits cross-legged on the end of the opposite twin bed. It's their spare room, but with the gaming console in the corner and the scattered Star Wars toys and action figures, it's clearly become Sadie's little brothers' temporary home. "My roommate hates me and got me thrown out of my dorm."

Sadie rolls her eyes. "Want me to hit her?"

The dry tone of her voice makes a smile pull at my mouth.

"Maybe." I shake my head. "I think I was just upset and wanted to forget for a while. It just feels like everything is spinning out of control."

Sadie nods, chewing lightly on her bottom lip. "Yeah. I get it."

I know she does. It might be the only reason I'm willing to talk to her about it.

"You can stay here as long as you need, but do you have anyone you can call?" Sadie asks. "I just don't want you to be alone right now."

For a moment, my mind flashes to blue eyes and a square jaw, fingers in my hair and a soothing, *"Hey, P. You okay?"*

I rush the thoughts away and sigh deeply, pressing fingers to my temple as I begrudgingly nod.

"Yeah. I know someone."

• • •

"This has to be a joke." Alessia's smoky tone reverberates out of my phone speaker next to me on the bed. "I'm being pranked, right?"

"Very funny." I shake my head, closing my eyes as I tilt my head back. "I need your help."

Silence—for nearly too long, chafing at my skin.

"You're cold-calling me after three years of ignored phone calls, texts—everything—and you're not even going to start with, 'Hello, Alessia? How are you? I'm so sorry I blew you off and made you think I was dead or worse.'" Her voice ratchets up higher with every sentence. "Seriously? God, Paloma, I—"

She cuts herself off with a muffled shriek.

"I'm cool, I'm chill."

"Sounds like it," I mumble, wincing when I hear another aggravated noise from far away.

"Let's start this over in a way that won't have me losing my job," Alessia says, before clearing her throat and brightening her voice. "Hi, Paloma, dear! How can I help you?"

I roll my eyes but settle back.

There's a giant lump in my throat that makes it difficult to swallow—and I never know if it's a buildup of regret or self-hatred. Or maybe the tears I've never shed. That I'll never allow myself to release.

Like the last dregs of fuel in a junkyard car. Sometimes that tight pressure is the only thing to remind me I'm alive.

I tell her quickly, almost clinically, about everything that's happened in the last twenty-four hours—never mind that I know she'd far rather know what's happened in the last three years. Even knowing there is no judgment I could ever face with Alessia, I'll never force my demons on her like that.

"I need to find an apartment," I finish. "It's—Sadie is letting me stay in a spare room at her . . . friends' house." My head spins a little at the thought of my proximity to the one constant fixation of my otherwise tumultuous life.

"I can stay here again tonight, but I just—"

My voice chokes off into nothing, a flash of blue eyes and slightly sharp stubble against my freshly showered skin.

"Does it have anything to do with Ethan?"

There's a moment where it feels like I'm being hunted, chest tight—just from the sound of his name. "No. It's— I can't—"

"Breathe," Alessia says, her voice tethering me. "It's all right. I'll take care of it, okay? Now, let's run the gamut. You've got money for food?"

"Yes."

"Have all your things or do you need someone to help you move?"

"I have it all in my car; it's still at the lot."

"Okay. Leave this with me, all right?" Her voice is calm and soothing in the same way it was when I was seventeen, sitting in her office with a small bag of my things, scared and crying. "I'll take care of everything. Do you want me to come get you?"

"I'm okay." As torturous as it might feel to be in this house with him, there is safety in knowing he's here. That nothing will happen to me.

"Okay, Paloma." She breathes, and I listen to the sound like a soft lullaby. "Take care of yourself today and I'll call you to check in tonight, yeah?"

"Okay."

I hang up before she can say anything else, or before I can break down in tears.

I sit in the spare room with the assurance from Sadie that she'll only say a friend of hers needed a bed for the night—and that Freddy wouldn't say anything either. I'd begged them both to keep my name out of it. Though they don't know why.

Gripping the velveteen rabbit I've kept nearby since I was six years old, I take comfort in the plush for the first time in years—the first time I've allowed myself to. My stomach growls and I search my backpack for a breakfast bar I know has been stashed in there for a while.

"Chicken nuggets? Really?" I can almost hear his voice, almost see the grimace. *"I said I could make you anything and that's your pick?"*

I remember my blush, warm over my cheeks as I nodded with a self-conscious laugh.

"Yes, please. With spicy ketchup."

His laugh was loud, more open than usual as he played lightly with a few strands of my hair. *"All right. Anything for you, P."*

It would be so easy. I wouldn't even need the usual *Walk me home?* text. I could slip into the room down the hall from me, the one that smells like clean sheets and sandalwood, with the lamplight on for me to sleep. He'd offer to run me a bath, braid my hair, feed me, take care of me.

If you cut open my skin, I think his name would be written across my veins, branded on the actual muscle of my heart. And I'd bleed for him over and over to keep him away from me, from the horrid, disgusting girl I became.

Still, I let the Bennett Reiner of my imagination lull me as I step into the unfamiliar bathroom to wash off.

CHAPTER 8

NOW

Bennett

The next morning, I start on the coffee and my own breakfast. It's a Tuesday, which means Ro is already awake and dressed when I come down, working on her computer at the counter. Our only other morning companion is usually Oliver, though it's a school day so he won't be here.

It's only quiet for twenty minutes before Freddy comes down in his boxers, half-asleep and looking for his girlfriend. I take the opportunity to step away and dress upstairs, grabbing my things.

Freddy's still in his boxers when I come back downstairs, though his girlfriend is quietly begging him to go up and change before they're late. He only concedes after a kiss that feels inappropriate to be privy to.

Sadie and Rhys come down soon after, both dressed and quietly talking over something that must be upsetting Rhys, going off the look on his face. My shoulders tense; the need to help is almost overwhelming—before it sinks away to nothing as Sadie stops Rhys and smooths her fingers over the dip in his brow, kissing him heartily.

He has Sadie. She's helped him more than you ever did. He doesn't need you—

I close my eyes briefly, taking a few long breaths.

We're all in the kitchen; the noise is loud but it feels *right*. Turnover plays from the speakers in the corner and most everyone grabs something off the breakfast platter I've prepared.

When the house is loud like this, warm and vibrant, I think of her most. The pain of missing her hits me hardest in the shower, when the water sluices over my skin and she's not there. But when I'm with my friends—my *family*—my mind floats into dreams.

Paloma in my sweatshirt, sitting at the bar top, warm brown eyes and flushed skin from an early morning shower. Feeding her. Making her coffee. Writing her a poem and slipping it into her bag before we leave. Together.

The way it was supposed to be.

Still, I smile because my friends are happy. I turn away before I can ruin it, reaching for my coffee as I back out of the kitchen area, when I stumble into someone in the hallway.

"Sorry," a voice whispers.

A voice I know more intimately than my own. For a moment, I'm sure I'm hallucinating.

I turn so swiftly I almost trip, coming face-to-face with a piece of my soul.

The love of my goddamn life.

Paloma Blake.

CHAPTER 9

NOW

Paloma

I knew I should have waited until I heard them all leave.

I want to regret it, only—I can't. Because Bennett Reiner is in front of me, eyes wide, hand half reaching for me.

Looking just over the peak of Bennett's bicep, I realize no one has noticed us yet. Bennett mimics my movement, checking over his own shoulder before pulling me gently away from the kitchen, down the hall, and into the garage.

"Are you okay?" he blurts out before I can say a word. His eyes scan over me once more before settling on mine, too severe and vibrant.

His hand is still on my wrist, hold firm and warm—not too tight. It's almost familiar, how often he's held both my wrists like that, above my head—

Stop.

My cheeks flush, eyes darting away from his and toward where he's still touching me. His focus on me, waiting for my answer, is too intense. Still, he doesn't notice my borderline inappropriate reaction to his closeness, his casual intimate touch that I haven't felt in months.

I take him in slowly: the large set of his shoulders, the furrow of his thick brow, the concern searing in his deep ocean blue eyes. My body aches to relax into his grip, to tell him everything and just let him fix it. But I know that he can't.

I'm unfixable.

And if this is my chance to turn over a new leaf, then I cannot use Bennett Reiner as my crutch to do it. I've proven time and again that it won't work, though my heart will never listen. Even now it reaches toward him, drawing me closer.

"Fine," I say, voice wobbly. "I'm fine."

"Then what are you doing here?"

He doesn't mean to be harsh—I know Bennett well enough to know that his intensity stems from care more than exasperation or anger.

It doesn't stop me from stammering as I offer my apology. "I'm sorry . . . I should've said something, but Sadie and Freddy said I could stay here and—"

"Hey, hey," he coos, putting his travel mug down and rubbing his hands over my arms. Gooseflesh rises in the wake of his touch. "You don't need to explain. It's fine. I just need to make sure you're okay."

I can feel myself drowning in his gaze, the way I always do in his presence. My body relaxes slowly, leaving the constant on-guard tension behind.

A voice booms, calling out something as they thump up the stairs—Freddy, I think. But it's enough to have me snapping back and away from his touch.

His hands linger in the air, like he's trying to catch smoke.

"I'm fine . . . promise." I offer, my voice a shade darker.

Shut this down.

"Are you sure?" Bennett's voice softens, and he steps closer, his concern palpable. He's so big, he blocks everything else out until all I can see is *him*.

"Yeah." I smirk, sinking into the only thing I know will protect me. *Myself.* At least, the thing that most people know me as.

Paloma Blake, party girl extraordinaire. A fucking beautiful girl and an even more beautiful fuck.

"Aren't I always?" I quirk my lips and dip my brow suggestively. "Did you pull me out here for something fun?"

His face shutters, like he's been hit. He's unable to cover the pain in his face or his voice as he begs quietly, "Don't do this, P."

"Do what?" I ask, biting my lip, hooding my eyes. My hands land gently on his shoulders. "Don't you want me? I can make it so good for you. Just like old times—"

"Stop," he snaps, eyes burning, hands locking on my wrists to stop them. Even as harsh as his voice is, it's in sharp contrast to the way he holds himself, like he's near to crumbling. "Just talk to me. Please—"

"Drop it, Bennett," I snap.

I turn away from him and head back inside and up the stairs before locking myself in the spare room. I don't open the door or respond to the quiet knocks I *know* are him. Because if he calls me *P* or *love* one more time, I'll fall right back into him.

And Bennett Reiner deserves worlds better than this.

CHAPTER 10

THEN: Freshman Year, August

Paloma

Intro to Poetry. I roll my eyes as I double-check my schedule.

One thing about being late in applications to colleges—which I was, severely—is getting the last orientation day and the leftover of class selections to go with it.

I'd take a musty art history lecture hall over the yellowed concrete liberal arts building that smells permanently like coffee and stacks of old books. And yet, as I make my way through the fluorescent halls that clearly don't have the funding that the other side of campus seems to, I'm still bubbling with excited first-day jitters.

I'm later than I'd like to be, only five minutes early to the 8 a.m. course when I prefer fifteen. Mostly so that I can pick where I sit and get an idea of what to expect.

Clipping the corner of the door on my way in, I rock back a little and peer into the classroom. Ten desks have been configured into a semicircle, the other desks haphazardly shoved away, nearly into the walls. Half of them are already taken, but my eyes immediately lock onto one in particular.

It's the boy from the other day. All large and imposing and sitting in a too-small desk in the classroom.

We're both aware of each other, but neither of us acknowledges it. Maybe it'd be more normal to sit next to him; knowing one person in this tiny class should be enough for me to try—friends, community, something.

"Bennett," he says, voice almost emotionless. But his eyes are sparkling.

Blinking again, I slump my owl-eyed expression into something more blank and waltz to a seat opposite him, nearest the door.

It's easy to tell he's hunched over, as if to make himself smaller, to draw as little attention as possible—which is impossible when he looks like he could be teaching the class, with his angular, strong jaw and nose. His eyes are a foggy turquoise, like a gem held out under a rain cloud. Or a distant misty ocean.

His eyes dart away as we catch each other staring. His cheeks redden to match the heat I feel across my own face.

"Good morning." A raspy chuckle reverberates in the small concrete room.

Dr. Nick Britton, our professor for Introduction to Poetry struts in with the heavy assistance of a curved, wooden cane. He's tall and reedy, with graying hair and a weathered, bespectacled face. If he was dressed more pretentiously, he'd resemble John Keating with a new Dead Poet's Society. Instead, he wears jeans and a wrinkled button-down.

While he settles in and hands out the syllabus, I'm distracted again by watching Bennett.

He's meticulous, careful with the paper as he flips the stapled corner and skims the entire thing briefly—as if in search of something specific. Too curious, I flip mine, trying to figure out what part he's reading through so intensely.

Bolded across the second page is "Required Texts," of which it lists "various" typed out with no proper capitalization. But below that, I find what I'm positive has captured Bennett's attention.

"Stopping by Woods on a Snowy Evening" by Robert Frost is printed over the last page of the syllabus.

I should be listening to our professor as he introduces the rules and code of conduct for the class, but so should Bennett. Instead, we both read.

It's familiar; I've read it before in one of my high school English classes. It's not my style, but it's an all-around crowd pleaser.

"Now." Dr. Britton claps his hands loudly, grabbing my attention back. "Let's start on our first assignment. Partner up."

He might as well have said "fight to the death" for the way my body reacts. Eyes dancing around the room, I hang back as a few more gregarious students grab a friend—or make a new one quickly—so as not to be picked last. And, since there's an even eight of us in here, there's no chance of waiting and asking to work on my own.

I find a girl who looks kind enough, if not very approachable, but just as I go to move, she's snatched up by the guy already seated to her right. Anxiety churns my stomach, a seasick feeling making my neck dampen with sweat.

Except, there *is* someone else without a partner. Someone else who didn't even attempt to ask someone. And the only person in here I even moderately know in some capacity.

I grab my binder and the syllabus, march over to him with short, efficient strides, and slide into one of the abandoned desks closest to him. I keep my eyes locked on our professor where he sits atop the large metal desk at the head of our circle.

Bennett keeps his eyes locked on me.

His gaze is searing, heating the side of my face like summer sunlight. And when I finally turn to meet it, it's just as intense as I suspected it would be.

Whatever I was going to say evaporates on my tongue, throat dry and neck still sweat damp.

"What did you think of it?" Bennett asks, his shoulders hiked and eyes downcast. As if feigning disinterest or hiding embarrassment.

He doesn't ask if I've read it. Maybe he was watching me as much as I was him.

"It's magical," I say. "Elusive in its meaning, but clearly intentional and structured."

Blue eyes that are just as magical and elusive dart up to meet my gaze, then shift just slightly to my nose.

"You—yeah." He clears his throat and looks back down at the papers. "What else?"

He won't offer his own opinion then, as if he's testing the waters. So I slump forward, edging a little closer to his rigid form. "I think he's talking about death."

A scoff works from his throat almost immediately, voice much louder as he insists, "It's not—if anything it's about *life*."

"Oh?" I smart, lip curling with well-restrained annoyance. "Did he tell you that himself?"

I wish I could say I'm being playful, but this is exactly what I hate about poetry. My teacher in high school did the same thing, tearing my interpretations to shreds if I offered something contradictory. As much as people preach about interpretation, my experience has been that there's always a right answer.

Bennett doesn't say anything, cheeks bright from either anger or embarrassment. I can't tell, nor do I necessarily care. Really, I shouldn't be as curious as I am about him.

"*Sleep* is inherently ambiguous. Is the tone exasperated? Or hopeful? I think I could argue both sides."

"You sound like my dad," he grumbles, but his face only burns redder, like he didn't mean to say it.

"Yeah?" I press him anyway. "He must be a genius."

"He's a lawyer."

A laugh bursts free, shocking us both. I can't remember the last time I laughed.

For a moment, I'm worried I scared off my surly partner, but then the corner of his mouth kicks up. It's nearly microscopic, but it's there. Just the hint of a smile.

Maybe we could be friends.

"What's so funny?" Our professor garners our attention easily, but there is no reprimand, only genuine curiosity reflected in his dancing eyes.

"Nothing," I rush to say, shaking my head and feeling chastised even without actually being in trouble. Dr. Britton frowns slightly and leans both hands heavily on the curve of his cane.

"All right. So then tell me about the poem."

We both stay silent at first, before I elbow Bennett and raise my eyebrows. *I did the talking. Your turn.*

He doesn't speak.

"Bennett should go first. I thought his views were very . . . sanguine." My partner's cheeks heat at my words but he's still grinning enough that I feel a bit like dancing in my seat with the victory.

"Yeah? Then tell me, Mr.—"

"Reiner," Bennett says, sitting up a little straighter. "We were just discussing the overall theme—life or death. We had a disagreement about the meaning."

"You and every other critic that's ever read the work. Did you find it uplifting or haunting? How about a precarious line of both? I think I've felt several different, contradictory emotions about this one."

"Isn't that the point?" Bennett asks. "To use the landscape and descriptions to lay out a greater metaphor and not explain what the metaphor is meant to be."

"If we can compare *Green Eggs and Ham* to the efforts of communism, I think that we can view intentionally obscure poems in whatever way we can defend."

Bennett's eyes are sparkling and he's smiling with teeth now. I get the feeling that he doesn't *know* that he looks so enthralled by the professor's words.

"See?" I say proudly, growing more comfortable next to this confident version of Bennett. "He's a poetry savant."

I've said something wrong by the way Bennett's entire face shutters. All my previous comfort dissolves like passing smoke.

Dr. Britton leaves us with a quiet, "Good work," muttered as he moves on to the next group. Bennett starts to pack up, which makes me furrow my brow until I check the analog clock on the wall and realize class is nearly over.

I watch him again, more blatantly than before. He's meticulous, just like he was with his hockey gear. Smoothing the paper's creases, tucking it into a dark blue folder, which then tucks into a greater binder and then into his backpack—big enough for his books, but almost too small against the broadness of his back.

A buzzer sounds the end of class just as he stands up. He walks away, three steps, before turning back to me and fidgeting, eyes staying glued to my sneakers and his thick brows furrowed.

"Have you read more of him? Frost?"

It feels like an odd question. Maybe it wasn't the one he intended to ask.

"Yeah, sure." I shrug, shucking the tote bag I brought over my shoulder and stepping over to walk ahead of him. "I don't hate him, but that one is boring."

"Then which one do you like?"

I spin on my heel and turn back toward him with a wide smirk. "'Devotion.'"

Bennett's eyebrows jump, like he's surprised I didn't name "The Road Not Taken" or "Nothing Gold Can Stay."

Shrugging my shoulders, I start walking again. He keeps stride with my shorter legs easily.

"What other poems do you like?" Bennett asks.

"I'm not really a big fan of poetry, especially like this. It's really . . . there's a lot of rules." His hopeful expression melts into deep disappointment, as if I've personally delivered the news of some tragic loss.

"It's . . . you should try it again."

It makes me smile for some reason, that Bennett wants me to *like* poetry.

Why?

"Maybe I will."

The honesty of my words haunts me long after I've returned to my dorm. I stare up at my bedroom ceiling and rethink every word I said.

CHAPTER 11

THEN: Freshman Year, August

Bennett

"What are you doing here?"

I really shouldn't be so surprised. In fact, I'm *more* surprised that he's managed to stay away this long before showing up unannounced.

"What are *you* doing here?" my dad asks as I open the door wider for him. He's still in a suit from work, sharply dressed as always with his thick curls combed back as best he can manage. "It's a Friday night. Shouldn't you be out?"

Behind him, still in the doorway, sits a full-grown black Lab with a little bowtie around his collar.

"Whose dog is that?"

My question goes unheard as Rhys shouts a quick "Hey, Mr. Reiner," from his spot at the kitchen table between bites of the lasagna I cooked.

"You two should be out, or at a party. What about your teammates?"

"We invited them," Rhys assures my dad, wiping his mouth and joining us near the doorway. "Whose dog is that?"

"That's what I'm trying to figure out," I mumble, eyes finding my dad's gaze again. "Dad?"

"He's yours."

My dad means well—honestly, he does. He checks on me often, never cancels on me, never shows up late. He's gone to therapy with me since I was eight years old, and I truly believe he wants me to be happy.

But as much as he doesn't want things to be different now—they *are*.

"I'm doing this because I love you, Ben." His words are the lyrics to a song that only ever plays in duet with my mother's crying.

"I didn't ask for a dog."

"He's a therapy dog," my dad says, meeting my eyes. "Not a puppy, so he's trained. He won't chew on your things or pee on the carpet. He's here to help."

Rhys grins down at the giant dog sitting quietly at our feet. "He will shed, though." His words are quiet, as if he thinks the dog will hear him say it and be offended. "Will that bother you?"

The question tells me that Rhys is already on board, which doesn't surprise me because my best friend has always tried to make life easier for me. While I've only made his more difficult.

"I don't know."

Cleanliness is a delicate situation for me. I can never explain it, and I have desperately tried. I *wish* I could. Maybe then I wouldn't have spent years crying over the way my mom served my food or the sickness I felt in trying to sleep in sheets I didn't wash myself. Maybe my parents wouldn't have fought so much. Maybe the divorce would've never happened.

"This has nothing to do with you, Ben," he says, standing in the corner by the door. *"I need you to tell me you understand."*

"I understand," I say, but I don't. Not really. And I hate changes. This one seems bigger than most.

"Until the custody agreement is made up, I have to keep my distance from the house. But if you need me—"

I shake myself free from the memory again, staring into the eyes of my dad in the present, not the past. Back then I couldn't meet his gaze. Now I find his blue eyes steadying.

"Okay."

Rhys winks at me. "Hell yeah, Ben."

"Great." My dad pats my shoulder quickly before pulling his hand away. "I have all his paperwork in the car, and I got him a tag and everything." His voice trails off as I look down at my new dog.

He's big, with wide brown eyes that look more forlorn and unsure than most dogs I've seen. He's quiet, a little unsure, and he still hasn't moved from the doorway.

"Come on in, bud."

"Does he have a name?" Rhys asks, kneeling to pet and coo at the dog as he slowly trots in. My dad closes the door and shakes his head, wincing.

"They had one for him at the children's hospital he worked for—Superdog." My dad smiles, lines crinkling around his eyes. "So I think you'll have to name him. Any ideas?"

Brow furrowed, I cross my arms and shake my head.

Rhys laughs a little, now fully sitting on the ground with him. "Maybe you should name him Gretzky? Or Crosby?" He shrugs. "Something hockey related, since he'll be living with us. Name him after one of your heroes."

"Seven."

The word pours out of me too fast, and my cheeks heat in the aftermath. I duck my head and scratch at the back of my neck.

"Seven?" Rhys questions. "I think—"

"It's a great name. A lucky number." My dad reassures me with another brief touch. "Welcome home, Seven."

I nod as if I agree.

The truth? I have one hero—and that was his number when he played.

Rhys's phone rings in the distance and he backs away from Seven apologetically, swiping his phone off the kitchen counter with a rueful grin.

"Miss me already?"

The phone is on speaker, so it's easy to hear the gruff voice of Max Koteskiy as he shouts to my dad, "You could've told me you were driving over."

My dad only grins at the sound of his angry best friend, walking over to speak closer to Rhys's phone. "I needed to see Bennett."

"And I wanted to see my son." He grumbles something in Russian, which Rhys replies to in the same foreign tongue, shaking his head.

The three of them continue to speak, but I don't hear it anymore, too distracted by a sudden warmth against my leg.

Seven, sitting nearly on my feet, head titled to my thigh. He looks minorly contented, enough that I can't tell who is comforting who. I reach my hand down slowly and pet his soft, smooth head.

I'm not sure how long we stand there, staring at each other, but the phone call ends and my dad walks back toward me. Seven stands at the intrusion and I spot the fine dusting of black hairs across my jeans and . . .

And it doesn't bother me. I don't feel the need to take them off and wash them now. If anything, it brings a hint of a smile to my lips, knowing he's leaving a mark in his own way. The warmth of his body on my leg, the heavy weight on my foot—it felt calming.

All right, Seven. Maybe this will work.

My dad leaves much later, after having dinner with us and checking on me a little heavy-handedly—again. I pretend I don't see him asking Rhys if I'm all right before demanding I follow him outside to his car. Practically pushing me down the sidewalk.

"You promise that you're—"

"I'm fine," I say for the four hundredth time. "Honestly. I'm . . . great, actually."

His eyes twinkle in the amber streetlights, seeming younger by years at my light confession. "Yeah?"

"Yeah," I skate a hand through my messy waves and step closer. "Don't tell anyone, but . . . there's a girl."

If possible, his eyes glow brighter. "Tell me about her."

CHAPTER 12

NOW

Paloma

"No fucking way," I mutter, slowing the car to a crawl.

"It's great, right?" Alessia calls through my phone speaker.

The street is nice, filled with homes owned by sweet families far out of my price range and a connected set of brick buildings with identical layouts—pretty brownstones that resemble a small Beacon Hill more than a strip of neighborhood closer to downtown Waterfell.

Something I could not afford in my wildest dreams.

"Yeah! If I was about fifteen tax brackets higher."

"I don't even think they have that many—"

"Alessia," I beg. "Be so serious right now."

"I am. Trust me. I talked to the girl renting it and she's a doll. Just stop being so stubborn and fighting me at every corner. Go check it out and call me back after. Okay? Okay! Love you!" She sputters out the last of her words and quickly hangs up before I can argue further.

I slam a hand on the steering wheel in frustration, immediately preparing to throw the car in reverse and hightail it out of there. I can apologize to Alessia tomorrow and sleep in my car tonight.

Before I can back out someone calls for me to, "Wait!"

Out of the least decorated of the townhomes comes a girl in tall black boots, nylons, and a skirt, with a thick gray coat and scarf bundling her up nearly to her eyes. Her auburn hair is almost in a clip, but it's lopsided, half fallen.

I recognize her immediately as the girl I ran into in the advisor building.

"Are you Paloma?" she asks, tripping over the end of the sidewalk and grabbing my rolled-down window with her gloved fingers. Blue eyes bright, she smiles and shoves her scarf down out of her mouth with her chin.

"I am—" I begin, but she cuts me off quickly.

"I've been waiting for you to show up all morning. Do you want to come inside? I can help you carry something?"

She looks like she's pushing five feet, barely able to reach up to the window of my old SUV. I think anything heavier than fifty pounds might knock her over.

"I'm good. This is—" I shake my head as I look around again. "I don't think I can live here."

My tone is more defensive than I mean it, but I try to soften it.

"Oh." She huffs a breath, biting on her lip and looking anywhere but my eyes. "But you haven't even seen it."

"It's—"

"Just . . . I really need a roommate. Can you come in and see? It's really nice, I promise."

That's the problem.

Something about her makes me pause. I want to leave. There's a shameful element to this for me. But instead, I nod and direct her away from the window so I can park against the curb. I tuck my sock-clad feet back into my clogs and hop down, not bothering to roll up the too-long legs of my jeans even as they graze the bits of clinging snow dusting the pavement.

"It's freezing." I say the words offhand, but she doesn't reply, only watches me over her shoulder as she leads us up the front entryway stairs. The door is cracked open.

I follow her in, nearly slamming into her as she stalls in the barren entryway. I wait for her to continue, to direct me through the house on a tour, but her big blue eyes are staring at me now in curious wonder.

"What's your name?" I ask.

Her mouth sinks into a frown. "I forgot to say that. It's Lily." She chews on her lip for a moment. She gestures vaguely behind her and says, "The kitchen and living room are down here. And the office—but don't go in there. It's . . . messy." It doesn't seem to be the word she was looking for, but she nods almost to herself and then looks back at me apprehensively.

I nod, mouth stuck because I can't think of what to say to the weird girl scuffling her feet in the entryway as if she's the guest.

"So—can I see the bedroom?"

"Oh, right. Yes." She cuts up the stairs, only stopping at the top to wait for me to follow.

I climb up behind her, noting the elegant ornate fixtures and knowing this entire place is far above my price range, but humoring her nonetheless. Though I continue cursing Alessia in my head.

As we pass by the first bedroom, I peek through the open doorway, quickly scanning over the half-unpacked room with things scattered all around, the walls covered in posters of famous paintings I'm sure I've seen before.

"That one is my room." She steps up beside me, glossing her eyes over the tornado-level mess of her bedroom. "Do you like van Gogh?"

"Hmm?"

"Van Gogh? He's an artist. He—those are mostly his." She fiddles with the hem of her skirt. "There's some Monet, Cézanne, and Gauguin, but it's mostly van Gogh."

I nod without really knowing what she's talking about, but it seems to please her. She walks with me to the other bedroom, which is much larger than any bedroom I've ever had before. It's empty, for the most part, but there is a full-size bed and dresser already there.

"We can move the furniture out. My dad bought it from the people that lived here, and they used to rent it. But I think—"

"It's fine." I cross my arms, staring a little longingly at the space. "How much does it—"

"How much can you pay?"

My brow furrows.

"However much you can, I'll take." Her words border on desperation, and I step back.

"Why do you need a roommate so bad?" I ask. "I mean, this place is amazing, I'm sure you have tons of—"

"My dad said I have to find someone to live with me by the end of the week or I can't stay here. And . . . I *really* don't want to move back in with him." Lily's words are a little too loud, but she doesn't seem to realize it. "And you're the first, like . . . nice person to show up . . . and the first girl." I nearly huff a laugh at her calling me nice but manage to smother it. Her expression sours, but she puffs her chest up. "I don't want to live with a boy, but I will if I have to."

Yeah, not gonna happen.

"Okay. Tentatively, I say yes."

"Really?" Her navy eyes brighten as her smile goes deliriously wide. She reaches out and takes my hand in hers. "When can you move in?"

I let out a laugh and shake my head, reluctantly already starting to like my new weird little roommate. Maybe this is exactly the kind of change I need.

. . .

"I told you, you didn't have to come with me," I mutter, slumping in the chair and feeling more like an angsty teenager than the twenty-one-year-old college senior I am.

"What was that?" Alessia asks, tapping her fingers against her chin. "Didn't hear you."

Alessia Baudelaire is otherworldly beautiful. Dressed like she's on a Parisian weekend getaway, smoky eye and blood red lips, I can't help but think she reminds me a little bit of Sadie Brown. She's got the build of a high fashion model, tall and leggy, with golden shimmery skin and dark brown eyes that are nearly black, even more intense with her near permanent scowl.

I might find her visually overdramatic now. But at eighteen, I'd found her intensity to be comforting, protective. She'd been my shield and sword that I trusted enough to hide behind.

And then I'd punished myself by shutting her out.

"I can do this myself. You don't have to follow me around like you're worried I'm going to off myself."

"Hmm," she mutters, still refusing to look at me. "I've blocked out the ability to hear bullshit actually, so—"

The door creaks open, the blond woman with kind eyes in the doorway watching as I stick my tongue out at Alessia. She smirks at me, murmuring "Very mature" under her breath as we both stand—her elegantly, me unfurling out of the chair like a clumsy house cat.

"Miss Blake?" The woman asks, eyes darting between the two of us. Alessia is in her late thirties, so no one would ever mistake her for my mother—which I'm grateful for. I don't think I could stomach that faux pas. "I'm Dr. Sutton. Or Sam, whatever you prefer."

"Yeah, hi. Nice to meet you," I say as I'm awkwardly half-shoved toward her by Alessia.

"I'll see you when you get out," Alessia says, smirking before spinning on her elegant heels and darting off.

I follow Dr. Sutton into her office, trying desperately to remind my racing heart that this is therapy I'm walking into, not a federal prison.

It doesn't work much.

. . .

The inside of Dr. Sutton's office is warm wooden walls, clean and well-enclosed except for one dark window in the corner, where winter browns and blues mix.

"Take a look around, if you want, and make yourself comfortable while I grab my intake form."

I nod, stepping slowly along the wall where multiple degrees are framed and proudly displayed. There are a few pictures of her with a beautiful redheaded woman, including a wedding photo of them both in dresses, sitting against a brick wall and laughing, eyes on each other instead of the camera.

My gaze snags on another photo as well—a team photo for Yale Swimming & Diving, a championship photo. Tucked in the more ornate frame is a Polaroid of three girls grinning broadly at the camera with a trophy in their collective grip.

"Do you swim?"

I jolt from the trance-like state the image seemed to put me in. "Sorry."

She shakes her head softly, gesturing toward the couch, loveseat, and armchair for me to choose a spot. "Don't be. I'm quite proud of that win."

Sitting in the corner of the long, dark red sofa, I try to get comfortable but can't. Not really.

"Do you swim?" she asks again.

"Oh, um . . . yes, but not like that." I nod toward her mini shrine across the room. She nods, sitting in the chair opposite me and putting a paper atop the side table nearest her.

"What do you mean?"

"I mean, not for a team or anything. I just like swimming."

She smiles. "What's swimming like for you?"

The question isn't what I expected. In fact, I was more than ready for her to begin with *So tell me what's wrong with you?* Or *Let's talk about your traumatic childhood.*

"I guess it's kind of therapeutic," I say, wincing as I realize my choice of words. "I mean, it's calming to me. I like being in the water, really, even without the swimming. But swimming makes me feel good."

"Do you swim a lot?"

"I used to," I say, feeling my shoulders relax slightly into the cushioned seat at my back. "But not as much lately."

She nods again, before letting out a pretty smile. "Have you ever been in therapy before?"

"Yes, but I was a kid, and it was court ordered."

Maybe I want to shock her a little, but she only nods politely again.

"Would you like for me to go over how today's session is going to go?"

I nod.

"I'm just going to ask you some general questions about yourself. If, for today, you don't want to talk about it, feel free to tell me that as well. You aren't required to talk about anything during our time together. You lead; I follow. For now." She winks. "Tell me about your family."

My shoulders stiffen before I can help it, eyes darting back to the photos behind her head as if just the image of the water will stabilize me.

Before I've thought of how to say anything without screaming *I don't want to talk about my mom*, she's moved on. "Tell me a little about Waterfell—where you live, what you're studying."

"I'm a sports management major," I say, blowing a breath to flutter the hairs fallen from my high ponytail out of my face. "And I . . . I'm moving to a new apartment today."

"Oh?"

A noncommittal noise rolls through my closed lips as I cross my arms.

I briefly recap my last three years in a quick summary of the woes of random roommates, before skipping eloquently over my complete spiral and into Alessia finding me an apartment. Which easily leads into a conversation about Alessia.

I'm leaving more gaps in my stories than I am offering vulnerability, but at least I'm talking at all.

The session finishes quicker than I'm expecting, and I start to follow Dr. Sutton out. As we pass her desk in the corner by the door, she stops to put away her pen and papers.

"Why haven't you gone swimming recently?" she asks, though she doesn't look at me.

"Just haven't had the time," I lie, shrugging, then crossing my arms over my chest again.

She tucks my paper into her file and nods, straightening back up. "I think you should try to go this week, if you can make the time for it."

CHAPTER 13

THEN: Freshman Year, September

Paloma

My job with the hockey team isn't what I expected—but it's not bad. Or difficult. I rarely see the team, spending most of my time in the laundry room holding my breath and ignoring Jeremy—my colleague—and his stupid mouth.

Though, I've imagined punching him in it several times.

"Honestly, Paloma," he says from his side of the laundry room, tossing one of the practice jerseys into the wrong bin. I snatch it quickly enough and toss it into the *correct* pile. "It's just kind of distracting."

When we'd met on our first day together, he'd shaken my hand and said, "I didn't think they hired girls for guys' sports." I'd tried to laugh off the immediate tension as I asked him why.

"You know," he'd said, smiling and elbowing me like we were already pals sharing an inside joke. "I don't think they want to worry about the guys sleeping with the girls, getting distracted or starting drama."

Since then, my anger toward him has only grown. I still haven't found the end of it.

"Distracting?" I ask, my voice louder than usual. I'm almost always the *nod and end the conversation* type of person, but he's made these comments three times in the past week. "I'm wearing the exact same thing as you."

"Yeah, but c'mon, Paloma. You have to know what you look like."

You look just like your mother.

With a body like that? What do you expect, Polly?

My stomach rolls with nausea as the words reopen old wounds I've fought hard to close.

Jeremy's eyes scroll over the school-issued track pants and polo—identical to his current outfit—lingering over parts of my body I wish he didn't even know existed. "Maybe you should get a baggier set."

"I don't even work with the team. We do laundry. We're—"

"Still." He waves his hand at me dismissively.

My body curves in, naturally wanting to hide whatever he's seeing. I swallow down the vitriol I want to spew, taking in a few calming breaths to push back the tears of frustration.

"Okay, Jeremy." I smile at him bitterly. "Actually, why don't you let me finish the rest by myself. You said you have a test, so you can get out of here earlier."

"No, you don't have—"

"I insist."

It doesn't take much more than that for him to cut out early for the day, a pep in his step. I don't give him my back, eyes locked on him as he salutes me and saunters out the door.

Screaming into the pulled-up collar of my shirt doesn't help.

• • •

It takes me twice the amount of time to prep without Jeremy's help, but I do it happily—

—until I glance at the clock and realize that practice has been over for nearly an hour.

"Shit," I curse, darting down the hallway and bursting into the locker room, expecting it to be empty. Expecting *him* to have left instead of waiting for me.

But Bennett Reiner is still here, standing stiffly where he always stands when I meet him after practice. His eyes dart to me at my rather cacophonous entrance, body straightening to his full, daunting height.

"I'm sorry—"

His fists curl for a moment, neck visibly tight as he shakes his head. "It's fine."

It clearly isn't, but I ignore it and reach for the careful pile of his uniform. I've hit my limit on male ego for the day—and if he's this upset about me being late when this isn't even technically my *job*—

"I got a dog," he blurts. It only surprises me because he's usually quiet, just observing while I practice his routine, never returning my polite smiles. "His name is Seven."

"Seven," I repeat, not looking up from my task. "Weird name for a dog. Though I'm surprised you didn't name him Sonnet, or after some ancient white man who wrote overly structured poetry."

My words are snippier than I mean for them to be, and the almost childlike hurt that moves across his face makes me feel *worse*.

"Sorry." I shake my head, head dropping. "I'm being mean. I just . . . I had a bad day today."

"What happened?"

"Nothing," I say quickly. "It's fine."

Bennett is always aware of his size, never crowding me, never touching me intentionally or unintentionally. He doesn't move closer, only stares expectantly.

"I don't really get along with one of the guys who works with me."

"Is he mean to you?"

There's a gruffer quality to his voice that wasn't there before.

I shrug. "Sometimes. He just . . . he thinks he's funny."

What a beautiful turn of phrase to say that he's a misogynistic asshole.

Bennett nods, arms still crossed as I finish the last of his pads. He helps me put them back in his cubby before we step back in unison.

His body is warm, heat still wafting off him where I'm close enough to feel it. The smell of him is heady, as it always is—sandalwood and bergamot, and something else, too, that reminds me of the water on a coastal beach.

Bennett always showers and dresses fully before meeting me after each practice, hair damp and body still flushed. His skin is always smooth, too, as if he's just shaved.

"If he bothers you again, tell me."

The words are steady and strong, more confident than any eighteen-year-old's should be. His expression is as serious as his tone. It might be the harshest I've ever heard him speak.

"Okay."

He waits by the door for me to gather my belongings, like he always does, before holding every door open for me until we're out of the arena and into the lightly crisp September air. A beat of silence hangs in the air.

"Have a good night, Paloma."

It's the first time he's said my name.

"You too, Bennett."

He pauses and turns back to me, calling my name under the glow of the parking lot lights. "I think you'd like Sylvia Plath," he says, a strange look in his eyes. But no smile, as if my relation to her might not be celebratory to him.

"Yeah?"

"Yeah."

Later that night, I read "The Moon and the Yew Tree" and quietly cry. He doesn't know, not really. He couldn't. But Bennett sees something no one else has.

I'm not sure if it comforts me or scares me.

CHAPTER 14

NOW

Bennett

"Great work today," Coach Harris says, stepping into the locker room—eyes darting toward the huddled, chatting pair of Holden and Toren. "Dougherty, Kane, Coach LaBlanc wants an extra twenty with the pair of you. Take five and head back."

They don't argue, but I can see their furrowed brows like matching marks on their faces. Still, something with the new coach must be going right, because they've never been cleaner on the ice together.

"Everyone else, get some rest."

I start to undress, slow as I remove my padding. Rhys slots in next to me, already half naked and dripping with sweat.

"All right?" I ask, because if he's not smiling post-practice my stomach sinks with the worry that I've missed something—again. That my best friend is drowning *again* and I'm not taking care of him.

"What?" he asks, half-distracted. "Oh, yeah—I'm good." He offers a dimpled grin and warm brown eyes. "Are you headed home?"

"After this? Yes."

"I think Ro and Sadie are already drunk." Freddy snorts, smacking a hand on Rhys's shoulder. "Hence why our captain is losing his usually calm demeanor."

"I'm losing my *usually calm demeanor*"—he mimics Freddy's

teasing tone—"because I haven't had a minute alone with my girlfriend in weeks."

My brow furrows. "Why?"

"Liam has been having nightmares." His face is serious, slightly heartbroken as he speaks softly about Sadie's youngest brother. "It's . . . it's not going well. And Oliver is . . . adjusting to my parent's house. He's too grown up for his own good."

He checks his phone again, closing his eyes and tilting his head to the sky with a whispered curse. I know it's something from his girlfriend as he mutters, "One more goddamn photo, Gray," he mutters, before tossing the offending device in his backpack while Freddy laughs.

"You coming with us, Reiner?" Freddy asks, stripped down to his boxers as he turns for the showers without even waiting for my answer.

Rhys looks at me. "You're more than welcome to. It would be nice, all of us together."

There's a moment of hesitation where I want to say yes—if only to be nearer to them. But I know the pain being the fifth wheel brings. I experience it at every family breakfast, even when I'm happy to see them happy and taken care of. But this might be too much.

"You guys go ahead," I say. "I've got a huge project to get ahead on."

It takes me twice as long to do my routine, so I haven't even showered by the time they're leaving, dressed for the bars downtown. Both smiling. Both incandescently happy.

I can't be mad, it's not fair to them—to be mad at their happiness?

It doesn't stop the longing, the pain in my chest like a wound, hollowed out and scarred over—but still so tender even just a graze against it is enough to send my hurt spiraling into memories.

The locker room is nearly cleared out by the time I'm done with my postgame ritual, before I start on cleaning my gear and pads, stacking them carefully as I always do.

Not always. *The thought comes unbidden, and unwanted. It draws me to my bag, unzipping it to grab my phone like muscle memory fused with tremors of anxiety as I check for a text that I don't want to see as much as I do.*

Nothing.

I take it as a sign that I'm safe to shower before dressing and grabbing my bag to head toward the nearly empty parking lot with a slap to Coach Harris's office door to tell him the locker room is cleared.

It isn't until I've pulled into the driveway of the Hockey House that my phone lights up in the cupholder.

A text, not a call—which could be better or worse.

P

Walk me home?

The words are familiar at this point. After hearing her weak voice whisper them that first night months ago, we'd treated the phrase like a code for help. A code that she needs me.

The call of her is impossible to resist. Like it always has been. As much as I waited with bated breath for her text, now I'm fueled by only anger.

Is it better to know her as this hurtful thing in my chest than to not know if she's breathing?

I don't know.

But I'm reversing out of the driveway and down the street immediately, following her location on the map until I pull up to some disgustingly overcrowded house, a half ripped-down sign congratulating the football team on another win. The front yard is covered with groups laughing and shouting, but it's all white noise.

My eyes find her immediately, sitting precariously on the overhang of the porch and swinging her legs back and forth. Blond hair bouncy and voluptuous, cascading around her pink-cheeked face. She's dressed in a dusty blue corset and jeans, enough skin on show to know she must be freezing. Or she's drunk enough not to feel the cold.

No one is around her, but that doesn't mean she's been alone tonight.

She spots me and hops haphazardly down, nearly face-planting— close enough to it that I'm shooting out of the truck and across the grass without preamble.

"Jesus, P," I sigh, grabbing her around the waist to steady her.

Brown doe eyes glimmer up at me, her entire body relaxing as she lets me take her weight and guide her to the passenger side of the car. I lift her by her waist into my truck, buckling her seatbelt before heading around to the driver's side.

Bon Iver croons in the cab, the gentle sounds sharply contrasting with the thunderous booming house music in a way that makes my head pound as I drive us away.

"Hungry?" I ask, voice gentle despite the pain of being this close to her.

"I want chicken nuggets," her soft voice sighs as she burrows into my bicep. "Can we?"

It's impossible to ignore the twinkling eyes she darts up at me. Her pouty mouth that's almost always scowling is smiling lightly. At me.

Paloma Blake might be the snarling, claws-out girl to everyone else, but to me she's something different.

Something softer.

"Yeah, I'll make you some while you shower," I say, pulling into the darkened driveway.

"With spicy ketchup?"

I ruffle her hair gently. "With spicy ketchup."

My roommates are out of the house commiserating our loss, so it's easy to sneak her in—especially when she hops onto my back with no complaint. Easier to get her inside and upstairs without the drunk stumbling into every piece of furniture we have.

I shut and lock my door before letting her slide down my back.

While she starts to take off her shoes, I head to the bathroom to turn on the shower, waiting until it's steamy-warm.

Stumbling a little, I grip the doorframe and dart my eyes to the ceiling to avoid searing the image of her—only in the blue corset bodysuit now—into my mind.

"Shower's ready."

I hear the light pitter-patter of her feet to the door. She ducks under my arms with a quick kiss pressed to the center of my chest, a distinct inhale from her like she's seeking my scent.

Once, she told me that the way I smell is comforting to her. That it makes her feel safe. Now, when I catch her trying to take in the scent of my clothes, I worry a little that something has made her feel unsafe.

I close her in the bathroom after leaving a pile of clothes on the countertop.

I keep my room cold because I can't stand sweating in my sleep. Which means I have to dress Paloma in warm clothes.

She emerges, swimming in the sweatpants I laid out for her. My sweatshirt, which has a near-hole chewed out of the right sleeve where Paloma likes to bite—a self-soothing tactic that makes my stomach roll every time she does it—covers her to midthigh. But she looks warm and cozy, skin still flushed from the hot shower, but eyes less glassy.

I pat the bed for her to sit, one of her brushes in my hand. Her wet hair lays in tangles, but I'm careful with each section as I brush through it until every strand is smooth down her back and she's nearly asleep in my hands.

"I thought you wanted chicken nuggets," *I ask, knowing she won't stay awake long enough for me to make it to the kitchen and back.*

"Goldfish, please," *she mumbles, sinking further into my chest. I laugh a little and reach over into my side table for one of the small bags of them.*

She lets me hand-feed her, laying pliantly against me, eyes closed softly as I press the fish-shaped crackers to her lips until she finishes the bag.

"Love you, P," I whisper, pressing a kiss to her forehead and rolling her to sleep on her side where I can keep watch over her until I fall asleep.

• • •

The kitchen is quiet, which years ago might've been fine—preferable even. But now it just fills me with a stifling sense of loss.

I've lived with Rhys nearly my entire life, at least in some capacity. As a child, my time with my dad was half spent at the Koteskiy house. As teens we attended Berkshire together, living together for over half the year in a dormitory. And now we're here at Waterfell.

Seven pads gently behind me, slumping against the back of my legs when I freeze by the stove before rousing myself and starting on the food.

When I check the fridge, a bolt of irritation rushes down my spine as I see Rhys and Freddy's meal-prepped food untouched. Rhys's has a note atop it that must be from yesterday.

Ended up having dinner with the girls. Sorry we let it go to waste.

Grabbing the containers, I toss the food and clean them until my hands are red from the heat of the water and the harsh chemicals of the soap. I take the time to dry them before putting the dishes away.

As I put a pan back, I get sidetracked for a moment by the one green pan that's different from my meticulous stainless-steel collection. Freddy's pan—the only one I allow him to use.

A smile pushes at my face, before another pang of loss replaces it. He hasn't used it in weeks.

My phone rings and I answer it without checking, too distracted by memories of Rhys and Freddy taking up space in the kitchen to realize who it is.

"Hello?"

"Bennett." My dad's half-shocked voice fills the line. He clears his throat. "How are you?"

Most people assume that the breaking of my relationship with my dad is centered around the divorce and his relationship with my mother. But no one knows the real situation, the real reason I've built walls between us, lost my respect for him.

"Fine."

I'm sure he was expecting a voicemail box he could speak to since I haven't taken his calls in months, but my stupid mistake has us both awkwardly silent, breathing into the phone.

"If you'd just talk to me—"

My head is already swimming, anger and frustration coating my voice. "Stop."

He does, immediately. "Sorry . . . sorry." Another unnecessary clearing of his throat, and then, "Max and Anna have invited us to dinner next week. Friday. Rhys is going as well. Will you be there?"

It's currently one of the last places I'd like to be—but with Rhys in the mix, I'll never say no.

"All right. I'll come."

He blows out a hard breath. I hang up before he can say anything else.

Instead, I spend the night with Seven asleep on my thighs and some Food Network competition on in the background while I check Paloma's social media like a stalker, frustrated when it reveals nothing.

I scroll through her photos until my chest feels so tight I can't breathe, then—even though I know it will hurt—I open the untitled folder in my photo album where photos of dirty blond hair in my hands and a beautiful girl asleep on my chest bring me more pain than comfort.

"Don't you want me? I can make it so good for you. Just like old times—"

"Sometimes I think you're not real. That I dreamed you up."

I barely manage to fall asleep; the want of her so intense I'm sure I can hold it in my hands. It's only the heavy calming presence of my dog that seems to do the trick.

CHAPTER 15

NOW

Bennett

P
Can we talk? Sorry to bother you.

I discreetly check the text once more, nearly fumbling the phone out of my sweat-slick hands as my knee shakes. I'm ready to burst out of the room the second my professor dismisses us.

Paloma texted me.

We haven't spoken since our run-in at the Hockey House, and she was gone when I tried to catch her again that night after practice. There were no signs of her ever having been in the house, to the point it almost made me feel more insane about her than usual, that I'd wholly imagined her.

The words of dismissal are barely out of my professor's mouth before I'm off like a shot, backpack swinging against my shoulder as I shove myself through the door in an out-of-character clumsy maneuver. I knock someone over but don't bother to apologize as my shoulder careens into the wall.

But she's there, leaning against the opposite wall with the windows highlighting the bright blond of her hair held back in a clip.

She's dressed like herself again, jeans and an oversized white long sleeve, a brown fleece vest overtop. Her eyes are locked on me; the warm feeling of being observed by her feeds my soul.

"Sorry, I didn't mean to stress you out," she blurts, pushing off the wall toward me. Student traffic packs the hall, so I crowd her back against the navy-painted concrete. I can almost see her anxiety clip off into nothing as I cover her with my body completely.

She's not yours, I remind myself, backing off just slightly. *Relax. Don't push her away.*

"Hey, Paloma," I say, unable to keep my lips from upturning, even only slightly.

"Hey, Bennett," she says, her voice melting down to softness.

I see then a million tiny flashes of this same moment, from age eighteen to now—nearly four years of memories, her voice multilayered in my brain.

"What did you want to talk to me about?"

She nibbles her bottom lip slowly. "I know you're about to go to the Wellness Center, but I figured I could walk with you?"

I should be anxious about the fact that she needs to talk to me about something this badly, but my brain is stuck on the fact that she remembers my routine.

"My lunch is in my bag."

It's not what I meant to say, to explain that I usually pack it because I prefer to eat the same lunch at the same time every day. Even knowing that she already *knows* that.

"That's perfect. I'll just walk with you. I already ate."

I don't tell her that it's hard for me to believe that, or that it doesn't quell the anxiety like watching her eat a meal might. I don't tell her that it doesn't matter if she *did* eat already, I won't be able to keep from wanting to slip her the childish snacks—a yogurt, crackers, fruit snacks—I always pack for her, just in case. Just to be sure.

Just in case.

"I want to talk to you about hockey," Paloma says, clearing her throat as I open the door to the concourse slowly, slipping on my sunglasses at the sight of the brightened sun glinting off the still-icy ground. "I—um, I'll be serving my last semester in an internship with ice sports. So, half pairs skating, half hockey with Coach Harris. It's just to shadow him, but if that would make you uncomfortable or . . . anything, I can figure out something else."

She looks a little seasick.

"Is that . . . okay?"

Is that okay? That I'll know where she is for hours? That I'll be able to see her? That I can watch her achieve her dream this close?

"More than okay," I say, eyes shimmering. I slow my stride just slightly as I see the Wellness Center not so far away, desperate to prolong my time in the warmth of her. "I'm so proud of you, P."

"Yeah?" She laughs. It's the same reaction she had to my words of praise three years ago.

"Yeah."

My eyes take her in again, the grip of her hand on the strap of her same blue backpack that she never lets out of her sight. The gentle swoop of her blond bangs across her temple, the icy strands bright against the sunlight.

How many years will this curse persist—me desperately in want of her? Am I so destined to become my father?

She follows me into the Wellness Center but stops just in the entryway.

"I got a new apartment," she blurts, cheeks flushing. "So I won't be at the Hockey House, invading your space and bothering you." It's an attempt at a joke, but I shake my head.

"You could never bother me." My voice is more serious than I mean for it to be. I double down, taking her hand in mine. "Never."

There's a long moment then, the air thick between us. The light from the wall of windows plays along her hair, her pretty, delicate skin, her peachy lips. It's hard, sometimes, to separate her mind from her beauty. To separate the girl I love from the girl I tend to lust after. Who I think of in the shower and often.

But at the same time, I am covetous of *her*, even from myself. I love her too much to sink back into the comfort of her body, to allow her to do the same.

I'm different now than when we first met. I have better ways of handling myself, of handling her. And I am even more determined than I was at eighteen that if she just gives me her hand one more time, we can be together. She'll allow me to hold her in the way I so desperately want to.

That she'll let me take care of her.

Slow and steady, I remind myself. It's almost an impossible feat with this girl, the woman I've been obsessed with since I was eighteen years old. The only girl I've ever loved, ever wanted in any way.

"I'll see you around, then?" she offers.

I nod, slipping a pack of Goldfish into her hand with a quiet, "Yeah, P. I'm not going anywhere."

CHAPTER 16

NOW

Paloma

It's loud.

I remember that much from freshman year, though I'd been *in* the locker and equipment rooms before. Now I'm seated in the chair outside Coach Harris's office, waiting for him to approve my schedule, so being able to hear the entire team from here tells me just how loud they are.

A door slams as I spot Toren Kane escaping one of the offices like a bat out of hell. Or Satan out of heaven.

Toren Kane—the new barnacle latched onto my side. The dark outcast of the hockey team I can't seem to shake, though my life would be far easier without him always playing both angel and devil on my shoulder.

"I'm not done," another voice snaps, drawing my attention to the well-dressed man standing in the doorway of the room Toren just left.

Toren spins on his heel and stretches his arms out wide, nearly touching both sides of the concrete hallway.

"Like I said," he sneers, "I don't give a fuck. Suspend me if you want to. Kiss the whole team's season goodbye."

There's confidence and arrogance in his voice, but he looks distressed. Head bent low and midnight black hair messy, he nearly darts past me without a second glance. As if he doesn't know I'm there.

The familiar man in the navy suit eyes me briefly and shakes his head, ducking back into his office and slamming the door.

"Does everyone hate you then?" I snip, making Toren pause in his steps.

Golden eyes scan over me; his brow furrows only for a second before a smile reveals his eerily sharp canines.

"It's my specialty, actually." He crosses his arms. "Here to try out for my spot? Or just to stare at Reiner until you feel sick?"

My stomach rolls and I scoff, looking away from him before his intense, irritating gaze can see more than he already has since last semester.

Though he's always seen right through me.

"You're drooling."

I rear back, away from the voice that snuck up on me in a corner at the Hockey Dorms Halloween party. I'm greeted by the sight of a tall figure in a Ghostface mask and a white button-down. Chuckling, he slides off the mask.

"Don't you have a summer camp to terrorize?" I snap out, heading away from him.

"Wrong movie," Toren grumbles, following behind. "And wrong direction—the Ninja Turtles you were so enamored with are back in there—"

"Stop it," I snap, spinning on my heel toward him and immediately regretting the move as my eyes lock onto the large green man in the kitchen just yards away. He's turned the opposite way, broad naked shoulders coated meticulously in green body paint and the tie of a blue eye mask half covered in messy brunette curls. He's so handsome it hurts, even now.

I usually avoid the Hockey Dorms when it comes to parties, because seeing Bennett relaxed or semi-drunk with a little smile on his usually frowning lips ignites an ache that pushes me toward him. That fills me with the false confidence of maybe *and* what if.

Bennett turns, eyes meeting mine briefly over his shoulder, the blue of them somehow more intense through his mask. My eyes grow as hot as my cheeks, gnawing want like a chasm in my stomach.

Turning away before I can do or say something to make this all worse, I grab the handle of the sliding door and step onto the lantern-lit patio. Toren follows me closely, tucking the mask into the waistband of his pants.

"Poor little Blake," Toren sneers, grabbing for my wrist and pulling me close. "So in love with a boy who loves her back but she won't let herself have him. Pathetic."

"You don't get it." *I feebly shove at him as he crowds me against the nearest wall, hiding me completely from the view of anyone else outside with us.*

"No?" *He tilts his head over mine and whispers in my ear.* "Self-hatred runs deep, Blake. And mine runs through every vein in my god-damn body. I bleed it."

I push him, harder this time, but he grabs my wrists to stop me. His hands move, fingers dusting over the strands of my dyed red hair, his golden eyes glazing over like a trance at the auburn color before he startles himself out of it.

"Poison Ivy?" *He smirks, scoffing as he runs disinterested eyes over my costume.* "Fitting."

"Fuck you."

His eyes sparkle. "You wish you could. But that's some twisted line you won't cross, right? You don't want to hurt him; you want to hurt *you*."

Like arrows to a target, the words easily find their mark.

"I'm not in love with him. You're just a psycho."

Something flashes in his eyes, and he slams a fist against his chest, like stabbing a knife into his heart.

"Yeah?" He laughs, eyes wet. "You're the one who has what you want within reach, and still, you treat him like shit. But I'm the psycho, right?"

Toren mumbles under his breath, shoving his hand into his pocket and pulling out a sucker. He unwraps it and pushes it between his lips, then presses himself into the wall, perched like the grim reaper watching the party with hate-filled eyes.

Even without the Ghostface mask, even sucking on a grape lollipop, he's terrifying. Most give him a wide berth as they move through the party, but I see the girls whose gazes linger a little too long. Like they want to see exactly what the bad boy has to offer.

I spend the night avoiding Bennett Reiner.

As much as I hate him for it, Toren is right. I don't want to hurt Bennett.

I want to hurt me.

Shaking myself from the memory, I open my mouth to respond to Toren.

But Toren has turned away, heading into the roaringly loud locker room. On his entrance, I hear a lull in the excitement before it starts up again, far quieter.

"Miss Blake," a voice says. I turn to meet the soft gray eyes in Coach Harris's kind face. He smiles at me, reaching out his hand to shake mine. "Good to have you back. Come on in and let's chat."

He leads me into his office, letting me settle in one of the chairs across from his large desk. Trophies line the shelves, and next to them are several photos of him with players of all ages. But mostly, of him with a woman—dark olive skin and almond brown eyes, smiling brightly up at him. His wife, I assume. His office is flooded with photos of her, of them together over decades.

"I'm going to have you shadow me on the days you're here," he says. My brow furrows deeply, mouth opening. "Is that okay?"

"Yeah, I just assumed . . . I thought I'd be with one of the assistant coaches."

"No, you'll be with me."

He examines me thoughtfully for a moment, hand reaching up to readjust his baseball cap. "I had no clue you were interested in coaching," he says. "If I had, I would've asked if you wanted to work on staff."

The fact that he remembers me at all feels . . . different. Flattering, though anxiety inducing in some measure.

Why does he remember you? I can think of a few reasons, Polly.

I cross my arms over my chest.

"Do you have any questions for me?"

I shake my head, eyes darting down toward my tapping feet. Coach Harris stands and grabs a bag from the corner, then tosses it to me.

"School-issued warm-up jacket for you. I'll get you some more merch. You can wear whatever athletic gear you want for practices, but I'll make sure they get you some jackets and sweats from the team gear." He sits back at his desk and signs off on my schedule paper, spinning it back to me. "And you'll work at least three games on the bench with me."

"Okay."

"All right." He nods his head and smiles. "Today is half strength and conditioning before on-ice time. Let's go deal with the pack of idiots I call my team." The words are sarcastic, but there's a glimmer of mischief in his eyes as he rounds his desk and opens the door for me. I follow him into the weight room.

I nearly trip and slam face first in the middle of the room at the sight that greets me.

Bennett, one leg extended to his side, the other bent back so his heel is nearly touching his ass. He's bent over the extended leg to stretch, but only briefly, before he lays flat forward and switches his legs.

Coach Harris starts writing a few things on his clipboard and speaking low with one of the strength trainers.

And my eyes are focused, ashamedly, on Bennett Reiner's ass as he settles onto the ground in a position like the splits, but with both legs bent at the knee, heels toward his butt. A frog pose with his groin flush to the ground, hands planted in front of him as he rocks back and forth into the stretch.

My mouth is bone dry, face hot.

"Feel sick yet?" A voice laughs, low in my ear. I blink at Toren as he walks by, grabbing a roller from the stack at my side. "Looking a little warm, Blake."

He sits near to Bennett's space and starts to dramatically roll out his hips, nearly obscenely humping the floor.

"Kane," Coach Harris snaps, eyeing him with an exasperated glare. "This is a gym. Not a sex club. And there is a lady present. Act right."

The same blue-suit-wearing assistant coach steps forward and snorts, muttering beneath his breath, "Toren Kane couldn't act right if his life depended on it. I'll take him to the ice early, if that's all right, Harris?"

Harris observes Toren for a moment before nodding. "Work your magic. I hired you for a reason, LaBlanc."

"Kane," Coach LaBlanc snaps out, voice booming over the blaring music. "C'mon. Show's over."

Toren looks like he's been handed a death sentence, his eyes ghosting over the crowd of his reluctant teammates. Holden stands up, adding a quick, "Need me, too?"

It makes sense—Holden Dougherty is Toren's defensive partner. They're a pair, so they should practice together. But LaBlanc shakes his head and follows a sulking Toren out of the room.

"Meet you all on the ice in a half hour," Coach Harris announces, turning toward me. "Hopefully they show you something actually impressive."

I can't help the grin that forms at feeling more a part of this team than I ever have before.

· · ·

After practice, I wait until I'm sure the locker room is empty, taking my time to stall and walk the arena halls before chancing a quick glance through the door.

Bennett is the only one left, slowly and meticulously working on his gear.

A rush of longing blares through me at the memory of so many nights like this—him and me, washing his pads and doing his routine together.

My eyes dart around the room as I stay hidden behind the doorframe for a smidge longer. I can see the past versions of us around me. The place where, arguably, we fell in love.

I miss him.

I leave before he can see me.

CHAPTER 17

THEN: Freshman Year, September

Bennett

It's the last week of September, which brings cooler weather and my usual anxiety surrounding the start of the hockey season, multiplied tenfold for the newness of this year.

It's also a Tuesday, which means I'm currently stuffed into the front seat of my dad's car, seat shoved back to accommodate my spread, shaking knees where I've dipped my head as I puff out breaths in a pattern.

Therapy isn't always like this, but sometimes it is.

"You could have brought Seven." His voice is kind, but I hear the words my dad wanted to say. *You should have brought Seven.* And he's right.

"I'll be fine," I grit out, shaking my head again and abruptly opening the door like I'll suddenly run with glee into the brownstone office building in front of me. Instead, as soon as the door shuts behind me, I falter again.

Go inside and tell her everything.

There's a small squeaking sound as my dad rolls down the window, and then his voice, calm and steadying. "I'll be back in an hour, and then we will have dinner at our usual spot." I nod in acknowledgment but don't turn back. "I love you, Ben."

He drives away before I take a step, but his words lead me up the well-kept stone steps and into the waiting room.

• • •

I've been seeing my therapist since I was first diagnosed as a kid. A mild-mannered but firm woman, Dr. Anya is the only one who knows my routines as deeply as I do.

"How has your week been, Bennett?"

She always starts with this question, while pulling her pen from behind her ear in a way that somehow doesn't disrupt the tightly slicked-back bun of ringlets she always wears. Her white shirt is so crisp I can hear the fabric as it brushes against itself, bright against the deep umber of her skin.

"Fine."

I always start with this answer, even if it isn't how I feel. Dr. Anya, however, is always immediately aware of my mood. A side effect of seeing me almost every week since I was eight. We spent the last several sessions talking about the "new shift" in my life, from boarding school to college, and she's allowed me to avoid the topic of my best friend slowly outgrowing me. Instead, we talk about hockey.

Mostly, the team's newest equipment manager.

"And how is the new routine there?"

This time I *know* she's talking about Paloma. We've spoken about her before, enough that I think I've painted a clear picture of exactly the level of my feelings for her, which inevitably climb higher each day. My cheeks blush involuntarily.

"Fine. She does everything right, so maybe I don't need to watch over her anymore."

Dr. Anya purses her lips. "Does that make you uncomfortable? Having her do it alone without your guidance?"

What makes me uncomfortable isn't relinquishing control to Paloma or trusting her—I already do. What makes me uncomfortable is the realization that not being with her would be the unwelcome change in this new routine.

"I like that time with her," I admit softly.

A weight lifts off my chest—only one of many, but it's a welcome relief to say it aloud.

Dr. Anya nods and taps her pen a few times. "Could you see yourself wanting more time with her? Rather than just in the arena for a few minutes?"

"She's in my poetry class."

"Outside of class and her work, Bennett. Would you enjoy doing something else with her?"

My brow furrows but I nod.

"Maybe you could ask her to get coffee."

There's an immediate discomfort that forces me to shake my head. *I take it back—I don't want to spend more time with her if that's the only way.*

"No—but maybe she'll ask me." The way it has always been. Rhys asked me to skate first. Freddy shoved his way headfirst into our group. Paloma asked to help with my routine. Saying yes is easier. Starting that conversation is nearly too much to even picture.

Dr. Anya readjusts herself in the seat across from me. "I think making a friend that isn't Rhys and isn't on the hockey team is really important for you. Why don't we practice how it might go? Then you can ask her to get coffee with you after your next poetry class *or* at the arena. Whatever comes first."

I want to say no. I think I'd rather talk about Rhys and my everpresent fear than this. Hell, maybe even Dr. Anya's favorite topic—the divorce.

Except—

"I'm not really a big fan of poetry like this. It's really . . . there's a lot of rules."

"It's . . . you should try it again."

Paloma smiles, eyes bright as she looks up at me. Her long, light brown hair is haphazardly pulled back in a messy braid, pieces falling over the smooth, dewy skin of her face. The back of my neck feels hot and damp. "Maybe I will."

"Okay."

• • •

I wait a week and one day before deciding to try it.

With my dad's encouragements as he went through it all with me again over dinner last night—mixed with the hidden disappointment of my therapist that I hadn't asked her yet—I don't think there is a possibility of feeling more ready.

My knee thumps in competition with my heart throughout the class, so much so that I barely hear a word our professor has said until he announces yet again, "We're partnering up."

Brown eyes find mine immediately, a smirk hidden in plush, pinkened lips as Paloma makes her way over to me. As if no one else exists—her first choice, even if we were originally the last two chosen.

Dr. Britton looks at us with a questioning expression, but I barely notice him or hear a word he says over the pounding of my pulse. It's so loud I worry she can hear it.

Step One: Compliment her backpack—

"Hey," she says.

I nod, sitting up a little straighter in my seat.

"So, listen, I—"

I'm cut off by our professor stepping up to our cluster of desks.

"Not the *best* listeners in the group, but somehow psychic." At our confused expressions he sighs. "I was pairing everyone up for the project—not that you two seem to have heard a word of it. But, that doesn't matter, since tah-dah—" he taps his cane three times. "I was already going to pair you two—the free-verse girl and the structured sonnets boy. Like a weird, poetry superhero duo."

Paloma snickers, so I laugh lightly and smile at him with a nod.

"Are you hoping we fight to the death? E. E. Cummings versus Petrarch?"

Again, I'm silent while our professor broadly grins at her quick sarcastic wit.

"I've chosen elegies for the both of you. Or odes, should you prefer them?"

Normally, I'd enjoy the verbal sparring performance between them, but I can't focus on anything other than the directions in my head, repeating them over and over so I don't forget.

Step One: Compliment her backpack.

Step Two: Give her time to settle into her desk.

Step Three: Make eye contact and ask her, "Would you like to go to coffee with me?"

I peek at her beneath my lashes, tapping my pen in time with my entire body's thumping heartbeat. She pays attention to our professor as he moves through each piece of the assignment. Her hands fiddle mindlessly with her hair, unbraiding and re-braiding the tangled strands. My hands flex. I want to brush them.

Focus. Step One—

The buzzing of the egg timer on Dr. Britton's desk sends an immediate shuffling frenzy through the classroom. Everyone might be moving slowly, but it feels like they're frantic with the way my pulse throbs and my adrenaline spikes.

Paloma stands and I mimic her quickly. She's slow as she sticks the papers in her folder and gently places mine in my open binder, smoothing the edges until they're crisp once more.

"You said you had something to ask me?" She eyes me, expectant but hesitant.

"No." I shake my head and look down at my shoes. "I don't."

We stand there for a moment longer.

"Your backpack is cool," I finally say, face overly warm as I dare another glance to her.

Paloma grins broadly, but her cheeks pinken. She seems mildly embarrassed. "Thanks. I, um, found it at the thrift store actually—brand new, too. Had a tag and everything."

She turns slightly, as if to show off the ocean-blue bag with a Waterfell Wolves hangtag. I grip my own bag a little tighter and reach for the binder she's closed for me.

"See you later, Bennett."

Say something. Compliment her backpack. Ask her to coffee.

Say something.

My mouth closes up into a tight-lipped smile and a wave that mimics hers as she heads out of the classroom.

CHAPTER 18

THEN: Freshman Year, October

Bennett

Another week goes by in our routine and I don't manage to ask her.

I'm almost certain both my dad and my therapist are frustrated with my inaction, but neither one has pushed me to do anything. And maybe that's worse.

As Dr. Anya put it, *"Avoiding this is only hurting you, Bennett."*

Now as we leave the classroom together like we always do, Paloma chatters away. She hasn't stopped talking since our group work started. I couldn't be more grateful for it.

First, it was about the poetry project. Then, about her most recent thrift shop trip, which she was very enthusiastic about. As we leave the halls of the Haley Center for the sparkling sunlight and crowded main campus pathway, I become more aware of how often people stop to look our way.

At first, I'm sure it's about me. I'm a big guy, just like my dad, and I'm used to the quick glances and intimidated eyebrow raises as I pass. But this is different. Men mostly, running their eyes over Paloma as she walks ahead of me, like she's some performative art piece for them to look at. Something about it feels more . . . sinister than the glances I'm used to getting.

I walk a little closer behind her, like a hulking shadow, as we near the spot we usually split ways.

Try holding her hand.

It sounds so much easier than it physically is—and maybe it's just me, but the thought of reaching for her makes my throat dry.

"Sorry. I'm talking your ears off," she says, sounding a little defeated. Paloma loops a finger through the end of one of the messy twin braids she's sporting today. I've paid enough attention to know she's talking about the first hockey away series this weekend and her frustration at not being chosen over Jeremy to go. "I don't even know if I necessarily *wanted* to go, but . . . I guess it's more that I do more work than him. I try much harder than him and I still didn't even get asked—"

"Do you want to get coffee with me?"

We both freeze at the words I've blurted out. A breeze blows a few loose strands of Paloma's hair into her face and she pushes them away hastily.

"Oh," she breathes, brown eyes wide and locked on me. "As friends? Or as a date?"

My stomach plummets, the question unexpected and terrifying. Cheeks burning hot, I open and close my mouth twice before looking for the best way to exit the entire conversation.

But then, Paloma smiles at me. Soft and warm.

"I wouldn't mind if it *was* a date," she offers, eyes dancing.

The sick feeling in my stomach doesn't disappear, but somehow only grows. It's warmer, like a buzzing sensation across my body. My skin is littered with goosebumps that I blame on the cool October breeze.

"A date then." I nod. "Tomorrow—seven a.m."

It's ridiculously too soon and too early in the morning. I didn't even pose it as a question. And yet—

"It's a date."

. . .

"Is that—both of your parents?"

Freddy is the one who asks, but only because I know the answer to *that* question. Anna and Max Koteskiy are in the stands of our practice—usually forbidden, but I'm not surprised the couple is making an appearance.

Rhys nods and laughs at Freddy's very hungover and very confused face.

Max is tall and domineering even from a distance, but as soft as they come for his wife and son. Right now, however, he keeps his face stony and intense, one hand resting gently on the back of his wife's neck. A pillar of strength at her back.

"That's Maximillian Koteskiy," one of the upperclassmen says. He elbows Freddy, who nearly collapses in a way that makes me question if he's showed up to practice not just hungover, but *drunk*. "He *still* holds the record for most Stanley Cup wins—the last great enforcer."

Rhys smiles, the proud son to match his equally proud father. "Yeah, that's my dad. He swore he wouldn't pop in for hockey, so it must be for my mom."

Anna looks soft, and she is, but she's also fiercely protective. Her hair is in a slicked ponytail and she's wearing a long turtleneck dress. As always, she looks much younger than she is. Which means I'm used to the comments that I *know* are coming.

"Holy *shiiit*, Koteskiy," one of them chuckles. "That's your mom? Goddamn—"

I'm grabbing for the guy before I can even figure out who it is.

"Watch it," I snap, eyes darting to everyone around us. "That's off fucking limits."

Rhys grabs my jersey and jostles me slightly, so I let go of the upperclassman in my grasp.

Coach Harris blows his whistle then and directs us all to stand or kneel near the benches as Rhys's parents step forward.

"Hello, boys," Anna begins, smiling gently and waving to her son, who waves back just as happily—never embarrassed. "I won't take up your time, but I want to talk to you about the charity I run. It's for affordable and free housing. And I'd love to have your help."

She speaks softly, as she always does, and looks so small standing next to the bench, surrounded by sweaty asshole hockey players, it makes something in my chest ache.

If I close my eyes, just the tone of her voice echoes memories of me—at six, seven, ten years old—even at fourteen and sixteen, making biscuits and chocolate gravy with me, or trying anything I cooked, even if it was terrible.

Another memory stirs, of a boy with tears in his eyes and trembling limbs.

A quiet request: *"Do you think I could practice? Will you help me?"*

"Of course, Ben." Then, arms surrounding me—in a way that, for the first time in my life, didn't make me panic.

I shake my head, almost too harshly, jostling Rhys. He steadies me without looking away from where his father is now speaking, hand on his mother's shoulder as she gazes up at him and kisses his knuckles.

The Koteskiys have always been overly affectionate—something I never saw growing up, even if it's too painful to admit.

My parents loved each other. They did—

"Ben?"

It's Rhys, shaking my shoulder.

"Sorry. Just lost in my head today."

My best friend smiles and skates backward over the quickly emptying ice. "I'm headed to dinner with my parents. I think your dad will come, too—do you want to come?"

Do I want to watch my dad watch your parents' open adoration of each other and pretend not to be sad for my sake?

"Yeah." I nod. "I'll catch up. I have to do my routine first."

"I'll text you the address."

I wait patiently for everyone to leave before Paloma comes in to help. We don't speak, but her presence is enough to soothe me.

I walk her to her car like I always do, but this time I open her door for her and wait.

"I'm excited about tomorrow," she offers. It warms my entire body, like stepping closer to the heat of a campfire.

"Yeah?" I ask. She nods. "Me too."

My fingers ease up toward her face, daring to tuck back a stray strand of hair, letting the glossy feel linger across my skin.

"Good night, Bennett."

"Night, P," I whisper. She blushes at the soft hush of the nickname before settling into her car.

CHAPTER 19

THEN: Freshman Year, October

Paloma

Because I am sometimes a complete *moron* and, more likely, because I lose track of time when I'm in the water—I'm running late.

Quite literally running—I sprint across campus, slip-on clogs slapping the pavement, before bursting through the doors of Brew Haven at exactly 7:05 a.m.

Bennett is already there, as I knew he would be, but he stands when he sees me. My stomach swoops.

He's in beautiful olive-green trousers and a white button-down, sleeves rolled up to his elbows. His mahogany curls are soft and set carefully along the angles of his face. A sleek watch adorns his wrist, an expensive one, gold gleaming against his lightly tanned skin.

I look down at myself, a little nauseous. A well-worn gray T-shirt and thrifted overalls. My hair is still damp, tied into a loose braid that smells strongly of my roommate's expensive conditioner I used this morning.

Embarrassment floods my system, and I'm tempted to apologize for being so underdressed before saying anything else.

But Bennett is smiling, ocean-blue eyes almost crinkling as he waves for my attention. As if my eyes have gone anywhere other than to *him*.

"I'm sorry," I blurt out anyway, hands to my reddened cheeks. "Should I change?"

His brow wrinkles sharply as he looks me over, seemingly for the first time.

"Why?" There is genuine confusion in his voice. "You look very beautiful."

"Oh." I laugh, blushing further as I slide into the booth. He waits for me to sit before he follows in across from me. "Thank you."

Bennett shrugs. "You always look beautiful."

He says it like it is the least interesting thing about me. My heart squeezes.

"Thanks—"

"Why is your hair wet?" he blurts.

I blush while Bennett pales.

Bennett Reiner is carefully controlled. I've seen him in enough environments to know he's meticulous about when he speaks and what he says. But with me, he seems to do this a lot: divulging his thoughts and feelings the moment he has them, not carefully controlled. It's refreshing, and a little selfishly, it makes me feel like I'm different to him. Somehow more than everyone else.

He shakes his head at his own question, grimacing as if he didn't mean to ask and would do just about anything to take it back. His hands flex in a quick pattern as he tries to apologize. "Sorry—"

"No, it's okay. I, um." I pull at my braid, lip trapped between my teeth. "I swam this morning, so I showered really quick before, and my hair didn't dry in time. So, it's kind of a mess."

"You swim? Like, for the team here?" His brow furrows and he tilts his head, almost distressed at possibly missing this detail about me.

"Oh, no. I just like it. It makes me feel good and alleviates stress. So, I just . . . do it for fun, I guess. It's calming."

At this, he nods understandingly.

"Do you swim?" I ask.

"Recreationally, in a pool, yes. But not like . . ." He fiddles with his curls, his other hand tapping along his leg. "I don't know the technical ways."

"I could teach you, if you ever wanted to learn. Might be good conditioning."

His brow wrinkles slightly, but he clears his throat and tries another question. "Um, how long have you been swimming?"

"Since I was a kid. I—I fell into a pool and decided I should probably learn so I didn't drown." I laugh, grinning toward him, shoving a few light brown strands of hair back. "But, yeah. I just never stopped. And then it became this peaceful thing for me, something that made me feel completely calm and safe. Weird, considering I almost drowned the first time."

Another laugh slips from my mouth, but Bennett just listens, his face set in deep concentration.

A quiet pause stretches between us, not uncomfortable but long enough that Bennett seems to be growing more anxious.

"Thank you for inviting me. I—" My gaze darts up to the empty counter where a girl with brown hair twirls the ends of her ponytail while slumped with boredom or sleepiness. "Should we order?"

"Right—coffee," Bennett says, almost to himself. Like a reminder. "I can order, if you tell me what you'd like."

I don't drink coffee; never tried more than a few sips of bitter black cups in a kitchen I'd rather erase from my mind. My mom didn't have a coffeepot to wake her up, instead reaching for an orange pill bottle or fifth of whiskey.

"Mom?" A flash of bright blond hair, messy and tangled. A little girl with a brush in her hand, half-hiding behind a stained sofa to ask her mom to help her.

My stomach churns as I shove the unwanted memories away.

"What do you usually get?"

"Iced black coffee, three tablespoons of almond milk," he recites, like reading off an instruction manual. His hand rubs the back of his neck as he looks at me. "But you shouldn't get that. I mean, I'm worried you won't like it. It's not sweet, if you like that."

I *do* like sweet drinks. Normally I'd just order a Dr Pepper and move on, but I want this moment to be something new. Something different; better.

"You should pick for me. Surprise me." I grin broadly, encouragingly.

Bennett looks apprehensive, biting down on his bottom lip for a moment as his eyes dart over his shoulder and scroll the handwritten menu. "Yeah, okay."

"I'll like whatever you pick. I promise."

Gregory Alan Isakov's "Big Black Car" plays quietly over the speakers of the coffee shop. Bennett hulks over the counter, even as he curves in his shoulders and speaks quietly to the barista. They talk back and forth for a moment, though he never makes eye contact, before he returns with a numbered placard for the table.

"I got you food, too. Since you swam this morning, I figure you're probably hungry."

My stomach flutters.

Don't get too comfortable, Polly. It'll only hurt.

"I'm starving," I blurt, as if the loudness of my voice will drown out everything else.

It isn't long before the mysterious dish and beverage are sat in front of me—something that looks a bit fancier than the breakfast sandwich I was expecting.

Bennett's plain coffee seems small in his large hand as he takes a long sip before eyeing me warily. It's only then I realize that I'm just staring oddly at the plate in front of me.

"It's—um, one of their best dishes. Eggs over medium, avocado, crumbled bacon, tomatoes, and feta over a hash brown patty. And that's a balsamic reduction drizzled over it. I think that's what makes the entire dish, really, so I got you extra. And the drink is pumpkin spice—sweet, but they make their syrups in house, so I think you'll like it. But . . . if you hate it—"

"It looks and *smells* delicious. I think I'll love it." I slice into the food, stuffing a too-big bite into my mouth and give him a quick thumbs-up.

It's an immediate burst of flavors on my tongue, decadent and salty and sweet all at once. I moan a little as I go for another bite, covering my mouth and bouncing excitedly in place as I relive the indulgent tasting experience for a second time. Then, grabbing the mug, I take a drink of the coffee, letting the nutmeg and cinnamon dance across my tongue.

"Do you like it?" he asks, urgency lacing the words.

I nod heartily, which grants me a gleaming smile.

Bennett's smiles are rare, beautiful things. I can count on one hand the number I've borne witness to. His lips tilt higher on the right side as his mouth closes in a softer smile. But his cheeks are still round and thick, dark eyebrows settled so that between them are oceans—so blue and deep I want to swim in them. His happiness is intoxicating.

This—me eating, enjoying the food he selected—it means something important to him.

Food. I log the thought away in my mental "Bennett's Interests" folder, next to poetry and hockey.

"So," I start, polishing off my meal in record time. "What got you interested in poetry?"

At this, he grimaces and messes with his hair before blowing out a breath. "I—are you sure you want to talk about poetry?"

"I mean, unless you don't?"

It's clear this—whatever it is—is really bothering him, hands back to fidgeting, shoulders shifting beneath the white material of his shirt.

"Poetry is our class together. Hockey is your job," he says. My brow furrows, trying to dissect his meaning as he speaks. "We're on a date. I'm supposed to ask you questions about yourself."

Something like relief floods through my body, and I take a moment to set my silverware on my now scraped empty plate. If I didn't think it would make him uncomfortable, I'd probably lick it clean. But this moment feels enormous, important, so I take my time before speaking.

"I've never been on a date before," I confess, tucking a few loose hairs back behind my ear. "So, maybe I don't know how it's supposed to go, but I think knowing why you like poetry is getting to know *you*. And I'd like to know."

The smile appears again, but broader, showing his teeth.

"This is my first date, too."

Again, the air hangs still while we beam at each other.

"I brought you something," he says suddenly, reaching into his pocket for a pressed envelope. "You can look at it later."

Taking his clear command, I tuck it into the pocket of my overalls with a light pat. "All right."

We never touch, but I can *feel* him. The soft guitar of coffeehouse music is the soundtrack to what finding something better, something good and safe, feels like.

That night, I open the envelope in the safety of my own room and read "Sonnet 227" under the soft light of glowing stars on my ceiling and the lamp by my bed. I almost laugh at the fact that it's literally a poem by Petrarch and not just in the form.

But the laugh gets caught in my throat as I read line by line, heart hammering and skin flushing. In my mind, I can hear Bennett's smooth dulcet tones whispering the words over my skin.

Happy air, remain here with your
living rays: and you, clear running stream,
why can't I exchange my path for yours?

The poem wraps around me like a blanket, soothing me gently as I fall asleep with the paper still clasped tightly to my chest.

From Paloma Blake to Bennett Reiner

What lips my lips have kissed, and where, and why,
I have forgotten

—EXCERPT FROM "SONNET XLII" BY EDNA ST. VINCENT MILLAY

Bennett,

A well-structured sonnet for you—you're welcome.
Though not so love struck as Petrarch.
I've never liked this one much either.

—P

CHAPTER 20

THEN: Freshman Year, October

Paloma

Bennett is late.

It feels like a lie, because Bennett Reiner is never late—but it's five minutes past our meeting time and I'm still alone in the private study room.

The door creaks open and I set my phone down on the table, smiling as Bennett enters, all broadness and height with a baseball cap settled low over his eyes. He's decked in a Waterfell hockey T-shirt today, with his backpack slung over one shoulder and a container of some sort cradled in his arms.

"Hey—"

"I brought you something," he cuts me off, pushing the blue Tupperware into my hands before scratching at the back of his neck and readjusting the hat he's wearing. His cheeks turn scarlet, but I grin broadly up at him.

"What is it? Can I open it now?"

"Yeah." He nods. "And, um, hey, Paloma."

"Hey, Bennett."

I pop the lid, the immediate smell of sugar making my mouth water.

"Cookies?" I ask, eyes wide. "Did you make them?"

"They're chocolate chip. But, um, yes. I was late because it took a little longer but—you should eat one now. While they're fresh."

I can feel that he's holding back from commanding me to eat a fresh, warm chocolate chip cookie. Not hesitating, I slip one from the container and bite into it, warm and soft, perfectly sweet with flakes of salt nipping at my tastebuds.

"God, Bennett," I murmur, eyes nearly crossing as the chocolate melts against my tongue. "It's *incredible*."

He's blushing, but he's smiling—bright and wide and wonderful. He's intensely handsome, the width of his features suited to the sheer size of him. He looks like a young Tom Welling, tall and broad with piercing blue eyes and a boyish cut of brown curls.

Lips usually pursed or frowning are pulled over brilliant, straight white teeth. There's a chip in the right canine; I can see it more this close. My own smile comes easily.

"Thank you for this. You didn't have to—"

"What you said, about swimming?" He cuts me off. "How it makes you calmer—that's cooking for me."

"Yeah? Well, you can cook for me anytime." I laugh with a quick shake of my head, pulling away and sliding back into my chair. "I'm kind of bad about remembering to feed myself."

And . . . frugal. Scholarship money is great, but the small included meal plan is potentially problematic. So I save when I can.

It's not hard. I'm used to making it work and going without. My mom was inconsistent in her care of me early enough that I learned to grocery shop and fend for myself before I got my first period. I learned to take care of myself as best I could.

Something I've said seems to bother Bennett, but he clenches a fist around his backpack strap and lets it go, maneuvering into the chair opposite mine and pulling out his laptop and notebooks.

I grab another one of the cookies and bite into it, a moan escaping my throat at the taste.

Bennett coughs, blushing red as he turns back to the screen of his laptop.

"These are amazing, Bennett."

"Thanks," he mutters, before pulling a black pen from his bag.

The poetry project is pretty open-ended—choose one poem each and trade, do an analysis, and then write a reimagined poem in any style. Dr. Britton told us to *think outside the box* and really *get creative with it*.

Today we focus on choosing the poems.

Before we can start, Bennett hands me a pack of ballpoint pens. I frown, staring at them on the table between us, then at the pen in my hand, and finally up at his eyes.

Anxiety is clearly written across his face. Bennett readjusts his hat before staring down at the pens.

Last session, I'd written across his work in my blue ink pen, not thinking much about it. But he'd been anxious the rest of the time and I saw him throw away the entire sheet during our break, starting over with his own black pen.

"I use these. So, I got you some. It's—" He cuts himself off, shaking his head and swallowing loudly. "It's embarrassing, I'm sorry. But I just..."

I don't say *I understand* because I don't. But if this helps him, it's fine with me.

"It's not embarrassing, Bennett. It's fine." I take the pens and break open the pack, tossing my usual dark blue one back into the front pocket of my backpack. I take one and draw a swirl over the end of my notebook.

"These things are fancy," I tease, trying to lessen the grimace still on his face. "Thanks for buying them for me."

He nods but doesn't comment, only resets his notebook by his laptop. I let it go.

Bennett works silently, as do I, but we both sneak glances at each other. I sit on my hands to keep from reaching for him.

An hour into the session, he suddenly straightens in his chair, grappling for his phone to check the time before softly cursing—a word I haven't heard from him yet. After throwing his things into his bag, he stands and looks at me a little panicked.

"I need to walk Seven," he says. "My dog."

I nod. "I remember."

He turns on his heel and leaves before I can say anything. But I've already started to pack so it doesn't take me long to run and catch up with his lengthy strides.

"Bennett?" I call, not stopping him but walking side by side. "Can I come?"

His brow furrows as his hands fidget. He slows his pace just slightly. "You want to walk my dog with me?"

"Yeah," I say brightly with a shrug. "Could be fun."

Bennett's mild concern melts into a gentle smile.

We leave the library and walk to the other side of campus, where the large, expensive "dorm" rooms sit. I shouldn't be so shocked when Bennett stops in front of one of the attached townhomes.

"Seven is . . . a quiet dog." It's all he says, but his fingers are twitching, drawing shapes on his thigh; a nervous habit I've seen from him before.

"If it's going to make him anxious"—*or you*—"I can come back a different day."

"No. Today is perfect. Just wait here," he says, walking away before turning back to me. "I can . . . hold on to your backpack? While we walk?"

I grip the bag a little tighter. "No, that's okay. I'll just keep it with me."

"You sure? I can—"

"I don't want you to," I snap. "I just . . . I like to have it with me."

There's a light flush of embarrassment covering my skin, but he doesn't see it, turning from me abruptly enough that I feel a bit bad for snapping at him. It's a long moment before the door reopens to reveal Bennett and a large black dog walking slowly beside him.

"This is Seven," Bennett says, voice calm. His dog, a handsome black Lab with big brown eyes, comes to a stop right by him, cocking his head slightly as he gazes up at me with too-intelligent eyes. "Ready?"

"I'm ready."

Seven approaches me before Bennett, butting his nose up against my open palm.

"Can I pet him?"

Bennett nods, watching us both closely as I bend down and run my fingers through his rich black fur. Soulful, almost sad eyes look up at me. It's strange how much he reminds me of Bennett, like that old adage of owners and pets starting to look alike.

We walk down the sidewalk and off campus, toward the strip of stores and Brew Haven.

"So, what made you want a dog?"

"Oh—um, I didn't, actually. My dad surprised me with him." There's a long pause as Bennett seems to wrestle with his thoughts. "He's a therapy dog. For my—um." He clears his throat. "For me."

He's silent for a long moment, eyes glancing like he's waiting for me to do or say something.

"For you?" I try to help him.

"Mmhmm."

I stay quiet, attempting to give him the moment.

But he never manages to elaborate, instead continuing on, stepping fast enough I have to take longer strides to keep up. I reach out for him, brushing his arm with my hand, but he jerks like he's been slapped and maneuvers slightly away.

Seven slumps against Bennett's now immobile legs.

"I'm sorry," I say, raising my hands. A breath puffs out of him.

I start to walk again and he follows, hoping the movement will help his clearly building anxiety. "You don't like touch, right? So maybe I should avoid touching you? I don't know why I—"

"No. I don't—" He huffs out an almost annoyed sound. "I like when *you* touch me." A blush forms on his face at his open, vulnerable words said a little too loud.

I turn my head away so he doesn't see my smile.

"I just prefer to know when it's happening. And I don't like light touches." He pauses again, physically and mentally it seems. I wait for him, and Seven bumps me with his nose. He steps around me, nudging my thigh so I scoot closer to Bennett.

"Like this?" I ask, reaching toward his hand but letting my own hang until he grasps it in a warm, firm grip.

Bennett stares at our intertwined hands for a long moment before letting the lightest of grins grow slowly across his face. A sense of pride, toward him and this conversation, spreads, along with a need to be as vulnerable, to open my own chest and hand-feed him my insecurities that I carry with me like tokens.

But I don't feel the bravery that Bennett seems to have. Instead, the fear is paralyzing, so I don't.

From Bennett Reiner to Paloma Blake

The sea can do craziness, it can do smooth,
it can lie down like silk breathing
or toss havoc shoreward; it can give

gifts or withhold all;

—EXCERPT FROM "THE POET COMPARES HUMAN NATURE TO THE OCEAN FROM WHICH WE CAME" BY MARY OLIVER

P,

Contrary to your beliefs, Mary Oliver is my favorite poet.
So, are you the ocean? And if so—
please don't withhold yourself from me.

Yours, Bennett

CHAPTER 21

NOW

Bennett

Rhys isn't here, running late apparently. Which has left me alone, slightly tormented by the sight of his parents and my dad at a wide, round oak table in the dimly lit back corner of some fancy steak restaurant.

While we'd normally meet in Boston, my dad has come to Waterfell tonight. The Koteskiys like to be closer to home ever since Sadie's brothers started to live with them.

Anna stands up when she sees me, eyes glittering as she steps forward with her arms open. It warms my empty chest, stepping into her embrace.

"I feel like I haven't seen you in forever," she says, pulling back to pat my cheek. Her husband and my father quickly join her on either side, only making my stomach sink further.

Still, I force a smile. "It's only been a few weeks."

"Way too long." She shakes her head. "Come sit. Do you want a drink?"

Max pulls her chair out for her, settling her in it with a hand planted on the back of her neck. I shake my head politely, taking the empty seat nearest my dad.

Max makes easy conversation about school, asking about my

classes and how practices are going, leaving my dad and Anna to interject with questions or comments of their own.

"And—with hockey? Any idea which teams are scouting you?"

I grimace, trying to hide it behind a quick gulp of my water. It's unavoidable at a table with Maximillian Koteskiy and Adam Reiner—to *not* talk about hockey would be a feat. But without Rhys here I don't have much to offer.

"I'm . . . not sure." I shrug. "I haven't met with Coach Harris yet."

What I've said seems to startle Max. His mouth opens, but before he can say anything else, my dad cuts him off.

"How's the gala planning going?"

They launch into small talk over the Koteskiys' annual charity gala—half discussion with a friend, half information for their main benefactor, Adam Reiner. I don't hear much, just tracing words along the napkin spread across my suit pants.

At one point, my dad reaches over to refill Anna's wine with the bottle they bought for the table. She continues to talk, smiling at him and lifting her hand to his bearded cheek, smoothing a thumb over his skin. The casual intimacy of it all, the smile my dad sends her way that seems almost *longing*, makes my chest hurt.

I wait for Max to say something, to stand or fight or *something*, but he just watches his wife with a small, closed-mouth smile.

Nearly ready to excuse myself, I clear my throat. Because I can't sit here and watch this.

Last year, when I'd first managed to recognize the looks of adoration my father sent his best friend's wife, I'd almost printed a copy of "The More Loving One" by W. H. Auden, as if it would show him that I understood.

And then . . . then I'd gone on a double date that night and it had changed everything.

This wasn't some beautiful love story. It was depressing and sad, and the idea of him loving her and staring across at her for his entire life made me nearly sick with rage at my own father. Until I couldn't stand being around him while he faked some strange happiness in my presence, then went home to be alone forever like some sick curse.

"I should—"

"Sorry I'm late," Rhys says, dimples gleaming as he slides into the seat next to us, straightening the suit coat he's wearing.

"How is everyone?" Anna asks, eyes softening at the sight of her son. "Oliver? Liam? Sadie?"

"All good," he promises, leaning over the back of his chair to order a Coke. "Promise. Liam and Oliver are playing video games, and Sadie made pancakes for dinner for them all."

Anna grins brighter. "I swear if that girl tries to clean my kitchen this time . . ."

"And how is my son?" Max asks, his eyes intent on Rhys.

Rhys nods, making stern eyes toward his father. "All good. Promise."

I'm grateful for the confirmation, too—because where I used to pride myself on being able to read Rhys, knowing my best friend inside and out, I'd failed him again.

"I understand," I'd told him, eyes watering, the morning after he'd gotten hammered and locked himself in a bathroom until Sadie came for him. *"If you'd told us, told me, we could've helped. Things would've been different."* It was all I'd dared to share, because part of me didn't want Rhys to know how well I understood—not just in an empathetic way, but in a way that explained how I felt all the time. Sad and angry and scared in a swirling mix. Like I was screaming underwater for *years*, and no one could hear me.

It's difficult for me to read people anyway, especially if they wanted to hide something from me.

It was the same with Paloma. I'd failed to see what was wrong and lost her for it.

Part of me feels like I've lost Rhys, too, in some ways.

"We told Sadie and the boys about the gala," Anna says, her eyes shining like stars. "They were the ones to pick the charity, actually. So it'll be a whole family affair."

"For us, too," my dad mutters, gulping back a heavy swing of his wine. He gives me an apologetic smile before adding, "Helen is coming. She's bringing Ethan."

Max's brow wrinkles. "I thought they got divorced."

"They did," he says. "Apparently, they're close again. Not sure. Helen just wanted me to know that she was coming and that she was bringing him."

My dad has never liked Ethan, though I never minded him. After a few arguments about him when Ethan was still married to my mom, we'd decided not to discuss it.

"Should we get you a hot date, then, Adam?" Anna smirks.

"Are you offering, Trouble?" he teases back, and Max laughs, shaking his head.

"Whatever you think you're doing to charm my wife," Max cuts in, "it won't work. Besides, you might have the looks and the bank account, but I have a better superpower." He leans closer to her, his voice dropping to whisper some long Russian phrase just loud enough for us to hear.

"Oh, god, I'm going to be sick," Rhys says. "Forget ordering, I'm losing my appetite."

It's a joke, but I want to wring his neck. To remind him how blessed he is to have two parents who *love* each other in that way. To point him toward the yearning expression on my father's face as he watches his best friends embrace.

Instead, I look at the menu and try to figure out what I can eat that won't make me feel *sicker* through this entire dinner. Food has always been a comfort for me, but maybe I'm losing that, too. Just like everything else in my life that I love.

CHAPTER 22

NOW

Paloma

"What about—"

"We cannot get both of those." I feel like a bad parent denying her, but the two brightly colored marshmallow cereal boxes in her hands are the same—one of them is just an off-brand. I point to one. "Just get those, they're better. Now focus, we need *meals*. Real food."

Lily grimaces but nods, stepping beside me next to the cart.

We look a little odd, I'm sure—her in her usual full outfit, like I picked her up from some uppity academy, the clack of her heeled boots in sharp contrast to the soft patter of my clogs.

"What kind of food are you good at making?" she asks, eyeing the candy aisle with slight interest, which I quickly divert. All we have in the cart is sugar at this point.

"Not much. I'm not the world's best cook."

"I've never cooked anything. Except mac and cheese, I can do that one."

I huff a laugh, shaking my head. "Yeah, me too."

We turn the corner and the front of our cart collides with someone.

"Oh—sorry—"

"Trying to run me over, Blake?" Sadie Brown says, cat-eyes taking quick stock of my oversized sweatshirt and leggings. "Is it because I stole your outfit?"

"Fuck off, Brown," I snap, maneuvering the cart around her, only to pause when I almost hit someone else. My stomach sinks.

Rhys Koteskiy, followed by Bennett Reiner.

My mouth parts at the sight of him dressed in nice navy slacks and a sport coat, white pressed shirt and no tie. Rhys is dressed similarly, and for a moment I consider if they had a game today I forgot about—but it wouldn't be over yet.

"Paloma," Rhys greets, eyes dipping to where Sadie is now grasping the bars of the cart. My eyes won't leave Bennett, even as I hear Rhys introduce himself to my silent roommate.

We're feet away from each other, but even in this god-awful fluorescent light, he's so ungodly handsome. Thick curls of brown and amber fall carefully around his face. He's shaved recently, jaw smoother than he usually keeps it, and his eyes are piercing as he looks at me solidly.

"I'm Lily," my roommate says. "I live with Paloma."

I look over at that. Sadie smiles, her gaze darting to me again.

Someone tries to maneuver around us, forcing us to back away into a tighter semicircle. It puts Bennett right at my side, the heat of his body smoldering against my right shoulder.

My arms are loose, hands flexing over and over—until I feel a finger along my palm.

I don't dare to look down to see where Bennett carefully rests the back of his hand against my own. So light I could almost say I'm imagining it.

But I'm not.

My stomach somersaults like he's kissed me; the touch is just as intimate.

"P," he whispers, looking straight ahead. "You okay?"

I nod, throat tight, eyes suddenly full up with tears I refuse to let fall. He runs his pinky over mine, linking them with such tenderness I feel him in my toes. Like a piece of his soul runs through my bloodstream.

He's everywhere all at once, and yet—

" . . . if you're interested," Rhys finishes whatever he was saying. "You are both more than welcome to come."

"Paloma?" Sadie asks, her use of my first name jarring enough to pull me away from the near mirage that Bennett has become. I snap forward, jerking my hands onto the cart. "Party at the Hockey Dorms, okay? Come. It'll be fun."

It might be one of the most genuine, un-sarcastic things she's said to me.

A saccharine smile stretches my lips, and I nod. "Thanks for the invite."

I pull Lily along with a hand slipped into hers. She stares at it like some alien thing has attached itself to her palm, but my heart is a roaring beast in my chest and I'm desperate to escape.

We hide in the produce aisle until they've left, booze in tow, smiles on all three of their faces. I even hear Bennett laugh, pricking at the back of my neck with the memories it brings.

• • •

It's strange, feeling so ingrained into the fabric of someone's life and yet so incredibly distant from them.

It's freezing cold and the entire party is in the massive, almost apartment-style house—affectionately, Hockey Dorms—sweating and gyrating to a wild mix of music. Lily didn't want to come, her anxiety clear though she lied and said she suddenly felt sick. I didn't push her, but against my better judgment, I couldn't stay away. So I'm here—alone, sober, and quick as I zoom through the party with one mission.

I shouldn't be here. Except I can't stay away from him. I never could, really. Even when it was my only goal.

The frigid late-January air blows in through the open back door where Bennett stands—still in his nice clothes, though he's discarded the jacket and rolled up his crisp white shirt despite the cold temperature. He's speaking softly to a beautiful girl. Gentle, with that intense listening expression I know well. It feels like knives, but I smile through the pain of them sliding down my skin.

He looks happy. So I watch him quietly.

There's a little version of myself inside, wailing constantly, trying to get out. The only time she isn't silent is when he's within reach.

"Paloma."

My eyes slide to the side, toward a small brunette in a silk dress, boots, and a thick leather jacket with two drinks in hand.

"Sadie." I nod, taking the proffered cup. "What is it?"

"Dirty Shirley." She smirks, dark red lips perking up. She touches her cup to mine in an almost sarcastic *cheers* before we both take a swig.

"You know, when Rhys told me you two dated, I was surprised."

A derisive snort leaves me.

"I imagine the same kind of surprise you had when you realized I was dating him. For girls like us? He's kinda out of reach," Sadie continues.

Thinking about Rhys and dating him and that awful night makes me want to be sick, so I shake my head and step away.

"You want to talk about me and your boyfriend hooking up?" I snort. "Really?"

"Watch it," she snaps, gray eyes heating as she looks at me. For a moment I wonder if she'll try her claws on my skin. Instead, she takes a deep settling breath and straightens her spine. "I'm trying to make a point."

"Save it," I sneer back. "We aren't the same. Don't play this stupid game, Sadie. We're not friends."

She shrugs as if everything I've said rolls right off her. She looks back out the window where my gaze has been all night.

"It wasn't ever about him, was it? That night at the party?" She takes a sip of her drink. "I'd say not once has your presence in this house had anything to do with Rhys or Holden or any of the guys who'd cut their leg off for a chance to sleep with you."

I shrug this time, mimicking her with a sip of my own drink. My eyes stray to Bennett again, shoulders tight at the happy, slightly drunken grin he's sporting.

"Do you love him?"

"No clue what the fuck you're talking about," I say, calm and collected. "Better get back to your boyfriend, Brown."

"Yeah," she snorts. "Have fun torturing yourself, P."

And then she's gone, and I'm all alone staring out across the back patio and trying not to cry. My chest heaves. It feels like mere moments later, though it could be hours for how lost in my head I am, that he approaches me out on the patio. Alone.

"I won't go with her," Bennett says. His body is so close, so warm, his bicep pressed against mine through layers of fabric. I don't look at him.

"It's fine," I say, desperate to make my voice sound anything but bitter. "It's good. I want you to be happy."

Something I've said makes him shake his head in my peripheral.

"Paloma—"

"It's fine, Bennett."

"I won't go with her if you don't want me to." He shakes his head. He moves closer to me, the heat of his body all-consuming as he covers my back. He ducks his head down so that his mouth almost touches my ear as he whispers, "Just say the word, P. You can have it all."

I don't say anything. This time, I force myself to be strong enough to leave him alone. He doesn't need this, need *me*. He deserves so much better than I could ever hope to give him.

I go home to my quiet room. My blue backpack and rabbit sit on the bed, but everything else is still packed up. Avoiding planting roots is my specialty.

And, like always when I can't sleep or get overwhelmed with the anxiety of a recurring nightmare, I think of Bennett and something softer. Of hands gentle in my tangled hair, a darker shade of blond. Of tentative fingers reaching for each other. Of steadying blue eyes.

The calm I feel in his hands is almost tangible as I pretend he's beside me now.

CHAPTER 23

NOW

Bennett

"Again," I hear the sneering yell of Coach LaBlanc.

Toren curses beneath his breath where he's sprawled after getting taken down by a sophomore on his way to the net. I stopped the goal, but it was a messy play on both parts—and still, it's Kane and Dougherty taking the blame.

"This time, Koteskiy—your line."

Rhys steps forward—Freddy on his left and Hathaway, our first line right winger, on his other side. I've watched Rhys from between the posts for most of my life, and he's still just as golden. I sometimes wonder if he knows that he skates like a more sophisticated version of his dad. He's fast and intense, but Rhys Koteskiy is always steady.

Toren and Holden, to me, work seamlessly together. But against their own line, it's a fierce competition. I keep my eyes on the puck currently on Freddy's stick, flicking my gaze to where the other forwards are—trying to make assumptions on what play they'll attempt, to guess at it faster than they can complete it.

I see the flicker of movement from Hathaway and angle toward him as Freddy passes—nearly intercepted by Holden—and then there's a mess of commotion as Rhys and Toren collide.

Everyone stops.

"Watch it," Toren snaps. Usually he's quicker with his snark, but today he just seems agitated. Holden stops short beside them, his free hand hovering to interfere if need be. I skate over, too, eyes watchful. Tension brackets the group, filling the air until it's suffocating.

Rhys frowns but doesn't take the bait, only knocking his shoulder against Toren as they pass.

After their near fight last semester, Coach doesn't like for them to play opposite each other. It doesn't surprise me when Harris blows the whistle and switches out the entire line before giving me a signal that I can switch with Mercer, the backup goalie.

I bump his glove with mine as we switch off.

Behind the boards, I see Paloma, and my breath catches.

I haven't seen her since the party at the Hockey Dorms, when she saw me with another girl from my class. I was too scared to guess at her expression, to give myself hope in the face of her possible jealousy. Was it terrible if I hoped she was? Knowing full well she had no reason to be?

It didn't matter. I hadn't been able to resist the pull of her—I never have.

We haven't spoken since then. I'd gone home alone soon after she left, indulging in my ritual of scrolling through her photos and stories.

As usual, nothing helped.

Neither did her warning about joining practices, because seeing her now feels just as much like a punch to the gut as it always has. She's so perfect, so beautiful, bright blond hair gleaming and pulled back off the smooth unblemished skin of her face. The thick Cupid's bow of her top lip slides between her teeth before she chews on the bottom one as well, distracting as she always is—though now she's not just in my sight, alone in the locker rooms after everyone has left.

Now, she's here, in front of the team. In front of so many of my teammates who have openly talked about her, flirted with her, shared stories that make me sick with envy and fury. Even now, I repress the urge to swipe my skate across the faces of guys I otherwise like as they stare at her along the boards.

Beside her stands a redheaded girl I recognize from the grocery store, though I wasn't paying attention enough to catch her name. And while Paloma looks dressed for her coaching session on the ice—leggings and a navy quarter zip with the Waterfell logo—the girl next to her does *not*, in a skirt and nylons with a plaid blazer overtop and heeled boots. She looks entirely in the wrong place.

"Holy shit," one of the freshmen mutters, eyes locked on the girls as the make their way down toward the benches. Toren's gaze shoots over his shoulder immediately. "Who the fuck is tha—"

"Who's who?" Toren asks, grabbing the guy by the collar with a shake. "Either way, close your eyes."

"S-sorry," the guy mutters, jerking out of Toren's hold. The freshmen may not respect Kane, since they know how the rest of the entire team feel about him, but they *are* afraid of him.

Kane locks his gaze with mine and nods.

Unease simmers. There's a reason Toren Kane has never bothered me as much as he does the others. And as much as I wish I could say it's the way he helped Ro last semester or how good of a defenseman he is, it's mostly centered around Paloma.

At first, I'd been almost raging with jealousy that I'd never show—but then I'd seen them at a party, him hovering over her like a protective brother. Helping her. And then it had been multiple parties—and it wasn't jealousy I felt, it was relief. To know that one other person in the damn town cared about Paloma Blake enough to defend her.

To be there when she wouldn't allow me.

The girls disappear before they come out of the tunnel and onto the coaching bench, close to me on the opposite end of LaBlanc and Harris, though the redheaded girl keeps her eyes on the newest coach for a long time.

My breath huffs out and I opt for pulling off my cage.

"Hey, P," I offer as she steps closer.

"Hi, Bennett," she says. "You remember my roommate, Lily?"

I nod to her, though she barely takes a glance at me before she's stepping forward toward the boards with a hissed, *"Hey."*

Toren looks at her over his shoulder and rolls his eyes. "Yes, doll?" he says, his tone sarcastic and cutting enough that I straighten at the pure venom.

"Watch it," Paloma snips. "Don't you have some puck to chase?"

Toren grins almost sinisterly, and I scoot slightly in front of Paloma, annoyed with him even looking at her like that. He tones it down just a bit but before he can reply, Holden slams into his side.

"A puck? Or a puck *bunny*? Gotta be clear with me here, Paloma."

My stomach churns, and I toss my water bottle back in its spot before slamming my cage closed. I've been privy to Holden's flirting with Paloma for three years now. Maybe I've reached my limit. Or maybe touching her skin again has awakened the possessive, desperate beast in my brain.

Lily looks almost close to tears, like the idiotic defensive pair have said something personally offensive, before her entire demeanor changes as Coach LaBlanc steps into the circle.

"Distractions in practice and you at the center, Kane," he huffs. "Wish I could say I was surprised. Let's go. Reiner, you're back in net."

We all break apart. But I do see Paloma take Lily's hand in hers and usher her out. I'm still minorly confused that she brought her roommate to practice in the first place. But there is a softer feeling beneath it—something in my heart comforted by the fact that, for the first time since I've known Paloma, I know she's not completely alone.

Maybe, for now, that's enough.

. . .

Everyone should be gone, but as I'm doing my usual after-practice routine, I hear a stumbling sound and the low grunt of voices. Then Coach LaBlanc comes through the room, straightening his tie.

He eyes me for a moment with a quick smile and nod. "Great work today in the net, Reiner. Reliable as always."

And then he's gone. But the sounds continue: an irritating spitting sound, then a sink turning on.

Nearly done and fully dressed, I round the corner to see Toren Kane, pads off but pants still on, skates shucked along the tile like he rushed to pull them off. He's spitting up blood, more of it dripping down over his eye like he took a blade or a puck to the face.

"Shit, Kane," I mutter, brow furrowing as I step toward him. "Are you okay?"

Golden eyes darken as he sneers up at me through the mirror. "Get that fucking pitying look off your face, Reiner."

He spits again, using his hand to cup water and splash it over his face.

"And get the fuck out of here."

CHAPTER 24

NOW

Paloma

"And how is therapy going?"

"Fine." I roll my eyes. "I told you last time we talked that it's going fine, and I haven't even had my third session yet. Can you relax?"

"When it comes to you?" Alessia hums. "No."

I'm sitting at the kitchen counter, indulging in a bowl of sugary marshmallow cereal for dinner while chatting on the phone with Alessia. It's an adjustment, but I feel . . . calmer. Happier in my own skin, a feeling I've chased away for years now.

"What about swimming again?" she asks.

"Oh . . . no, I haven't," I confess, swirling my spoon in the now-colorful milk.

"Maybe you should." There's a long pause before she huffs a sigh. "Talk to Dr. Sutton about it, yeah?"

"I already did," I mumble. "She said I should."

"Then you should, Paloma." She sighs again. "You can't deprive yourself of joy like this anymore. That's one of the rules."

"I think you just made that up—"

"Maybe," she says. "I'm just looking out for you. Now that you're letting me."

There's a smile on my lips that she can't see. She's the only one on this earth who knows *everything*. The good, the bad, the messy. The depths of my self-hatred and anger and fear. She saw me at seventeen—lost and scared, half dead in the eyes. And she never let go of my hand.

It was me who pushed her out.

"Maybe we can get dinner or something next week," I offer, feeling all at once shy and excited.

"Yeah?" I can hear the smile in her voice. "I'd like that."

We hang up soon after, and I settle comfortably at the table, opening my laptop to do my assignments due tomorrow.

The front door opens, hitting the wall with force.

"You're not the boss of me."

The sound of my roommate's annoyed yell—followed by our front door slamming—jolts me from the book I'm reading at the kitchen table.

"Wanna fucking bet?"

I swear I know that voice. I peek around the corner—only to be shocked by the sight of Toren Kane in my apartment, fuming mad, cornering my roommate in our living room. I step toward them, but neither one looks up from their heated standoff.

"Back off," I snap.

His ring-adorned hands tighten to fists at his sides as he towers over her.

Only, when I shove into him to push him away from my roommate, Lily grabs his wrist with both her hands—keeping him there, looming over her.

"Stay out of this, Blake." Toren snaps, eyes never leaving my roommate. She's not scared, matching his huffing anger breath for heated breath. "This is between me and Lily."

"You can't tell me what to do," she spits. His eyes lock down across her body and back up.

Toren's in his usual all-black ensemble, tattoos on display with a short sleeve shirt and jeans. A large black motorcycle helmet is at his feet like he dropped it there, with a faded sticker of swirling blues and yellow on the back. Lily, on the other hand, is dressed in a tight navy zip-up and leggings, an elastic headband keeping her auburn hair back in the slouching ponytail it's currently tied in. With her cheeks still pink from the cold, or exertion, it's clear she was doing something athletic.

"Like hell I can't. You're running around a busy-ass town with your headphones in blaring," he snaps, but his words are still quiet. Where Lily shouts, Toren doesn't raise his voice a notch over speaking volume.

"So?" I ask, crossing my arms, still halfway between them even if neither of them wants to look at me.

"So?" Toren laughs, but there's no humor in it. He turns to me then. "Lily can't hear out of her goddamn right ear, and she doesn't wear her hearing aids."

My eyes flare. "What?"

Lily looks more furious than embarrassed and stamps her foot like a little rabbit. "That's private!"

"Not when you're running with headphones in," he growls out. He shakes her off, arms flexing like he wants to pick her up and toss her over his shoulder. She'd probably go flying halfway across the room. "You wanna run all by yourself? Wear the fucking hearing aids."

"She's fine." I step down, a little reluctant to get in between them. Not because I'm scared of either of them, but because the energy between them is dangerously palpable. "She wears them all the time."

I'm lying through my teeth. I didn't even know she had a hearing problem.

Toren rolls his eyes at me and I catch sight of his bruised eye and butterfly tape across a cut there—one he didn't have in practice.

"Sure, she does. And I'm a fucking saint," he says, before taking his helmet in hand and storming out. Only, just at the doorway, he snaps his fingers at her, looking over his shoulder. "Wear them."

Lily is angry—furious rather than hurt by anything the towering defenseman has done. But she watches him with a quiver in her lips as he leaves, like she wants to ask a million questions and beg him to stay all in one breath.

"You okay, Lily?" I ask, stepping toward her. My words seem to break the trance that Toren Kane's presence put her in and she nods.

"I'm fine."

She steps to the sofa to sit down. Her hand comes up to touch her right ear, before untucking her hair to hide it.

My chest squeezes. "Is there a reason you didn't want to tell me about the hearing stuff?" I ask, settling myself at her left side.

"It's embarrassing."

"It's really not." I slump a little more comfortably. "You can't hear out of one of your ears?"

She nods. "Since I was a kid." She taps again on her right ear.

I want to ask her how Toren knew such an intimate detail, but I keep quiet.

The closest I get to broaching the subject is, "So you guys know each other well, huh?"

Lily bites her lip, thinks for a long while, but eventually nods. After his strangely impassioned reaction to her during the five minutes we dared to enter practice together, followed by *this?* Whatever is between them feels intense.

"It's why I talk so loud," she says suddenly. "At least, sometimes. People say I get loud, and I don't know it. And if I ask you to say something over and over again, it's . . . yeah. So, I'm sorry. I probably should've told you."

She's embarrassed, cheeks pale more than flushed—like this is some intimate secret she would've kept forever.

"I'm glad you told me," I say, though she didn't tell me. Not really.

Her shoulders relax. "And Toren knows because . . ."

"We're friends," she blurts, before her eyebrows furrow together. "Or. Well . . . we were. It's complicated, I think."

If anyone can understand complicated, it's me.

"I get it. You know, no one knows this but . . . Bennett? The big goalie? He and I dated before, freshman year." The words are an offering, hard to push through my lips at first. I've never done *girl talk* before. But it feels like maybe Lily hasn't either. "I was in love with him, and he loved me. But . . ." I clear my throat, "A lot of things happened, but it was mostly my fault. I hurt him a lot."

At this, Lily nods. "So you had to leave." She says the words with simplicity, as if that was a given. As if my actions make perfect sense.

"Yeah."

"I bet that hurt you, too."

The pain in my chest never eases, a permanent knife I refuse to withdraw. "It did."

Lily nods slowly, chewing hard on her lip, her brow furrowed. "I had to do that once. And it hurt a lot . . ."

She touches her hand absentmindedly over her chest, rubbing lightly. "It still does," she says, barely a whisper.

I nod. "I wasn't ready to be with him, I think, back then. But . . . I am now. At least, I'm trying to be."

I take her hand in mine across the flat of our sofa.

"But maybe don't tell anyone that. You're the only person who knows."

Her eyes blow wide. "A secret? You told me a secret? Just me."

"Yeah." I laugh as she jerks me upright, grabbing my hand in both of hers.

"Cause we're friends, right?" She asks, eyes twinkling. There's a slightly manic look in her eyes, but beneath it is fear.

Fear I know well, because I've been that girl. The one who wanted friendship so desperately she would've bent herself into every shape to capture it.

So I nod quickly, squeezing her hand in mine a little tighter. "Of course we're friends, Lily." I bite my lip for a minute before adding, "I have a weird idea—do you have a swimsuit?"

• • •

An hour later, we're seated on the ledge of the empty pool. The facility is only open for another half hour, but it's plenty of time.

Lily looks adorable and ridiculous in equal measure in a fancy one-piece swimsuit I'm worried to ask the price of, with a high swinging ponytail of perfect auburn hair. She keeps biting her lip and looking over the pool ledge like the Creature from the Black Lagoon will rise up and pull her down under.

"You swear you've swam before?"

"Mmhmm," she says, still staring down. "But maybe we can start in the shallow end."

I smirk. "Yeah—Lily? This is the shallow end. You're what, five feet tall?"

She grimaces. "More or less."

"You're not going to be able to touch with your head above the water. So if you can't swim, just tell me—"

"Can I just sit and watch you for a little?" She settles into the cold water of the shallow end with a shiver, scooting her butt to rest against one of the ladder rungs. "I just wanna spend time with you. Forget the swimming lessons."

A laugh bubbles out of me and my body feels instantly lighter. I loop my pigtail braids in my hand and pull my swim cap on. "All right. Why don't you use my phone." I arrow my head toward where it lays atop my sweatshirt in the messy pile behind her, "and time me? Just don't drop my phone in the pool."

She decides to sit with her feet in the water, lip between her teeth as I tell her my password and she opens the clock app. "Ready?"

"Ready."

CHAPTER 25

THEN: Freshman Year, October

Bennett

By midterms, Paloma and I have fallen into a new routine, working on the poetry project and walking Seven together. I always hold her hand. She always smiles and talks to me even when my own words don't come easily.

But, with her, I am finding it easier.

Today we're meeting with Dr. Britton for a progress update on our project. I'm fifteen minutes early to his office, and five minutes later Paloma rounds the corner. She's dressed in soft, baggy pants and an oversized, well-worn orange shirt with *It's the Great Pumpkin, Charlie Brown* emblazoned across the front, her backpack on her shoulder like always. I rarely see her without it.

"I like your shirt," I say, smiling. She blushes, stopping just next to me and reaching for my hand before boldly rising on her toes to kiss my cheek.

"Thank you," she says. "Good morning, Bennett."

A second date should be my next plan. I tried to talk it out with my therapist, but she insisted this is something I can figure out on my own.

I go over it time and again, tuning out most of what our professor is saying. This time, I'll hold her hand and compliment her. Then, a kiss on the cheek like she does for me so often. Or . . . *maybe the forehead?*

"All right, Bennett?"

A blush stains my cheeks as I look up. My hands are still floating slightly over my legs, tracing letters in the air, before I force myself to rest them on my thighs. "Oh—yes. Sorry."

"We've got it, Dr. Britton." Paloma covers for me, smiling gently while our professor stands and walks around his desk, handing us both our respective folders back. "As long as you like the ones we've chosen—"

"I think your choices are excellent. I cannot wait to see what you two come up with." As he says it, his hand grasps Paloma's shoulder.

And then everything happens too fast.

Paloma jolts forward as if she's been electrocuted, nearly falling out of her chair as she wrangles herself away from us both. A phone rings, distant in my ears, like I'm hearing it underwater. I stand— I don't know if it's to go toward her, to move away, or to leave. Only then I'm immobile, watching as she huffs a few breaths and gives us both her back, facing the door to his office.

"Are you all right?" Dr. Britton asks, concern coloring his voice. "Miss Blake—"

"No, I'm fine. I'm fine." The words are said half to us and half to herself.

Paloma doesn't look at me as she gathers her things and slides her ocean-blue backpack onto her shoulders. I want to reach for it, to hold it for her and walk out with her.

I should ask the same question our professor did. I should follow her and make sure she's okay, offer to walk with her, carry her bag— I *want* to do all of those things so badly my teeth ache.

Instead, I'm still frozen standing by the table, my tongue stuck on all the questions I didn't get to ask.

• • •

Paloma doesn't show up for practice that night. Or our usual meeting for poetry—she cancels over a quick text. My stomach rocks with nausea that only grows when I walk Seven alone, not used to the extra space without her beside me.

"Hey, Bennett?"

Realizing I'm frozen on the walkway to our dorm, I look up toward Rhys as he steps out and pulls the door closed behind him.

"Yeah?"

"All good?"

I bite down on my lip and glance back at the overgrown sidewalk. "It needs to be mowed."

"Yeah," Rhys agrees easily, reaching down to tap Seven on the head. It's only then I can feel the weight of my dog's body pressing into my legs. "You've been out here for a while. I know this is stressful, but I can call and see about getting someone to landscape it."

"It's fine," I say, attempting to ignore the way I try to straighten Seven's collar four times before I can pull him off my feet. "Have you eaten?"

Rhys shakes his head, smiling, dimples gleaming. "I waited for you."

"I'm going to make beef stroganoff then."

"My favorite," my best friend says. It's not his favorite—I know that. But I also know he'd say that to anything that came out of my mouth right now.

I've been in therapy since I was eight, long enough to tell when things are getting worse in my head. My anxiety is dialed up, which means I need the distraction and control over the kitchen. I need something that takes all my attention.

When Rhys leans over the small countertop space, I eye him again.

"I'm fine. You don't need to watch over me."

My words roll off Rhys like water, no effect on the set of his shoulders and intense watchfulness.

"Sure. You're making a complicated meal in our dorm kitchen after standing outside by the door staring at the grass for almost an hour." He doesn't wait for me to decipher the sarcasm or react to it, just continues on. "Something is bothering you. I know things are different now than they were at Berkshire. But you know I'm still here for you."

My heart clenches, mouth opening like I might be able to tell him how I feel. Tell him about Paloma.

Rhys is everything you have never been. He completes you.

My anxiety pulls tighter at my chest. I try to focus on the facts, the things I know are true, but it doesn't help.

1. *Rhys and Paloma are the best people I know.*
2. *Rhys has more girls chasing after him now than I've experienced in my life.*
3. *Paloma is the most beautiful girl I've ever seen.*

If I introduced her to him, would she see the way he fills my gaps? That in so many ways he is everything that I am not? That he would've taken her on several dates, perhaps even kissed her by now?

My stomach tosses again, and I focus on setting the cast iron skillet atop the stove. I shove the image of her into the back of my mind, a secret I'll keep from him for now. *Just mine.*

Instead of obsessing over Paloma, I spend the evening laughing and playing video games with my best friend. Rhys's never-faltering presence heals something in me, like he always does.

Everything will be fine.

CHAPTER 26

THEN: Freshman Year, October

Bennett

It's our first away game series of the season, about four hours on the bus and one night at a hotel, and I feel sick.

We're playing Vermont twice, back-to-back, which happens with the longer distance games. Still, as I load onto the bus, everything feels off.

"You sure you're good?" Rhys asks, tossing his bag next to mine in the lineup. "You seem . . . more tense than usual. You can talk to me about it, you know?"

"Yeah." I swallow hard. "I know."

Rhys would never shut me out. He would never do something to hurt me. But I can't stop the fear of his rejection engulfing me until I can't see the way out.

My best friend pats my back with a bright, dimpled smile. "Alright, Ben."

For a moment, I consider opening up—telling him that my anxiety in this moment is from something unknown to me—a girl. Maybe he could help. But then another wave of fear rushes my spine.

They're both too good for you.

It's startling enough to keep my own promise to myself: to keep Rhys and Paloma as separate as I can.

Though, maybe that won't be necessary if she's decided to remove herself from *me* entirely. I haven't spoken to her since that day in Dr. Britton's office. She hasn't answered my texts. And if I think too hard on it, I start fidgeting worse and spiraling through darker thoughts.

Two steps onto the bus and I stop, thankful that Rhys is far enough in front of me that he can't hear the audible huff of breath as I spot her.

Paloma Blake, light brown hair piled high into a messy bun, tendrils swirling around her face. She loops one over and over on her finger, tongue slightly out between her lips and brows furrowed while staring intently at her phone. I've seen the expression before; she's reading something. A book, probably, though the idea that maybe it's a poem spurred by the one I left in the Tupperware container makes my chest squeeze.

She's incredibly beautiful, tucked into a back row where some non-players sit and chat. And yet no one seems to notice her. She's good at blending in, but I can tell it's intentional.

No one notices Paloma. She isn't in our practices or the locker room except with me. And still, here on the bus, it's like she's made it that way on purpose. Unless she wants you to notice her, you won't.

For a moment, I consider going to her, sitting at her side.

But I always sit by Rhys. It's my routine, the one that relaxes me when it comes to hockey.

I look at her a little longer, memorizing the soft curve of her chin and the deep well of sadness in her brown eyes that makes the thing in my chest pull tighter, before turning and settling myself into the seat next to my best friend.

. . .

My entire world feels like it's crumbling. I'm not rooming with Rhys because the assistant coach screwed up the assignments. I played my worst game yet, letting in five to the opposite goalie's shutout.

Paloma wasn't there for our postgame routine, which should be fine, except it isn't. My anxiety is too high. Everything feels like it's breaking—which is most likely the reason I'm standing at the door of Paloma's hotel room, hair wet and dripping onto my shirt.

I shouldn't be here. It's an invasion of privacy.

Not to mention stealing the room assignments sheet was an obsessive, awful thing to do. Still, I raise my hand and knock.

It takes a long while but the door cracks open, just slightly. Paloma hesitantly peeks around the door, eyes going wide as she spots me.

"Bennett?"

She's in a big T-shirt but no pants. My eyes dart back to hers after a quick skim over her long, muscular legs. I've never seen so much of her skin before. To prevent my blush from growing, I try to inspect her face. Her skin looks a little flushed, and dark circles are starting to develop under her eyes.

"Are you all right?" I blurt out. "You look tired."

She grimaces and darts her eyes down, away from me. "You're not supposed to tell people that." Her words aren't reprimanding, however. She sounds exhausted—proving my point.

"But yeah," she continues. "I know I look terrible. I am tired. I've . . . I've been having nightmares again. So, I'm not sleeping." The words seem to come out almost accidentally and she shakes her head, rubbing her hands over her eyes and slumping against the doorframe.

Something throbs in my chest. She's so beautiful and sad. I want to fix everything for her, despite knowing logically that I can't. *Is this how my dad feels with me all the time?*

"What are you doing here, Bennett?"

I avoid the closed-off tone of her voice, shifting from foot to foot.

"I played horribly," I confess. "We lost. I—it was my fault. I screwed everything up for everyone and now . . . I don't know."

"You're the goalie," she whispers. "Not surprised you're taking all the responsibility. Though I highly doubt it's your fault. What was the score?"

"Five to zero."

She shakes her head. "That's a whole team effort to lose, Bennett. Not on you."

I let her words wash over me, absolving some of the guilt I feel weighing on my shoulders. Part of me wants to confess that this is one of the reasons I've never loved hockey like the others do, because it's a constant pressure in my chest when I play.

"You were gone."

Her eyes dart down, away from my gaze as her hand grips onto the door tighter. I wonder briefly if she might slam it in my face.

"Um, yeah. I just . . . I wasn't doing well," she says.

"Oh." When she offers nothing else, my mouth opens unbidden. "Did I do something wrong? I just—" A frustrated breath puffs from my lips. "I can't always read your expressions. I don't know if you're angry or upset with me. You have to tell me if I do something wrong or upset you."

"You didn't do anything wrong, Bennett," she says sincerely. "I promise. I just . . . with the nightmares again, I sleep a lot during the day to make up for not sleeping at night and I needed some time for myself."

I nod, biting my lip to not press for more.

"What would help?"

"What?"

"I just . . . Is there anything I could do to help you? To sleep?"

It's invasive, but I can't stop myself. The obsessive center point of my anxious thoughts has shifted to *her, her, her*.

"Oh." She darts her eyes back to the floor, biting at her lip. "I don't know. I—my—"

"Maybe I could stay awake with you?" I blurt again, unable to keep my damn mouth shut around her. "Or, if you are going to sleep and you have a nightmare, I could stay awake and wake you up?"

She's hesitant, standing a little straighter with effort and crossing her arms over her chest as if to hug herself. A long moment passes as she considers my offering.

"You can trust me," I vow, blue meeting brown in a rare show of direct eye contact. But I want her to see the sincerity in my gaze, the truth of my words. *I won't hurt you. Please, trust me. Let me help.*

"Okay."

. . .

Paloma is pacing in front of me now, quiet as she looks toward me and then away again. Over and over. Normally the movement might give *me* anxiety, but with her here, where I can see that she's okay, I feel calmer. If I could use that serene energy as a superpower, I'd encase her in it.

Finally, she stops and chews on her lips before speaking.

"I'm . . . I need to explain. My nightmares are bad. Dreams feel really *real* to me, but so do the bad ones."

My brow furrows. "Okay?"

"I just don't want to freak you out. I haven't . . . well, I've never slept next to or near someone when I've had a bad nightmare." Her eyes well, but she holds back the tears. "I'm worried I'll hurt you."

I look her over.

Paloma is maybe five-foot-six, give or take an inch, to my six-foot-six. If anyone could hurt the other, it's me. But something stops me from even hinting at that prospect.

Instead, I offer, "That's okay. I'm good. I'll wake you up faster than you could hurt me."

She's not convinced, but eventually Paloma settles on the bed nearer to the window, underneath the already-rumpled bedding. I sit atop the untouched bed closer to the door, propped up against the pillows and headboard, eyes trying to focus on the muted NHL season-opener game playing on the television.

But I feel her eyes on me every few moments. Her wary emotional turmoil is stifling in the air. She said she'd try to trust me, but she doesn't. And it's making it hard for her to sleep.

"You like hockey?" I try, pushing through my half-closed up throat, hoping the shift in concentration will help lull her like it often did for me as a child.

"Yeah." She blushes, turning on her side to look at me, tucking a hand beneath her pillow. Her hair is messy and long, looking brighter than her usually darker flat brown. I wonder briefly if it's dyed. "It's really fast and interesting. I've always enjoyed it."

"Did you play?"

She shakes her head. "I've never really skated before, but I like to watch it. I . . ." She pauses, swallowing and closing her eyes. "I want to work on a team—not as an equipment manager, but as an assistant coach or something. It's stupid—"

"It's not." My hand rakes through my curls, tangling lightly before I smooth them through my fingers. "I think it's great, P. You'd be amazing at it."

There's a small smile tugging at the corner of her mouth as she nods.

"And swimming?" I ask, desperate in so many ways to understand her.

"It's . . . yeah. It's important to me." She watches me with her same inspecting gaze, in a way I find more comforting than unnerving. "What about you? With hockey? You love it?"

"Oh." I pause. No one has ever asked me that before. Probably because my dad is Adam Reiner, and I've never *not* played hockey. "Um. Well, my dad played in the NHL before he got hurt. His best friend did, too. And then he stuck me in skating classes and hockey as soon as I was old enough. I was a big kid—"

"No," she says, perching her hands beneath her face, eyes sleepy but sparkling. "You? Big?"

My cheeks color as she rolls her gaze over me playfully. I know I look different than Rhys or Freddy, or most of the guys we've played with. I've always been tallest, but the biggest, too. Muscular, sure—I work out with the team. I'm heavily conditioned and trained. But it's muscle with a layer that's softer than the more cut forward and centers.

Maybe there was a time I would've been embarrassed by it, but with the way Paloma looks at me it's almost impossible not to be proud of it.

"Yeah. But I wasn't very aggressive with the puck. Not like the other kids. But I liked playing goalie. So I just stayed there."

"That's not really an answer," she mumbles, eyes fluttering.

The way I feel about hockey is different than Rhys or my dad— I've always known that. I stayed because it was easy for me. I'm good at it. But it's not my passion. It's not what I want to do forever.

I just don't know how to tell anyone.

Except . . .

"I don't love hockey," I admit into the quiet of the room, turning my head toward her. "I just play because I'm good at it. Because my dad loves it, and I feel closer to him and my friends when I play. But it's not . . ."

"It's not like poetry is for you," she finishes for me. "That's what you love."

For a moment I'm twelve and embarrassed to ask my mom to get me more poetry books because I've finished all the ones Dad got me the week before—knowing the look on my mom's face means something important, but I can't read it.

"Yeah," I breathe, a weight present for the majority of my life finally rolling off my shoulders. "Yeah, it is."

I was worried she might think the poem I slipped her on our date was too intense. Petrarch is known for only two things, really: the style of sonnet he created, and pining after the same woman for over three hundred of those sonnets.

Makes a little more sense now, I think as I admire Paloma's profile as she rolls onto her back. The angle of her jaw, the heavy pout of her full, peachy lips. Burnished golden strands mixed in the light brown of her hair, like clouds over a brighter color. Eyes like deep chocolate or the freshest soil around a blooming garden.

"Will you read me one?"

"Now?" My voice drags out the word. "Oh—yeah. Let me find—"

"Do you know any by memory?"

I know a lot from memory. But this feels intense. I'd prefer to have hours to figure out which one would suit her and this space between us best—but my mouth opens before I can think about it.

I recite John Keats's "Bright Star," my mouth moving leisurely and practiced across each word like a lullaby only for her ears.

She drifts off, her breath growing deeper, the rise and fall of her chest more drawn out. I don't take my eyes off her. I don't sleep.

An hour or two passes before the quiet whimpering starts, her brow furrowing deeply. I wait, hopeful that it might dissipate into nothing and she'll get more sleep.

But then she cries out sharply, hands shoving the pillow away from her.

Heart in my throat, I cross to her and try to wake her. I call her quietly, trying to avoid directly touching her. At first, she doesn't rouse, only cries silently, begging with an anguish I haven't seen before. Her hands grab onto my forearms, nails scouring my skin.

"Paloma," I call, louder than I mean to, shaking her upper body as I lean over her, trying to keep her from thrashing so violently she falls from the bed.

She wakes up, eyes wide before another terrified noise chokes from her and she tries to scurry backward away from me, smacking her head into the headboard in her haste.

"Shit." I rear back, slapping the nightstand between our beds to flick on the lamp. My hands hover in the air, heart in my throat at the image of her beneath me, curling slightly into a ball while fat tears make their way down her reddened cheeks.

"Bennett?"

"Hey," I say, voice calm and gentle. "Just me. I'm here—are you—"

I reach for her and she flinches back, scrambling away from me before sprinting off the bed and into the bathroom with a hard slam of the door.

I feel a bit like throwing up.

I stand before I mean to, stepping up to the bathroom door like I might knock. I can hear muffled, choked sobs from the other side. The sink runs for a long while. Then silence.

She emerges slowly, eyes pointed toward her feet.

It feels wrong, towering over her while she's so vulnerable. I want to hold her, but I don't know how.

Her face is soaked with tears and water that she's splashed herself with, wetting the collar of her T-shirt. She's still clearly distraught, but more embarrassed now. Paloma tries to pull at the now-tangled knot of her braid, gripping and yanking hard enough that new tears spring forward.

"Let me," I try softly.

Like a reprimanded child, she sulks as she moves forward.

My hand threads through her hair, pulling gently at the braid she was wearing and loosening the strands. It smells like her—juniper and fresh laundry—and feels soft like silk against my fingers.

The pad of my thumb swipes against the back of her neck, igniting a shiver through her body. But she only leans farther into me. Her body droops more heavily as my palms ghost over her shoulders and slender neck, into the base of her scalp.

Paloma relaxes almost instantly, hiccupped cries the only bit leftover as her eyes blink back open slowly.

"I'm sorry—"

"No," I murmur, tucking her tighter against me. Like that can stop the waves of self-hatred I can almost *feel* rolling off her. "Don't. It's okay, Paloma. Just breathe."

She follows my directions easily, as if just the command is enough to settle her.

CHAPTER 27

THEN: Freshman Year, October

Paloma

The intoxication of being wrapped in Bennett Reiner's arms post-nightmare is enough for me to miss what he says the first time.

"What?" My voice is scratchy with sleep more than screams this time.

"I have an idea." He smiles, despite having to repeat himself, but it seems to be more for reassurance than from authentic happiness. "I want to take you somewhere. Did you bring a swimsuit?"

I nod, trying to quell the sudden desperation that fills me. I *always* have a swimsuit, packed away in my backpack just in case. Bennett grabs a towel and lets me change in the bathroom.

Looking in the mirror after pulling on the tight burnt-orange material, I bite down on my lip and tie my hair back into a braid.

Normally I don't spend much time looking at myself, preferring to ignore the features that look too much like my mother's, despite my attempts at changing them. Dying my hair was important, but it's impossible to erase her in the wide bend of my hip or the height of my rounded cheekbones. Impossible to separate my doe-wide brown eyes and pursed deep peach lips.

Impossible to rid myself of the ample curve of my breasts, though I've tried for years to tamp them down.

Looking like that? What did you expect, Polly?

Feeling a little sick, I hunch down, like that might hide the obviously abundant features I've learned to despise about myself. I dress a certain way to shield myself from that, when I can.

I was twelve and terrified when I realized there was a reason my classmates weren't the only ones whispering about me behind my back. I'd overheard the comments from adults, condescending or pitying. Or horrifically inappropriate. So, I'd learned to hide.

It feels stupid to be so scared of showing my body in my athletic swimsuit. I trust Bennett as much as I can, more than I do most anyone else, but this still feels intimidating.

Taking a few deep breaths, I slip my oversized T-shirt back on and exit the bathroom.

I reach for his hand, and even though he didn't offer to hold mine, he grasps it back just as tightly.

• • •

The pool is *definitely* closed. But Bennett slips us in easily, confident in the face of my slight uncertainty.

"Are you . . . getting in with me?"

Shaking his head, he sets the towel on one of the bench seats.

"No, but I'm gonna sit right here with you. I just figured it might help you relax. Maybe help you sleep better."

I know that it will, so I nod and spin away from him, ripping off the shirt and sitting over the side before slipping into the lukewarm pool.

Surfacing just as quickly, I watch him and wade through the water for a moment. He removes his sandals, finding a spot to sit in the middle of the pool and slipping his feet in. His hands grip the pool ledge, the sleeves of his Waterfell hoodie rolled up slightly.

I swim and he watches me.

My nightmares have always been bad—my dreams haven't been

much better. They're too visceral, haunting me long after I wake up. But this feels different. There's a peace to knowing he was watching over me, which I usually wouldn't feel, let alone admit to.

And more than that, he doesn't seem put off by the entire ordeal.

The water is refreshing over my heated skin. And even obscured through the watery distortion, he's so beautiful. My heart thrusts in my chest, like it's reaching for him.

I follow the call, a sailor to a siren, swimming through the placid pool to breach for air by his legs. He's watching me, as he always does, the steady set of his blue eyes comforting, tracking every movement of my arms as I press by his hands and push my body *up, up, up* toward him.

Droplets fall like rain from my wet body across his shorts and hoodie. A rattling breath puffs from my lips before I press them to his, arms straining. He dips his chin so he can meet my kiss, lips soft and trembling in time with my racing heart.

He never releases his grip on the pool ledge.

I don't dare press further, only releasing him when my arms give out and I sink back into the water beneath him.

Bennett's eyes stay closed for a moment, head tipped, as if he's savoring the taste—of chlorine and peach lip balm and *me*. When he opens them, blue crashing down on me like a wave, there's something new.

Do you see me? Just me, as I am?

No one has before.

An image stirs of him surrounding me, holding me to his chest as he woke me from my nightmare. His hands combing my hair back over and over, little fretting touches.

Maybe he would be okay. Maybe he would be good to me. Maybe he's safe.

"I'm ready to get out now."

"Okay," he says. His fingers dance across his lips for a moment longer and he hesitates before standing and slipping his sandals back on, unrolling the towel at his side while I hoist myself up and out.

He wraps me in it, holding me closer than he might've before. It's possessive and comforting. I want to stay here.

My eyes close and I nuzzle into him a little before he lets me go.

I reach for his hand. He takes it. We walk quietly back to the elevators. Gooseflesh ripples across my skin, but I'm not cold—I'm . . . everything else. Happy, scared, excited, so full up that I'm bubbling like a bottle of champagne in anticipation.

Only to plummet into pure anxiety when we arrive back inside my darkened hotel room. Expectations and fear from the past mingle with interest and eagerness for this moment. *Does he want to* mixes heavily with *Will he make me?*

"Don't be an idiot," my mother slurs, eyes teary. "Men only want one thing from us."

"I'm not like you," I snap.

She laughs. "You could be my goddamn twin."

Bennett releases my hand. I fidget in the doorway while he slides off his shoes and sets them by the door.

"I'm gonna shower," I blurt, tripping over my own feet to get into the bathroom and shut the door.

Washing my hair calms me, as does the heat of the water. I take my time before dressing in soft pajama pants and another oversized shirt.

I exit shyly, eyeing where he sits on the bed with his back to the headboard. He's blushing already, fidgeting with his hands in a way that suddenly calms my lingering anxiety.

"Can I brush your hair?" he asks.

It's not the question I'm expecting, so I nod before I can think about it too deeply.

When I do, tears rush to my eyes. I turn back to the bathroom and dig through my toiletries bag for my well-loved boar bristle brush.

The sweetness of the sentiment . . . no one, not even my mother on a good day, has made that kind of offer.

I manage to pull it all in and hold back my desperation to be cared for in that way, eyes still glistening as I duck my head and walk toward him.

He plays Bon Iver's "Beach Baby" on his phone and waits for me. I crawl across the hotel bedding and sit tucked between his partially spread legs, handing him my brush.

"No one's ever—" I cut myself off. The confession feels too raw. "It's— I'm not tender-headed. So, you don't have to be careful."

"I'm gonna be gentle, P."

The words make me shiver; his voice is deep, his presence a solid wall behind me. He brushes through my hair slowly, careful not to pull. He hums low and soft to the music. The combination of it all has my eyes fluttering closed, and I slump into his warm arms just a bit.

I can handle anxious, timid Bennett. I can handle him when it's *me* catering to *him*. But this Bennett—he's overwhelming. Gentle and careful and dominant. Taking care of me.

It quiets the noise in my head, which feels good. But it makes me feel small and vulnerable, too—something that's harder for me.

I lose track of time, only knowing that he switches from the brush to his fingers, massaging my scalp and braiding my hair loosely.

"Will you stay with me?" I mutter, eyes closed.

A firm press of lips to the top of my head. And then, a quick huff of breath, like he didn't mean to do it.

"Always."

I fall into a deep, dreamless sleep and wake up with his hand in mine.

CHAPTER 28

THEN: Freshman Year, October

Bennett

Paloma slept through the night with my hand holding hers.

The next day, I play my best game yet—a shutout. I'm not naïve, I know they're related. I also know she watched it, sitting in the half-empty stands with my hoodie on. No one would know. No one even noticed her. But I did. Her soft smile of approval and excited cheering would be enough to sustain me forever.

I could live off the power of her peace alone.

My best friend racked up a hat trick even on the second line, though I know Coach Harris let him play more than usual tonight. Rhys's always been a star, and I've always had a perfect front-row seat to watch him shine.

So it's easy to smile as he taps his helmet to mine at the end of the line, yelling over the excitement of our teammates, "We did it, Ben! Let's fucking go!"

I smack his back as he goes in for a hug, tapping his thigh with my stick. "All you, Rhys."

The celebrations continue into the locker room, where Harris hands Rhys the coveted trophy—a length of rope made from championship nets. He gives me a shoutout in his happy speech. I can see even the older guys around him smiling, looking at him as if he's already their captain. Rhys covers the room with the shine of his goodness, his talent, his heart.

As happy as I am that we won, I'm more relieved that I didn't cause us to lose. I feel less excitement, and more the feeling of my shoulders finally relaxing.

There is a part of me that will always appreciate hockey. I'm good at it. It comes easily to me, and my need for routines works well within its structure. I just don't have the drive and want that the others do. I don't love it.

But Rhys loves hockey. And I love him.

Coach Harris grabs my shoulder as I amble onto the bus.

"Rhys told me about your usual routines, and—I'm sorry, Reiner," he says.

It doesn't surprise me. Rhys has always been an advocate for me, always understood. It was Anna who'd explained it all to him for me when we were both young. He's never faltered. I can always rely on him.

"I'll make sure you and Koteskiy room together next game." He huffs lightly before dropping his voice. "Anything you need, you can ask me, you know? I want you to succeed. As long as it's within my power, I will do whatever it is *you* need to get there. You know that?"

"I do," I say, swallowing the lump in my throat. He sounds too much like my dad. Enough that the second I'm settled onto the bus, I shoot him a text.

BENNETT
Lunch tomorrow?

DAD
Everything okay? Want me to call you?

BENNETT
Fine. No. Just need to talk.

It takes a long time, the bubbles indicating that my dad is typing. Then stopping. Then typing again, over and over. Before finally—

DAD
All right. Tomorrow at home. You can cook.

A smile takes over my face. I agree quickly before trying and failing to nap for the rest of the ride home.

• • •

Paloma's hair glints almost a bright blond in the parking lot lights outside the back entrance of the Waterfell arena. She's lugging a few of the equipment bags alongside the guy she usually works with— I've forgotten his name, but I *know* she doesn't like him.

Which must be the reason I follow behind them with my own bag, rather than sneaking it home to clean myself.

It's only the two of them sorting through it all, quiet until the smarmy-looking guy runs his eyes over Paloma where she's bent over one of the bags.

"Jesus, Blake." He laughs, crossing his arms and stepping too close. "I swear I've never seen someone with a better—"

I clear my throat, stepping in and shoving his body away from her with my own. My hand settles against Paloma's lower back slowly, but it still makes her jump.

"Just me, P," I say, trying to calm her. She straightens, eyes settling on mine over her shoulder as she stumbles slowly into my body. I hold her to me as my eyes lock back on him. She's still tense, but she stays in my arms.

"Hey, Bennett," she whispers.

"I'll stay with you until you finish up, okay?"

Her eyes are wide, happy and glistening just slightly as she nods.

"Yeah. Um, hey, Jeremy?" She turns back to him. "I can finish up here with Bennett if you wanna go."

"But I'm supposed to—"

"I've got it." My voice is all Adam Reiner, no room for argument. He leaves with little complaint after that.

Paloma steps from me almost instantly and my body mourns the loss of her. She tosses her hair over her shoulders and directs her eyes down toward her feet with a furrowed brow.

"You didn't have to do that."

My throat tightens, but I stay firm. "I know."

"Really." She crosses her arms. "I don't need you to just"—Paloma gestures vaguely around—"constantly swoop in. I can take care of myself."

"I know you can." I do know that. But the feeling of her relaxed and pliant in my arms last night still haunts me. Thrills me. I can *feel* the obsession creeping in, no chance to stop it or even quell it now.

In the quiet, Paloma steps away from me and continues to work. I take my bag off and start on my own things.

"Why do you . . ." Paloma begins, biting her lip before looking away from me. "I'm not judging. I was just wondering: Why do you like them cleaned and sorted a certain way?"

I know she's not judging me, because she's never asked *why* before. She's always just done it the way I asked her to, because she knows it makes me feel better. More comfortable.

"It's . . . I just have to have them that way. It's—"

"Like . . . OCD?" she asks, but keeps her eyes pointed ahead. My throat closes up as heat dampens the back of my neck. I'm not surprised she's picked up on it in some way. People use the term so loosely now.

"Yes." It's quiet for a long moment. "But not like . . . it's not like how people think."

Paloma looks at me then. "I wasn't thinking anything, Bennett. Do you want to tell me about it?"

No. I don't. But her eyes are so open, her posture relaxed. The call of her is impossible to ignore. "It's not about being clean. I don't wash my hands eight times or keep locking and unlocking my door. It's . . . there's a certain order. I need things to just be a certain way."

"Like your pads?"

I nod.

"And . . . the touch thing?" She bites her lip and glances away from me, arms crossing over her stomach. "I'm sorry if it's invasive. I just . . . after last night. I don't want to push or make things more difficult."

My stomach sours. "No. That's— I'm . . . that's different." I shake my head and look at the wall, pointedly away from her. "I'm autistic. I mean, when I was diagnosed it was still called Asperger's, but . . . yeah. I just . . . it's not a big deal and I'm not, like, different or anything."

I'm defensive and frustrated, and I hate it.

I drop my chin toward my chest with a heavy breath. "Well. I am, I mean. But you already know that."

"Something's wrong with me."

"No," my dad says, leaning down. He settles on his knees, arms enclosing the armrests of my chair like a wall. "Bennett, nothing is wrong with you."

"Mom is upset." My eyes try to bounce over his shoulder toward where I can hear her still, crying as quietly as she can. It feels like knives slicing my skin. I jerk my hands up and over my ears again.

Dad slowly raises his own hands, reaching for mine and pulling them away.

"Focus on me. This is important." Holding my palms in a tight grip,

he speaks a little louder. "You are perfect. Nothing is wrong with you. You just need things done differently, okay? And you and me—we're gonna figure this out. Okay?"

"Okay."

I clear my throat, still avoiding looking at her. Embarrassment and shame mix like a sickness in my body. "So sometimes things can be difficult for me. Seven is supposed to help me calm down and . . . other stuff."

"Does he help?" she asks, her voice loud enough that I know she's looking at me even if I won't look at her.

"Sometimes."

"And . . . are there things I could do? That would help?"

The question is soft, and it melts over my skin like a caress. Like her damp, smooth hair over my fingers. The catch in my throat is new, like I've swallowed a rock and can't speak around it, let alone breathe.

I turn toward her.

Paloma watches me all the time. I've grown used to the feeling of her eyes on me, surprised by the warmth and comfort her gaze brings. It still doesn't prepare me for the punch to the gut that is her warm brown eyes filled to the brim with concern and care for me.

"You do most things right."

My answer seems to irritate her. "Can you just tell me? How am I supposed to know if I'm doing something wrong unless you tell me?"

"I like to know when you're going to touch me," I rush to say. We've already talked about this, but it feels like a safe place to start. "And I don't . . . It's not always easy for me to read your expression. You might have to tell me how you're feeling, I won't always be able to guess."

"Okay. I can do that. What else?"

"Crowds. Loud noises."

"But hockey—?"

"That one isn't hard for me. Maybe because it's how I grew up, so

I'm used to it. Or because I have something else I'm hyper-focused on while I'm playing."

She nods as if that complexity makes perfect sense to her.

"Um . . . Sarcasm can be hard for me, too."

Poetry is easy. Recognizing idioms, figurative language, things that aren't literal. Talking to people, conversation—that's the harder piece. I don't always pick up on it, especially if the conversation is moving too fast. Locker room talk, hockey slang, they're all things I had to meticulously practice to understand. And even then, I never participate. Only listen.

"Anything else?"

I get a mental image of me at sixteen having a meltdown in my parent's kitchen, eyes blinking open, body sore as I realize I've blacked out. My mom's tear-soaked face and distant body language. My dad's arms tight around my body, holding me to his chest with his red-rimmed blue eyes. I can't remember what it was about, but I remember the effects.

But even the thought of telling Paloma that I might have a meltdown over something, explaining the way I'm careful with my own emotions to prevent it—it makes that overly hot, sick feeling rise again.

"No," I say, tone even. Quiet.

She nods before turning back to the laundry. As if nothing has changed. As if everything is normal.

Maybe, with her, it could be.

CHAPTER 29

NOW

Bennett

I'm not a fan of flying in general, but flying with the team isn't so bad. Maybe because everything is taken care of—I just show up, other anxieties easily expelled once I'm seated, all my things arranged correctly in and around my seat.

But I'm more calm than usual—and it all dials down to the blond girl traipsing down the aisle toward me.

The grin on my face is unstoppable, even at the set of her furrowed brows and beautiful frown.

I pull my headphones down to circle the back of my neck, daring to reach my hand to graze her arm and gather her attention. She doesn't jolt, only takes a steadying breath. Does she know she's leaning toward me, like she wants to be closer?

Don't make this something it's not.

It's impossible to crush the hope I have when it comes to Paloma Blake—so I stop trying.

"Hey, P."

Her brown eyes seem a bit lighter in the overhead fluorescence, her bag slipping off one sweatshirt-clad shoulder.

"Hey, Bennett," she says, soft and quiet.

Biting my lip, I look around. "Do you need somewhere to sit?"

Fuck my usual routine—I don't even care if it means we lose, if she will sit next to me.

Her features soften, mouth pulling into a slip of a smile. "I'm okay—I'm sitting with Lily." She nods behind her, where Lily is traipsing through the aisle unsteadily, Coach LaBlanc just steps behind her.

A long pause sits heavily between us.

"All right, well—I'm just gonna—" She nods her head forward, gesturing toward the back of the plane. "See you at the game, Bennett."

"Yeah. See ya, P."

I slip my headphones back on just in time to half drown out the sounds of my teammates tossing pickup lines and flirting with her as she heads to find a seat.

• • •

"Reiner! Reiner!"

I close my eyes, preparing for the inevitable rest of their godawful sieve chant.

"You suck! It's all your fault. It's all your fault! It's all your fault."

But I've played against this particular Michigan team before, in this particular arena. I'm used to it. I'm used to the sieve chants in general. They don't really bother or distract me. Though I can tell from here that Paloma's keyed up and furious. It makes me smile.

Tensions have been high the entire game, our teams neck and neck. Rhys, Freddy, and Toren have managed to make goals, but I've let in two, so closing in on the last few minutes of the second, the score is too close.

Right now, the Mt. Hart forwards are rushing my net, Toren and Holden both doing their best work while Rhys tries his hand at stealing the puck—one of the many things he's shockingly good at.

He just manages to snatch the puck from between the forward's legs, poking it toward Holden in the corner.

Head on a swivel, I keep my body pressed to my left post, leg extended to the right just in case I'll need to slide.

Holden misses his pass across, swept up by another towering Mt. Hart player coming in quick off a change. Too fast—he takes a shot I try to block, sliding into butterfly, before bowling over backward as the player knocks fully into me.

A muffled shout leaves my lips at the tearing sensation zinging up my inner thigh. *Fuck fuck fuck.*

The net has been tossed backward into the boards and my body is collapsed. Turning on my side, I put my hands up to protect my head where my helmet has snapped loose.

At first, I only hear yelling—Rhys, I'm sure—before my best friend appears over me, ripping off his cage. He looks terrified.

"Fuck, Ben—are you okay?"

I nod, but groan. "*Fuck*, I think I pulled something. Or a groin tear, I don't know." At least my words sound normal. He nods, turning and signaling for someone.

I move my head up, looking over to where Holden and Toren are locked in an all-out brawl. Kane is laying into the guy who hit me, gloves dropped, black hair sweat damp and half in his face, snarl still present. It's strange for a moment—I've seen the violence of Toren Kane close up and personal, relived the hit on Rhys in my brain like a nightmare more times than I can count, but not like this. Not in defense of me.

Holden is chirping as much as he is fighting another Mt. Hart player, both with their cages off, hands gripping each other's jerseys. It's a mess as the refs try to stop them all—I know heavy penalties and fines are coming, but maybe it'll be equal all around.

"Hey, Ben?" Rhys grabs my attention. "They've got the trainers for you. Can I help you skate off?"

I nod, letting them help me up so that I can take pressure off my groin even while balancing. Rhys slips a hand around my back, hooking my chest pad in his grip just in case I slip, before we all start slowly skating off together. The arena breaks into applause for me, as usual with an injured player.

Head ducked, breathing harsh, I wade through the pain.

"Let's get you the fuck out of here," Harris says when I arrive at the bench, before slapping Connor Mercer on the back and sending him to the net to warm up. "Get checked out. And then go back to the hotel and fucking rest, Reiner. Okay?"

I smile at his unusual doting. "All right, Coach."

CHAPTER 30

NOW

Paloma

I'm wearing a hole in the ugly patterned carpet, pacing back and forth in front of the hotel room door.

I took notes for Harris during the game, seated in the stands near the glass with Lily. I was already annoyed by the sieve chants at this particular arena, and then terrified when the player took out Bennett, knocking the net backward alongside the heap of their bodies.

My hand has risen and almost knocked several times, but I haven't quite managed it yet.

I really shouldn't be here right now. But the image of Bennett splayed on the ice, Rhys shouting his name in panic, and the sight of his head ducked as Rhys and an athletic trainer helped him skate off are stuck in my head like a nightmare I can't wake up from.

What if he—

I cut off the train of thought before it can even leave the station, shaking my head.

"You're being ridiculous," I mutter to myself, turning to face the door straight on and knock—

—only before I can, it opens, and Bennett Reiner fills the doorway.

My throat catches at the sight of him shirtless and damp, curls dark against his forehead. He leans against the entryway with one hand braced nearly on the ceiling, the other heavy against the wall, holding himself up.

God, he's so beautiful.

"Paloma?" he asks, attempting to straighten at the sight of me but wincing and relaxing back into his bracing hold. "Are you okay?"

"Am *I* okay?" I huff, crossing my arms tightly over the block letters of our university emblazoned across my half-zip. "You got hurt—I was so fucking worried about you. I just needed—"

"Hey," he coos, cutting me off and stepping closer. "I'm all right."

Closing my eyes, I take in a settling breath because I'm sliding into panic.

"I'm okay," he says, eyes still watching me too intensely. Like he can see everything I've hidden written beneath my skin.

"Okay." I nod, then shake my head. "All right, good. Then, I should—"

He grasps my bicep in his hand, warm and firm. A solid hold, like he's always had on me.

"Stay."

Blue eyes almost swallow me whole, devouring my anxiety and desperation to get away almost instantly. It's impossible for me *not* to feel settled in the grip of Bennett Reiner.

I shake my head. "No. I can't—"

"Please, P," he whispers, pulling me closer—so close I can almost feel the fiery heat of his bare chest on my skin. "Please. Let me—"

"Hey, Ben? I—" A voice interrupts, abruptly cutting him off. "Oh—sorry."

Rhys Koteskiy is barely a foot away from us, dousing the heated moment with icy water, clearing the almost rosy haze from my eyes.

"Sorry, I didn't mean to interrupt."

"It's fine—" I try to say, but Bennett slowly pulls me farther into his arms.

"Freddy's got an extra bed," Bennett says, his voice raspy and deep. "Mind staying with him?"

Rhys's eyes widen slightly, but he nods. "Yep. I'll just . . . I'll see you tomorrow, Ben."

And then he's gone. There's not a second for me to think before Bennett pulls me into his hotel room and shuts the door.

Alone in a hotel with Bennett feels dangerous. My entire body reacts to his proximity, heart racing and skin flushing. A pang of need sinks into my belly as his muscles bunch and move beneath the softer layer of his skin.

"I'm okay," he says again, sitting on the corner of his bed, legs spread wide and arms crossing over his bare chest as he looks at me again. "Just a groin sprain."

It's embarrassing how quickly I feel my entire body heat.

"Oh." I nod, feeling like a bobblehead as I manage to come up with *nothing* else to say. "And you're . . . that's all?"

He grins unexpectedly. "Hurts like hell, P. I think that's plenty."

"No." I shake my head, squeezing my eyes closed. "Sorry—"

"I'm just messing with you." He absentmindedly runs his hand down the inside of his thigh, and the reddened area moves beneath the pressure. "I just need to stretch it and rest. I already iced it for a while after I got pulled."

"You didn't get pulled." I roll my eyes, my shoulders relaxing as I step farther into the room. "You got injured. There's a difference."

He's still massaging the area, face grimacing every now and then, the muscles in his arm trembling slightly. And maybe it's that. Or the hypnotizing flecks of gray in his ocean blue eyes. Maybe the reminder of the last time we were in a hotel room together this close.

Or maybe it's just the desperation I always feel like a constant tug at my heart to be nearer to him that possesses me to offer, "Let me do it."

His mouth opens before closing slowly again, like he knows he should deny me—what have I done other than cause him pain and suffering over and over? Why should I deserve to touch him so vulnerably?

He nods.

I step forward slowly and he scoots back to sit more fully on the bed, arms behind him to hold him up. My body sinks next to his on the soft mattress, and I curl to my knees just left of his spread thighs. The position is almost too intimate.

"Can I . . ."

The question fades off into nothing,

"You can do whatever you want to me, P."

I have to stifle the sound that attempts to climb from my throat, working up the bravery to place my hands along the solid muscle of his thigh. I push down, focusing my eyes away from the swell between his legs visible through the athletic shorts he's wearing.

He grimaces, and I pull my hands back with apologies spilling from my lips.

"You're fine," he says with a lazy grin. "I don't mind a little pain if it's from your hands."

It's my turn to grimace with the weight of it. The sentiment would be flirty, but it feels deeper.

Still, he takes my hands in his again, spreading his legs farther until his injured thigh is flush with mine. He sets our joined hands on his upper thigh, moving his shorts up almost obscenely to continue. It's quiet, only the lull of a familiar playlist off his phone—Ben Howard and Bon Iver, the strum of guitars romantic and painful all at once.

A groan leaves his throat as he sinks farther into the mattress. My cheeks flush, but I follow him, using more of my body to work his upper thigh.

As breaths saw out of both of us, I realize I'm halfway on top of him, hovering, my messy ponytail nearly fully loose and hair hanging everywhere as I look at him. He's watching me, too, his hand reaching up to tuck a few stray hairs back around my ear—lingering there. I know he wants to touch it again, the slight obsession he's always had with my hair.

I should move away. I should take my hands off his body and excuse myself to a cold shower and restless sleep.

Instead, I rest my hand on his chest instead of the bed, drawing my other arm up. My hand bumps against the hardness of him we're both ignoring between us.

"P," he breathes out, eyes half-lidded and voice soft. "Please."

My heart is thundering, racing off to a place I know I can't go, no matter how deeply I want to.

Before I can second guess it, my hand grasps the length of him over the fabric of his shorts. Breath saws out of him faster, his stomach clenching and eyes closing tight.

"Is this . . . okay?" I whisper, afraid to break the moment. He nods, his face half pressed into the side of my neck as I curl closer and closer to his body.

My hand slowly rolls beneath his athletic shorts, no underwear impeding me from grasping the thick, heavy weight of him in my fingers. His skin is soft and warm, but hard as steel as I grip tighter, paying attention to his every breath—though arguably I know his body better than my own. I always have.

His hands roam my waist, curling around me like a protective shield.

"I want you," he breathes, breath shuddering against my skin. A faint kiss just beneath my ear, a longer moan. "Please, *please* let me have you."

"You do," I reply, almost a whimper as I squeeze my thighs together, shifting slightly like it might relieve the ache. He pulls his pants down, stretching them across the massive span of his thighs. I can see the reddened skin where he iced and I massaged.

He licks his hand before wrapping it half around himself, half around me—moving both our palms up and over the wettened veiny skin. My thigh slides over his hip and I rock slightly into his body, eyes rolling back.

"Are you aching, love?" he whispers. "Tell me you need me again, P."

The heady mix of vulnerability and dominance is too much, and my forehead slants against his temple as I nod. "Please."

"Come here," he coos, pulling me all the way atop him to straddle his left thigh as he continues to touch himself with both of our hands. "Use me, Paloma."

The command is easy, because he's said it before, in this exact way, letting my body move like it does in water, rocking and swaying delightfully against the solid muscle of his thigh. I'm on a hair trigger when it comes to Bennett Reiner; I'm close before I can even breathe in a full gulp of his warm, woodsy, showered scent.

My face lulls into his neck as I release a clenched cry. A near growl comes from his throat, his legs becoming more restless, jerking my body even more with their movement.

"Watch," Bennett grinds out, a hand reaching up and wrapping into my ponytail. He grips it so that it doesn't *pull* on my hair, only tightens, and holds that feeling of control over me.

My eyes lock onto the apex of his thighs, moaning as the sight and sounds of his orgasm trigger mine, both of us crying out almost too loudly.

In the aftermath, I feel the embarrassing sting of tears as I return back to reality. My body heaves. I try to hold it in, but it's impossible when Bennett tucks my body somehow closer, one of his hands combing through my hair as he quietly soothes me.

"*Shhh*, it's all right, Paloma. I've got you."

Tears leave my eyes easily, but I manage to keep back the sobs lodged in my throat, fingers straining as I hold him tighter.

Bennett carries me to the shower, washing my hair and brushing it like he's done a thousand times before. My tears never seem to stop, but he doesn't say anything, and I can hardly bear to look at him.

He gives me a well-worn sweatshirt to slip into, the sleeve chewed up by my mouth, I know. It swallows me whole, and it smells like him.

And then we lay back atop the sheets of his hotel bed. He kisses my fingers, whispering, "Nobody, not even the rain, has such small hands," into my palm. His arms tuck around me, pulling me to lay on his chest as he recites his favorite verses—E. E. Cummings, Pablo Neruda—into my flushed skin. *"Your mouth, your voice, your hair."*

My chest aches as I watch him silently.

"You should stay," he says, hands winding through my damp hair. "Just for tonight. You can go back in the morning."

"Bennett . . ." I start, my voice hesitant and somehow too loud in the quiet room.

A chuff of laughter, and then, "It's all right, P. This doesn't change anything, I know."

I wait until he's sleeping to leave and feel more rotten than usual at the quiet abandonment.

CHAPTER 31

THEN: Freshman Year, October

Paloma

There's another poem in my food, taped again to the inside of the Tupperware lid.

He's done this before, dropped food for me with a hidden letter—always a poem or song. But this one feels different. Not only because it's one I've read several times—Mary Oliver's "Wild Geese"—but because he's annotated it, marking it up with rhyme scheme and metaphors, as we usually do in class.

Beneath the last stanza is his carefully handwritten note.

This one reminded me of you.
Don't ask me to explain.

-Bennett

The note is simple as it always is, nothing too heavy or heartfelt, but it stabs me right in the chest anyway.

Before our next meeting, I carefully wash out the container and add my own note to the interior, fashioned in the exact same way. I can't keep back the sly smile as I hand it back to him, thankful he doesn't open it before we part ways.

Normally at the end of our time together, he'll wait for me to exit the study room first before following behind. But this time, I step forward, pushing nearly into his space and biting my lip, backpack strap tight in my right hand.

"So, you never asked me on a second date." I don't give him time to say anything before nervously prodding with, "Was the first one bad?"

Bennett's eyes go wide. "No. No, I was going to, but I didn't . . ." He trails off, letting out an irritated breath. "I couldn't figure out the best way."

It isn't a lie. I can imagine him sitting in his room, hand through Seven's fur as he thinks about the *best way* to ask me to go out with him again. The thought stirs up something giddy within me.

"Okay, well, I'm asking you out, then."

"Yeah?" He smiles, small with no teeth showing. I match him.

"Yeah. For coffee again, same place?"

He hesitates, mind working furiously behind ocean eyes. "No. We should . . . it should be better than just coffee."

I reach for his hand, and he takes both of mine in his grip. It feels odd and stiff, like a reluctant couple at the altar.

"Bennett, coffee is good. And comfortable. And it's close to where I swim." His face is still twisted up, brows furrowed. "I like going there with you. Can we do it again?"

"If you're sure."

I nod. "I'm sure."

"Okay." He squeezes my hands where they're still held in his. "But next time, we are going somewhere better."

"All right," I concede.

• • •

We meet at the same time in the same coffee shop, all the way down to the same booth.

I swam again, but took the time to dry my hair and wear something slightly better than our last date. Bennett, yet again, is dressed far nicer than me. I drink him in, broad shoulders covered with a flannel, sun-kissed brunette curls, ocean blue eyes and pursed lips. He's so handsome my chest aches.

"Good morning," I say as he stands from the booth and scans over my pretty thrifted cardigan and scrunchie-bound updo. Taking the initiative, I lean in to kiss his cheek, but he turns just in time to catch my mouth.

Breath huffs out of me, and my cheeks blaze at the warm feel of his lips.

"Good morning, P."

His voice is low and scratchy, still sleepy and unused. It makes my body tingle, enough that I pull away from him and try to regain my wobbly footing and hazy vision.

Bennett is more intoxicating than I'd imagine any drug or drink might be. And because it's so unintentional, it's somehow headier.

I feel a bit like blustering out *"Are you my boyfriend?"* but anxiety grabs hold of my tongue. I've never done *this* before. My only experience with romantic relationships is . . . not normal. And I watched my mom cling to every drug-addicted man who showed her an ounce of attention or affection. Or money. Drugs.

The blissed out, lovestruck version of my mother was more palatable, so selfishly, I didn't mind.

Until they turned their attentions to me.

I shake my head, clearing the dangerous thoughts.

There's a girl working—the same brunette with the scowl—but it seems like she's also babysitting two kids in a booth nearest the front, coloring sheets scattered across the table. We wait until she returns to the counter to order our drinks and food—which I let Bennett handle entirely, just standing at his side, his hand in mine, smiling.

It's like one of my Prince Charming fantasies, but *real*. How I'd imagined having a boyfriend might be like.

We haven't said the boyfriend or girlfriend words. It's only our second date—and yet, I feel like if I asked, he'd say yes. In my head, it's simple. He'd hold my hand and ask before he kissed me. Open my door and walk me home—without asking to come in or sleep with me. He'd take care of me without asking for something in return. He'd play with my hair and scratch my back. And he'd be just mine.

I think he already is.

Sitting back down, Bennett reaches for my hand across the table, thumb pressing circles into my skin. I smile so hard I think my lips might split from the force.

"I liked the poem you sent yesterday," he says. "Or, I guess, song."

"Did you just read it? Or listen to it as well?"

I'd taped a printout of the lyrics to "Roslyn" by Bon Iver and St. Vincent. Mostly because I love the song, and the lyrics are so interpretable. But also because Bon Iver's music has been my sleep playlist ever since the night in the hotel room. It's easier for sleep to find me with the lull of music and the memory of Bennett's warm, safe arms around me.

"Both. I treated it solely as a poem first, reading your annotations—"

"Checking my work?" I snark, but grin through the tease of my words. "How did I do, professor?"

Bennett blushes and ducks his chin, shaking his head at my antics. "You're brilliant, Paloma, I didn't need to check your work to know that."

He says it so simply, as if speaking of the weather or reciting hockey stats. Does he know it feels like a kiss to my skin?

"It works nicely as a poem, but there's an added level of emotional complexity with the music. A haunting, eerie element unfelt without it. Even the repetition is entirely different with the sound element. Which, I think, means you categorize a lot of music as poetry."

My eyes flutter closed as I nod, agreeing with his sentiment.

Thrilled that he treated my choice for our game with the intensity of a John Keats ode.

"*Which—*" he continues, smile growing as he almost tugs on my hand in his excitement. "—means you like poetry."

A laugh bubbles from my lips before I can help it, but I swallow down the sound with a blinding smile and shake my head.

"Maybe."

Bennett tilts his head and softly presses a kiss to my hand before releasing it. "I can work with a *maybe*."

"I really like you."

It spews from my mouth, embarrassment immediately clinging to my expression, warmth spreading over my cheeks and down my neck. The entire phrase is so juvenile and insufficient for how I've started to feel for him.

Something worse yawns in my stomach, clawing at every insecurity.

Pathetic. What's next? Begging him to like you? You're good at that, Polly.

My stomach churns, the heat on my cheeks and neck turning clammy so fast I feel sick.

"I—you do?" Bennett stumbles through the words, which only heightens my anxiety.

"*I like you,*" I whisper. "*A lot.*"

"*Yeah?*" *Ethan smirks as he tugs the sheet from my body just slightly. "You like me? C'mon, Polly, I'm not your middle school crush."*

My cheeks color, shame casting my eyes down as he pulls himself up and out of the bed.

"*I think you more than like me, considering what you just did for me.*" *He laughs and pulls on my hair a little roughly before leaning over to tug his jeans back on. I swallow down the confusion, still reaching out to nuzzle against him when he beckons for me before he leaves. Desperate for the touch. For the affection, even if it's mocking.*

"Paloma?"

I shake my head, pulling back and knocking my head into the wooden wall of the booth.

Bennett eyes me, fear and concern overshadowing the awkward anxiety that plagued his features mere moments ago.

"Sorry—got lost in my head for a second." I laugh, shaking my head and some of my lingering demons off. I try to bring up another poem, something else to talk about, trying to divert his attention from my weird display.

He doesn't speak for most of the rest of our date, lingering worry dancing over his face. It isn't long before our coffees are drained and my mostly one-sided anxious rambling stalls into tense silence.

Bennett walks me to my dorm like he always does now, but this time he pauses in front of the steps.

"Paloma? I'm not the best with talking about . . . this. But . . . I—" Again he trips over the word, face agitated.

I shake my head. "It was stupid. I don't know why I said it." I bite on my lip as my anxiety churns. "Can we just forget it?"

He frowns, shaking his head in a stiff denial.

"Please," pours from my lips before I can stop it.

"Paloma, what—"

Get out of here. I have to get out of here.

I stumble back a step. "I'll see you tomorrow, Bennett."

It's easier today to leave him on the steps in front of my dorm. I don't kiss his cheek, averting my eyes at his confused expression over the break in our routine, too focused on the swell of shame making my body feel hot and filthy.

I shower. Even as the water runs cold, I can't get the sensation of feeling dirty off my skin.

CHAPTER 32

THEN: Freshman Year, October

Paloma

Things return to normal and neither of us brings up my desperate confession.

We continue exchanging slips of paper like normal. He sends famed sonnets, ballads, villanelles, odes. I respond with free verse and lyrical poems, sometimes song lyrics with strict instructions to treat as a poem first, then listen.

I spend more time searching for the perfect ones to send than I do on my actual schoolwork.

Halloween falls on a school night, which means most parties are postponed to the weekend. I invited Bennett with a heavy advance, making sure he was comfortable with hanging out at my apartment for the evening.

"Just us?" he asked, biting his lip and hovering in front of the door to our study room.

"Just us."

"Does this count as another date?"

I laughed and nodded. To me, every minute I spend with him is a date.

And at 6 p.m. on the dot, there's a knock at my door. My roommate left earlier in the day with no information on when she'd be back, but I'm glad for it. I don't want to share Bennett with anyone. I want him to be only mine, at least for now. Even if it's only in my head.

"Hey, Paloma."

"Hey, Bennett."

Gorgeous as usual; I specifically instructed him to dress in comfort clothes, and he clearly obliged. A soft black long sleeve with Waterfell Hockey across the chest in bright blue is tight against his broad shoulders, and his legs are encased in long gray sweatpants that make my mouth water a little. He looks warmer and cozier than I've seen him before.

I want to make a pillow fort around him and cuddle by a fireplace.

Bennett's bright blue eyes scan over me slowly, taking in my oversized H is for Halloween T-shirt and soft black leggings.

Opening the door to my room feels terrifying. This place is my sanctuary, my one fully safe space: the blue walls covered with a floral tapestry, the glowing stars on the ceiling. A wooden skim board with multicolored hibiscus florals printed across it hangs precariously on one wall above my desk. I got flowers from the florist in Waterfell when they were going bad, hung them upside down to dry, and now they're part of my wall décor. Prints of every size and color and style hang alongside them, some taken from restaurants or coffee shops as free giveaways, some thrifted along with everything else in my room, all carefully styled.

I'd gone a little overboard with decorating, but it was the first thing that was ever completely *mine*.

Growing up, I went trick-or-treating around the trailer park with the other kids. I'd worn the same costume until the princess sleeves were so high and tight on my arms they left marks. My mother never decorated for the holidays, though I asked often enough. But she often didn't know what day it was.

"I bought a Halloween candle," I stutter out. "A-and the ghost pillow. I wanted to find a blanket, but . . ."

I trail off, rolling my eyes at myself because what in the *hell* can I say? *But I couldn't afford it because the other decorations already went over my spending budget for the month?*

I know that Bennett is much wealthier than I am. Granted, I might not know by *how* much, but he doesn't need to budget the way that I do.

"Anyway, it's . . . yeah." I shrug, spinning in a tight circle to face him where he's still lingering near the door. "This is my room."

Bennett examines every item as he steps forward into the space. It feels like he's seeing into a piece of my soul, closer than I let anyone else.

"I like it." He smiles.

"Yeah?"

"It's just like you," he says softly, affectionately. "We should come here more often."

"We can study here," I say, a little too animatedly. "If you'd like."

I grab for the stuffed animal sitting on my bed, considering tossing it under or into my closet, but as usual, Bennett's eyes are already on me.

"It's, um . . ."

I try to think of a more palatable way of saying what the stuffed bunny means to me. That it was something I found in my old room. That I thought maybe it was a gift left by my dad when he knew he wouldn't be there with me, for me to have a piece of him. It was more likely that my mother had found it or accidentally stolen it from some kid thinking it was mine. But it was hard to let go of the fantasy.

And it's just as hard to stuff this meaningful thing in a hiding spot. It's too similar to how I'd managed to keep it all these years.

"The velveteen rabbit," Bennett finishes my statement, nodding.

As if me hugging this stuffed rabbit so tightly in my arms, like he might take it from me, is highly normal.

"Oh—yeah, it is. At least, I think so? I got it a long time ago."

"It's special to you."

My tongue sticks to the roof of my mouth. I watch as he steps closer to me and reaches for it, nodding silently. He takes the bunny from my hand before propping it next to the ghost pillow I bought. Then he reaches for me.

Heart squeezing and eyes burning, I take his hand.

"We can sit on my bed together, if that's not uncomfortable."

"That's fine."

He follows me, sitting only after I have, eyes on me while I turn on my laptop to a stream of Halloween movies—nothing scary. The overhead lights are off, leaving only the soft glow of my lamp and the stars on the ceiling.

"I'd like to hold you," Bennett says, and our cheeks bear matching red stains almost immediately. "If that's okay."

I nod.

No one's ever asked if they could touch me. They just . . . did.

There's a wide grin across his lips, but his hands are shaking as he wraps one around my shoulder before pulling me back to lay against him fully. It's the most physical contact we've had in a while, my back flush to his warm, soft chest. It reminds me of the hotel room.

We settle into my bed, my blue blanket tucked around us both as I use his biceps like a pillow. *Hocus Pocus* and *Practical Magic* play back-to-back: "Two of my favorites," I quietly tell him.

By the middle of the second movie, I can't take much more. I pull on his arm a little, curling farther into him. His lips have pressed into my hair a few times, even daring to touch the skin of my forehead. But I'm borderline desperate for something *more* now.

I feel like a wriggling fish on a line.

"Bennett?"

"Yeah?"

I swallow a hard gulp and turn my face to stare up at him, neck supported by his large biceps. He pushes himself up a little to look fully into my eyes.

"Can you kiss me?" My fingers dance over my lips absentmindedly. "Here?"

A heavy sigh falls from his mouth, his breath minty and cool.

"It's all I think about, P, ever since the pool."

A sigh of relief barely leaves my throat before his lips are pressed to mine, almost too hard, but so perfect. I kiss him back quickly, hands gripping the bedsheets so that I don't grab for his hair.

My breath is almost too loud against Stevie Nicks singing "Crystal" off my laptop speakers.

His body is beside me, but with his lips on mine, he's half covering me. I want to ask him to press his weight over me, to let me feel completely sheltered and swallowed by him. Like I could hide in his arms and absorb the calm warmth of him forever.

It's safe here. I never want to leave.

His lips are deliberate, careful. With a slowness I'll never master, he raises his hand and tucks it behind my head, lifting my neck toward him. He's holding me entirely in his hands, his other reaching around to press against the center of my back, pulling me closer.

When we break for air, his mouth settles against the skin of my neck, his hands flexing against me. Now it's his breath that's loud, gruff in a way that makes my toes curl before he finally pulls back, kissing my cheek on his way.

"Was that good?"

I bite my lip and nod profusely. He smiles, sated and pleased—with himself or me, I'm unsure. Nor do I care.

When I try to settle back into our position from before, he moves me to lay across his front entirely, head resting on his chest, one leg settled over his thighs. His hand brushes through my hair, massaging the base of my scalp every few minutes, then trailing down my back.

I'm asleep far sooner than I mean to be.

The slight, quiet closing of the door wakes me hours later.

Next to me, there's a piece of notebook paper; on it, a poem: "somewhere i have never travelled, gladly beyond" by E. E. Cummings, one of my favorites. I *know* Bennett knows that. I know he picked the poem with the same gentle intentionality that he does everything.

Not to mention, it's handwritten from memory and annotated.

At the bottom, the last stanza is fully underlined with the word "You" written in his perfect script.

And beneath the entire thing is a simple note:

*Words don't come easily for me but
I care very deeply for you.*

-Bennett

Part of me wants to tuck it into the soft worn shoebox where I've kept every poem and note he's gifted me. But I can't bear not to see it, so I lay it on my bedside table, putting my new candle atop it to straighten the folded edges.

I drift back to sleep just looking at it.

CHAPTER 33

NOW

Paloma

I stare blankly at the folded notebook paper that's fallen out of my bag through a new hole I'll have to patch soon. My stomach somersaults again over how easily I might not have seen it slip from its usual spot of refuge.

Now it stares at me from the passenger seat, taunting me with the corner upturned where I can just make out the beginnings of "somewhere i have never travelled, gladly beyond" haunting and taunting me in equal measure.

Adjusting in my seat again, I try to talk myself out of this ridiculous, inane idea. But my desperation just to see him is too intense to ignore.

We haven't talked since that night in the hotel room. I sat next to Coach Harris to talk over notes, too afraid to look Bennett in the eyes when I saw him board. But I'd felt his stare. Since then, I haven't seen him in passing or at a practice—having spent the week with the pairs team.

Until today, when the anxious wary feeling of *not* seeing him threatened to eat me alive.

Staying in the wet swimsuit was a stupid move. Even beneath

long sleeves and sweatpants, the February wind threatens to freeze me as I jump out of my car. But I don't like showering in public.

I don't like the memories the pool locker room brings, either. My wet swimsuit stuck to every curve of my body; legs spread across the mass of his sweatpants-covered thigh. *"Move like you did in the water,"* whispered into my neck. Teeth in my shoulder as a low groan echoed against the tiles. *"I need you to keep going for me. I need to see you come like this."*

"I want to keep you like this. Do you trust me?"

"Let me hold you. Just like that, love. So good for me—"

Shaking away the warm, deep voice that's heating up my body, I duck my head into the hood of my open jacket.

I try knocking, hesitant at first, then insistently after gaining some bravery. It's a long length of silence, so long I step back to leave—before a dog barks and the door opens to Bennett Reiner, half slumped into the frame.

Broad and muscular, but with a softness that the other boys on the team don't have. Bennett is immensely tall, thick across his middle and chest, as well as his arms. Brunette curls more unruly than usual fall forward into his face as he takes me in sleepily.

He's so beautiful it hurts.

"You're swimming again," he says, eyes darting to my wet braid and the dark outline of my damp suit beneath the shirt I'm wearing. The cracks messily patched together in my heart yawn back open at his words.

"I—um, yeah." I nod. "It's been good for me."

The silence isn't relaxing this time, it's tense. Mostly from me. I start to back away. *This is a bad idea.*

Bennett's hand snaps out and wraps around my wrist, tugging me toward him. Seven peeks up from his spot at the top of the stairs, before raising himself up with more excitement and racing sloppily toward me.

"Hey." I grin, voice low and soft as I pet his fur. "Miss you, too, Sev."

"What—" Bennett coughs roughly, pulling his shirt up over his mouth. He clears his throat, but his voice is scratchy and worn. "How are you here?" He leans toward me, lifting a hand like he's in a daze, observing me like I'm some apparition from his brain.

"Oh, um—" I gulp down air like there's a short supply. "I came to see you, but—" A strange laugh escapes my lips as my face burns. "I'm . . . I'm sorry."

"No—wait." He clears his throat, voice raw as he steps backward away from me. I track my eyes over him again—sweat-glistening skin, reddened circles around his half-lidded ocean-blue eyes, slumped posture.

"Oh god, Bennett, are you sick?" I ask, stepping toward him on instinct. He tries to back away, like he's got the plague and he's terrified it'll infect me.

"Mmhmm." He draws out, eyes closing and breath heaving in his broad chest. "So, you should probably go now. I took some NyQuil and now I'm seeing things."

It almost looks like he's going to fall asleep right here, half leaned against the wall of the foyer. I bite down on my lip, smashing the threatening smile away. He looks so boyish, it's distracting.

"Can I help you get to your room? You need to sleep."

"You're always in my room, P." He slurs the words a bit. I approach anyway, slipping my arm around his thick waist. Even in his half-delusional, cough medicine–induced state, he doesn't collapse his weight on me. Like he's aware even now of his size and stature.

With my help, we walk up the stairs and toward his room.

The smell of it hits me like a brick wall, assaulting my senses all at once. Bergamot and pine, and something softer like fresh, warm sheets. It's the smell of home for me.

I untuck his sheets carefully on both sides of the bed. He watches me, eyes still only half open, but there's a softer set to his shoulders.

He's not as tense as he'd usually be when allowing me to complete one of his rituals for him.

"Get in, love." The old familiar word sneaks out of my mouth.

He smiles, sleepy and sated, and I don't have it in me to care about the line I've crossed.

Bennett's hands brush my hips as he passes me to slide into his sheets and comforter. He pulls the sweat-sticky shirt off, revealing the warm, pinkened skin of his upper body. He takes up so much of the bed, body heavy and limp before I've even flicked off his bedside lamp.

"Stay, P," he calls, voice whisper quiet. The window blinds are closed tight, casting the room in a peaceful darkness. "Please."

My heart tugs like the organ is trying to burst from my chest and into his hands, where it's always belonged.

Seeing Bennett like this feels wrong, the usual pillar of strength weakened by sickness. And knowing Bennett, I'm sure it's causing all sorts of anxiety by throwing his routines and rituals off.

I want to care for him. To do what I know he'd do for me, though he'd never ask me to.

"I'll be here when you wake up."

CHAPTER 34

NOW

Bennett

Light flickers between the slightly opened blinds.

And there's no sound of Seven.

I jolt up, hand coming to rub at my head as it throbs in earnest.

Hoisting myself up and out of bed, I resist the urge to shower just yet, needing to check on wherever the hell Seven is, too worried about him to care that I stink of sweat . . . even if my sweat-slick sleep pants sticking to me feel like knives in my skin.

"Seven?" I call, heaving myself slowly down the last few steps. I hear the pitter-patter of paws accompanied by feet and turn—

And she's there.

Paloma.

She pours into the doorway like the water drenching her body. She's in her swimsuit with sweatpants covering her from the waist down, also just as soaked, clinging to the curves of her body. Darkened blond hair drips onto the kitchen floor, framing her clean face and chewed-on lips.

The girl I've loved since the first moment she opened her mouth—even if I didn't realize it yet—is in my house.

"You're swimming again."

It's the only thing I can manage, even if I immediately curse myself for it. *Observations aren't greetings.*

"I—um, yeah." She nods, shaking the water off like Seven after a bath. He—just as soaked—mimics her. "You said that yesterday."

There's a small smile at those words and I want to grasp it tight with both hands.

"Right." I scratch at my stubble, feeling for how long it's been since I shaved. "I was a little . . ."

"Out of it?" She smirks. "High on NyQuil?"

"Yeah." I nod, blushing.

"Feeling better?"

"Yeah."

Another awkward silence floats between us until I feel a little nauseous over what to say next.

"I'm sorry," she blurts. "I shouldn't have stayed with you all night." My chest squeezes at her words. *She stayed with me all night? In my room?* "It's just—no one came home. And I didn't know if you'd walked Seven or fed him, and then I didn't want to leave you alone while you were sick. I just . . ."

Exhaustion settles into her expression.

A million questions form and die on my tongue; I'm terrified that something I say will send her running, skittish and fearful again.

"When did you start swimming again?"

It's not the question she's expecting, and maybe it's not the one I meant to ask, but for some reason it feels like the most important one.

"Um, this semester."

I want to ask more questions. I want to know everything I've missed. We've danced around each other this semester, and she's not reached out once for my help, called me to *walk her home.*

But she's swimming again. That's . . . that's everything.

There's something healing about the water, for Paloma. It's the reason I took the time to run her baths, to install the ridiculously expensive rain shower, to sit in the empty pool late at night and break a few school rules, to brave the irritation of wet socks and clothing sticking to me because watching the rain hit Paloma's skin looks like something divine.

Paloma was meant to be in water, or near it. Watching her deprive herself of it was enough of a heartbreak—but to know she's swimming now? Healing?

I smile before I mean to.

Seven steps forward again, nudging his soaking wet head against her equally wet sweatpants-clad thigh. He looks up at her like she hung the moon.

I imagine I look at her similarly.

"Did you give my dog a bath?"

Her cheeks pinken and her eyes dart down to my wet dog at her feet.

"Yeah—um, Seven got sick. I don't know from what, but he threw up on himself and so I cleaned it up and decided to bathe him." She picks at a tangle of blond hair and peeks up at me from beneath her lashes. "I just wanted to help, since you were sick. And I knew the mess would be . . . hard on you."

The last words flutter into the air between us, vulnerable and quiet.

"Can I make you food?" I squeeze my eyes shut and shake my head. "I mean, are you hungry?"

"Starving."

She hesitates for a moment; so do I. The pulling need to lead her, like I usually do, wars with the uncertainty of this moment. What are we to each other? How do we interact here, in this daylight vignette of something I've never had with her but always wanted?

I take a gamble.

"Why don't you go upstairs and shower?"

Her cheeks darken. I try not to ruminate on what *she's* thinking. "I didn't bring anything to change into. I don't even have my—"

"That's okay, P," I cut her off gently. "I'll lay something out for you."

• • •

I try to give her plenty of time to get into the shower before I creep up and into my room, grabbing for a sweatshirt with a chewed-up sleeve and a pair of sweatpants she's used before.

Just as I decide to leave them on my bed, rather than invade her space to leave them on the counter, the door opens.

My stomach hollows out at the sight of her in the doorway, towel tucked around her, shoulders bare and skin wet and flushed with the heat from the water. I bang my shin into the metal bedframe, nearly falling as I avert my eyes.

"Sorry," I mutter. "I'm sorry—I wasn't—"

"It's fine, Bennett," she says. "Nothing you haven't seen before."

It's meant to be a joke, to get rid of some of the tension. But it only makes my chest ache because it's *not* a joke to me. It doesn't matter if I've seen her naked before; her body is *hers*.

Why is that such a hard concept for her?

I'm terrified to admit that I know the answer. But still, I keep my back turned to her.

"I'm making you breakfast. Pancakes and an omelet. Some fruit and potatoes, too."

"You don't have to do all that, Bennett," she whispers. "But thank you."

Saying *I'll make you as much as I can because I live in constant fear that you don't have enough food* feels like too much, so I stay quiet. Though I did sneak protein bars and one of the kid's yogurts she likes into her backpack. Just in case.

"I'll just wait for you in the kitchen," I say, leaving and closing my door before she can say anything else.

CHAPTER 35

NOW

Paloma

Sitting at the countertop feels almost surreal, but not any more than watching Bennett Reiner cook for me once more.

He maneuvers in the kitchen like an art form.

Once I'd asked him if he wanted to be a chef, but he said no. That the environment of most kitchens would be unbearable for his anxiety, but that cooking was a way to say you loved someone without words.

"Words are hard for me," he'd said, sliding a plate of fancy tartines to me. "It's easier to show how I feel, I guess."

I love you. That's what he'd been trying to say.

"So, are you ready to tell me what happened the night Sadie brought you here? Why you stayed here? Why you haven't called . . ." His cheeks flush as he plates the pancakes with fruit and sets them in front of me. "If you told me last night, I don't remember it." I wait until he's returned to the counter, looking away from my face before I speak.

"I . . . I got kicked out of the dorms."

The soothing, rhythmic sound of his knife against the wood cutting board halts and he stares up at me, blue eyes shining.

"Did something happen?" he asks, followed quickly by a quieter, "Why didn't you call me?"

I hate that his first thought is that I would only come to him because I was in trouble or hurt. But I made it this way between us. He spent six months learning me, opening up to me, begging me to trust him in the way he was trusting me, loving me . . . and I threw it all away.

And now, I feel *wrong* still. Being here. Unworthy of his unwavering care.

I can see it even now, that he loves me. He's never hidden that from me. But it still feels far away, like I'll never really reach it again.

"Nothing happened," I assure him. "My old roommate was . . . terrible." I blow out a breath. "But I called Sadie, actually," I say, pushing a strawberry around in the syrup. "I just . . . it was a lot."

He nods, but I can see the near wince he tries to hide. The frustrated furrow in his brow. He begins chopping again, only it's more stuttered and inconsistent.

"Bennett?" He looks toward me. "I know you care for me and . . . and I know that you would have come for me, if I'd asked. If I'd called. But I needed to do this without you."

He stops suddenly and drops his hands onto the countertop, head dipping below his broad shoulders.

"Don't do this, P," he begs, barely a whisper. His shoulders shudder. "I *want* to be there for you. I . . . I *need* to—"

"I know," I cut him off, closing my eyes quickly because the sound of his pain, however faint, makes my entire body feel like lead. "Bennett, I'm not asking you . . . I'm not saying that you aren't there for me. You are. You always are."

"Then why haven't you called me?" he says, spinning toward me. Hurt bleeds from him.

I take in a slow breath, steeling my voice. "Because the past three years I have *used* you. And I know—I know it doesn't upset you, but it should."

"Paloma, I—" He pauses, clenching his fists at his sides. I can hear what he isn't saying. *I love you. I love you.*

He doesn't need to say it; I know it as clearly as my own heartbeat. He'd never let me doubt that, never taken those words away from me. Not the way I did from him.

"I know," I say. "But there *is* something I want from you."

He relaxes just slightly, crossing his arms. He nods, intent for me to continue.

"I don't know how to ask this, and I don't want an answer now, really. But . . . I'd like it if we could start over. As friends."

I can see that I've shocked him, his expression wide and unusually vibrant. "Friends?" The word sounds odd on his tongue. A disbelieving look crosses his face, his eyes hooding like he's remembering last weekend and the hotel room.

No. I'd really like to take you back into the shower with me and beg you to wash my hair so I can apologize and tell you why I've hurt you, and myself, to save you from something I was sure was worse. From something that terrified me at eighteen, but I think I could face head on now.

I want to say, *I'm sorry for not being stronger for you.*

I love you. I've never stopped.

But instead, I nod. "Yes. Friends. I'm . . . turning over a new leaf." I can feel Alessia Baudelaire's eye roll from here and internally, I roll my eyes at *myself* over the cliché. "I want things to be different. Especially between us."

Bennett only nods back at me with a gentle, appeasing smile. Like he's wary, but proud of me.

"All right, Paloma. Friends."

CHAPTER 36

THEN: Freshman Year, November

Bennett

I sleep at Paloma's for the weekend, faking sick for the Halloween party Freddy and Rhys invite me to and sneaking out with Seven.

It's much harder to sneak him *into* her dorm, but the sight of my dog curled up on her bed with her as I bring in the food I've heated up in her poor excuse for a kitchen is worth it.

Seven always sits between us, or has some part of his body on her leg or arm—always putting his weight on her like he does for me when I'm anxious. But Paloma is smiling and happy, so I assume it's because he likes her and not because there's something there I'm not seeing.

It doesn't stop another thread of worry and anxiety over her from taking root.

"This is so good." She practically moans the words through bites of the chili I made the day before. I fed Rhys and Freddy but lied and said I hadn't made enough for them to gorge themselves as usual. I was saving the rest for her.

"I'm glad you like it," I say. She treats every dinner I feed her as if it's a five-course meal at a Michelin star restaurant. Seeing her eat and enjoy my cooking fills me with warmth—and serves to chase away the concern that plagues me every time I open her barren fridge.

"I'm gonna leave the rest of the container, too." I put my bowl onto the desk she uses as a bedside table. "It should be good 'til Tuesday, so if you don't mind the same meal for a few days—"

"I don't mind. If I don't end up scarfing it all down by tomorrow."

My stomach churns. "I can bring more—"

"I'm kidding," she says, voice softer as she slowly places a firm hand on my thigh. "This would feed three of me for days."

There's a stretch of silence as Paloma finishes her bowl and sets it atop mine, before she looks up at me from beneath her lashes.

"You're always feeding me."

"I like feeding you." It's a better answer than *I obsess over you being hungry. I think you were, at some point. I worry you still are. Sometimes I can't sleep from worrying about it.*

Instead, I smile at her, reaching my hand out to touch her hair gently, looping it around my finger and back behind her ear. It's soft and silky, and my obsession with the strands only grows.

"Is this your natural hair color?"

Her cheeks darken, eyes darting away. I feel a little heat rush up my spine.

"Is that a bad question to ask? I'm sorry—"

"No, no. It's fine," she says, even if I'm almost certain it's *not* fine. "It's . . . close. I'm blond, this is just kinda darker."

I nod. She seems surprised that there aren't any follow-up questions.

"Do you like it?" she asks.

The question itself is surprising, because Paloma is intensely beautiful. At first, when I started to notice, it overwhelmed me.

I'd never really been attracted to anyone before. I could recognize objectively beautiful people based on typical standards and locker room talk.

I also understand that girls do find me somewhat attractive, because of my height or the fact that I'm on the hockey team. But I don't have the same build as the other guys on the team and never have. I've always been broader and softer than them. It didn't bother me.

But seeing the way that others often watch her, knowing how attractive and mesmerizing Paloma is to most *everyone* . . . it makes something like anxiety and fear churn in my gut, a sickening mixture. I can't distinguish the jealousy from the protectiveness.

I know if she spent *any* real time with the team instead of doing their laundry in separate rooms and hauling supplies to storage areas, this would be different. Because Paloma is exactly the girl that, physically, most of the guys would be panting over.

I want to keep her as just *mine*. At least a little bit longer.

"I . . . I love it," I say, feeling bolder. "I love your hair, Paloma."

Can I wash it? Can I brush it? Can I braid it and care for it and never let anyone else touch it?

I don't say any of the obsessive thoughts about her running through my head. I haven't even been able to admit them to my therapist.

Paloma smiles and pushes up on my thighs to kiss my mouth gently.

She lets me play with her hair all night as she slowly falls asleep on my chest.

. . .

The pool is relatively busy today—everyone active on a Saturday morning—but I spot Paloma easily. She's already finished swimming, towel wrapped around her body like a column, squeezing her hair out as I approach.

"Hey." She grins, eyes dancing with delight at the sight of me. The effect is a little heady. "What are you doing here?"

I clear my throat and tuck my hands behind my back.

"I wanted to ask you on a date. Tonight." I dart a glance down at my shoes. "Not coffee."

"Dinner?" she asks, patiently waiting as it takes me a moment to swallow and nod. "That would be great. What time do you want me to be ready?"

"I'll—at six thirty. That should give us time to get to the restaurant by seven."

She's still smiling, peachy lips flushed like they've recently been bitten. Like they sometimes look when I kiss her *harder*, the way I secretly like best.

"That's perfect, Bennett."

It feels like it is—until that night at 6:45, when I'm stuck in my car, too anxious to drive anywhere. Panicked and hungry, I check the time again, only to grow somehow more paralyzed now that I'm past my time to pick her up and off my scheduled plan.

"You can cancel," I whisper harshly to myself, batting my hand on the steering wheel. "She won't be mad."

It's the easy solution. Try again when I don't feel so terrified.

Only . . . I don't *want* to cancel. I *want* to be with Paloma desperately.

My phone rings, the noise blaring in the silence of my car. Stomach somersaulting, I let it ring almost until the end, answering just before it goes to voicemail.

"Hey, Bennett?" Her voice is calm and sweet.

I can't speak, throat dry. I'm not even sure at this point how long I've been sitting here.

"It's Paloma," she continues. I can hear the slight hurt, the anxiety I'm feeling mirrored in the sound of her voice dropping slowly at my continued silence.

"H-hey," I manage to wrangle out. "I'm s-sorry—"

"Are you okay?" she asks, voice losing all hesitation.

Tears sting at the corner of my eyes and I feel stupid and achingly ridiculous.

"No."

"Where are you?" There's shuffling and then the slamming of a door. "At your house?"

"Yes," I say. "In my car."

Every word I manage sounds half-strangled.

"Okay—stay there."

The call beeps, but I don't drop the phone away from my ear—as though if I listen harder, I'll be able to hear her breathing. The soft swish of her hair against the speaker. Anything to bring me back.

Focus. Remember your list.

1. Go to her dorm, to the door, and knock.
2. Tell her she looks beautiful.
3. Hold her hand and open her car door.

My hand hits the steering wheel again, a strange sort of grief welling up in me that I couldn't get to the first step because one thing in my routine went wrong and now nothing for this night will be okay.

I need to call her back. I need to cancel and tell her we can do it next weekend and it will be better then—

A knock sounds at my window, making me jump and drop my phone to the floor.

It's already dark outside, but the multiple streetlights illuminate Paloma against my car window. Her hair looks darker without the light, long and wavy. Her makeup is done—it might be the first time I've seen her with any—and she's dazzling.

So much so that I almost knock her over trying to open the door, forgetful of the state of my clothes and my eyes still wet with tears.

"Hey," I breathe, angling my body toward her without getting out of the car completely.

She's dressed in a long white skirt with a floral pattern and a navy cardigan, with little heeled boots peeking out from the ends of the skirt.

"You look beautiful," I say, words muddled. Her brow only furrows, making my stomach sink. *Why can't I get this right?*

I try to picture what she sees—my clothes rumpled and sweat-soaked, my eyes bloodshot and still teary, and my skin pale. Not exactly the image I want her to have of me. My eyes squeeze tight at the desperation to make it all stop, to go back in time and just be normal enough for this one goddamn night.

"Bennett . . ." My name sounds like a plea. "What happened? How—how long have you been out here?"

"Not long." I shake my head. "What time is it?"

Her eyes are wide pools of sad mahogany.

"It's almost eight."

My head spins, hands shoving through my once-styled curls until I'm sure they're a rat's nest atop my head.

"I'm sorry," I choke out, shaking my head back and forth. "I shouldn't have—"

"Hey," she whispers, suddenly close. Her scent works into my nose and mouth, stifling the apologies waiting on my tongue. Her arms slip up and over my shoulders as she presses herself into my body *hard*, stepping up to the cab between my legs.

"Can I—"

She doesn't get the question out before I'm hauling her to me, holding her as tightly as I need. My body is still trembling. I war over explaining myself or just letting her comfort me, which only causes more distress.

She coos into my ear, hands bracing me instead of attempting any soft touches—because she *knows* me now. Paloma has taken the time to understand what I need, what soothes me.

"What happened?" she asks, her voice muffled with her face pressed into the collar of my flannel.

"I don't know," I lie, only to immediately ramble on with, "It's— my plan was perfect. I just had an issue with Seven. He . . . it rained today, and he tracked mud in, and I didn't realize it until after. So, once I finished cleaning, I was off my schedule and rushing and everything just..."

"Spiraled?"

I nod.

"Okay." She pulls away from me and I feel the loss of her immediately. "Let's come up with a new plan."

My brow furrows, head already shaking. "It's— We can still go—"

"Maybe something a little smaller?"

"I don't want you to be disappointed." The words ache, raw and vulnerable.

Paloma's eyes soften, hand reaching out for mine. "I would never be disappointed. Please trust me, Bennett. I just want to spend time with you."

CHAPTER 37

THEN: Freshman Year, November

Bennett

About a half hour later, we arrive outside the large brownstone in Beacon Hill.

I've always loved my father's home, the warmth of the red brick exterior and the vibrant, well-styled interior. It's an older historic home that was passed down to my father through his father's side of the family, one of many Reiner family properties.

The Reiner family history traces back through decades of investment group funds, massive sports team owners, and one major private manufacturer—but it started back in the 1880s with massive success in mining businesses. And the Reiner family always had sons. Jonathan Reiner, my grandfather, had three sons—Jacob, Jonathan, and Adam, my father.

At this point, no one in our family technically needed to work for a living. But my uncle Jacob entered the family business of investment banking. My dad played one year in the NHL and went back to law school after his injury, starting his own immediately well-respected firm. It was only Jonathan who rebelled against the Reiner family rules and disappeared from family photos altogether.

Overall, most of my family is cold and distant. But my father is different, always has been.

"You're—" Paloma pauses and clears her throat. "This is your house?"

"My dad's." I nod, rubbing the back of my neck a little self-consciously. "He's . . . his family is generationally wealthy."

"Yeah." She snorts, stepping up at my side, eyes still running over the ivy-laden brick. "No kidding."

I reach for my keys, but before I can slot them into the keyhole, the door opens.

My dad is standing on the threshold, suit still on, sans jacket, sleeves rolled to his forearms.

"Bennett?"

I nearly swallow my tongue at his tone. "Sorry. I didn't call—I just thought—"

"No, no. You're fine. I'm glad to see you." He reaches forward for a tight, solid hug, before pulling back and glancing toward Paloma still in the doorway, with Seven sitting at her feet. It was her suggestion that we bring him.

"This is Paloma. We're—I'm going to cook for her, if that's okay."

My dad's eyes brighten, and a smile replaces his previous anxious expression. "Oh, absolutely. I'll let you show her around and just be in my office if you need me, all right?" He grins at my date politely before backing away from the door with a quick, "Pleasure to meet you, Paloma."

If she says something back, I don't hear, too focused on thinking of whether to show her around first or feed her.

But knowing I won't be able to focus on anything else until she's eaten, I guide her toward the kitchen.

Paloma follows me through the long corridor, coming to a brief stop at the sight of my father's one-and-only NHL jersey framed in the living room.

"Seven?" she asks.

My throat feels tight, skin heating. "Yeah."

Adam Reiner, lucky number seven . . . my hero as a kid. My hero *now*, who I named my dog after. She's the first one to catch it.

Paloma sits at the countertop while I start on our meal—braised beef with a quick garlic butter pasta and roasted vegetables.

"Do you want something to drink?" I ask, wiping my hands on the towel over my shoulder once everything is cooking. "We have a few things up here, but there's an entire wine cellar downstairs."

Her cheeks flush red, hands freezing where she was previously tapping her nails over the marble. "I don't drink, really."

"Me either," I say, feeling another strange stir of relief wash over me. "How about sparkling grape juice?"

It feels silly to suggest it, a children's drink for a New Year's party, but she lights up.

"I've never had it. But it sounds good."

I pour her a drink, the light pink liquid bright against the big crystalline glass, and hand it to her by the stem. While the beef cooks, I offer to show her around.

We trail slowly through the three-story building. I let her stop and ghost her fingers over the extreme number of baby pictures lining the walls and bookshelves. Before we leave the main level, I take her to the plot in the back where my dad cares for my herb garden.

Anna was the one to show me how to do it. She'd come over every day for a week, still in her work clothes, arms up to the elbows in soil as she helped me set it up so I could grow my own vegetables and herbs to cook with.

I'd mourned the little garden when I left for Berkshire, but my dad tended to it as if it was his second child.

It's too chilly in the evening to sit outside, so I take her back into the kitchen to check the food, then upstairs through the secondary living room, the library, and then—

"My bedroom." The words are rough in my throat. Paloma pushes the door open farther to one of my two childhood bedrooms.

This one is more *me* than the one at my mother's house. My bed is tidy, blue and gray flannel bedding tucked tightly with a white sheet just folded overtop. Two or three hockey trophies serve as bookends for the overflowing tomes of poetry and literature study littering the bookshelves.

"This is . . . quite the collection," Paloma says teasingly, hands touching the spines of my books carefully before her chin turns over her shoulder. "You've always loved poetry?"

I nod, hands shoved in my pockets so I don't reach for her.

The sight of Paloma in my room, golden lamplight dancing over her skin, her hands on my books—it makes something wild rouse within me. Something on the edge of feral. Terrifying enough that I ache for space, room to breathe without the scent of her in my nose.

"Stay here," I command lightly. "I'm going to bring the food up and we can eat in here."

I've said the right thing by the way she relaxes and slumps onto the end of my bed. I want to stretch her out across it, desperate to kiss her hard—harder than usual. To explore more of her. To beg her to show me how to make her feel good.

Instead, I nearly take the hinges off the door with the way my shoulder hits the frame as I stumble out into the hall.

By the time I return to my room with our plates, Paloma is laying against the pillows on the headboard, one of my books open under her fingers as she reads.

I can imagine coming home to this sight for years. And that thought is exhilarating and terrifying in equal measure.

"Which one did you grab?"

"*Dog Songs* by Mary Oliver." She giggles. "I'm reading to Seven."

Seven is asleep on her thighs, one of her hands on his head. I sit below her, putting her plate on the bedside table and mine on the floor beside me.

"Read to me."

She does, her words low and soft as she reads "Little Dog's Rhapsody in the Night."

"'Tell me you love me,' he says. 'Tell me again.'" She paces over the poem perfectly, making my heart pound louder, harder in my ears. "Could there be a sweeter arrangement? Over and over he gets to ask. I get to tell."

My affection for her fills the room until there is barely space to breathe. We eat and I let her give her opinion over each poem as she turns through them, listening more than speaking.

No one but her could make me feel this way in the aftermath of my spiral, to still make this feel romantic and intimate. She's the only one who would do exactly this with me, that would make sitting on the floor of my childhood bedroom with poetry and an old record spinning feel like a special occasion.

Only her.

Hours later, she helps me take the plates down and clean them. Our arms brush each other periodically, gooseflesh littering my skin beneath my flannel. I want to kiss her again. I almost do—

But my dad enters the kitchen just before I can work up the nerve, the moment fading like smoke in the air.

CHAPTER 38

THEN: Freshman Year, November

Paloma

Bennett's dad looks so much like him, it's almost unsettling. Both much too tall and well built, the beard and slight lines around his eyes and mouth are all that separate the man in the crisp suit from his son.

"I just need to grab a few things from my room. Can you wait here for me?" Bennett asks.

I nod despite the fear clogging my throat.

Don't be a baby, Polly.

Bennett kisses my forehead and moves past me to the hallway.

The quiet is awkward and unsettling, compounding the anxiety I'm already battling.

Adam Reiner steps forward, not even that close to me, to reach for something on the countertop beside me.

"Hey." A smoky voice. Male. Indistinguishable. "Need some help?"

Hands on my waist, holding me still. A punishing grip.

"You look just like your mom."

My stomach rolls, sickness threatening. I nearly jump out of my skin, flinching back and away from him, knocking my hip hard into one of the elaborate drawer handles. A hiss of pain explodes from my lips, skin burning so hot I'm sure I must be on fire.

Seven whines, pushing past Adam Reiner's leg to get to me.

"Are you all right?"

He isn't talking about my hip. That's obvious from the worried furrow of his brow, the tip of his chin and hunch of his body—the same tactic I've seen Bennett use before, attempting to shrink his massive frame.

"Yeah—I'm—"

God, am I about to cry? My voice is tight and scratchy. It feels like speaking through swallowed shards of glass.

Adam looks me over again, gaze assessing—seeing too much, too easily.

"Are you—"

"Ready?" Bennett calls, stepping back into the room with a few hangers of thicker winter coats tossed over his shoulder. I nod and nearly sprint toward him.

It's only when his arm is around me, his lips are to my hair, that I feel completely safe again.

. . .

We make it back to his place late, Seven quietly trailing us as we step into the pitch-black living room. I've calmed down, the rush of adrenaline and embarrassment both having faded out. In their place is a calm I only tend to feel in Bennett's strong presence.

And Seven's.

"My roommates are out for the night—since we don't have a game until Sunday evening. If you want to stay here."

I've never met his roommates or his friends. I don't even know their names; we never talk about them. Sometimes I think it's because Bennett's realized I don't have any friends myself.

It's not strange to me, like it might be to others. I'm used to being a secret; good at keeping them, too. Especially when it's something I want.

And I want Bennett Reiner.

The stereo in his room plays "You're the Only Good Thing in My Life" by Cigarettes After Sex—a band whose lyrics I used as a poem once in one of our letters to each other. The beat is slow, sensual. So is Bennett. His body is so large and warm, sturdy and unshakable— the same way he is to me.

He means so much to me—I think I'm falling in *love* with him, and he can barely admit to liking me. The cacophony of the self-conscious thoughts that plague me only ratchets up higher.

I reach for him, anxiety and excitement plaguing every sense until my heartbeat is rushing through my ears. Sinking to my knees between his massive, slightly spread thighs, I tuck my hair back over my shoulders and pull at his sweatpants.

"What—"

"I want to do something for you," I breathe, skin flushed and warm beneath his intense gaze. "Please . . ."

He swallows visibly, his throat working heavily, but he does nod.

He's hard as I grasp him beneath his sweats—and proportional to the size of his body. My stomach flips in anticipation and worry, but I continue, working him with one hand as I pull down his sweats and boxers just to expose him to me. Big and heavy, hot in my hand.

I spot his white-knuckle grip on the bed on either side of me, and roll my tongue to wet my lips before placing my mouth over just the tip of him.

A moan works from Bennett's throat, and he presses a hand to my shoulder. To . . . stop me? I pull back but keep my mouth mostly on him as I blink up at him.

He looks . . . almost in pain. No part of him seems relaxed or like he's feeling any sort of pleasure. My stomach plummets, ice searing through my veins as I pull up and off him, falling back on my butt in my haste.

"Is this . . . is it too much?" I ask, my voice small. "Or is it me?"

He doesn't answer right away.

Where my skin is likely ashen pale, Bennett's face is flaming red—not so much an embarrassed flush, but like an indication of pressure building up. Like everything inside him is too much, too overwhelming, and has nowhere to go. He won't look at me, his eyes fixed on the carpet between us, his hands covering his lap where he's hastily pulled up his sweatpants. As if he's shielding himself.

"It's—it's too much, I think," he admits, voice flat, eyes closing tightly.

A pang throbs in my chest, rejection sliding through my soft shield easily. I stay quiet, shrinking down and hugging my knees to my chest.

The weight of the silence between us is nearly unbearable. But my thoughts feel messy and harmful, half tossed into the past, and nothing will come out. I can't soothe him when I feel like this, the sting of his words and movement still fresh.

The sound of dark, taunting voices threatens in my head.

Finally, Bennett exhales a sharp breath and sits up straighter, his hands moving to grab tightly at his thighs. "It's not *you*," he says, his voice rough, almost defensive. "You're perfect. I—I just . . . I *can't*."

It's as if he's scraping my skin with the knife of his words. I flinch and nod.

"I haven't done this before," he says, the words harsh, like they've been pulled from him against his will.

My body settles. I'd entertained the thought that he might be inexperienced, but pushed it away—mostly because he's a collegiate hockey player. I made a stupid assumption and stuck to it, even in the face of glaring obvious hints. So his admission doesn't shock me.

If anything, it soothes me.

Bennett rubs the back of his neck with one hand, shoulders twitching up like they sometimes do when he's anxious. His face somehow burns even brighter. "Like . . . anything like this," he adds, the words tumbling out faster now, in a rush to rip the bandage off. "I don't know how to explain it right but . . . I've never *wanted* to do that with anyone before. And I don't know why. I don't know what's wrong with me, but—" His voice cracks, and he stops, clenching his jaw so hard it looks painful.

"There's nothing wrong with you," I whisper, wanting desperately to reach for him but knowing that until he can look at me, see me coming, I won't risk it.

"It doesn't feel like that," he says, the words almost mocking. "It feels like something *is* wrong with me. And . . . I've been okay with that." He nods, eyes squeezing closed again. Another twitch, his hands gripping his thighs harder. "But with you . . . it's different."

"That's okay," I whisper.

"It's *not*." This time the words are harsher, but all that anger is only directed inward. "And now *you're* stuck with an eighteen-year-old virgin who doesn't know what he's doing, and . . ."

His words hang in the air, sharp and self-conscious, and I can feel his embarrassment radiating off him. Like our conversations in the locker room or on Seven's walks, I stay quiet, allowing him to explain.

It's my only way of showing how desperately I want to know every part of him, deeply. Intimately.

"And that's not fair to you, Paloma. I want to make you feel *good* and I don't know how or where to even begin. And when you touched me just now? I felt so terrified of how good it felt that I stopped you? How pathetic is—"

"Stop it," I cut him off, fierce and protective. My hands are tight as I grasp his wrists, still kneeling on the floor beneath him. He finally looks at me, his beautiful ocean-blue eyes bloodshot and full up with self-hatred. It makes me almost seasick.

He's terrified of this.

"It's okay," I whisper. He grimaces and starts to jerk away from my hands. "You're not any different for that, okay?"

His lips part, but no words come out as he stares and stares at me. Finally, his hands relax from their white-knuckle grip, one drifting to sift his fingers through my hair—an act I know now calms him.

"You're not . . . ?" The question is nearly unspoken with how quiet he whispers it. "It doesn't bother you?"

"Never," I say, my throat tight. My hands slip off his wrists and onto his thighs. "We don't have to do anything, Bennett. But if you ever want to try—"

"I do." He nearly moans the words, half in pain, forehead leaning to press against mine. I push up, climbing to sit astride his lap. A blowjob was overwhelming for him, but this might be easier to start with.

"Is it stupid to say I'm scared?" he asks, raw and painfully vulnerable.

"No," I say fiercely. I grab his chin in my hand. "No, sex is terrifying. Even for me."

I don't mean for the admission to slip out, but I move on as quickly as I can so he won't read too much into my words.

"We can go slow," I say, pushing him languidly back into the mattress. "And you can stop me if you don't like it, okay?"

Bennett swallows hard, his eyes flicking up to meet mine. "I just . . . I don't want to mess it up," he murmurs, his voice thick with vulnerability.

"You won't," I promise. "There's no right or wrong way. Just *feel*." I rock forward along the still-hard length of him.

I'm torn between the desire to kiss him and the need to watch him.

A moan pulls almost unbidden from his throat, seeming to surprise him.

"Does that feel good?" I ask.

"I want to make *you* feel good," he gasps out, hands in the right place—along my waist—but tentative. I continue to move for him, dipping my head down to kiss his lips, along his jaw, and down to his neck.

His hands flex, jerking me a little harder over the mass of his bulge, and a long, low moan pulls from my mouth, breath against his skin.

"Like that?" he asks, taking a second to kiss my neck before whispering, "Please. I want you to make that noise again. Show me."

I shake my head. "It feels good because it's you," I say, the words a little huffed and vulnerable. "Everything you're doing feels good—touching my hair or my waist. I like it all."

He looks almost frustrated as I pull back and lock in on his eyes. And I know him enough now to know those words aren't comforting.

"I need you to show me," he begs again. "I can't... I can't always read your body language. And I never want to do something you don't want."

My throat sticks.

"You have to tell me. Please, show me." The words melt from a plea to a roughened command.

"Here." My breath hitches as his hand, tucked into mine, brushes against my clit over my shorts.

"Like this?" he asks, playing his fingers over the area like a pianist warming up. I nod, a whimper slipping out of my throat at the almost teasing touch.

"Yes," I pant. "Is it too much?" I ask, still riding across him. Still desperate. "We can stop—"

"No," he growls out. "Don't stop. That—the rocking feels so good." Every word is low, and the clear sound of his own pleasure has me threading closer to the edge of that cliff.

"Does it feel good to you?" He slows his movements for a moment. There's vulnerability and uncertainty in the question, and my hand comes up to cup his cheek, like I can soothe it away.

"Yes." His hand works its way up my back to the loose strands of dishwater blond flowing over his skin. In a moment of anxiety, I snap out a quick command: "Don't pull my hair."

Bennett freezes, only for a moment, before carefully brushing his fingers through the ends, the tingling effect on my scalp making me moan.

"I would never hurt you," he insists, words said into my ear as he tucks one strong arm around my waist, pulling me closer. His thrusts pick up, faster and more insistent. The hand in my hair glides carefully to my jaw, holding the side of it to pull my eyes to his, our foreheads nearly touching. "Tell me you know that. Say it."

"I do," I breathe, answering his command with shocking ease. "Please, don't stop."

"Are you going to come?" It's a genuine question, and I nod into his neck, pressing my lips to the hot skin there as I let myself go—crying and moaning out.

He shifts his hands to my hips, setting the pace, using his strength to move me up and down the length of him as he roars out his own pleasure in an animalistic, uncontrolled rumble.

That sound makes me come, my own pleasured keening pressed into his throat as Bennett continues to press and pull me until I stop him.

My eyes flicker over him slowly, affection pulsing from my heart, painful in its intensity. I want to keep him here, against my body and away from everything I know can hurt us. I want to tell him everything, my darkest moments, and watch as he holds them in his hands, careful with them as he's always been with me.

I want to—but I can't.

So instead, I press another soft, lingering kiss to his lips.

"Good?" he asks, breathless and still panting. I collapse on top of his big body, lax in his still-firm grip.

"Good," I whisper; such an understatement. He strokes his hands up and down my back, petting my hair, soothing me slowly in the aftermath. It's a level of care I've never experienced.

I keep my face pressed between his neck and the pillow to hide the tears it brings.

CHAPTER 39

NOW

Bennett

"You sure you don't want to come?"

Rhys looks back over his shoulder at me as I finish cleansing my left leg pad. He and Freddy linger in the doorway post-practice; nearly everyone else is gone besides Toren and Holden, who got held after for another extended practice session with LaBlanc.

Freddy hangs off Rhys's shoulder, a bright grin pulling at the smile lines around his mouth. "C'mon, Reiny—don't you love me?"

I shake my head with a smile. "I love my ears more."

Freddy frowns with a huff. "I'm not even a bad singer. Besides, it's karaoke—you're, like, supposed to be bad at it. That's the whole point."

"I don't know if that's true," Rhys says, but still gives the left winger another easy smile. Their friendship has blossomed into something deeper since last semester. I don't want to speculate that I'm being left behind—if I am, it's my fault. The truth is that it's easy for Rhys and Freddy because Sadie and Ro are so close.

But I still have to remind myself of that every now and then.

It's good to see them together. Freddy looks happier than he has since I met him, and Rhys seems settled again, unshakable, the way he's always been in my mind.

"It'll be fun, Ben," Rhys says. "Besides, Freddy bet me that if he scored the last goal at the game, I'd do karaoke with him. So you can come watch my public humiliation ritual. Just come."

The desire is there. It would be ten times easier to just say *yes*, even if I changed my mind on the way home. I'd probably even enjoy it, at least somewhat. But I just *can't*.

"Maybe," I say. "I don't know. I'm pretty tired. You guys go ahead."

It feels like disappointment even if they both attempt a smile for me, nodding as they dip out together.

By the time I make it to my car, the impulse to check my phone is only growing—though I've been avoiding the thought as best I can. I manage to wait this time until I park in the darkened garage. I'm surprised to see a series of texts from Sadie Brown at the top of my notifications.

SADIE BROWN
Didn't know if this would change your mind, but there's still room if you wanna join.

Attached is a photo: the amber lighting of a familiar bar, a few neon signs around adding a red cast to the yellow and orange hue. They're seated at a high-top, and at the center is Paloma Blake, gaze dipped over her shoulder. She's so goddamn beautiful. Blond hair spills over the blue long sleeve she's wearing as she glances toward something behind Sadie.

I want to be that something, the focus of her doe-brown eyes.

Fuck it.

I jump out of my car and head upstairs, feeding Seven and showering *again* before dressing in a T-shirt and flannel. I grab my well-worn Waterfell baseball cap and spin it backward on my head just to tamp down my unruly curls, then check the mirror one last time. My beard is a bit longer than the usual thick five-o'clock shadow I wear year-round now, but I don't have time to shave.

There's a riotous mass of butterflies in my stomach at the idea of seeing Paloma, and I'm a little ashamed to admit it makes me speed into downtown Waterfell toward the bar.

The Patio is as close to a country bar as one can get near Waterfell, which really means that once a night they play a Brooks & Dunn song and eventually somebody will probably sing "Tennessee Whiskey" at karaoke—which is currently being sung as I hand my ID to the bouncer and let them stamp my hand before heading inside.

I spot Rhys first, at the bar handing his card to the girl bartending with a dimpled, polite smile. He sees me as he turns, eyes lighting up in a way that makes my chest warm. It's not that I didn't expect that reaction. But it feels good to know he's happy I'm here.

"Need some help?" I ask, sidling up beside him. He nods in thanks, and I grab two of the amber beer bottles to take over to the table, helping him pass out everyone's drink orders. But my eyes are only on the girl across the table, her plump cheek smooshed in her propped-up hand, pulling her mouth up on the side.

She's watching the stage with a bored gaze, chewing on her perpetually swollen bottom lip, so I take the slight advantage and ease up to her side, setting one of the bottles next to her other hand.

Paloma looks up, the words "thank you" half out of her mouth before her eyes take me in.

"Bennett," she breathes, eyes wide.

"Hey, P." I smile, a blush tingeing my cheeks.

"What are you doing here?" she asks, but her eyes dart to Sadie briefly.

I sit on the stool next to her, still taking up too much space with my body, but not looming over her. "Singing karaoke, clearly."

She smiles, a slight chuckle leaving her lips before she takes a sip of her beer. "Clearly."

The word is low and smoky, the intoxication of Paloma Blake's unintentional sex appeal wrapping around me like a vice. I lean in closer.

"I heard Freddy was forcing Rhys to sing," I whisper. "I couldn't miss that."

As if on cue, their names are called. Freddy loops his arm around a bright red Rhys and they stalk off to the lifted stage in the corner. The bar isn't *packed* yet, but it's decently crowded. My best friend looks like he's going to sink into the floor, whereas Freddy's already unbuttoned his collared shirt nearly to his belly button and blows a kiss at his girlfriend.

"We should go up there," Ro says, eyes bright with affection and excitement. She's come entirely out of her shell since I first met her, much more confident with Freddy by her side. "To support them."

The girls head over, but I opt to stay at the table, not wanting to block anyone's view with my size. But the second they make it through the gathering crowd to the front of the stage, close enough that they could reach out and touch the guys, someone approaches Paloma.

I'm not surprised. She's beautiful, perfect—everyone knows it. Part of me wants to intervene. I've had to watch this for years. Should it be different now that we are *friends*?

We're just friends now. Leave her alone.

But brown eyes flicker over and find mine, a clear pleading look in them, and I'm heading to her immediately, cutting through the crowd with ease. The second I'm at her back, the frat boy wannabe takes me in and blanches, ducking his head and walking away.

I stand behind her like a sentry, covering her body with my bulk easily, trying to hide the smile that wants to pull at my face.

"This one's for our girlfriends!" Freddy shouts into the mic, making the feedback go off and several patrons flinch—including

Paloma, who scoots herself back into me before straightening again, staying close.

Sister Hazel's "All for You" starts up and Freddy and Rhys sing vibrantly into the mics. Rhys is tipsy enough to give something of a performance, but Freddy as usual steals the show. They both make a mess of the verses but manage to keep it together for each chorus.

Freddy is the loud one, but Rhys has the actually decent voice.

Freddy ends their performance on his knees, reaching for Rosalie's head to kiss her soundly in front of everyone, while Sadie shakes her head with a shimmering, rare smile as she watches Rhys blushing and singing.

It isn't until he climbs down off the stage that the figure skater runs to him, jumping into his waiting arms for a movie-worthy kiss as he holds her up, her legs around his waist.

"Feeling like the third wheel?" Paloma asks, leaning back so that her hair sweeps over the skin of my forearms where I've rolled up my flannel sleeves.

I look down at her, seeing the slight flush to her skin from the heat of the crowd and alcohol. The relaxed features of her face, the clear safety she finds in me.

"No," I say quietly. "I'm not."

The music interlude before the next karaoke performance is "With or Without You" by U2—I recognize it, almost certain I heard it in this exact bar three years ago, a more painful memory.

This time, I don't let it hurt.

Paloma turns, looking up at me with soft brown eyes. One hand still holds the neck of her beer tightly. My body is blocking her from the others nearly entirely as my heart thunders to the same beat:

Hers. Hers. Hers.

She can say that we're friends. I'll always be hers.

Her other hand falls from the protective hold across her middle, fingers curling deftly around my belt loop. She doesn't pull. She hardly moves, just sways slightly.

As if we're dancing, slowly, barely touching.

My desire for her has only grown, whether we're distant or she's asleep and safe in my bed, in my arms. It never goes away. I can't rid myself of it, and I don't want to.

I'll never pressure her for anything, but I will always long for her. Fingers in soft wet hair, hands on damp skin, and Paloma Blake soft and vulnerable and *trusting* beneath me. Moonlight and the sound of waves. A blue backpack and stuffed rabbit. Coconut cake and salt air. Damp skin warm against mine. Words pressed from my mouth and into hers, like I could breathe poetry into her lungs.

"P," I whisper. We aren't touching, but it feels like I'm buried inside her, just as overwhelming and intense.

Her breathing is somehow louder than the music, a pattern I recognize from late nights and early mornings and every single time she let me have her.

I step closer and the bubble bursts, a stricken look crossing Paloma's face. I feel her leave before she actually does. She takes her seat at our table, where Sadie, Rhys, Freddy, and Ro are, and smiles politely as Rosalie asks her something.

I follow her—I always do—standing next to Rhys at the side of the table and offering a clap to his shoulder.

"Great work up there," I say.

He shakes his head, tucking a few loose strands of shaggy brown hair back behind his ear. "Shut up."

I laugh and he beams.

"I'm glad you're here, Ben."

My gaze finds Paloma's, the eye contact just as intense as everything is where she's involved, and I smile at her, bright and warm. If being friends with her means having her here, with the people that have become my family, then I'll take it.

Rhys is still smiling at me, watching me watch Paloma with a twinkle in his eye, one dimple showing as he tilts the bottle of beer back. He's different, from freshman year, from last semester. A good different. We both are.

"Me too," I say, smiling at him, reaching for his arm to squeeze it.

CHAPTER 40

NOW

Paloma

"I'd like to talk about your relationship to intimacy."

My eyes don't move from the torn-up section of the carpet where the roller wheel of Dr. Sutton's office chair has pulled at the threads over and over. Brow furrowing, I bite down on my lip.

"You mean sex?" I blurt.

"Sure."

I shrug, playing with the end of my sloppy braid. "It's not a big deal to me. You can just say sex, it's whatever."

Watching her expression carefully, I can't help feeling like I'm revealing my cards without meaning to.

"What do you mean? Do you enjoy sex?" she asks bluntly.

A flash of ocean-blue eyes, a scratchy voice asking me to look at him. The feeling of hands in my hair. "Sometimes." I shake my head, attempting to double down. "It's just . . . it's not important, really. It's just sex."

Not with Bennett. I shut the thought down before it shows across my face.

"Right." She nods.

"I've been having sex since I was fourteen, so it's not that big of a deal, okay?" I say, feeling the defensiveness rise but unable to quell it. "We don't even need to talk about it, really."

Lies. Lies. Lies.

"Did you feel ready for that at fourteen?"

No. I shrug.

"I guess."

Dr. Sutton nods. "And when you lost your virginity, was it something you wanted? A boy you liked?"

Slowly, I shake my head, dipping my gaze toward my fingernails as I pick at them. "No."

She doesn't ask anything else for a moment, and I roll my eyes.

"Sex is fine. I've had times where I liked it and times where I didn't—is that enough?" I blow a breath heartily through my lips. "Can we talk about something else?"

"We can talk about something else," she says, voice calm. "Does something feel more important than this?"

My irritation with her only ratchets higher.

"You wanna know everything? Fine—when I was fourteen, I lost my virginity to a thirty-eight-year-old man. I had a relationship with him for almost three years. And then—" A ragged exhale. I close my eyes, trying to center my suddenly swirling thoughts. "And then, I had a boyfriend. My age. He was the first person who made me feel . . . I don't know, good? But I fucked that one up, too.

"And since then"—I shrug, half lifting my hands in the air with a smile that feels wrong and twisted along my face—"sex is just sex . . . I don't enjoy it. It hurts most of the time—I don't know what you want from me."

It's only when she hands me the tissue box that I realize I've been crying.

"Let's take a breath," Dr. Sutton says, voice soft and calm over the harshness of my hiccupped breathing. I take my time, breaths slow, deep. "Everything is okay. You're safe here."

I want to roll my eyes, but I can't. Because the words *are* making me feel calm and safe. Slowly, but it's happening.

"Why do you think you choose to have sex when it hurts or doesn't feel good?"

My stomach sours. I try to shrug again. "I don't know."

Dr. Sutton nods. "Try to think. You know yourself and your body better than anyone else. Think about those moments. Think about the times when it felt good, with your boyfriend. What is the difference for you?"

"It didn't feel like he was taking anything away from me."

"Who?"

"Bennett." His name pours from my lips before I can stop myself. I watch her vigilantly, but she doesn't write it down, just watches me back—steady in the torrent of my inner turmoil.

"And with others? When you choose to have sex now?"

My eyes feel waterlogged again, and I dip my chin. "It's . . . I don't know how to explain it. It feels better in my chest when I do it, even if I hate it. It's like . . . like I'm getting relief from something."

"From what, do you think?"

The word comes out before I can stop it. "Guilt."

My stomach churns.

The truth is that I feel like I'm paying some sort of penance. Like punishing myself feels better than allowing myself to sink into Bennett's arms—though I indulge in that more often than I should. But saying *that* out loud feels too raw. I'm just not ready for it yet.

"Paloma," she says, her voice firmer and more intense than it has been since I got here. "Sex is important, and it's complicated for you."

I shake my head.

"I wasn't attacked. I wasn't—"

"You were fourteen, Paloma," she says. Still that same firm voice, but it isn't harsh or scraping, though the words feel like knives all the same. "He was an adult. You didn't choose that."

"It's not that simple," I say, shaking my head. "He helped me. We were together. It wasn't like he forced me. It was fine—even if I didn't always like it. That's just how relationships are sometimes."

"So, when you were with Bennett, did you have sex when you didn't want to? Did he force you to?"

The words make me flinch, desperate to defend Bennett, to separate the two in my head.

"No, no—he didn't—"

"Relationships shouldn't hurt you. Sex should be your choice. It's your body, Paloma."

I shake my head. "I know."

"You didn't want that, Paloma," she continues. Her voice is steady. Not soft anymore, but firm and clear. "You were a fourteen-year-old girl. A child. You didn't choose that. You didn't have a choice. You need to understand that."

That little version of me that I keep deep inside peeks around the corners she lurks in, peering up. Even if I can't trust Dr. Sutton's words, that part of me *wants* to, desperately.

"What is intimacy?"

My brow furrows. "What do you mean?"

"What is intimacy to you, Paloma?"

There's still a part of me that wants to roll my eyes and shrug, but this feels too important.

I know my answer. I know what intimacy is to me. I feel it like the waves lapping over my toes across a beach I've spent every birthday laying on. Like the rainfall water of a shower I feel safest in.

It's hands in my hair, soothing, never painful. It's homemade food and the taste of salt air on my lips. It's hands on my waist only after asking *Is this okay?* It's eye contact with Bennett Reiner across a crowded bar top. It's him.

Him.

CHAPTER 41

NOW

Bennett

"Busy?"

"No," I say too quickly, stopping inside the door to the garage and turning to where Rhys is standing at the bottom of the stairs. "Why?"

"Thought we could ride to practice together," he offers, squeezing my shoulder as he walks past me for his bag. "We haven't gotten a lot of time together recently."

"You've been busy," I offer. Rhys winces and my stomach sinks. *Never can get this right, huh?*

"Right," he says. It's silent for a moment while we both climb into my car before he continues. "But you know that doesn't mean I don't have time for you, yeah? You're my best friend. Nothing is going to change that."

It feels so ridiculous. I want to snap at him that I'm not a kid and we're not in high school. He doesn't need to apologize to me for falling in love and having less time to be my crutch—because in so many ways that's exactly what he's been.

And that same fear rouses, rising like a tsunami in the back of my mind to crash over and terrorize every memory—that he sees me as a needy, pathetic, attached, and forced friend that he was never able to rid himself of.

I swallow it all down, though it feels like trying to swallow rocks. "I know," I say instead.

"Maybe we could get dinner or something, just you and me."

Another nod is all I can manage as I navigate the icy roads toward the arena. "That would be nice, I think."

We don't talk for much of the rest of the ride, our anxieties warring for space in the cab. I tell him I'm going to stay in the car for a little longer, and though he seems worried, he lets it go.

I fumble with my phone, the need to call my dad warring desperately with the need to avoid speaking with him at all costs. I can't talk to Rhys. I can't talk to my dad. I can't talk to *anyone* because everyone I try to hold closer seems to slip further from my grasp.

Just go inside. Do your usual routine and everything will be—

My hand is on the gearshift suddenly; I back up and drive out of the parking lot with no real plan. I dial the number I know by heart.

"Bennett?"

"P—" I breathe, hating that my voice sounds as shaky as I feel. "Hey, are you . . . are you busy?"

"Just got home from class," she says. "Are you okay?"

"Yeah, I just—can I come see you?"

Can I come over, was what I meant to ask—like a normal person. Resisting the urge to slam my forehead into the steering wheel, I stop a little too briefly at the stop sign before turning and idling on the corner.

"Yeah," Paloma says. I hear a door close before, "Bennett? Are you sure you're okay?"

"I'm fine, I just don't know where you live." I laugh, shaking my head.

"I'll send you the location. Just—drive safe, okay?"

She hangs up and shares her location with me, something that makes my chest feel warm. She used to do it all the time, so I could come get her wherever she was. So that I could always find her.

I march up to the front door of the pretty townhouse on shaky feet with trembling arms—like I'm running on adrenaline taken through an IV.

I knock twice before she answers, her beautiful brown eyes going wide at the sight of me in her doorway.

"Bennett," she greets.

"Sorry." I huff a breath, but a smile breaks through. "I didn't want to bother you. But I just needed to see you."

"You're fine." She smiles up at me. "More than fine. Come in."

It's warm in her home—and a thrill shoots up my spine that there's a place I can call that for her now. That Paloma has a *home* that's warm and safe, and that she seems to *want* to be in. The foyer is dark green and half-paneled with brown wood. There's a pretty woven carpet taking up most of the living room with a well-loved gray couch and several multicolored pillows—some that I recognize from her dorm freshman year. She has music playing softly on the TV.

And she's there in the center of it all, so warm and beautiful. *Happy*, I realize with a jolt.

"Is everything okay?"

I nod. "I just . . ." My voice trails off as I rock slightly on my heels, hands tucked into the pockets of my sweatpants.

"I don't want to be just your friend, Paloma." My confession is soft, quiet in the warm space as it floats over her. She basks in it slightly, lips parting with a puff of breath. "I never wanted to be just your friend. I *love* you." A short laugh works from me as I shrug my shoulder. "And that's just never going to change for me. I'm always going to want you."

"Bennett—"

I hold up my palm to stop her.

"I know," I say, eyes straying from hers toward my feet. "I am not trying to change your mind or *force* you to be with me, you know I'd never do that. But I want to be clear. I will be your friend if that's what you need. But I will never want less from you; I'm always going to hope for more." My voice drops lower. "For you to let me have you again. Take care of you."

"Bennett," she breathes, and I finally look at her. Her eyes look glassy and my stomach drops at the idea I might've upset her. But before I can try to fix it, she continues. "I do want a fresh start with you. But I . . . I want you, always."

"As more than friends."

She laughs, the sound wet but genuine. "Yes."

I nod. "Okay."

"Okay?"

"That's . . . that's all I came to say."

Her brow wrinkles as she watches me for a long moment, waiting for something. For once, I do what I want without overthinking it—stepping forward and kissing her. Hard and intense like I always crave to do.

Her hiccup of surprise melts into a moan as she latches her hands onto my shoulders. I scoop her up into my arms, heart thumping.

"Sorry," I whisper. "I've been thinking about that since the bar." *Far longer, if I'm honest with myself.*

"Me too," Paloma admits quietly. "I'm glad you're here. I . . . I missed you."

The words feel weighted. *I missed you.* How long have I waited for this from her lips? I've yearned for them. It's like water to my parched soul. I'm desperate for her.

"Can I see your room?" I ask with a grin. She giggles into my neck and nods, leaning back with bright eyes. *This is all I want. Forever, this is all I need.*

She directs me up the stairs and to her room. It's just as warm and cozy as I thought it would be. So *her* in every way. I want to stretch out across her bed and swim in the scent of her.

Instead, I splay her across the half-undone bedding of her queen-sized bed. Her blond lustrous strands twinkle in the lamplight. I brush a few stray pieces from her face before kissing her mouth, sweeter this time.

"If this isn't what you want, tell me," I say, half-kneeling over her. Her face is flushed and beautiful. I'm so in love with her it hurts.

My hand reaches up to rub at my chest.

"I want you, always."

I shake my head, closing my eyes and struggling with the words I'm desperate to say and terrified to admit in equal measure.

"The things I want to do to you, P . . ." My voice feels hoarse, almost raw in desperation. "I—I need you to promise you'll tell me if you don't like it."

"You know my body better than I do, Bennett," she whispers, almost shy.

"I don't want to hurt you."

"You never would." She reaches to hold my face in her hands. "But you have to trust me to tell you if I want you to stop."

"That's the problem, P," I whisper, hand covering hers where it still rests against my overheated cheek. "I trust you with everything." I lean down to kiss her forehead. "But not with your limits."

She sits up almost abruptly.

"Oh—okay. Yeah." She scrambles to kneel, pulling me a little by the wrist so I'll sit next to her. "Why don't we set them, then. You . . ." Her voice drops a little, eyes darting away from me. "You can decide what I need and when."

I feel like I should be ashamed of the way my cock hardens at the words she's saying, the desperation for control. To have her trust like that, to take care of her.

"Yeah," I agree. "Tell me what you don't want, P."

"Don't be mean," she whispers, and the words hit like an anvil on my heart. "I don't want to be called names or talked down to."

"Never," I whisper, but hold back the words I want to say, the anger toward the demons in her past simmering in my gut. "What else, love?"

"I don't . . . I don't think I like pain. Like, real pain. I don't want to be hit."

"I'd never hurt you."

She nods, eyes softening at the familiar words. "I know."

"What about tying you up?" I ask, the words choked but somehow more freeing than I anticipated.

"Yes."

"And . . . control?" I take a settling breath, because my entire body feels too tightly wound, muscles pumped like I could burst through a brick wall. "If I wanted to control when you come? Make you wait for it until you—"

"Yes," she says, but this time it's nearly a gasp. Her face is flushed, her chest heaving as the cutout sweatshirt dips lower off her shoulder, along her collarbone. "Please."

"Let's start like that, then. If you want this—"

"I do," she cuts me off. "Please, Bennett, I—"

"Shh," I quiet her softly, but firmly. "Take off your sweatshirt and lie back for me."

I've imagined this so many times. Done ample amounts of research over the years. Even talked to my therapist about it when I worried something was *wrong* with me for what I wanted—but I know this is everything *right*. The anticipation of it all is almost overwhelming, but then it's *her* beneath me and that changes everything.

Paloma Blake is naked from the waist up, laying across blue sheets like water. Her hair is wild, half out of a loose ponytail, her ample chest heaving with breaths as she trembles.

I reach my hand out slowly to run my knuckles across her stomach and between her breasts.

"You're so perfect, you know that?" I whisper reverently, before dropping my tone. "Push your tits together, P."

A noise sounds from her throat as her thighs press together tightly, desperate for pressure. I push them apart, settling my knee between her legs without touching her.

"Do you trust me to take care of you?"

She nods, eyes bright.

"Say it."

"I trust you."

"Good, love. You're so good for me, yeah?" I press a kiss to her warm forehead. "You take care of me without even trying. In the hotel room? When you helped me with my injury? You took such good care of me. And I was so hard for you. Only you."

"Mmhmm," she agrees through a puff of breath. "Bennett, *please*."

"Open for me, P." I shuck my pants and boxers off before pulling off my shirt and crawling back to the space between her legs, looking across the curves of her body as I touch myself leisurely. She's so beautiful—wide hips, thick thighs, sharp curved waistline, her tits large as she pushes them together, following my direction easily.

Paloma's always been unearthly hot—not just to me. The way people speak about her body has always filled me with rage. But it is a fact that Paloma Blake is the hottest woman I've ever seen.

She's starred in every fantasy I've ever had—and even now I need to touch her, to make sure she's real.

Her plump, peachy lips part as I press my cock into her mouth, inch by inch. I can't stop the groan that pours from my own mouth as I push in farther.

"That's it, love. Can you take me deeper?" She nods, peering up at me. I feed her another inch before her head bucks forward like she's trying to take all of me. She gags and her brown doe eyes water.

I pull back, popping her lips off me with a gentle grip on the side of her jaw and neck.

"Not in the business of pain or discomfort, P." My voice is tinged with a bit of anger, tone low. "I decide how much you get, understand?"

She nods. "I'm sorry," she sputters out.

I lean down and press an almost reverent kiss to her forehead, wiping away any stray tears carefully. "Good girl, P. So good for me, yeah?"

Another quick nod.

"Open. Let me in."

She obeys so beautifully, sweet and soft and pliant beneath my hands. It's her trust in me, her feeling safe with me that really gets me off.

Just as my tip presses to her bottom lip, she heaves a breath.

"Are you going to fuck my mouth?" she asks, a false bravado behind her words.

I shake my head. "Not tonight. Tonight, you're going to hold those perfect tits together for me and let me fuck them." A moan comes from her still open mouth, low and throaty and perfect. "But first, you're going to get me wet, sweet girl. Just going to lay there and relax and be everything I need, love."

A half-moan, half-cry works out of her lips, her back bowing slightly at my words.

Mine, mine, mine echoes like a chant in my brain.

CHAPTER 42

NOW

Paloma

He's intoxicating above me, all masculine and dominant. Another breath punches out of me as his hand ghosts over the spot I need him most. I feel like my entire body is throbbing, like I am a heartbeat in his hands.

And now, he's making a mess of me. He keeps my thigh pressed open into the bed—using it to steady himself as he mouths hungrily over my breasts.

"Has anyone ever told you how good you are?" he says, pulling back as he slides up my body, fingertips still swirling over the hardened peak of my nipple. "How you deserve to be worshipped like this?"

He slots his dick between my breasts where I'm still pushing them together, sliding slowly between them as I stare up at him in awe. The mass of his body is held off me but hovering so large and looming, like an ancient god to be worshiped.

Only, *I* feel worshipped by *him*.

"God, P," he grunts out. "Thought about this. For three fucking years." His breath huffs, blowing a few curls away from his eyes. "I'm always thinking about you. Always."

Again, his words tangle in vulnerability and heat—a mix that makes me mewl and restlessly grind into the air. He moves his body, using one arm planted at his side to keep his weight off me, the other reaching between my legs to cup me.

The position has him leaned back, giving me a perfect view of his soft chest, sparsely covered in dark brown curls. Everything about him is intoxicatingly powerful.

My moan is mirror-shattering, wanton, arguably unsexy—but he closes his eyes like he's hearing a symphony.

"That's it, P." His fingers pet against the seam of my lips, parting me with an expert touch—he's spent years learning my body, watching my every breath, to play me so easily.

Like fucking poetry.

"That's all I want, love—to make you feel good. Ride my fingers."

I do, watching him the same way he watches me. It's so intense immediately, as it always has been beneath his careful, calloused hands.

His mouth pours words over me like he's writing them in ink across my body. *So good for me, love* and *Ahh—no, P, not yet. Hold it*, in such a firm voice I can't help but obey.

"Please, Bennett, *please* let me—"

"*Fuck*," he grunts, tossing his head back, the muscles of his neck thick and tensed as his hips stutter, his come spilling messily between my breasts. Just seeing him completely undone makes me unravel faster, mouth opening on a low, breathy cry.

He shifts off me, curling around me entirely as he continues to fuck me with his thick fingers, my body building up and up. His mouth makes a new home by my ear, whispering sweet words, talking me all the way through it as I come hard—harder than in the hotel room, more vulnerable, but not rocked by the emotions the way I had been then.

No—now I feel warm, weightless, and whole. Like nothing bad ever happened to me. It's just me and Bennett, as if we've always been together, this close, with no pain.

"Good?" he asks, pressing a kiss to my cheeks and then the corner of my mouth. I smile, skin flushed as he checks me over almost obsessively. "Words, Paloma."

"Good."

He carries me to my bathroom, running the shower with one hand as he sets me carefully on my feet. But he still cradles me close, his other palm steady on the back of my head, keeping me pressed to his chest.

We shower and he washes my hair, gentle as always.

"I've missed this," I say, vulnerable and soft in his arms. My fingers play against his chest as he quietly tilts my head with a gentle command of *Lean back, P.*

"You know how I feel about your hair," he says, with an almost smoky chuckle. His voice is still thick, raspy in a way that has my body heating up, ready for him again. "I think about it all the time, imagine it in my hands, against my skin." He holds a hand at my forehead, attempting to keep water from my eyes as he washes away the conditioner he'd carefully combed through my strands.

"I'm going to brush it, too," he says, his mouth on my neck. I nod, though he didn't ask a question.

After he dries my body with the soft towel, wraps it around his waist, and slips his shirt over my head, he brushes my hair while we sit on the mess of my bed. I try to lay next to him, but he shakes his head with a soft, "Come here," pulling me to rest against his chest where he's propped up against my headboard.

I'm sleepy and soft, but he still feels tense. Almost antsy.

"Was that . . . okay?" he asks.

"Yes," I offer, pulling his hand to my mouth to kiss his fingers. "Are you okay?"

"Yes. Why?"

The question is fast enough that my brow furrows. "If something is bothering you, we can talk about it." A darker thought rises, and

I debate for a long moment if I should say it or ignore it. The girl I've been for years would ignore it. But I want something real with Bennett.

"If something is bothering you," I try again, "sex isn't going to make it go away."

"Do you regret it?" he asks, a lump in his throat.

I turn in his arms to look at him, eyes pleading as I lift his chin to meet my gaze. "*God*, no, Bennett. But I don't want . . . I don't want you to use—"

His eyes go wide, body sitting upright as his arms leave my sides. Head sinking into his palms, he begs, "No . . . God, no, P. I'm so sorry—I would never . . . I'm not using you. I swear I wasn't. I-I—"

"Bennett," I stop him, firm and loud. I slide to kneel between his thighs and sit back on my heels as I cup his entire face in my hands, pressing a gentle kiss to his lips. "I would *never* think you were using me. Never. I just want to make sure that you can talk to me, if something is hurting you."

"Like you did with me?"

I flinch back slightly. He shakes his head but continues to let me hold him. "Sorry. I shouldn't have—"

"No. I deserved that one." A breath chokes me, but I continue. "I'm sorry. I never meant to hurt you. I just . . . I wasn't okay."

"But you're okay now?" There's hope there in his words and I grasp it with two hands.

"Yeah. At least, I'm trying." I settle back against the headboard next to him, my legs over his waist as he skims his fingers over my calf and holds my ankle. "Actually, I've been going to therapy."

It feels ridiculous to be embarrassed by admitting it. Everyone and their mother goes to therapy now—it's normal; healthy, even.

A grin, however small, breaks across Bennett's face. "Yeah? That's . . . that's great, P."

I nod, chewing on my lip.

"How long have you, um, been going? If you want to tell—"

"I started at the beginning of the semester. I'm . . . I'm trying, to be different than I was."

"Did you go as a kid?"

I shake my head. There was a court-ordered therapist once, when my mom had been investigated by CPS. But I don't think that counts.

"No, but I think it's helping. So"—I shrug with a half grin—"yeah. Maybe one day I won't be so broken." It's a joke, but Bennett doesn't laugh.

"You're not broken, P," he whispers, squeezing my calf and dragging me fully into his lap. His hand reaches for mine, and he massages my palm and fingers as he speaks. "You're not. But I think therapy is great. It's always helped me."

I nod with a gentler smile this time. Because to know he still feels that way, that he sees me as something whole and wonderful, not the truly broken thing that I am. It feels like hope.

Like the first splash of cool water after a starting dive.

"We should get dinner tomorrow."

His eyes widen, body tensing beneath me. "Like . . . a date?"

I chew on my lip and hesitate, eyeing him as he dips his chin to meet my eyes.

A mischievous grin I don't normally see on Bennett suddenly appears. His hand tucks a strand of blond hair back.

"I wouldn't mind if it *was* a date," he says.

The words feel electrifying, so memorable. They're a perfect display of how intensely the power has shifted between us. It gives me hope . . . that maybe someday we *will* find our footing. Together. Maybe this is the first step.

"A date, then," I say, remembering his reply just as clearly as he remembered my teasing words.

He takes my hand. I can feel that touch in my soul, like the darkness is slowly washing away. Permanently.

CHAPTER 43

THEN: Freshman Year, November

Bennett

"And how is everything with Paloma?"

I sit a little taller on the comfy cloth sofa across from Dr. Anya for a rescheduled session. I'd had to move it around for a rare weekday game. Usually, sessions like this make me more anxious, less open to sharing, so I consider them nearly counterproductive. But today there is a whisper of excitement threading through time and space because I know what is coming after.

"It's good. We're going away this weekend."

"The whole weekend?" Her eyebrow raise is the only betrayal of her shock.

I'm breaking my routine and going somewhere not as familiar, doing something new with someone who also hasn't done this before—in more ways than one.

"Yeah—leaving tonight and back Sunday. I have an off weekend from hockey since we played Thursday this week."

"That's exciting. Are you two doing well then?"

"Yes."

"You told me last time that you opened up to her about your OCD, right?" I nod again, tapping my fingers hard against my kneecap. "Did you tell her anything else about yourself?"

Most people know I'm OCD, or at least they spot the compulsions and don't ask. Some even make jokes—about the way I wash my uniform or how I warm up—without knowing that it's serious for me. That my brain feels like it's attacking me with anxieties that seem ridiculous said out loud. But I can't shake the thought that something still *might happen*, so I have to do these things. I don't necessarily *want* to.

Sometimes, I actively *don't* want to.

But I don't really go around introducing myself as *"Bennett Reiner, autistic guy with OCD,"* so most people don't really know that part of me. I'm just Bennett Reiner, silent hockey goalie who doesn't like people.

It's not true, but it works for me. It's fine.

But I want Paloma to know, to understand me in the way she seems so desperate to.

"Yes. We talked about my thing with touching," I say, fidgeting further in my seat. "And I told her. About me, not just the OCD stuff."

Dr. Anya nods, tapping her pen once, twice, and then setting her notebook down.

"She's important to you."

"Very," I say, not hesitating.

"Tell me more about her."

"I like to touch her hair," I say impulsively, a blush creeping up my cheeks after. "Is that . . . is that wrong?"

Her brow furrows slightly. "Do you *have* to touch it? Do you get anxious if you can't?"

I shake my head. "No. I just like . . . I like the way it feels. I like touching it and washing it and . . ."

"Then that's okay," she says, a light smile over her face. "If anything, that's kind of beautiful, Bennett."

I fidget again.

"How are things between you progressing intimately?"

I've spoken about this sort of thing with Dr. Anya before. Several times. Opened up to her years earlier when I thought something was wrong with me for *not* being interested in physical intimacy. And then again about the things I *did* want with physical intimacy.

This weekend is important to Paloma, to *me*, and I want to make sure I'm doing this the right way the first time.

"They're . . . fine," I say carefully, reaching up to scratch at the back of my neck, wishing I'd let my dad cut my hair. It's getting too long—

"Can you elaborate on that?"

"We've . . . done things. It can be overwhelming, but I like that. It's a good feeling."

She nods again. "That's okay. Have you shared with her what you enjoy? With intimacy?"

That's a hard no—it's one thing dealing with my first experiences with sex and pleasure. It's another to bring up my proclivities, the need for control that bleeds into intimacy. Especially with Paloma . . .

I shrug, blood rushing hot in my cheeks. "I just want to make sure I'm doing things the right way."

There's a long pause, though I'm sure it feels longer to me than it truly is.

"Sex is complicated, for *everyone*—that part has nothing to do with your diagnoses, Bennett. Sex is probably just as scary and exciting a prospect for Paloma as it is for you. I think you need to remember that. Because there might be some awkward or stressful parts to being in this type of relationship with her. But that's okay."

Her smile is reassuring as she leans back and watches me for a moment.

"It's just like everything else. It gets better with practice."

"Yeah?"

Dr. Anya nods before straightening up, my cue that our time is over since I'm not allowed to have a watch or stress over time while in my sessions. "Yeah. I think you should just focus on communication. Ask her lots of questions. Don't be afraid to communicate, especially when it feels overwhelming. Trust her and yourself."

• • •

"The cleaners were just there last week, so everything should be good. And I called them to stock the fridge with the list you gave me," my dad's voice comes over my speaker as I pull into Paloma's dorm parking lot. "And if you—"

"I got it," I cut him off. "I promise, I'm good."

My dad sighs heavily over the phone. "All right, all right. I'm hovering. I get it. Just please check in and let me know you made it and when you're heading home, okay?"

"All right," I agree. "Love you."

"Love you, too."

We hang up just before someone taps on my window: Paloma, in her overalls with a colorful sweater slung over one shoulder and her hair in a loose bun at the back of her head. She's smiling brightly at me, face bare and eyes glinting almost caramel in the sunlight.

I unlock the truck door before she can pull on the handle impatiently, laughing as she stumbles her way into the cabin of the truck.

"Hey, Bennett," she says, half-climbing over the console and kissing my mouth before I can prepare for it. My heart pulses like it's reaching from my chest for her.

I rub at my chest before shaking my head and looking away from her. "Hey, Paloma."

"Where's Seven?"

"With my dad for the weekend."

Her eyes scan over me a little more intensely. "Are you sure? He can come with us."

"I'll be fine." But her worry over me and my dog makes another rope of obsession loop out from me and over her.

Her backpack is on the floor at her feet, but I grab it and carefully place it in the backseat before turning the music up and handing her my phone.

"I made a playlist for the drive," I offer, pulling away from the curb slowly. "Some of your *poems* are on there."

She's quiet, fiddling with my music app for a long while as Bon Iver plays through the stereo. When she finally hands my phone back, I see she's changed the name of the playlist from a number to "B + P."

My chest thunders, that same ache I've grown used to pressing hard against my heart. This time the smile she gives me as I glance over at her is softer, something more exposed and vulnerable. Like she's unsure.

I take her hand in mine.

She doesn't let go of it for the whole drive.

• • •

The house isn't as terrifyingly massive as some of the other Reiner properties, but it's my favorite. It's the one place my father laid claim to, even if we didn't visit here much other than a week or two in the summer.

It's winter now, too cold for much of the actual beach, but the little quiet town is close to Chatham and other popular Cape Cod destinations. Overall, the house is cozy, private, and perfect for this. Perfect for *her*.

I tell her to wait for me so I can get her bag and open her door. She doesn't fuss when I take her sweater and slide it carefully over her head, straightening it and fixing her hair slowly, gently. She spends most of the time staring over my shoulder at the house.

It's a family home, originally built for my dad's youngest brother.

An elegant sign over the entrance and a carved wooden one on the door state the year it was built and the name, Speyside. My grandfather named it after his youngest son's favorite place in Scotland.

I think it makes my dad sad that it's named after the place where his brother got his favorite whiskey, knowing it was the alcoholism that nearly killed him so young. Knowing it was the alcohol that brewed near-hatred between the sons and their father, before my uncle left it all behind.

But still, my dad has never taken the signs down.

It's New England classic, shingle-style architecture with an older feel in contrast to the well-insulated, beautifully updated interiors. The kitchen itself is far better than even my dad's home, as if he'd had me in mind when he renovated it. Three bedrooms, all beautiful and simple, and cozier than either my father's Boston home or my mother's extravagant mansion.

As I quietly tell Paloma where everything is, she looks wide-eyed across the large, pristine rooms.

"Paloma?"

"Hmm?"

Her eyes are fixed out the floor to ceiling windows overlooking the darkened beach. It's not far, but we're up on an elevated hillside. I flip the switch by the door, illuminating a pathway down to the water.

"I'm going to cook us some dinner," I whisper, stepping boldly up behind her, releasing her bun with my fingers and petting through the strands until they lay softly against her back. "Why don't you go sit by the ocean?"

"Really? I can?"

"Of course." I grab one of the thicker quilts out of a wicker basket by the sofa and step back over to her. "It's cold out, take a blanket with you."

"Okay," she agrees in an almost half-trance state as she stares at the stretch of dark ocean. I give her the directions to start the firepit as the sun sets in the distance.

It doesn't take long for me to heat up the warm ramen I'd already cooked this morning, the pork belly soft and warm, the noodles thick and from my favorite Asian market. I pour everything into thermoses from a high cabinet and shrug my flannel jacket back on as I head out into the bitter cold winds, which are only growing fiercer as the sky darkens.

"Hey, love," I say, pulling Paloma's attention from the nearby lapping waves. "Cold?"

She shakes her head. "All good."

I hand her the thermos, fingers feeling her palm to make sure she isn't frozen and lying about it.

I turn the fire up a little higher, sitting next to her on the bench seat she's chosen.

In the quiet, I observe her. The soft dip of her chin, the lithe upward curl of her nose. The perfect symmetry of her face, cheeks flushed with the proximity of the fire. She stirs the spoon around in her cup, taking a few noodle-forward bites, before looking over at me sheepishly.

"I'm not hungry."

I laugh, nervousness swirling. "Me either."

I am. But not for food. For her—all of her. I want to savor every inch of her skin and indulge in her until I'm overfull. Until the obsessive thoughts start to ebb away.

My fingers dust across her thigh.

"Can I run you a hot shower? It's cold."

She smiles. "Only if you'll shower with me."

I nod, standing a little abruptly and reaching to carry her. Her excited giggle rips through me like a burst of adrenaline. "Hold on to me."

CHAPTER 44

THEN: Freshman Year, November

Paloma

Bennett carries me through the house and up the stairs, sitting me down on the dark marble countertop of the master bathroom. He turns on the shower and steam from the warm water starts to fill the entire space.

I grab for his shirt when he walks past me to get a few towels, pulling him in for a devouring kiss. He smiles into my mouth and pulls back.

"I smell like a bonfire." His hand strokes my cheek, fingertips in my hair.

"Mmm." I pull him in between my legs, kissing his neck. "I don't care. I want you."

He laughs and the sound makes my soul feel lighter.

"You have me," he vows. "Always."

I let him go so he can fiddle with everything until it's exactly as he likes it.

"You can get in," he finally says before turning to face the wall so I can undress.

He follows in behind me, both of us naked, though neither of us looking. I stare toward the tiled wall, letting his warmth and size cover my back entirely as he steps into the steaming shower.

"I want to take you here, under the water," Bennett rasps into my ear, his hands slowly moving through my hair, washing it. "Where you feel safe and warm."

My eyes close, heart clenching, pliantly relaxing in his strong hold beneath the hot spray.

"But I can't be slow. And, selfishly, I want our first time to be in a bed." He nips at my ear, and I shiver. "But . . . next time?"

I peek over my shoulder at him to find a boyish gleaming grin blooming that I've never seen on him. He's so handsome it makes my chest ache. He turns me toward him, my chest to his. His fingers grip my chin lightly, tilting it up so that he can rinse the suds from my hair.

And I can't stop looking at him. The words spill, flowing easily from my lips.

"I need you to know that you are the first person I've chosen for myself. That this is the first time that I've . . . that I've wanted this," I confess. Maybe it's not true. Sometimes it's hard for me to remember what happened, to know it wasn't my fault. That even though I didn't fight outright, I didn't want that.

He hurt you, I try to tell myself, but the voice that's darker, more sinister, screams back, *You asked for it.*

My stomach swirls again, the heat of the shower making me feel dizzy. But I hold on to Bennett. His jaw is clenched tight, eyes swirling blue fire, but he doesn't interrupt. Every line of his body feels sharper, and I feel calmer, safer, at the change.

Having him here, with me, is enough to silence my mind into tranquil calm.

"I've never wanted anything more than this," I say, reaching up to press my lips to his hungrily, distracting him as best I can from the deep confession I've uttered in the safety of the water and his arms.

The water is still warm as he cuts off the shower, grabbing a towel and covering my shoulders, never once looking down. Even though

I wish he would. He wraps one around his own waist before looking back up at me, helping wring out my hair and pulling me close, hugging me in my towel to keep me warm.

"I'll give you a minute," he says before exiting the bathroom into the darkened bedroom and closing the door behind him.

I don't take a full minute; my heart thunders because I *can't* wait any longer for him.

He's there, using another towel to rub the water from his curls meticulously, but the sound of the door opening makes him pause. He tilts his chin over one massive shoulder, eyes dark and intense.

We stare at each other for a long moment, my heartbeat rushing in my ears like the ocean waves just outside the room.

He steps toward me, tentative. The floor-to-ceiling windows bathe his body in liquid moonlight.

Bennett is larger than most, but he's almost always hunched. Now, besides the slight curve of his shoulders, his body is fully extended. He takes up so much space, shoulders broad and back wide. His skin is glistening from the shower, muscular but not cut. Thicker and softer in his size.

The blue towel around his waist is only held by his hand now, mimicking my pose across from him.

I let go of mine first, revealing my body to him all at once. In the shower, he was careful to only stand at my back. I've never stood and faced him in my nakedness, bare and vulnerable.

Blue eyes to match the ocean outside scan slowly over me, intentional and careful. The way he looks at me doesn't feel dirty. It feels intense. Passionate, like the feeling of his eyes on me is feeding me power instead of taking it away.

He rewards my strength with his own, dropping the towel from his waist and stepping toward me.

My eyes move over his hips, the coarse hairs that lead down to the massive length of him, heavy against his abdomen. I knew he was big—he's too large of a person not to be—but the sight has my breath hitching.

We step toward each other, meeting in the middle. I sit on the end of the bed, inching back slowly as he follows me, not crowding or rushing me as he crawls over me *up, up, up* the bed. My head rests on the white silk pillowcase, curls messy and damp. His skin is warm against my goose-bump-covered body.

"Slow?"

"Slow," he says, his hand hovering over my hip. "Tell me if you want to stop."

"I won't want to."

"P," he says, his mouth soft, hovering over me carefully. Honeyed brown curls hang over his forehead. "Promise you'll tell me if you want to stop."

"I will." I nod as I say it. "And you have to tell me if you don't like something."

"I will." He nods back. "You're so beautiful."

"Please." The word is half whine, but no embarrassment surfaces. "Touch me."

Eyes wide, I watch his touch caress over my hips and up toward my breasts.

His fingers play across my body, sure and firm, as if he decided what he'd do and how before this. He's planned and thought this through more than I have—and it's only then I realize I'm slightly frozen beneath him. I am, for the first time, the one overthinking things.

"P?"

I've done this before. *It's just sex.*

The back of his massive hand trails over my collarbone, feather light up the length of my neck, reaching to tuck a few hairs behind my ear.

"Paloma?" he calls again, pushing his body up off me. The loss of him is like ice over my skin. I shiver, eyes watery as I look up at him.

"I'm sorry—I don't know what to do."

His eyes soften before a gentle kiss lands on my brow.

"Kiss me."

The command makes something loosen in my chest. I push up, reaching to pull him to me, lips pressing hard against his. Desperate and seeking.

He settles himself in the cradle of my thighs, spreading me wide with the broadness of his body. He soothes the stretch with his left hand, massaging lightly at the inside of my right thigh, while his other palm is pressed into the mattress by the side of my head—the only thing preventing him from crushing me with his weight.

Bennett disconnects from my mouth, kissing over my throat and down to my chest. His lips press over the hardened peak of one nipple before switching to the other as his fingers circle over the damp skin.

"Show me how you like it," he says as he releases the nipple he's been tormenting with slow smooth strokes. "I want to make you feel good. I need you to show me."

"They're kind of sensitive. Just some pressure—not too much." I swirl my fingers closed around and around, shivering from the shots of pleasure driving down my body.

"Okay." He presses a quick kiss to my mouth and ducks his head down, knocking my fingers away.

It's perfect immediately, enough that my hips arch up involuntarily.

"Feel good?"

"Yes." I buckle beneath him.

"Do you want more?"

"I want you to . . . to fuck me."

The language feels strange, like it's somehow wrong and right at the same time. Insecurity has me shrinking slightly under him, while trying to desperately grasp him to me in some feeble attempt at self-soothing.

"Not yet," he says into my neck, letting me pull him to cover my body. I kiss my fear and anxiety into the skin of his neck, lips almost vibrating with my worry. "I want to do everything with you. I've been waiting my whole life for this, and I want to take my time with you."

He pulls away again and my chest lurches, but I let him go. He smiles, hovering so big above me, and smooths his thumb over my cheekbone in soft, soothing strokes.

"Let me take care of you. Okay?"

I nod before biting my lip and reaching for him.

He laughs, the sound pumping through my veins like a drug, and settles back over me only lower.

Brown curls tickle my stomach as he stops and hovers just above my belly button.

His mouth is hot against my skin, my cheeks flushing because no one's ever done *this* before. He kisses and nibbles and licks at the most sensitive part of me. Bennett Reiner might be a virgin, but he's made an art of getting to know my body, taking his time learning where his touch unravels me the most. I come fast and hard, overly sensitive, back bowing off the bed. He reaches a hand to my low stomach to push me down. To steady me.

Always keeping me steady.

It's only after, when I sink back into the sheets to watch him carefully put on a condom, that his body raises to meet mine, settling between my thighs.

"Do you trust me?" he asks. I nod, eyes on his—always.

"Hold on to me," he says. The repetition of the words from earlier winds through me, relaxing my muscles and my mind in equal measure. He pushes into me in one strong thrust.

My back arches at the sheer size of him. I can feel him *everywhere*, as if he's inside every part of my body permanently. Deeply.

A cry bursts from my lips, hands grasping his meaty shoulders, nails digging in, and he stops fully. His brow dips, sweat and water from his damp curls dripping down smooth cheekbones, slipping over his swollen lips.

He watches me carefully. "Is it . . . too much?"

I laugh, my entire body relaxing around him so he can slide in farther. Only Bennett would casually ask that, unaware of the sexual undertone of the question—he means it genuinely.

"I just need a moment," I say, and he nods before dipping closer to me, using a hand beneath my neck to pull my body up toward him like an offering, pressing soft kisses along the tender skin of my throat.

His ministrations work like magic touches, relaxing my body to the intrusion of him. I'm not a virgin, but it's been over a year since I last had sex. And I've had no self-love intimacy, too scared to try anything. So, beyond Bennett's hands and mouth—and now the massive cock between his legs—nothing has touched me there in a long time.

And somehow where I thought I'd feel terror-struck and overwhelmed, I *don't*. I feel safer with him here, in his embrace, with him inside me, than I've ever felt.

"Okay. I'm ready. Please."

He moves and it's like electric shocks across my body. He's everywhere, no part of my body untouched by him—his fingers, his soul, his words.

It's slow, careful; despite how large and intensely intimidating he is, he's always been this with me. Careful. Gentle. His body is stretched over mine, so close that my nipples press against the sparse hair of his chest. His hands grasp the curves of my waist. Everything about him is manly, seeming older than his eighteen years—even his soul.

I want to be here, intertwined with him, forever.

The pace at which he makes love to me feels like he's searing himself into my marrow, unescapable and permanent. I've never been touched like this, taken care of like this, *loved* like this—if that's what it is. Maybe what it could be.

"Bennett," I breathe, eyes fluttering as an orgasm sneaks up over me—not so intense, but prolonged and filled with light.

"Oh *god*, Paloma—" he stutters out. "I can feel you squeezing me—*fuck*."

My entire body only tightens further around him, my orgasm rolling into a second one because he's panting and thrusting and losing his careful control. He curses so rarely; it works like a shot to my adrenals to hear it now. To know I make him feel that way.

I think I could get off on his reactions to me alone.

"Please, Bennett—"

"You feel so perfect," he breathes.

"Are you going to come?" The question is half stuttered, half moan.

"Yes," he breathes. "Can I? Can I come inside you?" A growl bursts from his lips against my ear. "I need to come inside you, love."

I know he's wearing a condom, but the words are intense and heady. I nod, fingers gripping the muscles of his shoulders, feeling the softness of his stomach against mine as his hips stutter before his abs contract and his mouth turns from my neck.

"You're the only thing I've ever cared about," I whisper, a broken confession spilling unwanted from my lips. I blink back tears, and he slows down. "*Ever.*"

He bites into my shoulder.

It makes me come again, fingers fluttering to the back of his head like I can hold him there. Like I can keep the mark of him on me forever.

• • •

We lie across rumpled sheets under the glow of moonlight, his body stretched out beneath me. His music plays softly from the speaker on the sill, Iron and Wine soothing and lulling filtering through my ears, competing with the thump of his heartbeat. Yet I feel energized while he looks sleepy and sated, beautiful. So handsome and so far above me, there's a piece of me forever shocked that he's here, underneath my fingers.

"How old were you? When you had your first kiss?"

He blushes at the question, despite being naked and entangled in my arms. "Sixteen. It was a girl who had a crush on my best friend. I think she was trying to get him to notice her or make him jealous."

I smirk, shaking my head and tracing my fingers over his brow. "Impossible. You're perfect. And way better than him."

He shakes his head. "You don't even know who you're talking about."

"I don't care," I whisper into his mouth. "I only want you."

I feel almost high on him. My heart pushes at my ribs, beating like it might reach from my chest and into his.

There's a giddy feeling in my chest, like butterflies. It like something from a fairy tale, and not the usual anxious sickness I'm more used to in the aftermath of sex.

"What about you?" he asks, hand brushing my hair back from my face softly as I nuzzle into his biceps where his arm is wrapped around me.

"What about me?"

"I want to know *everything*." He punctuates the word with a heady kiss. "When was your first kiss? Have you ever fallen in love with someone? How old were you when you first made love to someone?"

My stomach hollows, anxiety ripping through me like a whip. I jerk away from him, scrambling back slightly. He sits up, following me like he wants to grab for me, keep me close, but is fighting the impulse.

"Why—why would you ask me that?"

Stop. He doesn't know. He doesn't know.

It doesn't matter. I can't stop myself from snapping, "You're ruining this. You're ruining everything."

His face shutters like I've slapped him, but he doesn't move away. Instead, he looms closer.

"Wait," he commands, even with his voice soft as a whisper. He grasps my wrist in his hand, his other settling on my cheek, his pinky firm against the soft skin beneath my jaw, his thumb slowly caressing the swell of my bottom lip. "Paloma—"

"You don't want to know that." I try to shake my head, try to force myself to jolt away. But I can't. I don't *want* to, body pliant in the steadying strength of his hands.

"There is nothing you could say that would make me go, P," he says firmly. "Tell me."

A tear works its way down my cheek, falling softly over his fingertips.

"I was ten when someone kissed me for the first time," I say, throat full with a trapped cry. That little version of myself shouts in my head, hands over her ears—*Stop, stop, stop!*—as if she knows I shouldn't say this. He'll leave.

Good. He's better without this.

"He was . . . one of my mom's friends."

I see the words hit him. The implication.

A huff of his breath through his nose. He nods. "What else?"

My brow dips. "You—that's not—"

"Someone hurt you," he says, brow furrowing. He doesn't ask. He just says it, as if he can see everything I'm desperate to hide. "Tell me, Paloma. Let me be there for you. Trust me, please."

His words are a plea. The sob I'd tried to smother wrings free, pathetic and needy.

"What else?" he asks again.

"It doesn't matter."

"Paloma—"

"Stop," I cry, my voice louder than I mean for it to be. I move back away from him again. "Please, Bennett. I don't—I can't talk about this yet. Just . . . please."

"Okay," he says, hands up in a placating gesture that's meant to be as calming as his tone.

We sit quietly in the ruinous aftermath of the mess of my own making. *You ruined this. Like you ruined him. Like you ruin everything.*

Bennett stands slowly, naked but not desperate to cover himself in the way I am—the sheet drawn up over my body.

"You didn't eat," he says, eyes focused on his feet. "I know you're hungry. I'm going to make you food, okay?"

I nod, too afraid to ask him the questions burning in my throat—*Are you angry? Do you hate me? Do you regret it all?*

I reach out for his hand, but my stomach swoops and I pull back. It feels wrong to be allowed to touch him after I yelled at him.

"Can I . . . can I sit by the water again?"

"Of course you can," he says, voice exasperated. He leans in, hands in my hair, cupping my head in the massive stretch of his palms. "You can have anything you want, P."

His words feel intense, blanketing me in safety and warmth. Guilt and anxiety war in equal measure. I've never felt safer than I do with him. And yet, the terrifying thought of losing that is enough to drive me almost mad with wanting to keep it.

"Just wear something warm, okay?" He kisses my forehead long and hard, as if he can tattoo the feel of his lips on my skin.

It doesn't stop the pain from the physical loss of him and the safety of his arms.

CHAPTER 45

THEN: Freshman Year, November

Bennett

It doesn't matter that I'm only halfway to her spot on the illuminated deck; I can *feel* her distress.

Part of me wanted to rush down the second I heard her slip out of the sliding door, but I kept my focus on the plethora of snacks I was gathering for her. Things she likes most—applesauce and Goldfish, snacks I bought and brought with me because she'd grown up without the snacks most children love.

She deserves some space to be alone and calm by the sea before I try to comfort her.

And I know being near the water soothes Paloma. It's why I wanted to bring her here.

Paloma is completely still, silent, almost like she doesn't notice me there—which in and of itself is a bit nauseating. I don't like that she's so out of it, out here by herself. The worry that's been slowly building ratchets up to an almost insurmountable level.

"Hey, P," I whisper, sitting close as the fire crackles behind us. "You, okay?"

Her hair is unbound, tangled from the wind that seems to have stilled, like some metaphorical rage of her emotions has now settled, too. I pretend it was me that soothed her. My hands.

I can still *feel* the silk of her skin against my palms, the warmth of her body pressed to mine. My fists clench to not reach for her again.

"*Please, Bennett—*"

"*You feel so perfect. So perfect.*"

My stomach swoops like the rush of a freefall just *remembering* it. My world has altered fundamentally. It feels wrong that I'm not holding her now, that I'm not making her come again and again until she's soft and sleeping in my arms.

Instead, we're here. In the cold, with just the sound of the water to soothe her, the way I wish I could. The way I'll obsess over for years to come, until I can fix it. Make everything better for her. Never let her be hurt again.

"*I was ten.*" My stomach rolls with the knowledge. It's hard to understand it, to imagine her as a child, unprotected and scared.

Tell me the rest, I silently beg. *C'mon, P. Trust me to hold this for you. To never leave you alone in this pain. Be mine. Trust me enough to fall in love with me the way I am falling in love with you.*

"I'm so sorry." She swallows loudly. "I think I'm scared."

At her confession, she scoots away from me just slightly and my stomach hollows out.

Say something.

I try, mouth opening and closing—but nothing comes out. My palms feel sweaty despite the icy cold. I fidget with my sleeve where it suddenly seems to be cutting into my palm.

"Of me?"

It's not what I meant to say. It doesn't even make sense, but the slight anxiety roiling through me feels strange.

"No. Never," she says. Her voice sounds a little empty; her eyes are wide and watery as she glances at me before looking back out across the sea. "I just . . . I wanted this weekend to be good for you and I think I ruined it."

"God, P—no. No, you could never ruin this. But this isn't just—"

I cut myself off, head shaking. "You're perfect. I adore you. Why can't you understand that?"

I'm tripping over my words, carelessly flailing through this important conversation.

Paloma's hand presses hard over my thigh. "I want to trust you. I want to tell you. And—" Her voice starts to shake and she looks down at her hand on me, as if she's just realized it was there. "And I'm sorry, okay?"

Instead of consoling her or begging her to tell me, I sit quietly and allow her to speak.

She opens her mouth, but no words escape. Only silent tears. The fire crackles behind us, waves lapping at the sand just out of reach.

There's a beseeching look in her eyes, one I'm almost certain she doesn't realize is there. Like something inside her is *begging* me to find this answer so she doesn't have to, to speak it for her. *Come on, Bennett. Think.*

"Somebody hurt you," I try. "You already told me that. I think I've known for a while. But you're trusting me now, and I want to help. Let me carry this for you."

"I can't." She's breathing hard. Her voice trails off, but I can *feel* what she wants to say, like some third entity is nearby, looming dark over her usual shining bright light. Withdrawing in on herself, she curves her shoulders, making herself smaller.

Paloma bites her lip, eyebrows furrowed. As if she doesn't know the answer to my implied question—or won't tell me.

"Paloma?"

She finally nods and fury bursts in my chest, mixing with pain, threatening to swallow me. It's overwhelming, my vision fuzzing out at the corners.

My fists clench with the need to pull her into my chest, terrified to touch her and *not* to in equal measure.

"Paloma—"

"I'm . . . I'm sorry," she says again, helpless and small. She somehow sinks further into herself. "I should have just told you when you asked, but I was embarrassed—"

"Embarrassed?" The word booms out of me, angry. My voice is thick, torn between yelling and crying. I feel out of control. "Why? God— P. You didn't choose that."

Her eyes glance toward me. Like a cornered deer frozen but checking for danger.

"I— It's complicated."

"Did you want it?" Another hesitation. Another expression moving across her features like she's unsure and looking to *me* for the answer.

"I don't . . . no. I didn't," she says, as if the words are to herself more than to answer me.

Another piece of my heart breaks. I reach for her, taking her into my arms and bending down to kiss her forehead. I feel her flinch. It would hurt less if she had stabbed me. "That's not complicated, Paloma."

"Are you . . . Am I gross now?" she asks, vulnerability woven so deeply into every word.

"Never," I say vehemently.

"Do you regret it?" A choked half-sob works from her.

I put a hand on my chest, as if I can stop the pain.

"Never. Paloma—the way I feel about you is almost overwhelming," I attempt to explain. "I'm disappointed for you. I'm angry and hurt *for* you. I wish somehow, I could have known you then . . . protected you. Cared for you."

She holds my gaze, longer eye contact than I'm usually comfortable with.

She chokes out. "I just . . . I wanted us to have this together."

"Listen to me, P. This was just as much your first time as it was mine. Yeah?"

Tears threaten her doe brown eyes as she looks up at me. "Yeah."

"Was it good?" I whisper before wrapping her tighter into me, holding her tightly to my chest as she maneuvers herself to straddle my thighs. "Did I . . . did I make it good for you, P?"

She nods into my neck, then peels back with a wet-eyed smile. "It was the only time sex has felt . . . good. Thank you."

I shake my head, tucking her head back into my neck and holding her tightly again. Mostly so that she can't see the tears threatening at the corners of my eyes.

"Don't thank me, P. Just let me show you how it's supposed to be."

We stay in the cold too long. Paloma is tired but swears she can't sleep. I feed her Goldfish and applesauce, trying to quell the oncoming fixation with feeding her by hand, then carry her inside.

It's late, but I run another steaming shower and make good on my promise, taking her against the warm shower wall, her body wholly held in my hands, opening to me easier now. She complains softly of being sore and I apologize, ready to pull out of her—to let her rest.

But her nails sink into my back, holding me close.

"I want to feel it," she says, voice quiet. "I want the reminder of you when I move."

Her words make me ravenous, bucking into her harder and faster than before, chasing down her moans desperately until we come together.

I ask her what poem she feels like when we have sex. The question barely makes sense, but I know she understands me.

She shakes her head. "I don't know," she whispers. "Let me think about it."

I whisper, "I like my body when it is with your body," so she'll know. So she'll maybe understand.

This time when she says she can't sleep, her eyes are already closed, her body pressed to mine beneath the covers.

I watch over her for a long time.

In the morning, she grinds on top of me to wake me up. We make love, slow and sleepy. I make her come again under the shower spray, watching the way she unfurls from the warm water and the insistence of my fingers. I take my time, desperate to learn her every nerve ending. To perfect the art of pleasuring her. Of loving her.

By the evening, I recite lines of poetry in her ear when she lets me take her from behind, hand in her hair against the back of her neck, dominant but always gentle. Consuming her the way I want to so desperately. I swallow every cry of pleasure with my mouth.

The drive home the next morning is easy. We wind through the backroads with care as I drive slowly and deliberately. Adrienne Lanker plays on the radio.

I crack the windows to let Paloma feel the soft air flow. She takes turns pressing her feet beneath my thigh or laying her head on my biceps, which eventually turns to her sleeping on my arm. I'm even more careful as I purposefully drive slower not to jostle her.

I spend the ride just watching over her and feeling her skin always pressed to me in some way. It feels like a piece of her lives inside me now.

I don't think I'll ever be able to let her go.

CHAPTER 46

NOW

Bennett

"I said I don't want to talk about it," I snap.

It's the third session we've had that's been tense, and it's only gotten worse. But today I've hit my breaking point.

As usual, Dr. Anya has little to no reaction to my words or the harsh level of my voice—even if it is unusual for me. But I'm frustrated, enough that my knee is starting to ache as I keep bouncing it. "Paloma is good. She's back in my life again. Everything is great."

She nods. "Last time Paloma and you . . . broke up, I guess, you struggled severely. Enough that I think you need to talk about this, to imagine what it might be like, so that you have better control over your own life and situation if something does—"

"Nothing is going to happen."

"What would it be like if Paloma did leave?" she asks again, and the question hits like a punch.

"She won't," I grit out.

"You can't control everything," Dr. Anya says, clicking her pen again and setting it down in her lap, uncrossing her legs. "You can't control Paloma, or anyone else."

My heart is thundering, blood roaring through my ears like a constant wave across the shore.

Everything is fine.

"Paloma is my girlfriend again. Things with my mom are fine," I tell her. "My dad and I are . . . doing better. Rhys is back. Paloma is back. Everything is good."

I don't need this.

"Bennett," she tries again. Her voice is softer but it still feels like something is shredding me from the inside out. "You got through this once. You could do it again."

I'm standing before I realize it, fists clenching and unclenching as I stalk out and slam the door closed behind me.

I hear the sound of my dorm door closing three years ago. The sound of my childhood bedroom door when my dad left.

Everything is fine. I don't need this.

I grab my phone and call Paloma. A breath rushes out of me when she answers on the first ring.

"Hey." Her voice washes over me, icing out the heat but not the stress.

"Are you busy? Today and tomorrow?" It's hard work to keep the strain and frustration out of my voice, but I manage.

"No. I'm done with class—I just have a pairs skate tomorrow." Her laugh is like coming home. "Why?"

"Can you skip it?"

"Yes." She laughs again, more insistent this time as she asks, "Why?"

I clear my throat, picturing a cloudy, mist-covered beach. A girl with slightly darker blond hair and a campfire. Days that stretch over years of time, each one of them a precious, coveted memory for me.

"I want to go to Speyside."

CHAPTER 47

NOW

Paloma

Bennett and I have weaved in a constant dance around one another for three years—except in the first week before school, the August heat muggy and overly warm.

Because Bennett Reiner has never missed my birthday. Every single August 5, Bennett pulled in front of my dorm with a quick text, allowing for me to choose to answer the call. And I always have.

"I didn't celebrate my birthday growing up," I'd confessed to him once, stretched out in a bath he'd run for me, a little tipsy on wine.

He didn't comment, but his hands paused where he'd been smoothing the strands of my hair.

I hadn't hesitated to tell him the date when he asked, too unfocused to notice the determined set of his brow.

Every year, he would take me to Speyside for at least one night. Cooking for me, making me a coconut cake (which I'd discovered is my favorite after several attempts), and singing happy birthday in a low rasp. I swam most of the day, then sat close to him in front of the bonfire while he read poems—some new, some old favorites. It was the best day of the year for me; one of my only good days some years.

Bennett's birthday was a different story. Because unlike me, Bennett had friends who loved him, family who wanted to spend every June 28 with him, loving on him and making him happy. A bittersweet day for me as I spent the evenings watching his stories; Rhys and Freddy's, too.

Only once was I brave enough to show up, when the guys threw him a rager at their newly christened Hockey House. I spent most of the night in the shadows, watching them celebrate him and play drinking games. I was distracted by the strong column of his throat working beneath a funnel held by Freddy, though he'd had to stand on the table to reach the big goalie's mouth at the right angle.

I stayed all night, only slightly drunk. Holden spent some of the night trying to get me to play, flirting and suggesting we could go home together. But I stayed, waiting for the chance to sleep next to Bennett in his bed.

Instead, we'd only had one moment, outside of the bathroom in a dark corner. He'd run into me, blinking slowly while his entire face melted into happy surprise.

"You're here," he'd said, his finger running along my cheek. I blushed and smiled.

"Happy birthday, Bennett."

I took the frozen moment to kiss his cheek, watching his eyes close and a breath push out of him.

"Best birthday ever." He sighed before Freddy rounded the corner calling for him to join them for King's Cup.

I left after that, but the taste of his salty skin and genuine smile were enough to sustain me for a long time.

Now, it's icy cold and darkly cloudy, but still classic and beautiful. Speyside always has been—the small town surrounding it, the spaced-out houses weathered and lived-in. This place has always felt like a home to me; one I keep close to my heart like a secret.

"Hungry?" Bennett asks when we step inside. He flicks on all the lights and turns on the heat. "I can get the fireplace going and we can eat?"

I nod, watching him switch the Waterfell cap around backward on his head, curls spilling out from the bill against his neck. I pull the scarf off my now-heated neck and tuck it on the hook by the door with my thick jacket, following Bennett into the dimly lit kitchen.

Perching myself on the counter, I watch him cook, accompanied by the quiet lull of music from his speaker and the sizzle of a pan.

I follow his directions to make a salad in a pretty painted porcelain bowl while he cooks. He pours me a glass of sparkling grape juice, smirking as he offers me a *cheers*. It all feels so domestic.

Another piece of my soul latches on to him.

"I have something for you to look at," he says, leaving the steaks he's cooked us to perfection to rest as he grabs his backpack. He pauses briefly by my blue bag, noticing a bunny ear hanging out of the side where I zipped it up. I blush, my mouth opening to defend the childish, terrified impulse to bring it along, but stop when he grazes it with his finger and looks up at me.

"'Real isn't how you are made, it's a thing that happens to you.'"

I know the quote because I'd read the book over and over as a child, hiding in the far shelves of the library in elementary school where they kept the kids for after-school programs. Sometimes my mom never showed up and someone had to walk me home or call my neighbor. But I always had that stuffed bunny, half hidden because I was terrified the real owner would come back.

It barely looks like a bunny now—not even the same color it used to be, because I've loved it so much.

"You read it?"

He nods. "The first night you mentioned it, I did."

Something lodges heavy in my throat. At eighteen, being loved by Bennett was overwhelming. It still is, but not in the same way. This time, I'm not afraid. I'm only in awe of him and the purity of his heart.

He doesn't say anything more about it, grabbing a stapled packet of papers and handing them to me as he goes back to plating mushrooms, potatoes, and steak.

"It's a list of internships for your sports program." He clears his throat, avoiding my gaze before I finally glance down at the printed list—programs mostly in the surrounding areas, all age groups, almost all hockey. All the information is printed alongside it: start dates, requirements, brief pro/con lists.

"In case you want to . . . be here. Or close."

I want you here. I want you close. It's his way of saying words he's not ready to speak aloud. But I hear them all the same.

"Does this mean you'll be staying here?"

"At Waterfell," he specifies, taking my hand where I've frozen at the countertop and guiding me to sit on the floor pillows near the fire. He sits across from me, one thigh pressing nearly into the brick lip of the fireplace because he's so massive.

Bennett takes his hat off and tosses it on the sofa. He runs a hand through his hair, tousling his curls. "I switched, officially, to English with a minor in poetry. I talked with Dr. Britton last week and he helped me."

My smile is so wide my cheeks hurt, my eyes water. "Yeah?" He nods. "God, Bennett—I'm so proud of you."

We eat and talk quietly, about school and hockey and everything in between. And like always inside the walls of Speyside, it doesn't feel like we've spent three years running in circles, apart from one another. It feels like we've always been *this*.

After he returns to refill my glass, I grab my gift for him.

"I brough you something, too," I whisper, handing him the

folded note tucked away inside a yellowed, dingy envelope I know he recognizes.

His fingers are hesitant, but he reaches out and takes it, unfolding it slowly and reading silently in the glow and heat of the fire still crackling beside us.

> I can't write poetry
> But I can write it like this—place the words,
>
> Just so
>
> So that you read it like your favorite poem.
> So you trace your eyes over the pages, sensual and slow
> So that your teeth bite down on the words
>
> (bite down on my shoulder again and let me show you)
>
> Can I slip you into my brain? It would make it easier to show—
>   to tell
>
> The spaces inside my brain are filled with dust and fear and
> I never wanted you to see that. To know me as that girl.
> I always wanted you to just see me
>
> p. love. (*Your Love*)
> As I am. The girl who likes to swim and lets you wind your
>   fingers into her hair until we are just one string tangled
>   forever
>
> That is to say, I love
> I love you. I love you.

"It's . . ." I suddenly stammer, heart pounding the longer he takes, the more I track his gaze roving across my words. "I wrote it. For you. Is that so weird?"

His brow furrows and his eyes rise to mine reluctantly, like he's angry he has to look away from my heart on that paper.

"Every poem I've ever written has been about you," he says, almost exasperated. His breath saws out of him again. "You . . . you wrote a poem for me?"

"I just . . . I needed you to know. To understand—"

His body covers mine, pushing me against the soft pile of blankets. His palm braces the back of my head as he lays me flat so rapidly, I forget to breathe.

Bennett's hands make quick work of my clothes, an edge of roughness to his usual calm demeanor. His eyes are wholly black, chest rising and falling rapidly above me. I pull at his buttoned-up flannel until he nearly rips it off, shoving down his pants and underwear and tearing open a condom with his teeth—a fierce intensity I've never seen in him. Like he's unraveling before my eyes, nearly feral with desperation. For me.

"You write poems about me?" I ask, brain fuzzy with lust and want—but the words stick.

He thrusts into me, my entire body bowing to his strength, spine arching as he catches my waist and keeps me suspended.

"You're the only thing in my head," he whispers, eyes feral as they take stock of my body, the dips and curves and shadows. "I *have* to write about you." A kiss to my mouth, almost too harsh, too frantic. "I'd never written a poem of my own until I met you. I didn't think I could—and then, you."

His fingers dig into my skin, holding me still as he thrusts hard into me again. A loud whine bursts from my lips.

"Your hair in my fingers like silk," he says. "Let me inside of you—your mouth, your body"—he juts his hips forward, before bowing over me to kiss my temple and touch my hair—"your brain, your heart."

He's writing poetry with my body, his own like a pen and mine the paper. I can feel my walls tightening around him, fingernails gripping into the mass of his biceps as I struggle to hold on while falling over the precipice of pleasure.

"'Bite down on my shoulder again and let me show you,'" he growls into the skin of my neck, fucking me harder and my teeth lance his skin as I come; my words from his mouth.

Bennett flips me over in his grip, settling my knees against the cushioned pallet beneath us as he takes me from behind, covering my entire body with his bulk. He moves my hair and kisses the back of my neck.

His hips stutter, fast and slow, then give one last deep thrust as he comes and groans into my shoulder, his lips soft—before the slight sting of a bite that makes me squeeze him again.

"I love you," he mutters, repeated like a mantra into my hair as his fingers weave around the strands. "*Your mouth. Your voice. Your hair.*"

"Bennett," I moan, my body boneless, like a heap only he's holding up.

"Slip me into your brain," he says, his hands circling my ribs, cradling my body like an offering as he keeps his hips flush to my ass, dipping his head to kiss the center of my back so reverently. It's like being worshipped. "Keep me forever."

I want to.

CHAPTER 48

THEN: Freshman Year, December

Bennett

I stare over the papers again, fingers ghosting across the pages where my black ink markings are—her messier ones just across on the next page. Like a living metaphor of the poems.

Of us.

A hand slaps over the page, nails clean and short, skin peachy and half-covered with the chewed-up sleeve of my old hockey sweatshirt.

"We said we'd look at the same time," she says, shaking her head in disapproval. But her eyes are full of mischief.

I shut the binder and cross my arms, leaning back against the wall where I'm seated on her dorm room bed. "What if I don't want to wait anymore?"

"Too bad," she says, but the words are full of heat instead of censure. It makes me want to press her to the mattress and take her again, but we've already done it twice today. And she just showered.

The showering part is hard for me. Paloma's warm, pink skin . . . her hair in my hands as I wash and care for it—even if we've just had sex, it only serves to get me going again.

I kiss her instead, barely satiating the beast of my desire that has yet to leave me since the night at the beach house.

We've spent nearly every day together since. We studied for finals together in her dorm room, slept together nearly every night. And it never feels like enough, my thoughts circling *her, her, her* when I'm away from her.

"When do you leave for the break?" she asks.

My brow furrows again. She's asked this a lot lately, and Paloma remembers most everything.

"I've got a practice Tuesday, so not 'til after that." It's Saturday; half of campus left the second finals ended. "I'll be with my dad through Christmas. And then I do New Year's Eve dinner with my mom and stepdad."

"Is that how you always split it?"

"It wasn't. But . . . yeah, now we do. My mom is—" I shake my head. "She struggles with holidays, and I think I make her a bit sadder. So, this just works best for us. And I like Christmases with my dad."

"At the house in Beacon Hill?"

I nod, half distracted by the slipping of my old crewneck off her shoulder.

"Christmas is my favorite holiday." She says the words like she's admitting a little secret. I hold her vulnerable confessions close to my heart, just as protective of them as she seems to be. "It all just seems so warm and cozy—a fire in the fireplace, the multicolored glowing lights."

I nod again, but my mind snags on the words. On the fact that despite Paloma's usual affinity for dressing up her room for the season, there's no Christmas anything in here. Something heavy sits in my gut, gnawing at me slightly. A niggle of worry lodging deep.

You're obsessing over her and reading too much into it. Relax. Don't do this to her.

"I love it, too," I say. I kiss her forehead and tuck some loose hairs back. Her hair is getting blonder, whatever she uses to dye it washing out. Probably from the amount of times a week I insist on washing it myself, addicted to her hair in an obscene, relentless way. "Are you going home for Christmas?"

"Oh, um. Yeah." She nods, biting on her lip. Her eyes wander back to the binder at my side and she grabs for it. "Okay, are you ready to swap?"

I smile and nod, excited and a little nervous for her to read the romantic notions I've been putting toward her since the first day by the hockey lockers. I've been half in love with her since she told me her favorite Robert Frost poem. I hadn't let that go. It bled directly into my choice.

She scoops up my paper for herself, holding it close to her chest as she steps over to her desk chair.

After we turned in our project a week before finals, Dr. Britton gave us a "final" final—to choose a poem for our project partner.

"You've been spending an entire semester with them, getting to know them intimately—" The entire class had snickered, but he only raised his eyebrow and defended his words. *"Poetry and the way we view it—positively or negatively, the things we see in it, how we talk about it—I think it all represents the innermost workings of our brains. So yes, intimately."*

It made sense. Poetry was always intimate to me, especially with Paloma.

I wait until she's across the room and settled before I finally look down at the paper in my possession, still within the binder. My eyes widen at the title.

No fucking way.

Stomach tight, chest beating—like my heart is screaming *her, her, her*. I gaze up, seeing the same realization settling across her beautiful too-perfect features.

"Bennett—"

"I know."

She laughs, but the sound is wet, and I realize only then she's crying.

In my grip, I hold Robert Fanning's "Song of the Sea to the Shore," a twin to the poem I know she holds—Fanning's "Song of the Shore to the Sea."

I'd chosen my poem for her before discovering it had a twin, mere lines into my first read. To know she felt not only the same, but to gift me its mate? It feels almost surreal in its grand romanticism.

I love her. I'm in love with her.

She doesn't make me wait, running the few steps between us to collapse into my arms, her kiss frenzied. I calm her, holding on to the length of her braid—the one done by my hand earlier—and slow her with my own kiss. Harnessing the control I feel so desperate to hold when we are intimate.

She softens easily in my grip, like melting down her sometimes-frozen exterior to the watery vulnerability beneath. The parts of her I care for and always will.

. . .

"What's that?"

I nearly jump at the boom of my dad's voice as he returns from the kitchen to the main living room. A small Christmas tree sits in the corner, filled only with handmade ornaments from my grade school years, some cheesy hockey figurines, and a few framed ornaments of us and the Koteskiys.

"It's a poem, from my . . . girlfriend," I say, testing the word on my lips.

My dad's eyes glow and he tries to hide his blinding smile, lifting the wine glass to his mouth for a long sip. "Girlfriend? Is it Paloma?"

I nod. "We haven't said it yet . . . but yeah." I'm feeling a little ridiculous at not having asked her. "She's . . . really great." The words feel inconsequential for how she makes me feel.

"Did you want to invite her?"

The answer is easy—yes—but I never wanted to overwhelm her or force her to fit into my complicated only-child-with-divorced-parents holiday. We don't celebrate with some large, overflowing loud family. It's quiet and peaceful, just my dad, Seven, and me.

"Yeah. I might call her," I say, stepping toward the stairs. "Just . . . to say Merry Christmas and make sure she's good."

My anxiety over her hasn't calmed since I left. I'm not a text type of person, but I haven't been able to stop myself from bombarding her with texts every now and then. Just to check on her.

She answers on the first ring.

"Hey!"

Her voice is so happy, so pleased—as if my call is the one she's been waiting for.

"Hey, P," I breathe, a smile spreading across my lips. "I miss you. How are you?"

"I'm good. I'm just—"

A long, loud alarm starts blaring in the background. I almost drop my phone to get away from the noise, standing from my relaxed position.

"Paloma?" My voice is louder than I intend. Seven perks up at her name, leaving his bed in the living room to come sit near my legs. "What is that?"

"Fire alarm," she projects over the vibrant noise. I grit my teeth. "Sorry—they sent an email that they're doing maintenance and to ignore it, but it's very loud. I'm sorry."

"What?" The words feel strange and off. "Where are you?"

She's silent for too long; my fist grips the phone so tightly I'm afraid it might snap.

"The dorms," she confesses. "But I'm fine! I promise, Bennett. I'm good!"

"I thought you were going home," I say, already grabbing for my shoes and my coat, heading down the stairs. "Paloma—why wouldn't you—why would you lie about that?"

"I'm sorry—I know. I just . . . I don't talk to my mom. But I didn't want to crash another holiday for you. You have family, and I—"

"Paloma," I cut her off, fingers pressed into my now-aching temple. "Pack your stuff. I'll be there in a half hour."

CHAPTER 49

THEN: Freshman Year, December

Paloma

Bennett is silent for the first fifteen minutes of our drive to his dad's house. He plays his usual slow indie music and I try to relax, but I can't stop glancing over at him out of the corner of my eye, trying to gauge his frustration.

At me? Or at my lie?

Seven, on the other hand, sits in the backseat, his head between our seats resting on the center console, big brown eyes watching me too knowingly.

Finally, as we pull off the exit into downtown Boston, I ask, "Are you mad at me?"

"Yes," he huffs. My stomach sinks, but I nod. "I'm mad you lied to me. I'm mad you weren't going to tell me that you were alone for the holidays."

My head is already shaking, fingers biting into the soft leather of my seat. "It's fine. I don't mind it."

"It's not fine to me," he says, the words clipped and frustrated. He's angry but he seems like he's trying desperately not to be. Or at least, not to be loud or angry *toward* me. "You being alone isn't fine to me."

I'm quiet, unsure of what to do or what to say. As much as I haven't experienced romance, I've seen anger. I've been taught multiple lessons in yelling or condescending speeches. I know when to keep my mouth shut.

Only . . . it seems to have the opposite effect.

Bennett looks over at me as soon as he's parked in the driveway. His face looks almost sick.

"I'm sorry," he says, and my eyes shoot wide. "I'm just—I hate thinking of you alone. I hate it and I'm—I think I let my thoughts get away from me when I heard the alarm and realized you weren't going to tell me—" He stops, as if his throat closed up suddenly. Shaking his head, he rubs his hand over his thigh repeatedly, a self-soothing motion that's almost aggressive.

"Next time, please, Paloma. Tell me," he begs.

The words stick in my mouth, desperate to get out and stay in all the same. *Thank you. For caring about me. For wanting me not to be so alone.*

"I will," I finally manage to say. "Promise."

I stick out my pinky, a peace offering, however childish. But it works like a charm, Bennett's intoxicating half-grin etching briefly across his features. He links his pinky with mine and shakes it.

After telling me to stay put, he gets out and rounds the car, letting out Seven and grabbing my backpack from the back before opening my door. There's a part of me that's still clenched tight over him holding it, a desperation to take it myself and keep it close, but I trust Bennett. And that trust and deep feeling of safety has only grown.

"I'm really happy you're here, P," he says, and my entire body relaxes into the strong feel of his hand on my lower back.

Inside the Beacon Hill house, Adam Reiner is seated on the white couch. A twinge of anxiety rolls through my stomach at the memory of the strained moment we shared months ago. At the clear, frustrating understanding apparent even now in his blue eyes so like his son's.

"Paloma," Bennett's dad greets me first. "Happy you could join us."

I nod with a soft smile. "Thank you for having me."

Bennett kisses my temple with a quickly muttered, "I'm going to get you something to drink," before disappearing toward the kitchen. I stare quietly back at the larger-than-life man observing me, feeling somewhat wrong and out of place.

I bite down on my lip. "Um . . ."

"You're okay, Paloma?" he asks. His voice is low and calm. There's a slight beseeching look in his eyes.

I tense but give a quick nod before stepping toward the tree like I'm admiring it. He's too intensely observant, and I don't like the way it feels like he's seeing something I'm not showing. It definitely doesn't help that Seven is trailing me, watching me keenly.

"All good?" Bennett asks, stepping up beside me with a warm mug of hot chocolate, marshmallows covering the top so I can't see through the white, pillowy fluff.

"All good."

Bennett eyes me a moment longer before wrapping his arm around me. "I think we'll head to bed early. Dad?"

"Sounds good." His dad smiles back. "I think I'll head to Max and Anna's for a bit, all right?"

Bennett nods and takes my hand to pull me up the stairs, leaving his dog behind with his dad.

He lays me on his bed, the lamplight warm, the sight of his well-loved poetry books a comfort. I pull him on top of me, fingers pressed into his sweater-covered shoulders as I kiss him. He tastes like sparkling grape juice and sugar cookies. And *mine, mine, mine.*

"I need to tell you something," he says, pulling back slightly, just enough that his forehead is pressed to mine and I can only watch his lips move—turning up into a half smile before he says, "I love you, Paloma. So much. So deeply."

My stomach rocks. My eyes glimmer with unshed tears as the genuine care in his words washes over me. It feels the same as it did when I fell into the pool as a kid, awash in cold water and something new on the other side.

Something better.

"Bennett—"

"I'm not saying these words to hear them back," he says, pulling his head back farther to lock his ocean eyes on mine. "I'm saying them because I need you to know. To make *sure* you know."

I want to say them. I feel them; it's the only time I've ever felt them, really.

My mouth opens, ready for the intense, terrifying confession. *Just say it. Say it. Three words.*

Only I've said the words before. *I love you.*

I was sixteen and desperate for the scraps of affection that had been offered to me. Instead of being strong, of finding it in myself, I'd burrowed deep, lodging myself into the only person who seemed to want me, like that might make them love me.

We'd had sex, laid in his bed afterward, and I'd whispered to him those three words, eyes glittering, face red.

And he'd smirked, lips pulling so sharp I thought he might laugh. *"Sweet girl. Already in love with me?"* He'd tsked, before shaking his head and petting one blond curl back behind my ear. The affectionate move was so at war with the words, making my stomach toss and bounce until I felt nauseous.

"So touch deprived," he'd chuckled. *"Don't worry, I'm gonna take care of you now."*

It was easy, once he said that, to trick myself into thinking that was his *I love you.* That he cared for me.

Tears well in my eyes as I look at Bennett. He's so handsome, skin flushed and eyes glinting—the depths of the ocean there, my peace. My comfort. *Home.*

"I'm sorry," I say, wiping at my eyes. "I don't know why I'm crying."

He shakes his head with a saddened smile. "It's okay, P."

It's not. He takes me into his embrace, a tight grip that calms my body.

"I do, too," I whisper into the safety of his arms. "I love you."

"Yeah?" he asks, and I can feel his grin against my hair.

"So much. So deeply." *More than you'll ever know or understand.*

I stay with Bennett and his dad through Christmas and it's just as magical and perfect as I'd imagined it might be. Time passes slow and fast all at once, like stars winking out against the inky sky, and I can't quell my desperation to keep this memory close and unmarred, to make this moment last forever. Bennett gifts me a complete set of Mary Oliver books from his own collection, littered with his black pen script from years of reading. It's like holding a piece of him.

The days bleed together until it's the day before New Years and we're drinking expensive champagne and sparkling grape juice, dancing to music off the stereo in the main room—celebrating the holiday early as his dad insists on.

I step over to the CD player, flipping through the selection in their "favorites" basket. My fingers ghost over a few familiar ones before settling on one I love.

"That's a good one," Adam Reiner says, stepping up behind me slowly. He's always overly cautious now, as if that moment in the kitchen has stuck with him. I wish he'd forget it.

"You have a thing for CDs?"

He nods with a smile, taking it from my hands to insert it into the old system.

Stepping away and back toward Bennett, I observe him for a long moment in the silence before the music starts up again.

"Sky Blue and Black" plays, the gentle piano adding cadence to my steps back toward where Bennett is watching me.

"Want to dance?" he asks. We've all been dancing and singing along to music all night, at Adam Reiner's suggestion. Where Bennett is stoic and calm, his dad is openly affectionate toward him and a slight goofball.

As much as I don't want to admit it to myself, Adam Reiner is exactly the father I dreamed up for myself in my quiet moments alone, when things were bad enough that I'd imagine my dad was somewhere out there, trying desperately to find me. That he hadn't meant to leave and that at any moment he'd burst through the door to our trailer home and pick me up. Take me away from it all.

Adam ruffles his son's curls as he passes us and quietly excuses himself for the evening.

I raise my left hand to the swell of Bennett's shoulder, my right hand held gently in his grip as we start to dance. My head rests on his chest and he hums, low and soft beneath his breath. I can feel the vibrations more than I can hear his voice.

Bennett and I dance, slow and careful as the CD plays. It feels like magic. It feels like love.

My heartbeat thumps in time with his—*him, him, him.*

Later that night, he makes love to me in the bed I once read to him from. He asks me again as he cares for me afterward what poem I'm reminded of when we have sex. I tell him I don't know. He recites a line from a sonnet I've never heard of and kisses a pathway down my spine through each word.

"I crave your mouth, your voice, your hair," he says, his fingers obsessively caught in the strands I know he adores.

"Your mouth," he says as he presses a kiss to my lips.

"Your voice," he says, kissing down my throat.

"Your hair," he says, pressing a kiss to my forehead at the edge of my hairline. "Your hair." He repeats as he presses me back into the mattress, intent to take me again.

I look into his ocean eyes as he pushes gently into me and my heart learns to beat at his command, reaching for him from my chest.

Even if I don't get to keep him, I will never love anyone the way I love him.

CHAPTER 50

NOW

Paloma

After we've showered, Bennett starts the firepit and bundles me up.

"You know, we could've waited to wash off," I say, smirking as he zips up his jacket to nearly cover my chin. "We're about to ruin it all and smell like a bonfire."

He shrugs, taking a beanie out of one of the baskets by the door. I spot the old Winnipeg Jets logo on the front as he sets it on my head. "You know I have to care for you after sex. It's part of it, for me. Sometimes it's better than the sex."

My eyes blow wide. "Better?"

"Sometimes." He shakes his head, exasperated as he reaches out to pull the beanie down to cover my eyes with a laugh. "Warm enough?"

I pull it back up and watch him with a bright smile. How many people get to see this side of Bennett—the playful, smiling, slightly goofy version of him? The piece that resembles his dad most.

Does Adam Reiner know how much of himself is present in the happiness of his son?

I want to ask about them, about what happened between them. But instead, I slide on the gloves Bennett's laid out for me and follow him out the sliding glass doors, into the whipping night wind and down toward the beach.

"You sure you're not too cold?" he asks, and I nod.

"I'm good." The flames illuminate the side of his face. The soft sound of the waves is enough to have me relaxing entirely in the familiar setting. "I like being near the water."

He smirks. "I know, love."

"I'm really happy for you, about the major change. I think you'll be a lot happier."

His smile is bright and wide. "I already am."

Chewing on my lip, I tuck a few strands of my hair—dry, because Bennett didn't want me to be cold, though I could tell it was difficult for him to *not* wash my hair—back over my shoulder, fiddling with the beanie.

"Actually, I have something to ask you."

I nod for him to continue, cocking my head to the side. "Yes?"

"There's a gala coming up. The Koteskiys do it every year, with a new charity. I don't usually go, but this year I guess Sadie and her brothers are involved in it—so I told Rhys I'd go. Would you . . ." He trails off and clears his throat, hitching his shoulder up to his ear in one of his usual nervous ticks. "Would you want to come with me?"

It's both funny and endearing, that Bennett Reiner can be so dominant and commanding in the bedroom—that he just finished fucking me brainless into the floor of the living room—but finds this question terrifying to ask.

"As your date?"

His smile warms me far more than the fire. "Yes. As my date."

I half stand, leaning over to kiss his mouth. "I'd love to." Sitting back down comfortably, I ask, "Why was that so nerve-racking? You had to know I'd say yes."

"I never know with you, P."

My stomach churns a bit at the honesty of his confession. "I'm sorry."

He shakes his head, playing with his curls for a moment. They're messy and boyish after being in a hat all day, then from the grip my hands had on them earlier.

"It's fine. I don't think I was prepared to take no for an answer on this one." He grins, all playful, and it's so intoxicating. I can feel my body warming again for him.

"No?"

"No. It's going to be the first time my parents will be in the same room since my mom got divorced, so I need you there—as my date or as my friend. I would've accepted either."

I freeze, trying to absorb the information he's spilling without some massive outward reaction. "Oh? Are you worried about that?"

"A little." He shrugs carefully. "But it'll be fine. And you'll be there, as my *date*. That makes everything better."

My mind is flying, thoughts swirling so that I can't focus on one point.

"Maybe we should talk more," I offer. "About everything."

His brow furrows, smile sliding slowly off his face. "No—no, we don't need to."

It would be so much easier to let it go. To go back to happy smiles and playful gestures, to let this beachside paradise be an oasis—but the reality is that it will become a mirage. It's not *real* if we're only like this together here. And to be *real*, it might have to hurt first.

"I'd like to," I try. His jaw works, eyes staring toward the fire now, away from me, as he nods in concession.

His hands press together, squeezing—I imagine he's trying to keep his fingers from tracing words across his thigh. "Okay."

"Is everything okay with you?" I ask. "Not that—I just have never seen you skip class before, or practice. Just want to make sure."

He smiles, but it's brittle, like a push could break it to pieces. "I'm okay. I mean, for me, I guess." The mass of his shoulders rolls with his shrug. His voice drops low. "You know how it is for me. It's always difficult."

"Is it?" I ask. It doesn't matter if I *think* that I know him this way. It's not enough. He has to tell me.

Another shrug. "Just keeping my head above water, P. It will pass, you know." He looks out across the black expanse of the darkened ocean. "It always does."

There's a long moment of soft silence between us. My eyes graze over the golden light bouncing off his face, making his stubble-lined jaw sharper, his thick, furrowed eyebrows casting shadows over the ocean-blue eyes I could paint from memory.

"I don't want to talk about me right now," he says softly—nearly whispering. "If that's okay."

"That's okay. But you promise you'll tell me if things aren't okay, right?" I ask. My hand reaches for his, intertwining our fingers. "Promise."

"I promise."

A chilled burst of wind blows through my hair, and I shiver. Bennett unloops his scarf and wraps it carefully around me so I can burrow into the warmth of him. The smell of him.

"Was it . . ." he starts, before looking down at his shoes, away from me. "I know you said it wasn't me, but I just—I have to ask. Did I do something? To push you away that night?"

New Year's Eve, three years ago. That Night—the one I've blocked out with every power inside my mind, until it's a distant foggy memory I refuse to revisit.

Still, I find my voice, though it sticks in my throat for a long time. "No, you didn't."

He nods, contemplation and relief swirling across his face.

"I think I just got it in my head for a while, that maybe it was me." He clears his throat, working through a knot there. "That I was too much or I couldn't read you the way you needed and that . . . that you wanted someone more normal."

My eyes close as I take his soft, vulnerable words like knives to my heart. And I deserve every single one.

A flash of a midnight-blue bedroom. A dog whining. A soft, half-broken confession—*Someone like you could never love someone like me, right?*—and a door slamming in the absence of denial.

Stomach churning, I let the cold wind settle me again.

"It had nothing to do with you," I breathe. "You were perfect, Bennett."

A breath before, "Then why did you leave me?"

Because you were never going to understand what was wrong with me. Because I was eighteen and terrified enough of losing you to sabotage everything. Because I needed to hurt myself before you hurt me.

And then I kept doing it. Hurting myself over and over and over. Like it would erase what I'd done.

Am I still the monster I was trying so hard not to become?

"I never wanted to," I try to say, squeezing my arms around my middle. "I just—I was so broken and scared, Bennett. And I'm sorry. I'm so sorry for what I did to you. For how I hurt you over and over—for Rhys—"

"Don't." He stops me, hands in the air and eyes closed tightly, in pain. "I can't . . . not yet."

Everything I've considered with Bennett was a path forward. But I've forgotten that there's a chance that won't be on the other side of this pain. That I've caused too much wreckage and it'll be impossible to clear it all, to fix it enough to pass through to the other side.

Speyside has always been a dream. Maybe it will continue to be.

"Sometimes I worry that leaving you was the smartest thing I could've done," I confess into the quiet. "But it was me not really letting you go that made things worse. Maybe if I had, you could have moved on. Been happier."

And then he's there, kneeling on the stone patio, backlit by the fire like a deity with a great halo of flames. His hands hold my face, tender and careful—constant and unmovable.

The steady shore standing unshakable and firm against the ebb and flow of my sea, like he always has.

"It wouldn't have mattered," he confesses, his voice just as whisper-quiet as mine. "I was never going to be willing to let you go. You're all I've thought about since that day in the locker room. I breathe and you're in my lungs." His breath huffs out, almost agitated as he looks back up at me with watery blue eyes. "Why can't you understand that?"

We stay there, frozen in some distorted beach vignette of pain and longing, desperation and yearning.

I want to show him the darker parts of myself, to display the scarred pieces of me, the smaller, little version of me that lurks in my brain—that has found everything in this world to be painful and terrifying. Except for him.

But I just . . . I can't.

The words are sewn into the sides of my throat, the threat and the promise of relief in equal measure. So I let him hold me closer, press kisses into my hair.

I watch the flames of the bonfire and wonder if there will be a day when I can show him everything. Or if we are, like so many beautiful poets and the subjects of their affection, doomed to burn out into ash and never get the things we want.

CHAPTER 51

THEN: Freshman Year, New Year's Eve, 3:45 p.m.

Bennett

"What if . . ." Paloma's voice trails off. "What if they don't like me?"

She's in my passenger seat, a light freckling of snow out the window over her shoulder as I park in front of her dorm. We've spent nearly a week with my dad at Beacon Hill and I'm more obsessively in love with her than I thought possible for a person to be. Especially me.

Last night, with the muscles of her back under my hands while she lay across my bed in the lamplight, I convinced her to stay with me longer and go to my mom's for New Year's Eve dinner. Our one holiday tradition.

My relationship with my mom has always been complicated, difficult. She opted out of therapy when I was a kid, something that displeased both my dad and my therapist. I knew that it was me that made her sad—though she might hedge that it was my autism, my sensitivities or difficulties with things she saw as simple or straightforward. Things that "shouldn't be so hard."

It got better when she met my stepdad. She and Ethan had exchanged emails after meeting online, which worried me, until he moved a few cities over to live with us. It wasn't long after that they got married.

My dad hated him. Still does, which then makes *me* irate when it's brought up. Having to play the go-between for my parents is a personal hell of mine.

"What?" My brow furrows, eyes darting toward her. I flick on my hazards, parking and unbuckling quickly to shift completely toward her in the seat.

She looks so small, delicate against the black leather. Knees pulled to her chest, scribbled Converse with a hole in the side rubbing squeakily against the other as she chews on her plump bottom lip. She releases it into a pout as she finally glances at me underneath long lashes.

"I don't think they're going to like me."

"They'll love you," I try to assure her. "You met my dad and he adores you."

She nods, but there's no change to the clear worry drawn across her beautiful features. "I just—it's your mom." She huffs a breath and whispers, "I'm not great with moms."

"No?" I ask patiently.

She shakes her head. "My mom is . . . difficult. She was . . . she had a lot of problems."

I nod. I've gathered that, try to shove away the obsessive, intense questions I want to ask her.

"But—I didn't . . . She didn't like me."

Heart aching at her vulnerable quiet confession, I shake my head.

"Then it's her loss," I say. "My mom will be kind. If anything, she'll be too excited. She'll definitely want to hug, since I don't really—" I clear my throat. "I don't hug, really."

"You hug me," she points out. "And your dad."

"It's easier with you," I huff, drawing back from her slightly. I feel overexposed, skin burning a little, but I know I should explain more. "My mom struggles to . . . accommodate me." I grimace. "It's almost like it upsets her. So I try to be better, when I'm around her."

Be better. The words feel wrong.

Dr. Anya and I have spoken about it repeatedly. How I shouldn't have to apologize for the way that I am, especially with my mom. But my mom's life is difficult, and she's perpetually sad. And my dad was the one who broke her heart.

And that's your fault. If you'd just—

I shake my head, reaching for Paloma again to settle myself. We didn't do Christmas presents, but I did take Paloma this morning to swim as a semi-gift. The peace written on her face when she jumped into the pool was enough to sustain me for years to come.

Now, she's dressed in sweatpants, a sweatshirt, and a jacket. I'd even slumped my own beanie over her damp hair, desperate to keep her warmer.

"It's easier with you. Hugging, physical touch. Probably because I trust you."

She blushes.

"Yeah?" There's an innocence to her question that makes my heart punch in my chest. I nod. "Me too. I trust you, too."

"Good," I say, grabbing her hand in mine and kissing her palm as I hold it to my face firmly. "Go shower, get dressed and whatever else. I'll pick you up in an hour?"

"Okay."

"Love you," I say, unbuckling her seatbelt.

"Love you," she whispers back.

> I slept there the night you said 'I think I'm
> falling in love with you,' igniting a great unendurable
> belongingness, like a match in a forest fire.
> I burned so long so quiet you must have wondered
> if I loved you back. I did, I did, I do.

—FROM "THE PILLOWCASE" BY ANNELYSE GELMAN

From Paloma Blake, never received by Bennett Reiner

Bennett,

I'm sorry.

P

CHAPTER 52

THEN: Freshman Year, New Year's Eve, 11:52 p.m.

Bennett

Seven is whining.

He's done it before, when Paloma was having a nightmare—so that he could wake me. But that hasn't happened in a month or so.

And yet—

"Quiet, please," a voice begs.

Seven whines again, louder, his paws soft on the carpet, but his collar jingles. My eyes open, spotting Paloma standing near the door, trying to shove Seven back so that she can . . . leave?

"Paloma?" She pauses, her face shadowed and hard to read in the darkness of my room. "What—what are you doing?"

"I didn't want to wake you," she whispers. "I need to go."

My brow furrows. "Is everything okay? I can drive you wherever, just tell me what's—"

"No, Bennett," she cuts me off, voice harsh. "I'm . . . I can't do this anymore."

Shaking my head, I sputter out, "Talk to me. What's going on? Where are you going?"

"Isn't it obvious?" she asks. My stomach rolls, cheeks flushing in embarrassment because *no*, it's not obvious to me. Maybe she doesn't mean it that way, but I've felt something was off since we left dinner at my mom's and my brain started spiraling the entire ride home. Something is wrong.

"Explain it to me. Why—what's happening?"

I try to run through the last twenty-four hours in my head. The dinner with my mom and stepdad. It was awkward, sure—but not more than my usual dinners alone with them. *What is going on?*

"You wouldn't understand."

"Try me." The words feel more like begging than I mean for them to.

Frustrated, she runs a hand through her tangled blond hair, swooping it up into a knot with an elastic from her wrist

"I can't do *this*." She stresses the last word, gesturing between us. I stay seated on the bed, desperate not to alarm her more than something clearly already has. "Us—this weird thing between us? It has to stop."

"What are you talking about?" My throat hurts, words sharpened like knives against my mouth as I push them out. "I thought . . ."

"Bennett," Paloma says calmly, though her eyes close, hiding from my gaze. "You don't know me. Not really. We've been friends for barely five months? And we think we know each other well enough to say we love each other?"

My stomach sinks, and I can't stop the flinch.

"I . . ."

I know everything I need to know and nothing you say will change my mind.

I have told you more about myself than anyone else before.

I love you. End of story. Please . . . don't go.

Before I can decide on anything to say, she continues.

"This was fun. But the real me? Who I am really? You wouldn't even *recognize* her. And you wouldn't like her."

"Let me decide," I plead, my voice cracking. I'm spiraling as I speak, the careful threads of my control unraveling. "I should get to decide that, right? Show me—whoever you think you are—I'm not going anywhere."

There's a strange sort of smile on her face before tears spill from her brown eyes. My own bleary sight has just focused in the dim light, and I can't stop from inspecting her over and over. As if I can *see* some physical manifestation of whatever this pain is, so I can make it right. Fix it.

"Bennett. We don't know each other. It's been five months," she repeats the words slowly, like I'm a fucking child, and for the first time, I feel *anger* toward her. Red hot, with warnings flashing in the back of my mind still—*wrong, wrong, wrong.*

"Talk to me. Tell me what's going on," I beg, though there's a bitter, choked quality to my voice that I loathe. "Five months? That's enough time—we *know* each other."

"Do we?" Her arms grip either side of her, hugging herself. I try to take another calming breath. I've never felt this out of control around her before; her presences has always centered me, calmed me. Now . . .

I stand, stepping forward because she's crying.

She steps back, hitting the door softly, and I freeze.

"I know you feel that way." Her voice is all placating whispers. "But how much do we actually know? About each other? About what we've been through or what we need?"

"Then tell me." The words are a desperate demand. My feet slip as I fight the urge to step toward her. "We can figure it out, together—"

"Bennett," she snaps, cutting me off. Her voice fills with a sob. "You don't get it. You *can't.*"

You can't. My head spins. *Wrong, wrong. This is wrong and you know it.* I cycle back through the last twenty-four hours—it has to be something that happened.

Your mom. Your dad. Your family.

They think something is wrong with you, they always have. Your mom can barely speak to you without bringing it up—she finally saw the piece of you that you were so desperate to hide.

"Maybe," she says, and though she's whispering, her voice feels too loud. "Maybe we aren't right for each other."

A sharp twist, like a knife shoved deeper into the center of my chest. "You mean *I'm* not right for you, yeah?"

"That's not what I said," Paloma bites out, anger and frustration parting through the tears. Her face is red, all the softened pieces now angular and sharp. Defensive. But beneath it I can almost see a flicker of guilt.

"You didn't have to," I snap back, throat tight. I've never raised my voice at her, I'm desperate *not* to even now, but I can barely stop myself. It all hurts too much, and I feel like I'm losing the slipping control I had over this. Over us. "I get it," I say, raising my hands toward her in surrender, head ducking to hide the pain I know I'm unable to mask from her. "I'm not normal."

Can't hug your mom without flinching?
Can't leave the arena without your goddamn rituals?
Can't have sex with her without needing control?

I rake a hand through my hair and squeeze my fists at my side, voice raw and broken.

"I thought you wanted me."

The words are vulnerable but covered in the sting of my own fury. She flinches, back hitting the door again. Fireworks burst in the background—loud and abrasive against my ears, illuminating Paloma's face over and over like a spectacle spotlight from my bedroom window.

"Bennett—please—"

"It's fine," I cut her off. "It's too difficult for you, yeah? It's—I'm—" A frustrated noise leaves my throat "You're right. Someone like you could never love someone like me, right?"

"Bennett," she pleads, voice heady and intoxicating. I want to apologize and beg her to stay—but I can't do this. I *can't*. It'll kill me—and I'm not going to get any better. If anything, my obsession with *her* has only gotten worse with every day that she's near me, every strand of her hair over my fingers, every piece of her ingrained in me.

She doesn't deny the words.

"Just go, Paloma."

Seven whines, standing between us, like he's unsure of what to do.

"Go."

This time, it's almost a shout, my control slipping.

She does, the door swinging violently shut as she sprints out.

The rush of adrenaline leaves me just as quicky, making my legs shaky and weak. My stomach sinks, my body following as I melt to the floor, back against my bed. *Wrong, wrong, wrong.*

Heart racing and fingers shaking, I reach for my phone and call her. To apologize.

It goes straight to her voicemail.

I call her again. And again. Obsessively, trying over and over to reach her. Fireworks continue on, making me flinch with every burst of noise.

Stop. Stop. Make it stop.

Seven sits almost entirely in my lap, pressing his weight on my thumping heart. A deep well forms in my throat, a sob ready to rip free, but I try to hold it back.

Hours pass. I only know because I see the sunlight stream through my windows. I hear the front door open and slam again as Rhys calls for me.

I don't answer.

After a long moment, he steps into my doorway, eyes widening. "Ben? Are you all right?"

"F-fine."

Clearly, I'm not fine. The pain is so intense I almost feel numb.

"What can I do?" Rhys asks. He doesn't pester me with further questions, doesn't try to discover what's wrong. Only sits by my side patiently as I ask him to stay with me.

We call out of practice. He stays with me all day.

"I don't know," I manage to push out. My hands feel numb and cold as I flex and curl them, as if it will help. Everything feels glacial and raw.

Rhys nods. "That's okay." He hesitates a moment longer, then asks, "Do you want me to hug you?"

I nod, tears slipping down my cheeks as I break in my best friend's arms, tight around me to slow my erratic heart.

She's gone.

CHAPTER 53

THEN: Freshman Year, January

Bennett

Three days later and she's still in my lungs.

Every breath I take is a burst of juniper and sea breeze, like the first scent of the ocean, until I can't be in my goddamn room anymore. I try staying at my dad's, but it doesn't make it any better.

In some ways its worse, the memory of her on my bed, in my room, the words *I love you* between my teeth. My poetry against her skin. I can't escape her—until it's almost suffocating.

"If you want to talk—"

"I said I'm fine."

We exchange the same angry, pain-fuel words twice more before I leave.

. . .

She's not here. In the locker room alone, I'm frozen, scratching the back of my scalp, tapping my foot measuredly against the floor.

She's sick. She's just out because she's sick.

She's not avoiding you. You can talk to her and everything will go back to the way it was.

The repetitive thoughts are so soothing and completely enthralling that I barely notice anything else.

It takes me two hours to get through my post-practice routine.

• • •

One month of pure adrenaline and a pathetic number of attempts to call her. Then a month of panic attacks and seeing my therapist twice a week because my compulsions get bad enough that I have trouble leaving the house.

Then it's March, the snow sticking heavily to the ground and the barren wasteland of the Northeast finally starts reflecting my soul.

We're at a bar, the entire team celebrating before regionals begins. Rhys stands with me in a corner of the front room, as close to outside as we can be. The speakers are loud, a cover band playing an old U2 song. It's too loud, too crowded, and I'm just about to tell Rhys I'm going home when I spot her.

At first, I'm convinced it can't be her. Bleached, almost white-blond hair in bouncy curls, eyes smoky with shadow, and lips in a cruel twist of a smirk.

"Shit," I mumble, standing. I've had a beer or two; I'm not really drunk by any means, but I'm a lightweight despite my size, unused to the effects of alcohol.

"You okay?" Rhys asks. I nod and step away from him, mumbling something about the bathroom as I watch her walk toward the back bar.

She's alone, but I'm not sure if it makes me feel better or worse. Her tight jeans and strapless chocolate brown corset draw the eyes of everyone around her—her cleavage pushed up high. She's so goddamn beautiful, so perfect, and yet no one looks anywhere away from her chest.

I clench my fists.

Some guy approaches her and she leans in to speak with him. I know I should turn around, leave—

He tucks her hair behind her ear. *He touched her hair.*

My vision swirls with fury and hatred, so heady I feel out of control, on the edge of an attack. I want to step in, to remove his hand—maybe cut it off and cuff her to my side.

Instead, I run to throw up in the dingy bar bathroom. I wash my mouth out in the sink and try desperately to gain back control over my own body.

But when I leave, she's there.

Her. Only her—forever.

Some sound comes from my throat, a punch of breath but louder. I try to memorize her again, eyes obsessively scanning her over and over. She's so beautiful my chest aches.

"Paloma?"

She looks up at me. But her eyes make me pause. Red and watery, dazed as she slowly takes me in. She bites her lip, head tipping to the side.

"Are you . . . Paloma, are you drunk?" *She doesn't drink. This is wrong. Help her—*

She stumbles into the wall. "I'm fine."

"Come on, I'm taking you home."

"No," she snaps out, eyes lighting up.

For a moment, I don't know her. She's not the same, and every second of this moment feels like a splinter in my skin. Seeing her again but not really seeing her, my Paloma—it's like loss.

Like grief.

"Leave me alone," she says. Her voice drops further. "Please."

The last word is a whimpered plea and it runs across my skin like water, cooling down my surprisingly overheated temper.

"P," I breathe, and because I can't stop myself—"Please, let me take you home, love."

The word pours from my lips. She flinches away from me, eyes going dark before she tips them down, away from my beseeching gaze.

"Bennett, stop."

"You don't drink, Paloma." I seethe, temper rising again. "Something is wrong."

"You don't know me. I'm—I'm not—"

"Please just let me take care of you." It slips out before I can think, before I can even *realize* what I've asked.

"I don't need you," she spits. The words are angry, like we're both feeding off the pain of this moment in this stupid dark hallway. "Fuck. Off."

She stumbles away from me, eyes wide. As if she's just as shocked by her own words.

I watch her leave again. Somehow, I think it hurts worse.

• • •

We win Frozen Four.

I get black-out drunk and hate myself when I wake up in bed with someone new. Two things I've never done before, all in one night. I check my phone obsessively all day and night, cleaning and mowing the lawn despite the frozen ground, avoiding the worried looks from Rhys, the only one to notice how many of my compulsions I'm indulging in.

I don't sleep.

Paloma shows up to the party at the Hockey Dorms when we get back. I watch her quietly from my usual corner spot, heart aching. I'm desperate for her, even if it's only like this.

Did you see me on TV? I wonder. *Do you miss me? Do you long for me, too?*

She finds someone to dance with. I call a car home.

I don't see her again for six months.

CHAPTER 54

NOW

Bennett

"Ben?"

I'm not sure how many times Rhys has said my name before I realize I'm in my closet, still half naked. I don't know how long I've been standing here, lost in my head. Everything's felt fuzzy lately, hazy around the edges.

I grab a shirt off its hanger and slip it on, then reach for my phone—like I might call Paloma again—before pocketing it. *Let her have her night. She's with Sadie. She's fine.*

She's fine. I'm fine. Everything is okay.

"Sorry." I shake my head, eyeing Rhys as he slips on his belt.

His mouth opens, but before he can speak, a little voice calls out, "Can you please help?"

Liam's eyes are wide as he opens the door to my bedroom where Rhys has decidedly made himself comfortable.

The youngest of Sadie's brothers is small and sweet, but usually rambunctious. Right now, however, he's frustrated, seeking out the comforting presence of my best friend. He holds out his hands to Rhys with a little navy tie with a pattern of wolves printed on it. Rhys kneels in front of him with a smile, talking quietly, softly to the kid as he knots the tie for him.

My gaze tracks movement at my door again—this time, the middle child of the Brown family, Oliver. He's fully dressed, but his tie is stretched out and knotted incorrectly—and he keeps pulling at it.

"He reminds me of you," Rhys confided in me one day, when he realized Oliver was doing his homework at the counter on the mornings he stayed with us, enjoying the quiet time with only me, and sometimes Ro, downstairs.

I heard everything he didn't say, too.

"Oliver," I say, half in greeting, half to garner his attention. "Lose the tie."

He furrows his brow—he's Sadie's twin in most ways, dark hair, freckles and pale skin, gray cat-like eyes. He's distrusting and skeptical like her, too. But it only takes him a moment to realize I'm not wearing one either—I never do—before he pulls his off and tucks it into his pocket with a quiet, "Thanks."

Oliver comes to collect his brother, telling him their sister is waiting for him to send a photo of their outfits.

"Tell your sister we're leaving soon," Rhys calls to the boys, ushering them out and leaning against the door after he closes us in.

I watch him, eyes guarded and cautious.

"We should talk."

"About what?" I say, cheeks flushing as I step to the other side of the room for my suit jacket, then into the bathroom, checking my hair and washing my hands.

"About Paloma," he starts, and my eyes shut involuntarily. "Listen, I'm sorry—"

"Don't," I snap, before pressing my palms to the counter and hanging my head for a minute. I've dreaded this conversation, but I know Rhys enough to know he wouldn't be able to put it off for much longer. My best friend is a good person who cares deeply—but he's also a martyr. And it's the exact reason I never confided in him about Paloma, especially after they dated.

I don't like to think about it now, but I know that as much as it pains me, it hurts Rhys, too. The guilt of the betrayal he feels responsible for is blatantly painted across his face.

"Bennett," he chokes. His arms are crossed, and he stands barely a foot away from me in the doorway, watching me through the bathroom mirror. "If I had known..."

"I know," I whisper, eyes closing tightly. "You couldn't have known. I didn't tell you."

He nods, and I know it's not enough to rid him of his remorse. But for now, it has to be.

Rhys only gives me another moment before he sighs heavily and asks, "How long have you two..."

"It's recent, us dating again."

"Again," he huffs. "Bennett, you're my best friend. I know you, so I'll ask again. How long have you been in love with Paloma Blake?"

"Since freshman year. Fall semester." Probably since I first laid eyes on her in the hockey locker room. "A long time," I say, sending him a bitter smile.

"Jesus Christ," Rhys mutters, hands rubbing at his eyes. "No wonder Seven lost it that night."

My brow furrows as I tilt my head up.

"What night?"

"You don't remember?" He laughs and shakes his head. "I think it was... spring? Sophomore year? We threw that big party here for the first time—nearly got out of hand with all the people who came."

I barely remember the night he's talking about. I'd never been much of a drinker, but I had indulged that night. Too much—and I'd *hated* it.

"Anyway—Paloma was there. I remember, she was by herself, and I think she was wasted, but some asshole wouldn't leave her alone.

And I was about to intervene, before your big ass dog slammed past me and *tackled* the guy. You really don't remember this?"

Eyes wide, I shake my head.

"Seven attacked someone?"

"It was a mess—I can't believe you don't remember this. Although now that I'm thinking about it, I think Seven was only out because Freddy helped walk you upstairs to your room and you both passed out in your bed."

The smile that pushes at my lips is mild embarrassment but also just a warm feeling of friendship. That might be the closest, at least physically, Freddy and I ever were.

"But yeah, Seven just went *after* this guy, barking—and I'd never heard him bark before. He was growling and yelping. And then after I pulled on his collar to get him off, he just collapsed himself on top of Paloma where she was sitting. I think he slept there with her that night—I mean, I *know* you remember us all waking up to fifty-something people in our house."

He's right. I do remember that absolute nightmare of anxiety and terror. Rhys nearly had to lock me in his bedroom—the one room somehow untouched by chaos—while he conducted everything.

"It just . . . makes a lot of sense now." He shakes his head. "And I'm sorry. I never wanted to hurt you. With Paloma or by shutting you out during my panic attack stuff. I just . . . I'm sorry."

"It's okay." I grasp his shoulder. "All good."

"Is it?" he asks, stopping me before I can pass him by. He's quieter, even though we're alone in the room together. "You . . . you skipped practice. Twice. That's not . . . the last time you did that was with me, freshman year, when you were drowning and wouldn't tell me why."

I don't say anything. I barely move.

"Was it her?" His voice drops, softer. "Was that night, New Year's Eve, when I found you having a panic attack—was that because of her?"

"It wasn't her fault," I insist. "We'd just broken up and I wasn't . . . I didn't take it well."

I'm still not taking it well—I've never gotten answers to that night, but I'm not going to ask about it now.

"You're my best friend, Ben," he says. "I just want to make sure you aren't going to get hurt like that again."

Bitterness and resentment gnaw at me. I jerk my shoulder from his grip, eyes dipping down toward his feet. "Yeah? Well, at least you'll know if *I'm* the one hurting. Considering I don't shut you out."

He flinches like I've hit him, but don't have it in me to regret it.

"Ben—"

"It's fine," I say, waving my hand as I step past him and grasp my door. "It's all good, Rhys." I smile over my shoulder at him.

It *is* all good, at least to me. The past is in the past and I'm tired of everyone wanting me to focus there, when Rhys has Sadie and is okay now; when Paloma is *here* now—and happy.

That's enough.

It has to be.

Rhys and I will be fine; we always are. But there are times when I wonder what it was that broke the constant chain I thought would link us forever—the hit he took last year, or the one he dealt me junior year.

CHAPTER 55

THEN: Junior Year, November

Bennett

"You have to try."

There's an irritation to my dad's voice that isn't usually there. He fiddles with his silverware anxiously before swirling his Americano around in the glass mug and swigging it down in one go.

"It's not because of—"

"It is, and you know it," he snaps, but I let it roll off me.

I have a date tonight. And just the thought of it is enough to have me spiraling into a panic only Adam Reiner seems able to pull me from—despite the tension that's only festered lately, heavier now as I'm back at Waterfell for junior year.

"It's one date, Ben. Why don't you ask Rhys to bring a girl and make it a double date?"

I'd thought about it, several times, but hadn't worked up the nerve. Rhys didn't know about *her*, my first girlfriend—and letting him in on *why* I needed a buffer on this damn date with a girl from my class would only lead to more questions than I could answer.

"I might," I say, but my dad is distracted again. Normally, this would irritate me, but he seems . . . upset.

He looks over my shoulder again just as a figure moves into my periphery.

It's Anna Koteskiy, pulling her strawberry blond hair from beneath the neck of the deep blue overcoat she's just shrugged on. My dad runs his eyes over her like he's checking her over, as if she's just escaped certain death.

"Bennett, Adam," she greets us both. "Surprised to see you here."

"Are you all right?"

My dad's voice is soft but adamant. I quietly sink back, sipping my water.

"Fine," she says, smiling at me again before turning slightly narrowed eyes to him. "I take it Max let you know what I was doing today."

"Possibly," he mutters. "I take it you're okay, then?"

"No need for you to beat anyone up this time." She smiles, but there's a softness as she rests her hand on my dad's shoulder, close to his neck.

A long moment of silence draws out while they seem to have an entire conversation with each other, lost in memories of their youth.

"I'm okay," she offers quietly.

My dad closes his eyes and huffs a quick heavy breath. "Good."

"Good to see you both," she says, before the click of her heels on the marble flooring signal her departure.

My dad's eyes follow her, a desperation in the way he watches her. It's not the first time I've clocked it—but it's the most blatant I've seen it. As I get older, I can spot the aching familiarity all too well.

My dad looks . . . tired, I realize. Like he's lived a thousand lives and never had one where he was truly happy. There's an ache in my heart again as I watch him more closely.

Mirrors. Doomed to love from afar.

. . .

"He's not usually late," I stammer, fidgeting a little in the booth.

It was the only seating option they had, but it puts Hannah too close to me, especially for the first date.

The restaurant is crowded and loud, cacophonous noise echoing off the high ceilings. I check my watch again—fifteen minutes late. *Goddamn it, Rhys.*

I grab my phone to text him, beyond the point of being relatively polite, before a soft, low voice speaks.

"I hate being late." The words seem to carry over the other noise, the soft, low voice igniting goose bumps across my exposed forearms.

Throat dry, I manage the courage to look up—

—only to have the wind knocked out of me by the sight of my best friend ushering Paloma Blake into our booth.

My Paloma Blake.

Her hair is beautiful, the *real* color I always suspected lurked beneath the faded brown—a bright, vibrant blond in bouncy curls. But I barely recognize the rest of her. A full face of makeup, accentuating her deep brown eyes and pouty dark pink lips, which are the same dusty rose as her tank top, which puts all her golden glowing skin on display. She's tanner, especially for the winter, and I can't stop my eyes from dropping to the tight material pushing up her chest.

God, she's beautiful. She's also a goddamn walking wet dream. I don't know why I'm surprised Rhys found her—*of course* he did. She is . . . everything. Good and kind and brilliant.

They're two of the best people I've ever met.

Admitting they might deserve each other was my nightmare years before, when I thought she'd be only mine, forever. Now, it feels like I'm being stabbed under this table.

I smile at them both, trying to shove back the gnawing pain in my chest.

"Bennett?" Rhys asks, and I realize they've been talking. "You know Paloma, right?"

Know her? Sure. If by know her, he means that she is half of my soul. The tumultuous sea to my constant shore.

"Bennett is my best friend." Rhys smiles, all glittering and golden, arm sliding gently around Paloma's shoulders. The move is casual, gentle and effortless. Like he doesn't have to plan it ahead, practice the movement of his arm so that it's seamless.

Touching is easy for him. It makes me sick with envy.

"Best friend," Paloma repeats, voice the same semi-sarcastic sound even when she doesn't mean it. "You never mentioned him. Ever."

Except, she isn't reprimanding Rhys—she's talking to *me*.

Her eyes are locked on mine, almost pleading, and I can't look away. My stomach hurts, the semi-assuredness of *she didn't know* warring with the more sinister sentiment of *would it really matter if she did? She deserves someone better. Someone like Rhys.*

"Sorry." Rhys smirks. "He's too handsome. *And* he can cook—didn't want him to charm you away before I got a chance to."

I laugh, almost too loud, but my eyes feel like they're burning. Rhys turns his grin toward me, a grateful look in his eye, as if I'm playing the perfect wingman like I never have before.

Can't you feel my heart, Rhys? You're pulling it from my chest.

"I'm Hannah," my date introduces herself. "Nice to meet you both."

"You too," Rhys says. Paloma and I still haven't broken eye contact. "How did you two meet?"

I can feel Hannah smiling at me, but I don't speak, the words catching on my tongue, so she tells it.

"We're both pre-law. We had Mass Media Law together last semester and we were project partners." Paloma huffs a breath. I look away from her. "And then we're in another class this semester, so . . ." Hannah shrugs. "I'd been waiting for him to ask me out, but eventually I just took the initiative myself."

Paloma blinks and rips her gaze from mine, smiling more like a predator than prey now.

"Way to go," she offers, before reaching for one of the empty glasses and the large jar of water. She's barely touched it before Rhys bats her hand away and pours it for her. "Almost meant to be, huh?"

"What about you?" Hannah asks, biting lightly on her lip. She's beautiful, dressed tonight in a floral dress and cardigan, auburn hair swept up into a ribbon-bound ponytail. "What's your major?"

"I'm undecided." Paloma takes a distracted gulp of water.

"Let's make a deal, then," she whispers, words soft against my heated, sticky skin. "I fill out my declaration as sports management. You fill yours out for poetry."

I smile and shake my head. "That's not a major."

"Okay, then creative writing. Or literature. And then you can take all the poetry classes and have it as your minor." Her laugh is intoxicating, as is the feel of her when she collapses back on my chest, the burst of post-sex energy she usually displays finally giving out. "I'll make it mine, too, so we can take the classes together."

"Yeah?" I ask, heart thumping beneath her ear. I brush a hand through her hair gently.

"Yeah. I don't want you swapping poems with anyone else."

Another huff of a laugh, before I pull my head up off the pillow to kiss her head and pull her closer. "Never. Those are only for you."

We stare across the table at each other again, two halves of an unfulfilled promise.

A hand tapping my shoulder has me jumping in my seat like a live wire, knee slamming into the hard wooden oak.

"Sorry." Hannah laughs, nervously eyeing Rhys and Paloma before ducking her head closer to my ear. "I just needed to get out, for the restroom."

"No, I'm sorry," I say, exiting the booth so she can scoot out. I rub at my knee for a moment while standing up, matching my date's smile as best I can, before sliding back in.

Brow furrowed, Rhys settles his forearms on the table and leans toward me. "You good? Is it from last night?"

"What happened last night?" Paloma blurts, cheeks blushing a little when she realizes how loud she's asked.

Her eyes roam my face, then look down at the table like she can somehow see through it and my pants to the bruise on my knee.

"Bennett's our goalie," Rhys explains unnecessarily. "Some asshole from Yale hit him last night while he was in a bad position—"

"Butterfly," I say, knowing Paloma too well not to explain. "But I'm fine. Just tweaked it."

She's upset, clearly, and something in that makes me feel better. But it's like putting a Band-Aid on a fatal wound.

Rhys settles back against the wood of the bench seat before he tilts his head down to kiss her cheek gently. Every touch they share is familiar, like this isn't a first date for them. And maybe it's not.

I know my best friend isn't the *sleep around* type of guy. I know Rhys Koteskiy is the three-date-rule golden boy that girls don't just thirst over but romanticize—and accurately. He's always been easily romantic and loving to the few girls he's dated.

So, as much as it feels like a fist to the gut, there is a comfort in the fact that I *know* how Rhys treats Paloma. That he walks her to her dorm and always gets her car door for her. That he foots the bill for any date. That he would never pressure her for something she didn't want to give.

Bittersweet. I finally understand the word.

I don't go home with Hannah—I don't go home at all. I find a bar, drink too heavily, and try to drown out the sight of Rhys's hands on Paloma's skin. The sight of my father looking toward Anna Koteskiy.

Is this some kind of Reiner curse?

Burying my sadness and anger, I go home with someone I don't know. The alcohol makes my head swim enough that it doesn't bother me. I try to focus on my hands in her hair, the tight control I exude over her body—the way I want so desperately.

But her face bleeds into soft doe-brown eyes and brighter, voluptuous hair. Until it's Paloma beneath my grip, letting me hold her tightly.

Shame eats at me until I stop prematurely, apologizing and kissing the woman's forehead. I don't know her name and she doesn't know mine, but she lets me shower and offers to call me a car home.

I choose to walk, hoping I won't make it all the way.

Nearly sure that the pain and anxiety will devour me first.

there are no poems anymore—no words
only the memories tangled like strands of hair that I can't
    get out
of my shower, my pillowcase—
only relentless memory woven into every facet of life;
    the endless pain;
the loss of her

I try to breathe. And only salt water and juniper are in my
    lungs
I don't want to write anymore

—"UNTITLED" BY BENNETT REINER

CHAPTER 56

NOW

Bennett

As with everything the Koteskiys do, the charity gala is beautiful: a careful balance of wealth, to garner the monetary support their asking for, and focus on the actual groups they're here to help.

Anna, Oliver, and Liam are at the greeting area. She gives me a tight hug and kiss to my cheek before fawning over her son.

"There are two lovely girls in there waiting for you, gentlemen." She smiles, eyes twinkling as she nods toward the grand entrance to the main ballroom. "Tell them both thank you again, for helping me."

Rhys and I both perk up, heading in that direction like following the North Star. I grin slightly at the way my best friend takes off in a jog to swoop his girlfriend up from behind, her squeak echoing in the semi-barren area as she slaps at him.

"God, hotshot. You need a collar with a bell, I swear," she snips, elbowing him lightly, but I can see her cheeks flush as he whispers to her.

"You wanna keep me on a leash, *kotonyok*?" He presses another kiss to her temple. "Fine by me."

"Where's Paloma?" I ask, before they can forget I'm still here.

"Right over there," Sadie offers, jutting her chin toward the other side of the room, where a curvy blonde is resetting the silverware on one of the gaudy tables.

The navy silk of the dress moves like water over the curved lines of her body, strapless so it shows off her shoulders, a long piece of matching midnight navy silk wrapped around her neck like a scarf and hanging down her back nearly to the floor.

She turns, hair bouncing loose in buoyant curls around her face, held back by a simple black pin on one side.

"Bennett," she breathes, eyes warmer as she looks at me. "Hey."

"You look beautiful," I say, voice catching. My fingers reach out and touch the fabric of her dress where it lays across the generous curve of her hip. "I missed you."

"You too," she says, stepping back and turning back to the table—almost anxiously.

"You okay?"

She nods. "Just finishing up." Paloma nibbles on her bottom lip and pulls her fingers in. "Do you think Mrs. Koteskiy will think this looks nice?"

"I'm positive she told you to call her Anna," I whisper, stepping up behind her. "She'll love it. She'd love it no matter what you did, you know. She's—she's a good mom."

"You're really close?" she asks. "To the Koteskiys? Rhys and his family."

The tone of her voice means something more than she's saying, but I can't figure it out; can't quite read it or see any of her expression to guide me as she's still turned away.

"Yes," I offer. "Rhys and I grew up together since birth, and so Max and Anna were like my second set of parents. It was . . . especially good during the divorce. I stayed with them sometimes. And—and Anna has always been more accepting of me than my own mother," I add the last words quickly, as if I can skim over that part of my history as well.

Paloma frowns, her head tipping over one delicate shoulder. "I'm sorry, you know—that your mom makes things difficult for you."

I shake my head. "I'm the one who—"

"No, Bennett. You aren't." Her tone is harsher than I'm expecting. "She's your mother. That's not how mothers should behave."

I don't press her with the questions I want to ask—about her own family, her mother. She's mentioned so few details and all of them seem to make her more upset, so I push it away from the front of my mind.

"You sure this looks even?" she asks, worrying her bottom lip. "I want Anna to think it looks okay."

"She'll love it. Come here, P." The command works like a charm, bringing her body against mine before she turns in my arms. Her heels bring her closer to my mouth, so it's easier to kiss her skin, her lips, her hair—careful not to mess up even a strand.

"You look beautiful," she says, eyes glimmering. "Very elegant and regal. Like a prince."

It should be a teasing sentiment, but it feels genuine. Real. I stand straighter.

"Hey," another voice invades our space: Sadie, readjusting her heels with a hand for balance on the chair beside her. "I'm gonna go wash my hands—do you wanna come with?"

Paloma presses a quick kiss to my cheek and nods, stepping away to follow Sadie across the ballroom. I watch them exit—then pathetically watch the darkened hallway, like she might immediately reappear.

A hand firmly wraps around my forearm, yanking me closer to the wall. My dad, I realize with a shock. He's dressed in a black tux and bowtie, curls slicked back with gel, eyes dark.

"We need to talk."

I shrug out of his hold but stay close. "Then talk."

His voice drops lower, a whispered hiss. "You want to tell me why I got a no-show charge from your therapist?"

Damn it. A no-show charge alert for him, because it wouldn't be covered by our insurance—an alert to tell him I've missed therapy three times in a row.

I keep my face impassive, careful with every twitch of muscle, because my dad has always been the person in every room who understood me most. If I even *blink* oddly, he'll pick up on it. Taking a sip from my glass, I dip my chin.

"I'll pay you back."

Like lighting a match, his expression boils over—though it's more hurt than anger spreading across the lines of his face.

"Pay me back," he mutters, almost breathless. "You've got to be fucking joking. What the hell is going on, Ben? Why are you missing therapy?'

"I'm fine."

"You're *not*," he snaps. "Talk to me. Please, Ben—"

"Honestly, you're the last person I want to talk to right now, Dad." My words are cutting, harsh, but I turn away before I can see the blows land. "Besides—"

"Adam Reiner," yet another voice interrupts. I raise a hand to the bridge of my nose, rubbing my thumb there as a headache starts to form.

The newest Waterfell coach is standing opposite us, invading our circle with a small redheaded girl—Paloma's roommate, Lily, on the arm of a well-dressed young man that I don't recognize.

My dad's brow furrows, and he eyes me for a moment longer before straightening with a sharp smile. "Sorry, do we know each other?"

"Christopher LaBlanc," he introduces himself, one hand on his chest and the other wrapped around a wine glass stem. "I'm the new assistant coach for the Wolves; more of a favor to Harris than anything else, but"—he shrugs with a wide grin, all gleaming teeth—"here I am."

"LaBlanc, right," my dad says, reaching his hand out to shake my coach's already outstretched palm. "Good to officially meet you. You're back to coaching, then?"

"I like to have my hands in every part of the business, you know."

With the quiet lull in conversation, I nod toward Paloma's roommate. "Lily, good to see you."

She looks mildly startled that I've acknowledged her at all. "Hi, Bennett."

LaBlanc looks between us. "I had no idea you knew my daughter, Reiner."

The reality is that I'm only putting together the connection just now, but I nod anyways. "Her roommate is my girlfriend," I say to my coach, before my eyes scan back to Lily. "Paloma's here, too, and I'm sure she'd love to see you."

Her eyes dart to her dad, as if asking permission, but he shakes his head sharply.

"Stay here," he says, voice different than I've heard it before. "You can talk to her when you're back at your apartment."

My dad furrows his eyebrows, watching carefully.

"Lily?" I ask again, but she only bites her lip and stares directly at the breast pocket of my suit jacket.

"I'll talk to her later," Lily says, before her eyes turn back to the polished floor. "At home, I mean."

I offer her a smile and nod my head; Lily is important to Paloma, kind to her, one of her only friends, I think. And therefore, she's important to me.

Excusing myself, I turn to head across the room.

"Ben," my dad calls, careful with his tone. "We still need to talk."

I nod, but don't offer much else. There are too many people—and with the ballroom filling more and more with guests, I feel a desperate edge to my need for an escape.

Crossing the ballroom quickly, I head down the hallway to the men's room—my shoulder slamming into someone as I stomp forward.

"Sorry," I offer.

Holden shakes his head, eyes downcast. "It's fine. I'm—you're good, Reiny."

He stalks off without another word. I want to focus on him, to ask and make sure he's all right, but I *can't*. My heart is still racing, the threads of panic making themselves more known.

I just need a few minutes to calm myself.

Turning on the sink, I wet my hands with cold water and pat my cheeks, carefully dabbing the back of my neck while I box-breathe to calm down. The anxiety feels like it crept up out of nowhere, but it's undeniably strong. Maybe it's been building for weeks. Still, I manage to get it under control.

In for four. Hold for four. Out for four. Hold for four.
Again. Again.

Slowly, the haze around my vision disappears. My heart feels calmer, slower in rhythm—back to my baseline.

Everything is fine.

The creak of a stall door echoes in the otherwise empty space.

"Shit," I mutter, eyes up, clocking Toren Kane through the mirror.

He's in all-black like an idealized version of Hades himself—his button up slightly undone and tie hanging loose around his tattooed neck, and matching onyx suit jacket slung over one shoulder. His russet skin is bright under the warm lighting of the chandeliers in the polished marble bathroom, making his eyes seem like pools of pure gold—striking and unsettling like always.

"You good?" he asks, no teasing or biting tone. Just mild concern, brow furrowed.

"Fine," I say, washing my hands.

He smirks, his free hand pressing a thumb along his bottom lip, the silver of his rings glinting. "Yeah?" He snorts. "You and Blake are both *terrible* liars."

I don't say a word. Don't acknowledge anything.

He takes the silence as an invitation. "Sounded like you weren't okay—"

"I don't need your help," I snap. "I'm fine. Leave it, Kane."

Before he can add anything, I spin on my heel and leave the bathroom, feeling moderately worse than before.

CHAPTER 57

NOW

Paloma

He's so perfect, brutally handsome. Raised to be exactly this, a suit-clad gladiator in some make-believe boardroom. Under the twinkling starlight, I watch as he nods and sips a glass of sparkling grape juice, talking with adults twice his age as if he's the one with the power.

Bennett Reiner is gorgeous, strong and steady. Hair styled perfectly, suit pressed, no tie because he hates the way it feels around his neck. I'm not sure where he found a suit so expensive looking to fit his massive frame.

But he's perfect.

He's kind and careful, gentle with everyone. He's steady and unmoving, trustworthy. Someone I know I can lean on, and he'll always, *always* hold me up. Bennett Reiner has taken care of me when it yielded him nothing. Carried me home from my worst nights, held me through nightmares, fought my demons without knowing who they were, the extent of the damage they did to me.

He chose me. He loves *me*.

And I'm just . . . *this*, forever. It only takes the small reminder to reignite the fear that I can't have him, not really.

I might be beautiful, but it's nothing more than this body. And being beautiful is the thing that's hurt me most.

Bennett exits the conversation he's engaged in, then eyes me and struts to my side without a moment's pause, his hand gracing my hip so he can pull me completely into the shelter of his body.

"You okay?" he asks.

I open my mouth to reply, but pause because I spot someone first. Graying blond hair, slender build, severe all-seeing gaze.

My body flashes cold.

"Why is your ex-stepdad here?"

"Oh—I forgot," Bennett says, sipping at the sparkling cider. "My mom decided to bring him as her date. I guess they've grown close again recently. She told me she thinks they'll be getting remarried." He presses a kiss to my temple and hugs me tighter. "The year of rekindling, huh?"

I practically swallow my tongue, tripping backward—except Bennett is holding me up. I don't stumble.

My eyes trail Bennett's open, gentle expression again, trying to memorize the way he looks now so I don't forget it. *Just in case.* Despite every layer of growth I've had, I'm almost too ready to run.

"Are you sure you're okay?" He leans down to kiss the shell of my ear and then press his nose to my hair. "We can leave whenever you want."

I shake my head. "I'm fine." The lie slips painfully from my mouth. "I'm going to get some water. Promise you'll be right here when I get back?"

"I won't move," he vows.

My hand grabs for my purse off the back of my chair, reaching for my phone to call Alessia. Just for a pep talk. Or maybe a getaway car.

I start toward the other side of the grand ballroom and spot Anna Koteskiy with two young boys. She's kneeling in her beautiful dress, fixing the tie on the younger one while the older of the boys surveys the room. He looks like a mini bodyguard.

Smiling lightly, I relax a little. *Ethan will not scare me this time.*

Things are different now. Look at Sadie and Rhys. You can have this life.

"You deserve better," I mumble to myself under my breath, tucking my phone back into my clutch.

A shoulder bumps mine, followed by a quiet, "Excuse me," from a taunting voice I know too well. Ethan Marks, shoving into me intentionally as he makes his way over to the bar, right toward the only solo patron there.

I do a double take, scanning over the girl anxiously twittering at the bar, where Ethan has just stepped up arguably too close to her.

God fucking dammit.

My weird little roommate, Lily.

She's teetering on her too tall heels, but the girl barely reaches five feet. She's dressed in long white silk, stark against her pinkened pale skin. The fabric clings softly to the thin shape of her, built more stick-straight and column-esque in contrast to my curves. The only thing holding the fabric up is the halter tie around her delicate neck, trailing down her back a little unevenly, like she tied it herself. But it leaves most of her pale back exposed, and just as she starts to falter on her heels again, Ethan moves his hand to the low pointed dip of her dress.

I'm moving before I can stop myself.

I can't hear what he says, only that he's laughing in that same condescending way.

"Is that right? Lovely girl—"

"Don't talk to her." I almost growl the words. My eyes lock on Lily and I pull her wrist so she stumbles in closer to me. "Lily, what are you doing?" I snap, a little gruffer than I mean to be with her.

"I just—I wanted to order a drink. But I don't—"

Her eyes widen, welling a little, and my chest tightens. Still, I'm too anxious to apologize.

"She wants a sparkling rosé," I order for her. The bartender nods, a look of relief flitting my way as he pours her drink into a tall, thin flute.

Lily beams at me, anxiety forgotten as she takes a drink of the bubbling pink liquid. "Thank you. I was looking for you. I didn't know you were coming, but I'm so happy you're here." Her words are bright, eyes starry as she looks at me.

Ethan steps in closer, opening his mouth to speak, and my shoulders climb to my ears.

"Excuse me," a deep timbre rumbles. A tall figure looms over Lily as Adam Reiner steps up next to Ethan, nearly casting the smaller man in shadow. My heart turns over in my chest, thumping hard and fast.

"Everything okay?" Adam asks.

"Fine. Good to see you, Adam," Ethan grimaces, gulping down his drink. My body steps closer to Adam, a comfort in knowing Bennett's dad won't let anything happen.

"Girls," Adam says, turning to where I'm half in front of Lily. "I think your dates are looking for you."

He's clearly rescuing us, but I take the out.

Pulling on my roommate's hand, I smile politely at Adam and waltz backward away from them.

I eye Lily. "You brought a date?"

"Oh, um, yeah. My dad made me. He doesn't like me very much." The statement is said on a laugh, but her eyes wander away from my face, trailing to my cleavage in her usual way that makes me want to smirk.

"Where is he?"

"What?"

"Your date. Which one is he?"

She straightens, looking over her shoulder and tilting her head. A handsome, reedy man in a charcoal gray suit stands by one of the farther tables, chatting animatedly with Coach LaBlanc. The guy looks mid- to late twenties if I had to guess, which surprises me, but I don't say anything.

She takes another sip of her sparkling rosé, and I catch the glint of a massive diamond on her right hand. "Jesus, Lily—you're gonna blind me with that thing."

Her eyes go wide and she follows my gaze to her own hand with a deep blush. "Oh—yeah. It's big."

It's gaudy for sure—and also kind of ugly. It definitely doesn't look like anything she'd wear.

"My dad made me wear it," she says with a shrug, finishing off her glass before letting one of the passing waiters take it.

It's a brief reminder that this is the girl who told me to "pay whatever I wanted" for a nice townhouse in downtown Waterfell. Whose outfits I've suspected would cost more than a semester's tuition any given day. Coach LaBlanc has Reiner kind of money, if this jewelry is anything to go by.

"I'm gonna go hide in the bathroom," Lily mumbles. "Do you wanna come?"

My eyes gloss over the circle of Bennett and his friends and parents. *Running away hasn't gotten you anywhere good. Stand and face it.*

"I'm going to go back to Bennett," I say. My hand rests over her pale, bare arm and squeezes. "Do you want to come with me?"

She shakes her head. "I'm okay."

I tuck a fallen piece of her hair behind her ear, checking to see she's wearing her hearing aid. "Come find me if you're not."

She smiles and touches over the place my hand was before trotting off. I wait until she's in the hallway toward the bathrooms before I head back to Bennett's side.

He wraps his arm around me, pulling me in and kissing the top of my head briefly as the conversation continues on. Rhys's father, Max Koteskiy, and Adam Reiner are talking plans for the next phase of fundraising for the new charity. And everyone is listening, quietly watching and only contributing when asked.

Rhys says something to Bennett from his side as Sadie attempts to slip out of his hold. He doesn't even pause, grabbing her back in his arms as he continues whispering to my boyfriend.

"Will you be giving a speech?" Ethan suddenly asks, directing his question to me as he steps into the circle alongside Bennett's mother.

"W-what?" I've zoned out, watching the silent struggle for dominance that feels half real and half foreplay between Sadie and Rhys, so I've missed most of what's been said.

"I just assumed—I'm sorry, Paloma. I thought you might be partially invested in this particular charity, considering..."

He lets the word hang. A ringing starts in my ears, the warmth of Bennett's palm on my waist disappearing as my body goes numb.

"Considering what?" my boyfriend asks.

Ethan's brow furrows, but I can see the slight upward curve of his lips hidden behind his glass as he takes another sip. "Did Paloma ever tell you that we actually know each other?"

Ice shoots through my veins and I stagger slightly in my heels.

"No," Bennett says, eyes confused and almost hurt as he looks down at me. "P?"

"I—"

Ethan smiles and reaches his hand out toward me, patting my arm lightly. I barely hold in a flinch.

"It's okay, Paloma. No need to be ashamed," Ethan says, serious. The same caring intensity he had when I was thirteen and terrified.

Then, to the entire circle—Adam, Max, Helen, Rhys, Sadie, and Bennett—he tells the story. *My* story.

"I met Paloma when I was still a cop, assigned to the area where she lived—a trailer park we tended to frequent. Her mom was hooked on several drugs and usually had some lowlife guy or other in and out of the house. And Paloma was so young—god, how old were you? Ten?"

"Thirteen."

"Thirteen. Wow." He smiles at me. And I know that the web he's weaving is ensnaring them all—that he took pity on a poor little girl. I feel sick. "Anyway, I didn't recognize her before, but with the blond hair . . . it's impossible not to see that same girl. And I am just so happy to see you doing so well now."

He turns his chin back to Mr. Koteskiy and nods. "Paloma is exactly the kind of kid this new charity will help. I'm so thrilled that you two have put this together."

I stumble back, away from the group, barely keeping down the vomit I can feel coming up.

"I-I need to go," I say, words garbled and half-formed. "Sorry. I-I—excuse me."

It's the best I can get out before I take off across the ballroom as fast as I can in my heels, transitioning into an all-out sprint the second the doors open to the refreshing cool night air.

So much for not running away anymore.

Pathetic, the hateful voice whispers. Only this time it doesn't sound like him.

It sounds like me.

A hand wraps around my shoulder.

CHAPTER 58

THEN: Freshman Year, New Year's Eve, 5:30 p.m.

Paloma

"P? You okay?"

I nod. "Just nervous."

Bennett's music is soothing and soft in the cabin of the car but I'm distracted, folding and unfolding the bottom of my maxi skirt with its ditsy floral pattern. It's a little too cold for it, but I want to make an impression—modest, but girlish. Pretty.

I desperately want them to like me.

When he notices I'm still fidgeting toward the end of our two-hour drive, Bennett reaches over and smothers both my hands in one of his massive paws.

"It'll be perfect."

"Yeah," I agree, easy under the weight of his calming, intense presence.

Adam's house in Beacon Hill is smaller than this one by quite a bit—this mansion is wealth in a different way.

Bennett explained, albeit briefly, that his parents were both from wealthy families. While his dad is from a long line of extravagant and continuously building wealth, his mother's family came into money more recently. I wonder if his parents' marriage was arranged for business purposes.

They're not a family drama show, I chastise myself, focusing back on the ornately gated driveway and beautiful fountain that is currently covered in a thick blanket of snow.

Bennett's mom is just inside the entryway, beautiful and tall with a waterfall of honey curls that she's perfectly styled into waves. Her eyes are crystal blue, lighter than Bennett's, and she scans them over me once—twice—and then rushes to greet her son with a gentle hand to his cheek.

There's a moment where Bennett almost flinches away from her, but he settles into the quick touch and grants her a closed-lip smile.

"Mom," he greets, then turns toward me and pulls my hand from the clenched fist at my side and entangles our fingers. "This is my girlfriend, Paloma."

"Nice to meet you, dear." She eyes me for a moment before blurting. "Are you all right with hugs?"

"Yeah." I smile and open my arms. She engulfs me quickly, tight.

"You don't know how hard it is to not hug my child—but you know, he's different." She pulls back and shakes her head. "It's just difficult, sometimes."

The comment feels wrong, brutal and hurtful despite the gentle tone.

I spare a glance at Bennett, his hands in the pockets of his fancy slacks and bottom lip thoroughly bitten. He looks ashamed. Stepping back, I reach for his hand and tuck it into mine.

My mouth opens—to defend him or to yell at her, maybe a combination of both—before Bennett stops me with a tight squeeze of my hand and a subtle shake of his head.

His mom says something I don't hear over the slight pounding in my ears—a little fury mixed with confusion and frustration.

Bennett kisses my forehead and pulls away, nodding to his mom. "I'll help him bring the food in."

Him. Bennett's stepdad.

I quickly straighten my spine, reminding myself that I'm not done with the first impressions just yet.

"Do you drink, Paloma?" Bennett's mother calls as I follow her into the expansive dining room. She's pouring herself something from a bottle that costs more than a year of my tuition, I'm sure.

I shake my head demurely. I'm eighteen, but more importantly, alcohol reminds me of things I'd rather forget. There are a lot of reasons I choose not to drink.

"No," I say. "Thank you, though, ma'am."

"You can call me Helen."

She winks and ushers me into one of the seats at the grand table. It's meant for a large group, but she's only set the four places in the center. Taking a seat diagonal to me, she hands me a glass with a minuscule pour of white wine swirling in the bottom.

"Try it, sweetie," she urges. "It's not every day you've got the opportunity to drink this fine of a vintage."

I don't want to, but I want his mother to like me, so I take it and swallow it down brutally.

If it tastes any different than a boxed wine, I'm not the one to know, but I paint a charming smile over my pinkened lips.

"It's good," I muster. She nods approvingly, lipstick sticking to the rim of her glass as she takes down another large gulp of her bubbling champagne.

Her mouth opens to speak again, but just then Bennett comes through the door with a large platter of salmon on a thick wood plank. It looks delicious and fresh, beautifully cut into sizable portions. He serves all four plates before returning to the kitchen.

"This looks—"

The words halt half out of my mouth, throat going bone dry as the empty glass in my hand slips from my grip, bounces off the table, and lands heavily in my lap.

Blond hair slicked back, a graying goatee, and haunting pale green eyes.

Ethan Marks, my nightmare in the flesh, stands across the suddenly too-small table with a cheshire grin and a bowl of grilled vegetables. He's staring at me happily, like I'm his surprise birthday present. I want to stand, to excuse myself and run, but instead I'm frozen. A deer in headlights; prey caught, frozen in a predator's snare.

"Ethan," Helen says, smiling over her shoulder at him. "This is Paloma, Bennett's beautiful girlfriend. Paloma, this is my husband, Ethan."

Her husband. Bennett's stepfather.

My stomach sours; tears fight to spill free. I clear my throat and blink rapidly to push them back.

"Pleasure, Paloma," he says, setting the bowl across the table.

"Isn't she a doll?" Helen says, grinning brightly at me. It's a compliment, and maybe I should say *thank you*, but I can't hear anything besides my own heartbeat thundering in my ears. It feels a little like I'm dying.

"That she is," he agrees easily, reaching his hand out to shake mine. "Nice to meet you."

I don't want to touch him—but they're both staring at me and Bennett is still gone.

I reach a shaky hand toward him and he grasps it in both of his, almost massaging the skin with his thumbs in the overly tight hold. The desire to wash my hands is so overwhelming, I stand and stumble back over my chair.

"I—um—" My voice is shaky at best as sweat pools on the back of my neck. "I need to use the restroom, please."

"I can—"

"Sit, Helen," he commands lightly, kissing her cheek. "I can show Paloma where it is. I need to change my shirt anyway—I smell like a grill."

"All right," Helen concedes, giving him another sparkling smile as he refills her glass so she doesn't have to move.

Suddenly, I don't want to go—not knowing he's with me—but I don't see how to get out of it. I stay guarded, a few steps behind as we trek through the long hallway, right to the sharp turn from where I can't see back toward the kitchen and living room. My heart hammers against my ribs as he opens a door and stands, waiting for me.

"Right here, *Paloma*." He speaks my name like an unwanted caress. I hesitate before swallowing hard against the thick lump in my throat and walking in, trying to grab for the door before he can—

He slides in, shoving me back and closing the door tightly behind him.

"Get out," I try to snarl, but it comes out a weak, squeaky plea.

"Look at you," he says, taking a step toward me with each word until my body is back against the wall of the half-bath. It's a small space; bright light from an extravagant chandelier above makes everything harsher.

"S-stop—"

Ethan reaches toward my face and my limbs finally react. I grab his wrist, stopping the movement just before he can touch my hair.

"New hair color?" He yanks his wrist from my grip and reaches for my hair anyway—like he owns me, the touch all proprietary. "I love the change. Makes you look all grown up."

I pull back, slamming my body into the opposite wall.

"You need to leave, now. I—" I swallow loudly, trying to imbue my voice with strength I don't feel. "I'm going to—"

"Tell Bennett?"

My snarl is half-baked, like a hapless child facing off against a cruel adult. "What makes you so sure I haven't already?"

"Because I know you, *Polly*." He smirks, watching the taunting nickname hit me like a slap. "Did you tell him?"

"I will." It's a lie—I don't think I *could* tell Bennett if I tried. Risk having him look at me with disgust? Knowing the girl he's cared so gently for isn't who he thought?

Ethan steps closer, hands raised like a peace offering. I press myself up against the far wall, a terrified, cornered animal.

"I'll tell Bennett," I say again, begging my voice not to wobble.

"And what would you say?" He smiles, head tilting to the side. "That you seduced me? Begged for me repeatedly? You want to tell Bennett that you used to fuck his stepdad and beg to sleep next to him, so you didn't have to go back to that trailer?"

My stomach rolls so violently, I worry I'm going to throw up. Heat swelters against my neck and face, head shaking.

It's not true. It's not true.

And that same small voice screaming inside of me *Stop! Stop! Stop!*

"I was fourteen." My voice is weepy despite trying to make it cold and defensive. "Y-you—you took advantage—"

He laughs and the sound makes my nausea worse.

"All right, Paloma. You were fourteen, sure. Fourteen and begging a man more than twice your age to save you, to take you away, right?" He laughs. "Playing the victim since day one, are we? Tell him if you want, but don't go around telling him a lie."

He's right. I hate how easily he paints the picture of it all—because I *did* beg him to take me with him, called his number and cried for him to carry me away from it all. But I was scared and—

You asked for it.

Shame settles sharply between my ribs; my heart aches with the pressure.

Tears pour down my cheeks, my body giving up, losing the fight against it. I go slack, hand grasping the sink counter like it will hold me up.

"I know you best. And Bennett is my stepson." Every word is

a strike to my heart, a kick to my already beaten body. "And you, Polly," he coos, "are not who you're pretending to be."

"Okay," I acquiesce.

It feels like I'm thirteen again, staring at an older, handsome cop who's offering me his coat because it's the middle of winter with a foot of snow outside and there's no heat in our trailer. My hands are over my ears while my mom screams and begs them not to arrest her current deadbeat boyfriend—

"Do you have somewhere to go for the night?" he asks.

"Sometimes I sleep at the school," I admit, then feel ridiculously stupid because I just admitted to something illegal to a cop. "Please don't tell."

He chuckles and swipes some melting snow from his ashy blond hair. "I won't. But I really don't think you should stay here tonight."

"Oh." I nod, swallowing hard. "Okay. Yeah. I, um, can maybe ask our neighbor?"

The officer grimaces. "No. I don't—" He huffs a long breath and then looks around at the other officers, one of whom is trying to calm my mother down while the others shove the strung-out addict into the back of a cop car.

"What's your name?" he asks, the question so abrupt I gape for a second, like I can't remember.

"Um, Paloma."

He smiles. "That's a really pretty name, Paloma. I'm Officer Marks, but you can call me Ethan if you want."

"Okay." I nod, but choose not to, huddling tighter into the thick coat. "Thanks, for this."

He shakes his head. "Sure." Glancing around again, Officer Marks squats into the snow so I'm no longer staring up at him. He's handsome, much more than the guys that hang around our trailer or the men my mom dates—probably because they're all gaunt and drugged up. He looks clean, safe. Like a real adult.

"Listen, I shouldn't offer, because it's inappropriate, but I really don't think you should stay here. Especially with your mom this upset."

I peek over at her again. Everyone says we look alike, blond bouncy curls and dark brown eyes, a golden undertone to our complexions and apricot lips—even with her reckless lifestyle, everyone says she's beautiful.

And I'm her twin—a fact that gives me more anxiety than it does any complimentary feelings.

"Yeah."

"So, if you can hang here for a bit, I'll come back and get you. I have an extra guest room you can sleep in just for tonight, okay?"

Hesitancy has me biting down on my lip. Men have offered this before, or something similar—to take me from my mom, to go on a little trip with them while she's high. But it always leads to them trying to take something I don't want to give. An exchange I didn't agree to.

I curl in tighter at the thought. He looks safe, but assumptions have gotten me nowhere good.

It must be written all over my face, because he raises his hands in surrender. "Just a warm place to sleep—safe, I promise. I won't touch you, okay? I just want to make sure you're safe."

Part of me wants to say no, self-preservation and fear riding me hard. But it's freezing, and I don't want to go back in the trailer with Mom while she cries all night and yells at me—finds a way to blame me for it all.

"Okay," I agree, nodding my head. He smiles and it makes me feel a little warmer in the icy snow.

Panicked breaths saw out of me, and Ethan's eyes widen just slightly.

"Relax, Polly," he whispers. "Breathe."

I can't.

"You need to cry? That's okay—they can't hear it in here, okay? Just calm down."

I shake my head, wanting to scream and cry and rage. "Stop it," I beg instead. Hatred for myself only grows.

Tears work down my cheeks for a long moment, but I'm too scared to look away from him. Ethan steps forward, hands still raised as if to placate me. He grabs the hand towel off the hook by my head, reaching out slowly to wipe away my tears.

It's worse. At one time, I would've begged for this affection, when it was the only touch I knew. The confusing swirl of comfort and fear only serves to make me sicker.

"All better," he sighs, releasing my chin and stepping back. "God, Polly—you still look so much like your mom. Just more beautiful."

Just like your mom.

"I'll let you wash your hands," he says. "But hurry. You better get back to your sweet boyfriend. I'll go keep *my* wife and *my* stepson company until you're all put together."

The reminder is as sharp as the *snick* of the door.

I let a few silent sobs rake out, ugly and harsh as I run the tap to cover the noise just in case. Closing my eyes tightly, I pull it all back, slow and sure. Until everything is sealed behind my comforting barrier of ice. Walls of adamant steel are cracked but strong where they've protected me for so long. I hide behind them now.

It's like mourning myself as I stare in the mirror, knowing that I have to let go of who I've been since arriving in Waterfell—the image of myself I'd finally created that was *good* and nearly whole, without the darkened shadows of my past. And I have to let go of the one person I've ever tried to hold on to for myself.

Bennett.

Stop it. You knew this would happen. It was stupid to try to hold him. Stupid.

I try to shake the thought from my head, ripping a few pieces of toilet paper to dab below my eyes.

CHAPTER 59

THEN: Freshman Year, New Year's Eve, 8:45 p.m.

Paloma

It's quiet, almost somber in the cabin of Bennett's car as we drive back to Waterfell.

I'd barely spoken more than three full sentences through dinner, answering all Helen's well-meaning questions with simple, one-word responses. I'd almost thrown up when Ethan squeezed Bennett's shoulder as he served our desserts.

Bennett reached for my hand at one point and I flinched, pulling it back and away from him, which only served to make us both more upset.

He sits quietly, carefully driving one-handed while his other palm rests firmly on my thigh. It's only when we're closing in on the downtown streets that he finally asks, "Are you okay?"

"Fine," I snap out. He looks at me, pulling to a stop at the red light. His hand reaches forward to wipe an embarrassing stray tear from the corner of my eye and I flinch back.

"All better."

I grab the handlebar above me, suddenly feeling like the entire car is spinning.

"Actually, do you think you could drop me at the dorms?" I don't ask until we're pulling up to Bennett's townhouse, feeling even more ridiculous since we're already *here* and I'm asking him to cart me around like a car service.

"Oh." Bennett shakes his head a little as he parks on the curb. "I—yeah, of course. If that's what you want?"

He wants to ask more, but he's scared to—enough that his hand on my thigh retracts and squeezes the steering wheel over and over, treating the leather like a stress ball.

"I'm just tired," I lie.

Bennett nods again, like it makes complete sense. His fingers release their white-knuckle grip as he angles his body toward mine. "Sorry, I think . . . I've just gotten used to our routine now. I sleep better when you're in bed with me."

From anyone else, it might sound like a line. But Bennett's words are dripping with a sobering mix of anxiety and honesty, a deep blush staining his cheeks at the admission.

Bennett likes his routines. When I first started staying over at his place, he'd had to adapt to me being there, in his space. Now, to take that away from him feels wrong. And I desperately want to be nearer to him, even if it's wrong for me to want that.

My throat tightens, tears that I've held back all evening threatening to spill again. A war rages in my heart—is it better to give him this or to break it cleanly?

And the inevitable questions of *what if?*

What if I did tell him? What if he believed me, if he understood why I did what I did? What if it was all okay and he wanted me anyway?

"Okay." I nod. "Yeah, I'll stay with you. I like our routine, too."

The beautiful, rare smile is enough to make the pain of it all worth it.

Once again, no one is home when we get there. It's only when we're inside his spacious room—nearly triple the size of my dorm room on campus—that I finally feel myself starting to lose any grip

I had on the idea of this new life. This dream of something different than what I came from.

"Can I shower?"

"Of course," he says, not pausing in his movements as he heads to the shower and starts it for me, making the water just the right temperature and laying out a towel and clothes for me.

Taking such gentle care of me it aches.

"Do you want me to join you?" he asks, an edge of vulnerability slipping into the words.

I shake my head, turning away from him before I can see the hurt of my rejection. Before he can see the tears in my eyes.

Playing the victim since day one, are we? Tell him if you want, but don't go around telling him a lie. Ethan's words play on a loop, only cementing my decision.

You are not who you're pretending to be.

My stomach swirls, tears joining the water as it cascades over my face and arms. No matter how hot I turn it, I can't erase the feeling of being *dirty*. I feel unclean again, the same way I felt at fifteen, sixteen, seventeen—my body turning from something I cherished into this thing I hate.

I hate myself.

And for a moment, I thought I could have it all be different. That I'd found my way with a full scholarship to a school I'd never afford otherwise. That I would be smart and start a future that wasn't like my mother's—so that no matter how much I looked like her, I would never *be* like her again.

I'd gotten out, and even if that was all the good I got to have, it was enough. I didn't need anything else.

Only . . . I met Bennett.

And I saw the promise of something greater in his eyes. The kind of gentle care that makes me feel sleepy around him, like I can finally rest and *know* with certainty no one can hurt me.

Trust him. Tell him everything.

I've told him bits and pieces. I know he's brilliant and has put some of them together.

But this is his *family*.

I can't hurt him like that.

And selfishly, I won't risk seeing betrayal or disgust in his eyes when he looks at me.

There's only one real choice.

CHAPTER 60

NOW

Paloma

Bennett is holding my arm, loose but firm. Tethering me to this moment.

"Slow down, Paloma."

I can't.

"I want to leave," I say, my voice a hateful whisper. But never directed at him, only myself.

Bennett's eyes are searing sapphires as he looks at me, nostrils flaring and hand tightening on my bicep.

"Fine," he says, his voice raspy, like he's actively fighting to stay completely calm. "But I'm driving, and you're coming to the house. We need to talk."

A maniacal laugh spills from my painted lips. "There's nothing to talk about."

"You said things were different this time," he says, pulling me closer. "You made me a promise. This is your chance to prove it."

Don't leave me, a small voice cries out in my head, my hand latching onto his forearm as I manage a nod.

"Okay."

He takes the lead immediately, staying steady and constant while the ebb and flow of my internal turmoil threatens to drown me.

My head pounds, enough that when the valet brings Bennett's car around, I barely remember getting in; I have just the slight memory of hands around my waist, buckling me in.

I try to focus, but my mind is caught up in the past, tangling and twisting me into knots.

"Loving you hurts—"

"Pathetic, Polly, honestly—"

"You look just like your mother—"

"P, please, don't do this—"

"I think I'm going to be sick."

"You need me to pull over?" I don't say anything, eyes glazed as rain starts to fall, making the streetlight glassy against the wet pavement. "Paloma," he snaps, louder. "Tell me if you need me to pull over."

"I—no, I'm okay."

I'm not okay. And I can tell from the near growl of breath and the slam of a hand on the steering wheel that Bennett knows it, too.

"You gotta let me help you, P," he says almost softly as he pulls up to the darkened Hockey House. "Please—"

The second the car is in park, I hop out. My heart is thundering in my ears as I sprint through the garage and into the house, taking the steps so fast I slip. A door slams, but it sounds distant enough that I'm unsure if it's happening now or if it's an echo of the past torturing my brain.

Every memory is spilling out around me like broken glass from a mirror I shattered. Bennett tries to reach for me again—

CHAPTER 61

THEN: Sophomore Year, October

Paloma

Something is wrong.

It's the middle of October, sophomore year, at some dingy party scene. There's a reason I don't drink—but I barely remember it now, buried beneath shots of tequila and the burn of lime and salt on my tongue. Nothing distracts from the constant sting of being back in Waterfell without him.

Lately, I've been drinking a lot.

But tonight, something is different. Wrong. I can feel it.

"I need to use the bathroom," I say, but the words feel loose on my cotton-dry tongue. The guy whose name I've forgotten entirely smirks and tries to touch my newly bleached hair. I shove his hand away, hard, but I miss entirely.

"This way, babe," he says, using his hands on my waist to lead me through the party and to one of the doors in the long stretch of hallway.

My stomach sinks again as I realize it's a bedroom, not a bathroom.

This is what you wanted, right, Polly? It's what you deserve.

I grasp the doorframe and shake my head. "I'm gonna be sick,"

I threaten, which seems to work enough to get him into action. He takes me through to a conjoined bathroom and I shut the door quickly, nearly slamming it in his face.

I grab for my phone, tears blurring my vision. I can barely see enough to click the contact, and with the panic racing through me, I take a chance.

He answers on the first ring.

"Bennett?" I call, before he can even breathe into my ear.

"Paloma?" he asks, his voice a disbelieving cry. "What—"

"I need help," I beg, soft and quiet. A soft curse threads through my ear. "I'm—I'm sorry to call. But I'm scared."

I hear something loud, like an engine roaring to life, before Bennett's voice comes back over. "Tell me where you are. I'm gonna come get you."

My eyes droop lower, head swimmy and fogged up with alcohol and . . . something else. I barely have enough in me to tell him how to find me.

• • •

"—the fuck out of here, before I kill you."

"Take it easy! She didn't say she had a boyfriend—"

I can barely lift my heavy eyelids. Eyelashes fluttering, I try to blink to see what all the distant yelling is about.

No. Not distant. I can almost *feel* the rumble of one of the voices, as if it's coming from *me*.

My hand flexes out, grabbing for something and closing around soft warm material—a shirt. A warmer, stronger hand covers mine, lips to my forehead briefly as I realize that I'm in someone's arms, outside—the October air cool against my heated skin.

Bennett Reiner's arms, as he carries me out of the house like a goddamn superhero.

"I didn't do shit—" someone yells. The voice makes me tremble, hunching down farther into Bennett's arms, as if I can burrow myself into the bulk of him.

"You better fucking *hope* I can't find proof that you drugged her," Bennett snaps. Though I almost second-guess if it's actually him—I've never heard Bennett sound like that, as if he's near to feral. I've never heard him even raise his voice. "You have no *clue* what I'm willing to do when it comes to her."

"Listen, man—"

"That's Bennett fucking Reiner, dude. What the fuck did you do?"

Someone else must've come outside, the owner of the new terrified voice, because Bennett tenses further, pulling me closer as he drops his voice.

"I'm taking her to the goddamn hospital—so you better get your shit together because I'm *sure* campus security and the IFC would love to hear about this."

The IFC—Interfraternal Council. He's threatening them.

I squeeze his arm as tight as my loose, drugged grip can and whisper, "Can you walk me home?"

It's not what I meant to say, but he seems to understand it.

"If I ever catch you even *looking* her direction again," he says, half over his shoulder as he's turned away to block me from their view, "I'll kill you."

His voice is terrifying enough that a jolt runs through me, only soothed by the fact that I *know* Bennett. He's not like this—but he's panicked.

It's not until we get to the car that he manages to let go of me. I feel his hands buckle me in, shaking as he maneuvers and settles my body in place. But my eyes are fully closed, nearly completely passed out.

I swear I hear him crying softly as he drives.

• • •

I jolt up and sprint for the bathroom, groggy, slipping and falling to the tile almost immediately.

Though it's mostly dry-heaving, I can't stop trembling over the toilet, eyes barely open and awash with tears.

A hand gently pulls all of my hair up and out of my face, keeping it carefully snug as I continue to be sick for a long moment. Eventually, the heaving turns to soft sobs, head drooping—but before I can rest my cheek on the seat, my entire body falls back to rest against Bennett's warm, solid chest.

"I'm s-s-sorry," I try to mutter, words still half-caught in my dry, achy throat.

"Shh," he coos. "It's fine. I'm gonna take care of you, P."

I take the suddenly proffered bottle of water from his hand and sip slowly.

"Do you want to shower?"

When I nod, he slowly releases me to walk over and carefully turn the knobs to get the water to the right temperature for me. I try to join him, but everything feels sludgy and heavy.

"Paloma?" Bennett asks, renewed concern in his voice as he sees my tears start up again.

"I . . . I can't move my arms," I whisper. "Everything feels numb."

His jaw clenches tight, eyes closing for a moment before decision stamps his face with conviction. Unwavering in his movements, he cuts off the now-steaming shower and begins to run a bath.

It makes my heart throb, affection for him that's never waned racing over my body like a wave.

In the quiet, I realize this isn't his usual bathroom—it's newer, larger than the townhouse dorm he used to stay in. Probably some nice off-campus housing. My chest aches for the time lost with him, for the differences and the way that I feel like I know him so deeply and yet . . . he's different. His life is different.

It's a pain I didn't prepare for.

"Do you want me to help you?" he asks; the words seem pained. Still, I nod.

With anyone else, I'd suffer through the night with sweat-damp skin and vomit sticking to the strands of my hair. But no matter the circumstances, I feel safe here, with Bennett.

He undresses me carefully, slowly, but keeps me facing away from him as he helps pull off my jacket and dress. My feet are bare—which I assume Bennett did himself when we first got here, so that I could sleep more comfortably.

Then, he takes my arms in his massive hands, moving his chest to hover over my back as he helps me into the steamy hot bathwater.

Bubbles froth at the edges, and that deeply hidden little girl within my heart peeks out of her shadowed safe space.

Once I'm safely settled against the porcelain, Bennett steps back and closes the toilet, flushing and sitting atop the lid to watch over me. In the last nine months, I haven't relaxed my shoulders once. This may be the first time I've even taken a full breath.

"I . . . I'm sorry—"

"Don't apologize again, Paloma," he says, voice fierce and loud in the echoey bathroom. "I can't take it."

"I think he put something in my drink."

"Thought so." Bennett nods, wiping his hands over his eyes and massaging his temple. I can feel the anger, the fury quietly brewing beneath his skin. "I thought you didn't drink," he says, aggressive.

"People change." My back is up, the words flying from my mouth before I can stop the bitter reply.

Silence stretches between us. Not the usual kind that makes me relaxed, that doesn't need to be filled. But a strained, angry kind. One filled with fury and anxiety and fear.

"What time is it?" I ask, desperate for something to fill the space.

"Six in the morning," he says, voice flat. "I'll get you some clothes and when you're done, I'll drive you home. You still live in the dorms?"

The question hurts. "Yeah." He nods and leaves the room.

I bathe and wash my hair quicker without his assessing gaze. I cry silently, yanking at the tangles in my hair with the brush, too terrified that he might offer to do it . . . even more terrified that he *won't*. He leaves a pair of sweatpants and an old long sleeve that I've slept in before, given the chewed-up, frayed sleeve from my teeth; I dress in them quickly.

The car ride is silent, the approaching dawn making the blue and black sky slightly lighter. But when he parks and I grab for the door handle, he reaches over me and pulls it back shut.

Eyes still on the empty road before him, Bennett huffs out a slow breath and swallows hard.

"I won't pretend to know what happened . . . why you didn't want to be with me anymore. And if I did something to hurt you . . ."

"You didn't," I interject, desperate to stop his self-hatred but too petrified to give him another word beyond that.

He nods, but still has that aching, burning look to his face, eyes reddened more from pain than lack of sleep.

"I love you. That doesn't just go away for me, okay? So . . . I can't *worry* this much about you."

"You don't have to. You—I promise—"

His eyes dart toward me, scanning over me once before they're back to glaring at the road. "I don't believe you."

My hands wrap around my middle, hugging myself, just barely resisting the urge to pull my knees up to my chin and sink into his seat. To tell him everything. To ask him to believe me, to take me home and hold me until I feel clean again.

"I need you to do something for me," he says.

"Anything." It's a vow.

"I'm not asking for anything more. I'm not trying to get you to change your mind. But *please*, Paloma. If you need me—if you're scared or worried or just need something, anything at all, please call me. *Use* me. That's . . . that's the only way this anxiety over you won't eat me alive."

I can't speak, tongue-tied and words turning to ash over and over again in my mouth.

"Okay," I say. My hand reaches back for the door handle; I'm suffocating in the warmth of his steadfast affection and care. Feeling continuously unworthy of it all.

He still looks hurt, eyes downcast and fingers gripping the steering wheel as I look back over at him.

I want to ask him: *Do I haunt you?*

Do you still think of your hands in my hair and the sleepy feeling that invades my every muscle in the safety of your presence?

Do you remember the night you told me it felt like poetry to be inside me? Before you kissed along my spine and took me again, hard and insistent, and dominating my soul in a way that I was sure would brand me as yours forever?

Instead, I stand in the cold fall air and stare at him, lingering at the open car door for a too-long moment.

The wind chafes my skin, but I barely feel that pain. It's nothing compared to the way my heart begins to eat itself.

CHAPTER 62

THEN: Sophomore Year, May

Paloma

"Come home with me," Bennett whispers.

It's May. They didn't win Frozen Four, but they made it to the semifinals, losing the first round. Bennett took it personally. He called me but only let it ring once before he ended the call.

Stronger than me. I would've answered if it had started again.

But he's here now, at this party, on the alcove of the stairs just behind the wall, catching my wrist as we brush past one another.

"Come home with me," he says again, and this time it's a plea.

"Okay." I nod. His flushed cheeks pull higher, a smile tugging red lips across white teeth until I can see the chip in one.

I pull my hand away. His fingers follow, gripping me tighter and then reluctantly, slowly releasing me. "Just meet me in the car, ten minutes."

The sentence dims his light, and my own nails dig deep into my palm, paying penance for his pain.

"Sure." He nods. "If that's how it's going to be."

It has to be, I want to say.

I don't say a word. I want to say, *Never mind, it's not worth it. It will only hurt us both even more.* But I can't.

I can't say no to him. And I don't want to.

Ten minutes later he presses me to the side of his car with a heavy, burning kiss. His tongue slips into my mouth, tasting like whiskey and saltwater and every piece of myself I've tried to destroy.

"Are you drunk?"

He shakes his head. "Are you?"

I shake mine. We crawl into the backseat of his car, and he kisses me slower, pulling my body into his lap and curling his hands into my hair.

We don't have sex, despite the situation others might read if they saw us slipping away. Instead, he lays my head on the expanse of his thighs, hands combing through my hair in gentle soothing strokes. We watch each other breathe. I fall asleep there, only waking when I feel the movement of the car coming to a stop. Only opening my eyes to the sight of his room, Seven gently nudging my leg.

He sleeps beside me for an hour, my hand in his. I get up and leave before the sun has risen.

CHAPTER 63

THEN: Junior Year, December

Paloma

It's early December. I can't decide who has been avoiding who, but when I catch him on the balcony by the dimming fire, it's late and he's drunk.

At first, I'm sure he'll see me and turn the other way. That I've finally snuffed out the light that's always burned for me inside of Bennett Reiner.

That's what you want, right?

But he doesn't. He just stares for a long moment, before finishing his cup of whatever alcoholic drink he's been indulging in.

"Bennett," I say, biting my lip. I've had *zero* sips of alcohol. "Listen—"

"Rhys isn't here." He slurs the words. My stomach cramps, hand raising to my heart like I can rub the sting away.

"I need to talk to you—"

"I'm not surprised." He laughs, but there's only pain in it. "That you like him. Rhys is—"

"Stop it," I whisper, stepping closer to him. "I didn't know. And . . . once I did it was over."

I'd barely made it to the car the night of our cursed double date before telling Rhys I needed to go. I texted him that I was done quickly after. It was callous and rude for a boy that had only been kind to me, but I'd never meant to hurt anyone.

Even if it seems like that's the only thing I'm good at.

Bennett nods, but his face still bleeds pain. "I slept with someone else," he says, bitter and angry. I nod.

"I know."

"Just the same as you," he sneers. He's drunk and hurting. I can feel the turmoil, the knowledge that a part of him wants me to hurt, too, but he's still *Bennett*. Kind even when he shouldn't be. Good, right down to his soul.

"You're not," I say. "You're so much better than me."

We stand in charged silence for a long while.

"I don't want to do this anymore." His words are a wrangled sob, blubbery as he wipes at his eyes. "But I don't know how to be without you. I've tried. But . . . Goddamn it, Paloma, loving you *hurts*."

I know. I want to cry. I know. I'm sorry.

I should let him go. I should use this moment, here and now, to release him from the pain we both feel. That's what a *good* person would do.

Instead, I drive him home—and then to my door when he begs me not to leave him there. I tuck him into my too-small bed as he grasps me tight around the middle.

"I know you're asleep," I whisper. He doesn't stir. "And you probably won't remember this in the morning. But . . . when I was fourteen, a man told me he would take care of me. I just had to give him . . . something I didn't want to give. And I was too scared of everything to stop it, even if I wanted it to stop. And then, when I met you? I was so ashamed of who I'd been before."

I lean in and kiss his forehead, watching his lips kick like he can feel me in his sleep.

"I love you. I'll always love you, Bennett. I just wish I was someone else, better and more deserving of your kind of love."

I sleep in my car that night, so that I don't have to watch him leave in the morning.

CHAPTER 64

THEN: Junior Year, Sometime Spring Semester

Paloma

"—aren't you, baby?"

Whatever the guy has said to me is barely an echo in my head. Instead, I let the beat of the music roll through my relaxed limbs as I splay myself back on the bed.

His name is lost on me by now, my brain swimming as he strips himself down to nothing and climbs over me. I wince a little at the tight hold he takes on my throat, but he doesn't notice. And if he does, well, maybe he likes it.

I smirk, eyes glimmering with the alcohol spreading in my system.

Tonight, I'm doing something worse than usual. And I wonder if it will be the thing that breaks me.

Aren't you already broken enough? Cracked and splayed on the floor. Forgotten.

Worthless.

My eyes flicker to the door again, wondering if he'll show. If he'll break the door down and scoop me up and away from this fucking nightmare. As if he even knows where I am.

A fantasy—with him *as your knight in shining armor? How pathetic, Polly.*

The voice in my head is louder tonight. Angry. Bitter. It's accompanied by the image of Bennett, smiling and drunk and happy, hands around the hips of a girl I've seen before. Pretty, brunette, smart. Put together.

Not broken.

I roll my hips, tightening my knees around his waist.

He's barely done a thing to me, but the moan leaves my throat unbidden. I watch the happy smile overtake his face as he slides hard into me—hard enough that my stomach lurches. It's not that he's big, it's that I'm not prepared and dehydrated and—

"God, no wonder everyone in the goddamn school is half in love with you," he whispers hard into my ear, huffing. "So fucking tight."

I roll my eyes, but hum beneath him, gripping my nails into his shoulders like a minor punishment.

I wish he'd shut up.

"Yeah?" I mewl out like a kitten. Playing my part perfectly, flawlessly.

Completely iconic.

"Surprising," he chokes out with a laugh, but it fades to a moan. "Considering the sheer number of guys you've let in here. Thought you'd be—"

"I'm gonna come," I say, whining and high pitched and so fake it makes my skin crawl.

He starts thrashing harder now, sweat beading on his brow as he furrows it in concentration. It feels the same as it always does. Painful, like knives swimming deep through my skin to the middle of my chest.

Sometimes I grip my heart to check that I'm not bleeding, because it feels so much like I am.

For a moment, my head swimming, his brown eyes melt away into only *blue*. His body grows in size, covering me. Comforting me like a weighted blanket. And if I close my eyes and really try I can almost feel two-day stubble scratching at my cheek.

"*Paloma.*"

The whisper of my name on his lips is only a memory but it feels so real tears well up in my eyes.

I want out. I want this to stop.

But I do nothing, just let everything continue to crash over me in waves.

It doesn't matter. I know that now.

I could scream for whoever it is on top of me to stop, and he'd probably think I was playing a game. And no one in this house would care if it wasn't. If I was truly hurt.

No one cares.

No one except Bennett. And I destroyed him just like I do everything I touch.

So, I close my eyes and pretend.

He's almost real in my head. Because I'm an expert at pretending.

• • •

Later, after I've made it back to my dorm room and showered off as quickly as I can while still feeling as clean as my brain will let me feel, I stand and stare into the dark, dingy mirror for a long time.

And I know that she *is* me—that the girl reflected is myself—but the disconnect I feel toward the blonde in the mirror . . . Black mascara stains across cheeks where she carelessly scrubbed her makeup into her skin. Peachy skin raw with the intensity of the fast and uncaring scrub she's done to her own body. A few fingerprints across her breasts where she let someone pull and tug and *hurt* because she doesn't care.

It's not me, I swear. Only it is. And I've played this game before, pretending the things that happened to me were happening to someone else.

There's a numbness to it, down to the unfeeling grip of my hands across my arms as I curve in on my own body, watching as the girl in the mirror mimics the movement.

If I closed my eyes now, I could almost feel him behind me. Combing my hair, touching my shoulder, kissing the side of my neck, my cheek, my forehead, my hair. Looking at me like I'm something *worth* his love-filled gaze.

Instead, I stare at the girl I've abandoned in the mirror. I smear her image with my hand on the condensation, like the blurred, messy picture will be easier to deal with. It's only when Sadie knocks on the bathroom door that I even remember I'm not alone. I should be, I think, entirely alone. But I can't remember if it was her or me who insisted she stay here.

There is a part of us that's the same, that finds a relief in the way we do things together. Hers is different, though. Where Sadie seems lighter when we reunite after one of her quick hookups, my shoulders only feel heavier. I've paid my penance, but it only makes me feel worse. Maybe that's what I deserve.

After Sadie showers, she lays in my small bed next to me, lightly snoring only seconds after her head hits the pillow.

Sleep never finds me, but pain keeps me constant company.

CHAPTER 65

NOW

Paloma

"P?" Bennett's voice mixes past and present in my memory. "Just—"

He keeps speaking to me, but I can't make out the words. They're more like distant sounds. I'm in his room. A pang of loneliness hits and I'm desperate to chase it away.

"What do you need?" Bennett's gravelly voice breaks through the pounding in my head. "Paloma, please—"

I yank at my dress, nearly ripping the seams at my chest, until I manage to pull it off. Standing before him semi-naked, my head swims.

"I want you."

Bennett shakes his head at me, brow furrowing and eyes turning to turquoise wells of pain, so deep I find myself lost in them.

"No, P," he begs. His eyes dart around, hand flexing—like he's looking for Seven. His eyes close for a moment and he breathes deep. "Let's talk. You're upset—please—"

"I told you. You asked me what I need. What I want. I need you." I reach for him again, planning to grip his button-down hard and rip it down the middle so I can smooth my hands against his chest, the tuffs of curls and strong hard muscle beneath. "Just this—"

He steps back again, nearly tripping as his shoulder hits the wall and his hands jut out to grasp my wrists.

I freeze instantly and just *that* makes him swallow hard and gasp in pain. Like my reaction to his touch is as effective as a physical blow.

He drops my hands, raising his in the air like he's surrendering, like I'm pointing a loaded gun at him.

In a way, maybe I am.

Tears work their way into my eyes as I look at him, the beautiful man I've destroyed with my ugliness. And yet, I can't fucking stop myself from reaching for him again.

"Paloma, please. This isn't what you need right now."

"It is," I try to growl, but it comes out as a breathy sob. "Please."

"Don't do this, P. I'm begging." He *is* begging, pleading for me not to use my one-time ask for something that will hurt us both, leave both of us in ruins. I know neither one of us will recover from the aftermath of what I'm pleading for.

"It's just sex," I snap.

"It's *not*," he breathes. "Not with us. You know that. Tell me you know that." The words seem as painful for him to say as they are for me to hear.

"What does it matter?" I spit. "This will mean *nothing* when you're inside of me, Ben." I try to make my tone different, to bring out the breathy smoky seductive voice I keep on me like a knife. My protection. "I'll make it so fucking good for you."

Devastation settles over his features.

It's like watching myself from a cage, unable to stop the fury and anger from hurting the one person I love more than anything. The one person that's ever cared for me.

I wait to see what he'll do. Hoping he'll just give in.

Instead, I watch him build his armor, quiet but stable. The constant shore of unwavering love to the tumultuous sea of my own self-hatred.

"You're upset because of what Ethan said," he begins, eyes downcast. His voice is matter-of-fact, like he's working through it aloud, trying to understand. "Maybe embarrassed, too, even if you shouldn't be. But him talking about you as a kid? It hurt you, and you won't tell me why."

I flinch.

His voice has no emotion; his face is steel as he speaks. "You're upset because of me knowing about your past. Maybe because of your mom, or what Ethan said about her . . . reputation. About the trailer park you lived in—"

"S-stop it." I manage to find my voice, backing away as he starts to advance toward me. "Bennett—"

"Someone hurt you in that house. Maybe more than one person, and just talking about that triggered you. You want sex because it'll distract you. Make you feel better—"

Bennett watches my face intensely, and I see the slow realization overtake him. His eyes flare.

"No—fuck, Paloma." His voice breaks over my name. "Y-you . . . you want sex because it makes you feel *worse*?" Bennett's knees give out and he falls onto the edge of the bed. His breath shudders faster, eyes shining like he might cry. "All this time . . . You thought that . . . that you deserve that? To feel bad?"

I slam my hands over my ears, tears flowing.

"Stop." I want to scream, but I sound like a whimpering child. *No, no, no* —I grip hands into my hair and pull slightly. "Please, I—"

"Shhh," Bennett tries to soothe me, reaching out to hold me up, and I realize I've stumbled toward him. His arms wrap around me, hands gently finding mine and pulling them from my scalp. He tucks them into his, our fingers interlocking. "Please, love. Just breathe."

I do. He pulls me slowly, like coaxing a dog whose been beaten and chained, into his lap. Desperate to save it, as Bennett's always been desperate to save me.

I press myself into his chest, ear to his heart, and breathe.

He's crying, I realize, sobs wracking his body. It makes my hands go numb.

"Bennett?" I ask, pulling back. But he only holds on tighter.

"Paloma," he breathes into my hair, hands pressing like he's memorizing my body, inch by inch. "*God*—I didn't know. I thought..." he stalls, but I hear him anyway.

He thought when we were apart I used sex as an outlet, a distraction. But I wielded it like a razor, crawling deeper into that dark pit every time. And Bennett stood there and watched it happen, thinking he wasn't enough. Thinking I wanted a release, just trying to feel good—and was looking for something he couldn't give. Something I wouldn't take from him.

I know he blames himself entirely, as if he stood back and forced me to go upstairs and into dark hallways and further down the rabbit hole of my self-hatred.

"I'm sorry," I whisper into his skin, pressing so I can feel his neck against my lips. "I didn't mean to hurt you. I just want you, just you. Just this. I'm sorry."

There are broken pieces of us scattered on the floor. Raw. Vulnerable. And for a second, the thought of running and hiding feels like a comfort. I want to—

But then he kisses me. And it makes everything right, even just for a moment.

We stay there for a long time before Bennett stands and carries me to the bathroom. He turns on the bathtub and pulls open the drawer of all my favorite soaps and hair products he keeps around.

It feels silly, to be so comforted by the idea of a bubble bath at the hands of Bennett Reiner, but as soon as the overly warm water conceals my naked body there's a loosening in my chest.

Bennett stands for a moment, easily taking up too much space in the small room, still in his suit pants and button-down, sleeves rolled up, hands tucked deep into his pockets.

"I should . . ." He trails off, eyes downcast.

My hand reaches out, wet against the dark fabric of his pants. "Stay?"

Bennett nods, eyes finding mine as he kneels by the lip of the tub, his palm touching my cheek. I nuzzle into it with a soft, contented sigh. And then it's nothing but the sound of water moving as I shift beneath the sudsy curtain.

"I was an only child," I suddenly confess. My eyes shoot down, watching my own fingers play and swirl. "I don't really talk about my mom—and I don't want to. She didn't care about me, never protected me. My childhood wasn't . . . it was bad, Bennett."

Bad is an understatement. But telling him this is hard enough.

"My mom was in trouble a lot—drugs, violent boyfriends, anything you can think of. And sometimes the cops that came were . . . 'friends' of my mother. Sometimes they were worse than the assholes she brought home. And . . ." I shake my head, words trailing away. But the pain-soaked intensity of them hangs behind.

Bennett's hand reaches out, grasping mine with a gentle, reassuring squeeze.

"Don't. Not if it hurts."

He seems to wince at his own words, shaking his head like he knows. *It all hurts.*

"There was someone, though, who was kind to me when we met." I want to tell him. I want to let the name spill from my lips, but I *can't*. "He was older than me. He knew I'd been sleeping in a house with no power in the dead of winter or sneaking into the school to sleep."

"You slept... at the school?"

"All the time." I laugh, no humor in it. "It's... it was warm. And no one tried to get in my room." I stop there, swallowing hard. By the time I met Ethan I didn't trust anyone—man, woman, child. It was me versus everyone else.

"Goddamn it," Bennett mutters, eyes darting down before wiping at his eyes. "Sorry. I'm sorry. I don't know why that..."

I stay silent.

"I just... picturing you alone and scared, and sleeping in a fucking school?" His voice is still whisper quiet, soft and gentle despite the harsher language.

"It's okay. It wasn't that bad."

He shakes his head, eyes darting to me like he wants to tear those words from my mouth and lay his anger into them.

I wait and Bennett calms, stays quiet while I tell the rest. But the tears slowly tracking from his ocean-blue eyes never quite stop.

The words pour from me like water, and he absorbs them all. The unshakable, constant shore bowing to my fraught waves.

I explain Ethan's treatment—how his demeanor ran so hot and cold. How he was the first adult to take care of me, how I trusted him. The way he showed me affection when I'd never had any before. I might as well have been touch starved.

Desperate for anything. And he knew that, used it against me.

"I'd never had anyone pay attention to me like that," I say, voice bitter and resentful. No amount of time changes the way I feel about myself at fifteen, sixteen, and so on—desperate and so *stupid*. "I was grateful, that he seemed to care for me. I thought I should be glad... but then he changed, and I didn't realize he'd never looked at me like a daughter."

The words dredge up the usual nausea, tenfold at having to confess this to Bennett.

"He—" My throat closes and I wipe away a few silent tears. "I didn't want it, *any* of it. But I wanted someone to . . ." *God*, this hurts most of all. "I just wanted someone to care about me. Even if I didn't *want* to be with him. And I didn't."

A sob stabs at my throat, voice sticky. "Please, believe me."

Bennett's arms loop around me, tugging me into his warmth so I can sob into his soft chest and release everything I've held back from him since I met him.

"I do," he whispers. "I do. I believe you. God, Paloma."

"I'm sorry I didn't tell you," I breathe, shame casting my eyes down.

"Don't," he nearly cuts me off. Water sloshes over the lip of the tub as Bennett picks me up and steps to sit in the bath, still fully clothed. He settles me onto his lap, facing him. "Please, P. I believe you. I believe you."

He whispers the words like his own form of poetry, soothing and protective in equal measure.

"You're okay—you're safe now.

"I'm so sorry, P.

"I won't let anything happen to you again."

We sit like that for a long time. I try to focus on anything but the torrent of emotions still plaguing me—the left-out detail of my story that's begging to be told. Instead, I take in the movement of the water. His big body taking up too much space. The soft damp fabric of his shirt against my chest where he's got me crowded into his body.

My fingers fiddle with the button of his shirt.

"Can I wash your hair?"

The question is as soft as his fingers as he tips me back by the neck, until my hair swirls in the water. He keeps hold of my neck in one hand, using the other to grab for the shampoo. I turn in his arms, still naked and vulnerable. He spreads his legs to pull me closer between them, my back to his chest now. Bennett presses a soft kiss to my temple before sudsing his hands and massaging my scalp, careful and slow so he doesn't get anything in my eyes.

He does the same slow movements with the conditioner. It's our routine, at least a version of it—and I can feel that it soothes him arguably more than me.

Maybe this is the moment—a fresh start. A clean slate, all my darkened secrets finally in the light.

Not all of them.

"Take your time," Bennett whispers after he's wrapped me in a towel and shucked off his wet clothes, grabbing his own towel off the bar on the wall. "Take as long as you need."

Calm settles over me like a weighted blanket, like Bennett's massive body might. I wring out my hair, using all the luxury products that I haven't allowed myself in years, taking the time to plait my wet hair into pigtail braids before slipping on his massive Berkshire shirt and forgoing the rest of the clothes he left out for me.

I still feel raw as I emerge from the steamy room, but my throat catches as I see the pretty lights he's plugged in along with the usual lamp.

Bennett turns from his computer, Ben Howard plays softly through the speakers as he steps toward me. He's changed, too, soft pajama pants and no shirt like he usually sleeps.

I stand there blankly, unsure what to do now. Unsure of where I belong.

My fingers play at the stiff wet end of one of my braids as I chew on my lip.

"I'm not tired," I blurt. "I couldn't sleep if I tried."

Bennett smiles, small and quick, but I hold it close to my heart, warming myself from the inside out. "I know, love. I want to show you something."

He walks over to his dresser, just past the golden lamp on his bedside table. Tucked against the wall is a tall, full-length mirror. Tall enough to capture the hulking form of the 6'6" goalie—and me.

I look down at the ground quickly, but Bennett sweeps up a hand to my chin.

"Look," he whispers. "Tell me what you see."

"I see . . . something bad. Someone who hurt you," I whisper, ashamed of the words but needing him to know. To understand that I hate myself for it all.

"Stop it," he whispers, his head dipping to nuzzle the crook of my neck. I go nearly boneless as he scoops an arm around my middle. "Look."

"Bennett . . ." My eyes cast down just slightly, avoiding the glass.

"Just look, P. *This* is the girl I've loved for four years of my life. Steadfastly adored. My *soulmate*." He tilts my head again to look in the mirror. "You. Exactly like this."

I look.

His body encases mine, and it's hard not to focus on just him—on the rugged lines of his face that mix so well with the aristocratic nose he broke when he was twelve. Of the clean cut of his stubble, the soft waves of his chestnut hair that look like warm coffee or the freshness of fall in the city. The long, thick muscles of his arms, the grip of his hand on my hip—

On the generous curve of my hip. I follow my own body down to my ankles, seeing the tightness of my legs that allow me to swim every day. To run away, when I've needed to. I see the way Bennett's shirt falls over me like I could live in it forever. Like it was made for my body. *Mine.* I see my face, bare and clean, looking youthful and content. Beautiful. My skin, pink from the hot bath that the boy I love made for me. Warm from the way the boy I love holds me.

"You're so beautiful," he whispers, kissing my neck. "So strong.

You aren't that little girl trapped in that house anymore. You're so smart, clever. Kind and wonderful."

"I'm not. I'm mean."

"Your meanness has kept you safe. I don't care if you've used it against me, because it's kept you *safe*." He emphasizes it again, hands crawling up my body to grip the small of my waist.

"I've been so horrible to you," I whisper. "I don't—"

"I would crawl through broken glass to get to you, P."

His voice is breathy and soft, but the words build pillars in my mind, making something new in the rubble of destruction. I turn in his arms.

"I would for you, too," I say, feeling ridiculous at the repeated sentiment, but I don't know how else to say it.

He presses a hard, fierce kiss to my lips.

"I know," he says, before kissing me again, gentle and slow, as he backs up to his bed, scooping me into his arms and settling me on his lap as he sits.

His hands smooth against my skin, leaving chilled bumps in their wake as he pulls my shirt up and over my head. Music plays. His eyes sparkle like living waters, and I feel the last piece of my armor break.

I push my hands against his shoulders, letting him settle into the mattress slowly as I rock against him and kiss him again.

He rolls me beneath him, my thighs stretched impossibly wide around the bulk of his body.

The way Bennett looks at me feels the exact same as the first time, on soft blue sheets with waves crashing outside and soft moonlight along more boyish features. When this pull between us was unmarred and pure. Something soft.

Maybe for him, nothing ever changed.

His pants come off and I can feel him against me. Skin to skin.

We kiss, touch, push into each other for a long moment, before I press against his shoulder and roll until I'm on top of him again. I lift up, looking at him for approval as I reach back and hold him in my grip. He's so fucking big it should be frightening, but I've never wanted anything more. Because it's him.

Him, him, him, like a silent chant.

"Are you sure?" I ask.

He nods, but his lips press to my cheek, his hand caressing lightly against my skin. "Please don't break my heart again," he begs, then follows it with a watery smile and half chuckle. "I don't think I can take anymore."

"Never," I vow. "I love you," I breathe, as my hips slip down and I take him slowly into my body.

He jolts, hips arching, and I moan a curse at the sheer size of him.

"Say it again," he begs. "Please."

I push up on his chest when he's still only halfway inside me.

"I love you."

I breathe in and sink the rest of the way down, huffing and moaning as he takes up every inch of space and then some.

And we stay there, hips flush. Completely connected.

His eyes shine with tears; his cheeks are wet. He reaches up to touch my cheek and I realize I'm crying, too—for the first time, happy tears.

"You're so beautiful," he mutters again, eyes in awe of me even as his gaze doesn't dip to my body. He's only looking at me. Me.

"I love you."

"You're so perfect."

"Just you."

"Just you," he whispers back, picking up the pace. "Just you and me, forever, love."

Falling in love with Bennett was like jumping into the ocean, expecting the water to be icy and painfully cold, only to be completely encompassed in comforting warmth. A warmth that has never faltered.

"I love you," I say again, because I can't help it. He slows again, savoring the feeling of us this close, before he presses his lips to my neck, just below my ear and whispers poems into my skin as he makes me come again and again, until we're both wrung out.

Love from Bennett Reiner will always be this—perfect and warm. It's homemade versions of my favorite food, warm blankets, firm hands on sore muscles, and gentle fingers in my hair. It's slow indie music that's just soft enough to be a lullaby, but with lyrics so beautiful my ears ache to listen. It's poems ripped from his favorite books lying on my pillow, with the words he struggles to say splayed on softly crinkled paper.

"You're the only person who has ever had me," I breathe, tears still spilling quietly over my cheeks. "All of me."

My words make him moan into the curve of my neck.

"I'll take care of you forever, P," he says, angling his neck to press our foreheads together in the quiet dark. "You just have to let me, love."

I release a hiccupped cry, overwhelmed by how I feel about him, distraught over the cycle I've felt perpetually stuck in that wouldn't allow me to have him until I could defeat this evil thing I've let live in my head since I was fourteen.

Bennett tucks me against his chest and pets my hair, soothing me, whispering soft poetry that I'm almost sure is *his*, until I'm calm again. Until I fall asleep with him still inside me.

CHAPTER 66

NOW

Bennett

I can't sleep.

I've propped myself up against the headboard, eyes focused on the rise and fall of Paloma's chest. As if her breathing controls my own breath.

It feels as if I've been split in two—the Before and After. Flashes of moments from the past three years, comments she's made, little glimpses she unwittingly offered into her past race across my mind. I've always found the softness in Paloma, the pieces of her she's hidden from everyone else. The pieces of her that have been *just* mine.

Now, it's like trying to put her back together in my mind. She is a shattered glass sculpture, and I have all the grace of a child with a glue stick and construction paper. Nothing feels like it will fit—nothing makes the pain lessen.

And the anger . . .

It's almost overwhelming. And she didn't offer a name—not that I'd be able to find this faceless villain anyway. And if I did? What could I even do?

Nothing. Just like you've done before—with her. With Rhys. With—

I shake my head. Maybe it would be easier to have something physical I could lay this rage and anger into on her behalf.

"I was ten when someone kissed me for the first time. He was . . . one of my mom's friends."

Her voice is a never-ending echo of torture in my head. But I welcome it like a penance to be paid. I've always known someone hurt Paloma—maybe more than just someone. But to hear her force herself to relive those memories so I could understand what I didn't really know . . . the pain of the last three years feels worse.

Worse because, no matter what . . . I can't fix it. I can't make it better.

For the first time since the gala, I check my phone. Texts and missed calls spill across the screen—Rhys, Freddy, Anna, my dad—all in multiples, times overlapping. Seeing it all at once threatens to send my anxiety spiraling further.

Focus. Most important item first.

It doesn't help—because my only thought is still the girl curled into my chest, using my pec and upper abdomen like a pillow.

Instead of replying or trying with any of them, I open my thread with Rhys and Freddy and type out a quick message.

BENNETT
Family breakfast in an hour. She needs routine.
Be normal and don't ask.

Their responses are nearly instantaneous.

RHYS
Got it. Whatever you both need, just tell us.

FREDDY
Yes, Chef! 😇😇😇

I slowly roll Paloma to her side before snapping my fingers for Seven to take my place on the bed. Still, my girl stirs and blinks bleary eyes up at me.

"Bennett . . . ?"

"Shhh, love," I whisper, kneeling by her and tucking some of her hair back. "I'm going to go start on breakfast. Sleep as much as you can. I'm leaving Seven here with you."

"Mmkay," she mumbles, turning on her back and letting Seven crawl and settle half on her stomach.

I close the door to the bathroom quietly, following my routine more stringently than I usually might with her in the next room. It takes almost too long, which makes my stomach churn about breakfast not being ready before everyone is downstairs to eat.

By the time I've finished the pancake batter and omelets, Ro, Rhys, and Freddy have joined me, talking and laughing as the sound of family permeates the room. *This is what she needs. This will show her that she's cared for.*

"Good morning, Reiny," Freddy greets brightly, seated shirtless at the table next to a fully put-together Ro. "Food smells amazing."

I nod. "Don't eat anything. I'm serious, not until I get Paloma from upstairs."

Stepping past where Rhys is making two lattes and taking his time with the artwork, I head up the stairs—only to see she's already on her way to me, dressed from head to toe in my clothes.

"Hungry, P?" I ask, taking her face in my palms. She nods, biting down on her lip. I want to ask her a thousand questions, but she still looks exhausted from last night. It doesn't help that my own emotions feel a little shot—all over the place all at once.

"Yeah, I think I could eat."

"Good." I press a kiss to her temple and bring her closer under my arm. "We're having family breakfast."

There's a brighter look then in her eyes, a twinkling of excitement and hesitant wonder.

"Really?"

I think I'm only just now understanding the depth of Paloma's loneliness. That it's more than how she's been at Waterfell, strangely isolated despite her popularity and well-known name. Her kind of loneliness goes further back. It makes a well of regret start to form, and how much I wished she'd been here at our table for breakfasts all along. Even as a friend—somehow included.

Wrong. I've gotten it wrong too many times. I'm determined now to never let her suffer again.

Once she's settled at the table, Freddy and Sadie already bickering to provide the entertainment, the doorbell rings. I hold a hand up to Rhys and offer to get it—nearly sure that Adam Reiner is about to make an unexpected appearance, if his frantic texts are anything to go off.

"It's weird. If she wanted me here, she would've asked."

The voices are muffled, but I can hear the girl clearly because she's slightly loud. I look through the peephole to see Toren and Lily side by side, arms crossed as they stare at each other.

"She wants you here," Toren says back quietly, his voice soft and unconcerned in sharp contrast to the almost-frantic, too-loud tone of his companion.

"You don't know that! You don't have friends, Tor. You don't know—"

I pull open the door, greeted by the ridiculous picture the two of them make: my defenseman towering in his black slacks and black button-up from the night before, sleeves rolled up, tattoos on display covering almost every inch of exposed skin. And next to him, a redhead barely half his size in brown boots, stockings, a pleated skirt, and turtleneck sweater.

"Toren." I nod to him. "Lily."

"Hi, Bennett," she whispers, suddenly shy as she ducks her head to stare down at my shoes.

"Lily wanted to check on Paloma after she didn't come home last night," Toren offers, a hand slipping to her back and pushing her a stumbling step forward. "I figured I could drop her here and I can pick her up later, or Paloma can take her back."

I nod, stepping to the side to let her in.

"Paloma is in the kitchen and would love to see you."

You might be the only friend she's ever really had. The only one she's made on her own.

Lily scurries off toward the kitchen, arguably too fast. Toren watches her go with a softer look on his face than I've ever seen—something almost serene.

"You should stay," I say, clearing my throat and gripping the doorframe. "Have breakfast with all of us."

"No." He smirks, but there's nothing happy in it. "You don't have to be nice to me, Reiner. It's fine."

My brow furrows. "Come inside. Eat with us. You're a part of the team."

A huff of a laugh blows from his lips and he shakes his head. "Right."

"You are," I say, more intense than the first time. My voice drops as I add, "And you look out for Paloma. You always have. I owe you for that at the very least."

He doesn't say anything, eyes down toward the dewy morning grass and damp concrete. He looks . . . young, and almost lost. *Is this how I looked all those years ago? Is this what I'd be without Rhys? Lonely and lost and rejected by everyone who doesn't understand me?*

Lily is a lot like me, I think, and Toren sticks close to her. Takes care of her.

There is a part of me that believes Toren is like Paloma, a bleeding heart and full up with love he doesn't know what to do with.

"I know you hit Sadie's coach that night, defending her. And I was there when you protected Ro from her ex-boyfriend. And I think you've done more for Paloma than you'll even share with me." I take in a slow breath, voice dropping. I don't mention the locker room, but it's all I can see when I look at him now.

I know what people said about him, the rumors that spread. I know what his old teammates have taunted him with on the ice and off it. But I also know what I've seen of him, how he's defended and protected these girls without even knowing them.

"You're not a bad guy, Kane."

He doesn't look at me, eyes firm on the ground, guard still up.

"So, I think you should come inside and eat with us."

Slowly, with a slight tremble in his hands, Toren nods and steps over the threshold to follow me inside.

. . .

"So, Toren?" Rhys asks, helping me clean up the kitchen after everyone's gone—Sadie to practice, Lily and Paloma back to their apartment accompanied by Kane, and Freddy and Ro to inevitably roll in the sheets upstairs.

"Yeah." I nod, rubbing the pan with the buffer scrub, careful as I set it to soak in the warm water. "I should've asked you about it. How you feel about him now."

Rhys shrugs. "I don't like him. But . . . he did punch that asshole Kelley, not even knowing Sadie. Maybe he's got more in him than I thought."

I nod again, shrugging my shoulders—though it does nothing to diffuse the tension in my muscles there.

"Doesn't make it easier to be around him," he mumbles and my body freezes, eyes shutting at the stabbing pain that reignites. I turn toward him almost too quickly, like running my eyes over him will erase the image of his body lying on the ice, the sound of his cry: *"I can't see. Where's my dad? I can't see anything—"*

My stomach churns again, but I shake my head and grip the back of my neck.

"I'm sorry," I say. "I should've asked. He just seemed like he was struggling."

"No kidding," Rhys mutters. "He was a wreck last night at the gala, too, after you left."

I should ask. But I can't think of anything besides, "Are you okay?"

The question seems to shake my best friend, his eyebrows furrowing as he looks at me. He's leaning against the stovetop, wearing a well-worn Berkshire sweatshirt I also own and a pair of flannel pajama bottoms, hair a mess.

"Me?" he asks, but nods. "I'm fine, Ben."

My nostrils flare and I close my eyes tight. "I can't tell sometimes. And it's a fucking mind game, trying to read you. Between you and Paloma, I feel like I can't breathe."

It isn't fair to put this on his shoulders—I'd argue it's counterproductive. But I can't help it. I still feel raw from last night, every emotion overwhelming.

"Bennett, what—"

"You didn't tell me anything last semester. You shut me out, and I keep trying to move on and be okay with it, but it's like stepping on a minefield. I don't know if you're actually okay or if you're just saying that, and I don't *want* to feel like I'm measuring every breath you take to make sure you aren't hurting and just won't tell me about it."

Rhys stands, arms crossed as he listens.

"And I'm sorry I didn't say anything about Paloma when it all happened—but you have always been the best in my eyes. The best hockey player, the best friend, the best guy I know. I'm so thankful for you. But I wanted Paloma to be mine, from the first time I saw her, and so I kept her to myself."

A bitter laugh works from my throat. "And you found each other anyway. And it doesn't matter that it was for barely a few dates or nights or whatever, it still *hurts*, and it's my fault. If I'd told either of you about each other, it never would have happened. But it did.

"What is so wrong with me that no one wants to tell me what's happening? Do I seem so fucked up in the head that no one wants my help? Paloma spent three years shutting me out to punish herself, hurt herself over and over, and I didn't see it. And you? You did the same thing. And I'm terrified every single day that you'll do it again, and because I can't read your goddamn expression, I won't know!"

In the silence of my loud confession, there is a strange relief.

"Bennett," he breathes, brown eyes watery as he looks at me. "I—I'm so sorry. You are my *best* friend. It had nothing to do with you. I didn't tell my mom or my dad or anyone. I would have never told Sadie if she hadn't found me mid-panic attack on the ice." He steps closer, hands outstretched. "It had *nothing* to do with you, okay?"

Another step, and then he grabs me in a tight hug. My dad, Anna Koteskiy, Rhys, and Paloma are the only ones I enjoy being touched by; I've missed this. I've missed my best friend. It feels like I haven't really been close to him since that hit. But maybe the fractures started earlier, that night sitting across from him and the girl I wanted more than my next breath.

"Just don't do it again," I say, half into his embrace.

He laughs, shaking his head. "Never." We break apart and he squeezes my shoulder. "Now, tell me the whole story, Ben. I wanna know how you met Paloma. Tell me everything I missed."

CHAPTER 67

NOW

Bennett

We win our regional semifinal—a hard-fought win, but I play nearly perfectly, only letting in one goal through the three periods. Thankfully, Rhys carries the team well—though the winning goal was scored by Toren, who was quiet and almost somber in his acceptance of the award from Coach Harris.

Paloma worked the game on the bench, eyes twinkling as Harris kept her close and spoke with her often, including her entirely in the real coaching experience. She was glowing by the end of the game, cheeks pink.

Now, she's standing in the line of coaches as Harris finishes his speech, hands tucked into the pockets of her oversized navy blazer, hair slicked back tightly into an elegant ponytail I'm desperate to tug on.

Rhys takes over as soon as our coach is done, announcing the Final Bash at the Hockey Dorms this weekend but being very clear on the usual rules: party as hard as you want, but then zero tolerance policy into the Frozen Four stretch.

Cheers erupt and Paloma breaks away from the line, stepping carefully toward my spot on the bench where I've removed most of my pads and am wiping off my neck, only dressed in my compression pants.

"Hey," she says, hesitant, picking at the sleeve of her jacket.

My smile is soft, eyes glimmering as I mumble, "Come here, P."

She steps forward into my embrace, letting me kiss her mouth in front of them all. We aren't usually the public-display-of-affection couple, but I feel possessive of her—always, but especially here in this locker room. I know how many of my teammates feel about Paloma, know the way some of them have fantasized vocally about her, have tried their hand at having her, so I *want* them to know.

She's taken. Forever, if I can keep hold of her like this. And *God*, am I going to try.

There's a few hoots and cheers, Rhys smirking next to me as he smacks my shoulder. Freddy catcalls us, shaking out his wet hair. Paloma pulls back from me and rolls her eyes, but her cheeks are pink, and her eyes are full up with love.

For me.

"You and Reiner now?" Holden smirks, shaking his head. "Come on, Paloma. Just give me a chance. When is it my turn?"

"Knock it off," Rhys says, still lighthearted, but clearly a warning.

"You're only saying that cause you already got a chance with her, Cap." Holden laughs, seemingly not noticing the shift at his words. "Paloma, baby, let me try. I bet I can—"

Paloma leaps for him suddenly, like she might hit him. Before I can move, Toren's arms wrap around her waist and yank her off Holden and back against him.

"Calm the fuck down, Blake," he whispers to her.

Holden wrinkles his brow, sobering quickly. "What the hell—"

"Shut the fuck up," Toren snaps, eyes darting toward his partner. "For one goddamn minute, Holden, shut up."

I'm crossing to them, half-dressed and sweaty, but it only takes a second for Paloma to realize I'm there. Toren lets her go, eyes staying on Holden even as he looks thoroughly apologetic.

"You okay, P?" I ask, voice a whisper as I move my hands to bracket her face and turn it toward me. She nods but huffs a breath. Angry tears build in her eyes as she hides her face in my chest.

Paloma sinks into my embrace easily and I pet her hair, kissing her temple. I don't say anything, but the way we move together seems to be enough.

"Why don't you go get your stuff and meet me right outside."

She agrees, her heels clicking loudly in the silence of the locker room.

My eyes scan over the entire room, where everyone is focused on me. I might not be the shimmering captain of gold or the terrifying defenseman who snaps at the drop of a hat, but I've made my place here. I have my own stoic, intense reputation.

My words aren't a yell, but they don't have to be. "Talk about her again like that, see what fucking happens."

My voice is solid and plain, no growl, no fury—just a threatening calm.

Most of them nod—Holden still watching me with a clear remorseful look on his face. And I know that he didn't mean to hurt either of us, but I've spent three years watching him shamelessly flirt with her. I just need a minute.

"See you all tomorrow," I say, tossing on my track pants and sweatshirt. For the first time, I leave without cleaning my pads or doing a single one of my postgame routines.

. . .

"Please—"

She's panting, eyes glazed and looking at me adoringly. It's a shot to my heart, as it always is with Paloma. But here, with her stretched out like an offering over my bed, arms tied together and held above her head—making her beautiful tits push forward even more—my gaze on her is almost worshipful.

"Bennett," she cries, body jerking as those same wide brown eyes shut tight.

My hand slides across her cheek to her mouth, covering it briefly with my finger to quiet her. I'm not surprised by the way her body curves and arches into even my smallest touch—I've been playing with her for ten minutes already, and she'd been dripping since I tied her hands.

She was fucking *made* for me.

"Can you be quieter for me, love?"

She nods over and over.

"Good girl," I say, dragging the word along her skin as I run my finger over her chin, down her neck, into the valley between her breasts. "You're holding it in for me, aren't you? Waiting for me to tell you to come?"

"Yes," she breathes. "Please—"

"Shh," I coo. "Tonight is going to be different. I'm going to make you come with my fingers, my mouth, my cock—" She moans so loud, I cover her mouth again. "And you can come as much as you want, without asking for permission, okay?"

Her nod is like a bobblehead, hair spilling from the tight ponytail it was in before. Unable to resist, I reach up and tug the elastic carefully, running my hands through the blond strands until they lay like water across my sheets.

"Do you know why?"

She doesn't say anything, grinding into the air—so keyed up. So free beneath my hands, trusting me so thoroughly. It's intoxicating.

"Paloma? Answer me, love. Do you know why I'm going to let you come as much as you want?"

She shakes her head, eyes tracking back to me.

"Because you *deserve* this. Because you are so good and strong and *perfect*. I want to make you feel good—to show you exactly how good you always are for me."

The words are softer than anything else I've said. And her body stills, eyes welling slightly with tears, mouth tipping into a soft smile.

I'll pour praise over her again and again for as long as I live, or as long as she lets me. Because *this* is how it makes her feel. And when she's so vulnerable beneath my hands, tied up and splayed in her purest form, I want her to *know* that I will care for her, love her, *worship* her.

"Are you going to let me take care of you? The way I want to?"

"*Yes*," she says. It's almost a plea. "Bennett."

Pulling her closer, I kneel on the floor between her spread thighs, tossing each one over the bulk of my shoulders, hand down my sweatpants as I lick at the seam of her pussy, pulling moans from Paloma's mouth.

I take my time with her, pressing my words into her skin, using my fingers to keep her suspended in pleasure while I praise her. I'm finally able to say everything I want to her, no fear of scaring her away or waking up without her beside me. She's *mine*.

"You're so beautiful. So smart.

"I've dreamt about these thighs, entangled with mine.

"When I fantasize about you, you're soft and warm in my embrace, letting me take care of you—just like this. Come again for me, P. I know you can."

I give her my fingers, my tongue, even my thigh so she can grind into it—making her come over and over again.

Her face is flushed, eyes bright and waterlogged, shimmering with release and need and the aftereffects of my praise I've come to expect. But still, I don't stop. I won't, until she *understands* how desperately I love her.

It's heady, my own pulse thrumming as I fit another finger into her, watching her body arch and pushing down on her abdomen lightly as I curl my fingers inside. She goes off again, clenching around me as I lean over her body and coo, talking her through it the way I know she loves.

"You are everything to me, Paloma," I whisper. "You breathe; I breathe. All I want is to make you feel good—here and everywhere. To keep you here, safe, if you want. I'll give you anything you want."

"I love you," she sobs out, body arching again and this time, I come, too—untouched, in my fucking pants.

Sitting back for a second, I huff out a few breaths.

Paloma stares at me with tears in her eyes before her mouth cracks open to whisper, "Can you untie me, please?"

Scooting up by her head, I carefully unfasten her hands, massaging her wrists as I check them over carefully. But the second I let one go, she leaps toward me, arms encircling my neck, her naked body attaching tightly to my clothed one.

Holding on to me. Whispering still, over and over, "Thank you. Thank you."

Something in my chest burns, the pieces of my once-shattered heart remade by her love and care of me now.

CHAPTER 68

NOW

Paloma

"Are you sure you want to wear that?" I ask, cringing at the question. "Are you gonna be comfortable?"

Lily nods, but her eyes scrunch a little in the mirror where she tries to pull up the slightly gaping cups of the corset top she's borrowed. I'm letting her have her moment, but she's not leaving in this ridiculous top.

Partially because it covers none of her. But mostly because it's the most *not* Lily thing I've ever seen her attempt to wear. She looks uncomfortable, messing with it continuously, chewing on her lip with a frustrated divot between her auburn brows. She's trying, for some reason, to be someone else. And I don't want that for her.

She's perfect as she is—and maybe no one has told her that.

Except for a large, usually hovering defenseman.

Biting my lip, I turn back toward her closet to rummage through her messy stacks of clothes, most of which aren't even hung on the slightly empty rack.

"What about this?" I ask, pulling out a spaghetti strap black dress with a thin scarf of matching material looped over the hanger. It still has the tag on, with a price higher than I've ever paid in *rent*, let alone for clothes.

"Oh," Lily breathes, fingers tapping over her lips as she settles onto the edge of the bed facing me. Her blue eyes are comically big with the work I did on her makeup, lips shiny and rosy. "I forgot I had that."

I let out a small, low laugh and pull the dress off the hanger.

"Maybe with your stockings and heels?"

She nods as if in a trance, takes the dress from my outstretched hands, and heads to her bathroom to change. There's a cacophonous sound of stumbling before she reemerges with the scarf in hand, biting her lip.

"Can you do it?"

I pat the seat at her vanity, deciding to pull her auburn locks up and out of her face into a bouncy ponytail. Then, I carefully wrap the scarf securely around her neck to drape down her pale, slender back.

"You look very pretty, Lily." My smile is real, bright next to my best friend. "This is going to be fun. Are you ready?"

She nods. "You look really hot," she says, eyeing my plain black dress. "And we match."

"Like twins."

Her smile widens, eyes twinkling. The moment feels vulnerable, like we both want to stay here and prevent the inevitable cracks and breaks we're both so used to. Lily is a little weirdo, but she's my little weirdo.

So it doesn't feel cheesy to tease her with a, "C'mon, bestie. Let's go," as we stand and slip arm in arm out the door.

. . .

The party is already in full swing when we arrive. I wanted to show up earlier, just in case Lily decided this wasn't her *scene* and wanted to go home. Or . . . if it was too much for me and I needed to make an escape.

But it's nice. Comfortable, because for the first time I'm not here to punish myself with hate-fueled sex or upsetting hookups. I'm here for a boy I'm in love with.

Bennett is against the far wall, huddled with the other guys from his line—Holden, Freddy, Rhys—and dressed in a black long sleeve and jeans. Somehow, he looks bigger. More powerful. More all-consuming. He's sporting a backward hat to tamp down the unruly brown and amber curls pouring out the back. He's so beautiful my breath catches, chest tightening like if I step too close, he'll disappear.

I take Lily's hand in mine before heading toward them, because without even looking back at her, I know her gaze is all over the place. Probably looking for a six-foot-six defenseman, though she won't admit it.

Bennett's eyes are on mine the whole way over, like a magnet pulling our gazes to each other across lifetimes. Only, this time it doesn't hurt.

Holden notices us next, eyes brightening with a playful, flirty edge.

"Ladies. Paloma, good to see you," he greets with a beaming grin. There's an apology in his gaze, but I nod toward him.

"Dougherty," I say. His smile renewed, he turns his eyes toward the girl at my side.

"Lily." He nods to my roommate with a sharper edge to his smile.

Lily blushes and wrinkles her nose. "Holden." Her arms cross, then release at her sides, hands flexing like she's not sure how to *stand*, let alone talk to the flirty defenseman.

"Hey, Bennett," I whisper as I step into Bennett's already open arms. He's so soft and warm, so resolute and solid as his hands slip over my hips and to my lower back with a heavy pressure.

"Hey, P." He smiles. His eyes are half-lidded, and he smells like citrus—no doubt from the IPAs he's drinking. Like he's at a fancy brewery and not a college hockey party.

And then, as if we've done this a million times before at a million other parties, he kisses me. Bold and sensual, his tongue slipping to open my lips. My heart thumps so hard I can feel it trying to pop out of my chest and into his hands. Like it always feels with him.

His hand slowly climbs my spine and into my hair.

I laugh lowly as he releases my lips but keeps hold of my hair.

"How early did you start on the beers?"

He smiles lazily, more relaxed and boyish than I'm sure I've ever seen him. "Like . . . five o'clock."

A brighter laugh pulls from me then as I shake my head at my slightly drunk boyfriend. "You're drunk, love."

"Drunk on you," he flirts, pulling me in for another kiss before sliding his nose against mine affectionately.

His hands grip my hips in a way that has me blushing more than the kisses do, mostly because it brings back flashes of last night—the way he held me so solidly as I begged for him. I'm sure there are still slight marks on my wrists from the tie he used to keep my hands tethered.

Bennett spins me to settle with my back to his front. His hand sits low on my abdomen, possessive and warm, as he continues to chat quietly with Freddy about something hockey related. I can barely tell. My mind is floating too far above me.

No, I think. *I'm the one drunk on Bennett Reiner.*

"Want a drink?" he asks, head tipping down to my ear, his lips and tongue lightly brushing the skin there. "I'll make it for you."

"Yeah?" I grin.

He nods, boyish and handsome, his hair a mess as he pulls off his baseball cap and readjusts it, pushing the mop of his curls back again. "Anything you want. I'll make it for you, P. Anything for you."

His words are slightly slurred, but he's not wasted yet—just enjoying himself with his friends. And with me. My cheeks warm as he spreads his hands across my waist and presses behind me to march us across the hall and into the kitchen.

A couple of the guys holler his name, and he nods politely, but his body heat never falters from my back, fingers squeezing on my hips.

The kitchen is dimly lit and crowded, an entire table dedicated to shots of different kinds. Bennett moves behind the makeshift bar where the freshmen are working and shoos them out of his way when they try to help him.

"My girlfriend—no one else touches her cup," he says when one of the guys says something. I feel light and airy—almost giddy with affection for him.

The playful side of my serious, stoic poet. Every facet of him beautiful and shimmering, like spinning a diamond in the sunlight.

I tell him to make me whatever he thinks I'd like, and he goes to work—only minorly spilling the liquids. I get distracted when he spills the tequila across his hand, because it makes him giggle before he licks the side of his hand and sticks his thumb in his mouth to suck it off.

My entire body flushes with heat and I discreetly cross my legs.

Whatever strange fruity cocktail he's made, it's delicious and I can barely taste the alcohol. "It's not much," he promises. "I know you don't like to feel out of control."

Another burst of warmth from my chest, affection swirling because I didn't have to explain it. He understood. He read me like his favorite poetry book, as he always has.

We stay in the kitchen, sipping on my drink together. I spend most of my energy trying to stay upright with Bennett Reiner whispering filthy words into my ear. It feels so good I want to freeze time.

Us. Here. Young and goofy and in love.

"Stay here for me?" he asks, leaning me against the bar top. "I just need to pee."

A blush takes over his face, head shaking as his hands come up to cover his eyes. "Why did I say that?"

I laugh, full and open as his hat topples off his head—though I catch it easily and slip it onto my own voluptuous curls, spinning it backward. I feel like I'm flying while flirting with him in the dingy light of the Hockey Dorms kitchen.

"Need me to come with?"

"No—if I get you into a room alone right now, P . . ." His voice rumbles off as he crowds into my space, dipping his head to kiss my cheek, my jaw, my neck. "Just stay here. Don't move."

He steps away, mussing his curls with one hand as he hangs on to the doorframe with the other. In his absence, another massive shadow appears—Toren Kane in his usual all-black fit, tattoos fully on display.

"Blake," he nods.

"Kane," I say, hip checking him as he settles next to me at the bar. He smiles but tries to hide it with a sip from a bottle of beer, not his usual alcoholic beverage. His rings click against the glass.

Music thrums in the silence between me and my substitute shadow. Someone yells loud enough to draw my attention toward the shots table—where my little roommate has become the center of attention, whether she realizes it or not.

Lily grabs for Holden's hair, jerking his head back a little roughly where he kneels patiently for her to even reach him. Toren straightens, shoulders tight, jaw locked.

"Stay still," Lily's bell-like voice rings out. Holden nods excitedly, eyes wide on her as she tilts the bottle to pour into his mouth for a long pull. He swallows, gasping for air with a rough pant as Lily pulls her hand away from his hair.

I watch Toren for a long time, though his eyes never leave the odd couple in front of him.

"Feel sick yet?" I ask.

His jaw somehow locks further, eyes flaming gold as he darts them toward me. My smirk is uncontainable—but before I can say anything else, a stumbling six-foot-six handsome man makes a reappearance.

"Blake—"

"Sorry, I gotta go," I say sarcastically with a laugh tossed over my shoulder. I point my thumb toward Bennett. "That's my ride."

CHAPTER 69

NOW

Bennett

"Hate to say it like this, but you're glowing," Freddy says, clapping me on the back.

Toren laughs and shakes his head. "He's not a fucking pregnant woman, Fredderic."

Freddy frowns up at the defenseman like he might want to start something, but Holden shoves in between them to settle against the kitchen bar we're all standing around.

"You gonna kiss him again?" Freddy asks, eyeing Holden's shoulder pressing into Toren's bicep where he's squished into the group.

At Ro's birthday party in February, apparently they'd played spin the bottle, which resulted in a kiss between the defensive pair.

Holden smirks. "If you're jealous, I can plant one on you, too."

Rhys and I laugh, while Toren merely smirks and rolls his eyes. Holden makes a kissing face toward Freddy who shoves him off.

"All this"—Freddy gestures to his body—"is a Rosalie-only zone."

It feels good to be here with my friends, drinking and laughing. Rhys is near to wrestling Sadie where she's standing in her tall boots on top of the counter, him crawling up after her. They're both drunk and giggling—blissfully happy.

Paloma, Lily, and Ro are dancing, laughing, spinning in a circle.

Mostly, they keep Lily in the center, the slip of a girl nearly disappearing between them.

Suddenly, Rhys is back on the ground, Sadie slung over his shoulder before he slides her down his body and toward the group of girls, whispering something into his girlfriend's ear that makes her blush bright red before he heads toward me.

"We're gonna Uber home soon and get some pizza. Do you guys want to join?"

I nod, and Freddy joins in, until eventually our entire line, including Toren and Holden, all agree to head out together. We call the cars and gather the girls. Rhys, Sadie, Paloma, and I pile into one, while Freddy, Ro, Toren, Holden, and Lily opt for the other.

Our car arrives first, just in time to grab the pizza that Rhys had the presence of mind to order ahead. Paloma stays outside to wait for her roommate, so I cuddle her close. Seven joins us once someone opens the door, settling at our feet after we both give him a scratch.

"It looks like a clown car," Paloma whispers with a laugh, watching leggy Ro and Freddy get out of the front, revealing Lily squished between Toren and Holden in the back bench seat.

They all hop out, Lily darting for Paloma the moment she's free, cheeks flushed to nearly match her hair. Paloma loops her arm around her roommate's shoulder as they strut ahead, heads leaned together.

Sadie plays her music, and we all lounge across the sofas and chairs in the front room. Rhys scoops her up in a bridal carry and sits on one end of the couch. He unzips her heeled boots and massages her feet as she eats her pizza and queues up more music.

Freddy sits at Ro's feet after giving her one of the chairs, head tipped back while she plays with his hair and feeds him a slice of pizza upside down, drunk and giggling.

And maybe it's because we're all drunk and sleepy, but I don't read too much into the odd trio in the other plush chair. Toren sits with Lily perched on the edge of his thigh, legs dangling. He's not touching her at all, but her scarf is half wrapped in Toren's fist.

Holden is on the ground, his shoulder pressed to the side of Toren's leg. Lily's legs keep swinging toward him, while Holden tries to catch one of her ankles with his hands as if they're playing a little game.

Paloma settles at my side on the sofa, resting across my chest, sleepy and soft, her fingers dancing over my pec. I feed her pizza with one hand and comb my fingers through her hair with the other. Seven lays down happily against the edge of the sofa.

It makes me remember all those months ago, when I'd wished for exactly this—her in my arms, with this family we've built all around me.

Safe. Here. Real.

Later that night, I tuck a sleeping Paloma into bed. Seven climbs in after her and huffs a contented breath. I try to sneak back down to clean up, but as I turn, Paloma's fingers grasp at the hem of my shirt.

"Can you just stay? I don't wanna fall asleep without you."

She's so beautiful lying against my sheets, amber light from the lamp that I always keep on for her glowing across peachy skin. Her hair is a mess from my fingers and her twisting and turning.

"Yeah, P. I'll stay."

I don't think I could love her more if I tried.

• • •

I feel a bit like Superman standing next to Paloma's car, getting my final moments with her before we load up to head to Connecticut for regionals. We're playing Dalton. I know a few guys from the team; we've played them before in season and partied with them after. But this game has more riding on it.

"You sure you want to come?" I ask again. Paloma worked three games on the bench as part of her internship already, but Harris gave her tickets to the rest of them if she wanted to attend. "You don't have to."

"Hush it," she snaps. "I'm all decked out beneath my jacket; you just haven't seen it yet." She smiles brightly up at me. "Besides, I'm going with Sadie. We're gonna shop around a bit before heading to the game and we will meet up with you after."

"Are you driving?"

"On the way back. We're taking my car, but Sadie's gonna drive us there." She reaches a gloved hand to my cheek. "Everything will be great."

The normal anxiety and heaviness on my chest are only multiplying with the weight of this game, the pressure to make it to Frozen Four one last time. But here with Paloma, I feel a modicum of calm. Like standing on the beach at Speyside, letting the waves lap at our toes.

Everything will be great.

. . .

We win. *Thank god.*

It's a hard game—low scoring on both sides because we're so evenly matched. Kane gets in another fight with the same guy from last game, which only seems to irk Holden, who goes after him the next play. Still, everyone mostly plays a clean game.

It's all thanks to Rhys that we end the game 2-1, securing our spot in the Frozen Four tournament.

After the game, we head to a bar Rhys found online—one that we could get to easily in an Uber while avoiding enemy territory. It's a country-style bar, all wooden with neon signs and something twangy playing on the speakers.

Freddy opts *not* to go, to stay at the hotel and call his girlfriend. It's different, a break in his usual away-game celebratory routine, but I couldn't be happier for him.

"Jesus Christ," Rhys mutters, ducking his head, a groan pouring from his mouth.

My eyes shoot wide with concern. "What? Are you okay?"

"No. My girlfriend is trying to kill me."

Brow furrowed, I look up, seeing Sadie pushing her way through the crowd with a twisted-up smirk. She's dressed in jeans and a very cropped shirt that shows off the solid plane of her stomach . . . and makes me slightly worried that if she lifts her hands, she'll flash the whole bar. The kicker is that I recognize the shirt—Koteskiy is printed across the back in big bold letters, but it has to be from when we were kids and cut most likely by the girl wearing it.

Laughing, I shake my head at my best friend. "And you're not happy about this because . . . ? Are you two in some competition?"

"Back to my usual build-up routine for Frozen Four."

Meaning he won't have sex with her. I almost snort out my beer.

"You've been playing fine, Rhys. Why punish yourself now?"

"Hey, regional champions," Sadie greets, refusing to slide into the booth with her boyfriend. "Hotshot," she whispers, hand doing something I don't want to know.

I nod to her, and flit my eyes away from the display when I spot who is right behind her.

The love of my goddamn life. Paloma Blake, dressed in an oversized jersey with my number and name on the back, baggy jeans, blond hair pulled back into a slicked ponytail. She smiles softly, relaxed as she approaches my side and slides into the booth with me.

"Hi."

"Hey, P."

I press a soft kiss to her temple as she curls her hands around my biceps and cuddles into me.

"Good game today," she offers.

"Yeah?" I grin. "Thanks for cheering me on."

She rolls her eyes before leaning in toward my ear. "Maybe you can read me poetry in bed when you get back. So I can see you really perform."

I'm hard as a goddamn rock—from her words, from the feel of her breath against my skin, from *her*.

"Anything for you, P. 'I do not know what it is about you that closes and opens,'" I whisper, before pulling her clasped hands to my mouth, kissing her fingertips and adding, "'Not even the rain has such small hands.'"

She shakes her head with a fake frown, skin flushed. "You forgot the line about my eyes."

"I'd rather talk about your hair."

"Yeah?"

I nod. "Let me touch your hair. Wrap it around my fingers, tightening the farther from my grasp you wander. Let me inside you. Let me sew my soul to yours like some great patchwork quilt across a sandless beach—just you and me. And the water between us."

I pull back from her ear, inspecting the contours of her face cast in shadowy light.

"I like that one. Who wrote it?" she asks.

"Me," I say, my own blush rushing up my neck and into my cheeks. "Every poem I write is about you, remember?"

She nods. "Will you let me see them all?"

I kiss the corner of her mouth, pulling her closer into this little bubble of bliss around us. "One day."

Forever will *never* be enough with her. I've known that since I was eighteen years old. But I'll take whatever she's willing and ready to give.

CHAPTER 70

NOW

Paloma

I'm almost back into Boston when I spot the car tailing us.

My brow furrows, but I don't say a word, just let Sadie play ABBA and scream-sing along to it. My enthusiasm dwindles the closer the car gets, until I see who the driver is through my rearview.

Oh my god.

Heart in my throat, I speed up just a bit, anxiety shoving my foot farther down on the gas.

Red and blue lights shine bright across the darkened pavement.

I speed up again.

"Jesus, Paloma," Sadie curses, her hand grabbing for the handle above her head. I check my review mirror and my stomach drops.

It's him. I know it's him. And I've done nothing illegal—not for a detective to pull me over. He's trying to scare me.

"Paloma?" Sadie says, her voice steady, calm. "Maybe you should pull over."

I can't. I try to explain, but my mouth won't open, jaw clenched tightly.

"Paloma, please." Sadie is more frantic this time. "You're scaring me. I can't get in trouble. My brothers—"

I slow down, because the truth is he'll follow me all the way home and I won't let him near Lily. Or my one safe place. It opens too many old wounds.

Pulling to the side of the road, I park and roll my window down.

He pulls up behind us, the isolated street cold and damp from the previous rain. I look over at Sadie's wide, terrified gray eyes. I've never seen her like this before.

My fingers are shaking, gripping the wheel, eyes glued to my rearview and side mirrors.

"Sadie, I need you to listen to me." I keep my voice steady and firm. "I need you to get my phone out of my bag and call Alessia."

Her eyes bug out as she looks at the man heading our way—out of an unmarked car, wearing dress pants and a button down, gun holstered, hair slicked back. "Is that—"

"Yes. Listen to me. I need you to call or text Alessia. Tell her Ethan Marks just pulled us over and I need her, okay? She'll know what to do."

"Paloma—wait. What is going on?" Sadie asks, taking the phone from my hand. "You didn't do anything wrong. You weren't drinking or speeding—"

"I know," I whisper, trying to calm my racing heart. I spare a glance at her, my hand reaching to grasp hers for just a minute. "I'm so sorry, Sadie."

"Good evening, ladies," Ethan says, ducking his head into the space of my car. "Do you know why I pulled you over?"

Because you're a fucking creep.

"No," I say, keeping a tight leash on my fury. I'm not scared of him anymore—I'm just *angry*.

"You were swerving all over the road."

"She was not—"

"Sadie," I snap, cutting her off. "Everything is fine. Let me just—"

"License and registration?"

I grab the documents and shove them into his hands roughly, huffing out, "Just let us go. I'm not trying to cause a problem."

He smirks, handing me back both my ID card and the papers for registration. "Right. Step out of the vehicle, Paloma."

Fury ignites like a match. "Fuck you," I snap. "I didn't do anything wrong."

As if it was what he wanted all along, he yanks on the door handle. "Do you want to do this the hard way?"

I look toward the rearview mirror again, seeing another figure under the streetlight move toward Sadie's side of the car. She looks terrified—enough that my stomach twists and I unclip my seatbelt. I push on the now unlocked door, sliding off the seat and into the den of a lion.

"Leave her alone," I say—not a plea, but a command.

Ethan grasps my arm and spins me toward the vehicle like he's going to pat me down, eyes blazing, intense. I press my own hands against the side of the car to steady myself. His hands run up my calves in quick succession, then over my thighs, across my ass—lingering slightly, but not fully—before touching my stomach. He presses his fingers up, up, up—before his body comes closer, his chest nearly flush with my back.

"Easy, Polly," he says quietly. Like a haunting lullaby I remember.

I can feel his breath against my neck, making my stomach churn with renewed nausea and rage like I've never known. For a moment, I see flashes of a girl—at fourteen, fifteen, sixteen—terrified of him and yet desperate for *someone* to care about her.

And maybe it's their rage, or maybe it's mine, that has my grip on my control unraveling as I spin to hit him as hard as I can.

. . .

The sterile, cold lights make me feel more exposed, but it's Sadie I'm the most worried about. She's next to me, one hand in mine, her other arm wrapped around her torso as Max Koteskiy stands behind her trying to calm her down.

"But—" she blubbers. "The boys?" Her voice is watery, like she might be crying. My stomach clenches and I stare down at my shoes. "Am I gonna be in trouble? What if—"

"You're okay, Sadie," Max whispers, kneeling and tucking her into his arms, which pulls her grip from mine. It might be the first time I've ever seen Sadie hug anyone that wasn't Rhys, Ro, or her brothers. "It's fine. Just calm down for me, *dochen'ka.*"

"Water, Paloma?" Adam asks, stepping up with a cup in each hand. I take one gladly, nibbling on my lip as I obsessively watch the door Ethan entered when we arrived. "Do you need something for your hand?"

The question makes my eyes dart away, looking down at the split skin over my knuckles. Is it strange that it makes me smile?

"I'm okay."

Adam nods. "Everything is gonna be fine. I'll take care of it—"

"Oh my god," a voice shouts, followed by the sound of clicking heels.

It's Alessia, running toward me at breakneck speed. Her arms fling around my shoulders. She's in black boots, a red coat, and black gloves, with perfectly styled hair, like she was in the middle of a high fashion shoot and not out to dinner with friends. I melt into her, breaths sawing out of me.

"Are you okay? God, Paloma—tell me you're okay."

"I'm okay," I manage, before slinking out of her embrace and back against the wall. "Alessia—"

"Who the hell are you?" she snaps, deciding that Adam Reiner is too close, towering over us both. Her eyes run over his messy brown curls, graying at the temple, and across his slightly rumpled suit and tie getup, brow furrowing.

"This is Bennett's dad. He's here to help." I shake my head, eyes dropping. "I'm fine. I didn't mean to scare you. I'm sorry—"

"Don't apologize. You did nothing wrong." Her eyes go cold and she turns to look around the room before she sneers. "Where the fuck is he?"

She's the only one that knows everything—though I'm sure Sadie's figured much of it out by now—so when her eyes connect with Ethan as he steps out of the office, she takes off again.

Heart in my throat, I can't even manage to shout for her. But Adam seems to figure it out fine, his legs moving swiftly behind her—

"Hey," Alessia shouts, grabbing Ethan's biceps to spin him toward her. But before she can hit him, Adam swoops an arm around her waist and scoops her backward against his chest. She wrestles against him, but he says something in her ear that has her eyes shooting up toward him, fight leaving her body. He lets her go after a moment, both ignoring whatever Ethan is shouting as well as the cops surrounding him.

Adam takes over, speaking swiftly and calmly—low enough that I can't hear.

"What the fuck?" Ethan spits. His face is red and I wonder if it's from me. My arms were swinging wildly. I know my elbow caught his jaw, and he's got a patched-up cut on his eyebrow, so maybe that's where my hit landed.

"*Fuck you*," Alessia shouts.

I take another sip of water, hands shaking, eyes never straying from the scene.

There's another burst of noise and all our eyes are drawn to the entrance, where Bennett and Rhys are shoving their way through.

"Gray!" It's almost a frantic shout as Rhys makes it to us first, reaching down and grabbing Sadie out of his father's arms. He scans his eyes over her, making sure she's all right, before picking her up and tucking her head into the crook of his neck for a long moment. Her legs wrap around his waist and I see relief pour over him before he turns his face away, kissing her hair and whispering quietly as her shoulders shake.

Bennett stops right in front of me, head ducking to look into my eyes. My stomach somersaults.

A long moment passes, both of us just looking at each other—searching for something. And I let my walls fully down, pouring everything I have into the string that seems to bind us.

He nods, like he understands some great truth.

Bennett closes his eyes only for a moment, breathing slowly, before tucking his hand under my chin. "Are you okay?"

I nod. His brows dip as he glances over me again, his hands moving my body like a doll, inspecting every inch before—

"What the fuck?" he snaps, voice louder. His nostrils are flaring like an angry bull, shoulders hiking with tension. "Who did this to you?"

My gaze flutters past his body anxiously, toward where Ethan, Alessia, and Adam are still standing off. Bennett tracks my gaze, a punch of breath leaving him as his eyes close tightly and then open over me. They drop back to my bruised hand again.

"Was it him?" His voice sounds like gravel in a blender.

My eyes dart away, only for a second, before Bennett's hands bracket my face. Gentle, but firm.

"P," he breathes.

"Yes," I say, my voice quiet.

"You hit him?" he asks, his voice still steady, but overwrought. I can feel the intensity he's holding back like a wave. "Because he . . . Paloma." He swallows, his throat working against strain. "Is that who—"

My eyes squeeze shut. I know what he's asking and I don't want to say it.

"Tell me, P. Please." He swallows hard. "Was it my fucking stepfather? Was it Ethan?"

I nod, biting down on my lip and taking in a shaky breath.

Bennett's face cracks—just for a moment, pure anguish and grief, guilt, flash across it clear as day. I have a front row seat to the confession that I always worried would break him.

But then he straightens, body somehow growing bigger and taller as he nods heavily. His eyes stay glued on my bruised hand as he juts his chin toward his best friend.

"Rhys."

That's all he has to say. Rhys, Sadie still in his arms, steps to my side as Bennett storms heavily across the room toward where Adam is still holding Alessia, looser now, and Ethan is talking to an officer.

He eyes Bennett's approach, and I swear he looks nervous. But there isn't some kind, simpering look. It's a sinister, mocking smirk I recognize. One that makes me back up just a step, before I steady myself.

Bennett is here. Alessia is here. Adam is here. No one is going to hurt me.

As if she knows where my thoughts have gone, Sadie's hand dusts over my shoulder and squeezes. I'm grateful for the support, more than she knows, but my eyes are locked on Bennett as he approaches my nightmare of the last seven years.

Ethan opens his mouth and spits something at Bennett. Something vile, clearly, by Alessia's reaction. Adam, jaw clenched, fury bright on his face, has to cage her in again as she reaches to hit him.

But no one is there to stop Bennett.

My boyfriend lets his fist fly.

Blood sprays from Ethan's nose and Adam let's Alessia go, shoving her body behind his and grasping his son's biceps. Though Adam doesn't look disapproving so much as protective, pulling Bennett closer to him.

Bennett doesn't say anything to Ethan—only stares at him for a long time, nostrils flaring, jaw locked, as if there's so much he wants to spew at him, he can't get it out.

Instead, Bennett turns away, shrugging out of his dad's grip and quickly walking back to me.

He looks intense, like an avenging angel, a bit of blood splattered across his shirt as he stalks toward me quickly. There is a practiced calm there, covering the simmering fury underneath.

"Come here, P," he whispers, opening his arms and pulling me into his embrace, tucking his hands into my hair as he presses a kiss to the top of my head. "You're okay. Everything is gonna be okay."

He keeps whispering phrases over me as I sink into his body.

"You're okay." Fingers combing through my hair, careful of a few knots I've created. "Nothing is going to hurt you again. Ever." A kiss to my temple, the scratch of stubble. "I'm not leaving you alone. I'm here." His fingers on my wrist, pulling my right hand to kiss around the busted skin, careful, as if I'm made of glass.

Adam is still calming everyone down in the corner, conversing with an older officer who I assume might be in charge. Alessia appears next to us and speaks quickly to Max and Rhys, who both nod and then leave, Sadie sandwiched between their tall forms. Then she ushers me, still in Bennett's arms, into an empty conference room. Adam follows in after us.

"They need to talk to you—to open a report," Alessia says, sitting on the lip of the table, crossing her legs. "After that, we can go home."

I nod, not bothering to ask for any clarification, but a little rush of worry sneaks up my spine. "I don't want to go in alone. I don't trust—"

Adam raises his hand and nods. "Alessia has made everything quite clear to me. That won't be an issue. I promise." There is a vow in his words, the same steadiness I see in Bennett now clear in his father's eyes.

"You're not alone, P," Bennett whispers, pressing another solid kiss to my temple, hand moving beneath the curtain of my hair to massage lightly at the base of my skull.

"You'll come with me?" I ask, eyes finding Alessia's.

She smiles and nods. "I always have you, Paloma. You know that."

I step forward to her, letting her take my hand in hers. Bennett watches me vigilantly before clearing his throat. "I think maybe my dad should go, too—just . . . just in case. He's a lawyer and—if it's okay with you, it would make me feel better, knowing he's there to look out for you."

I nod—but if I expected Adam to deny his need to be there, I'm wrong. Instead, he's locked in a long, intense look with his son.

"You have to take care of her," Bennett says. A moment passes between them: identical blue eyes, matching hard lines of their body, intensity in equal measure.

"I will, Ben," his father says. "I promise."

They step just outside, giving me a moment alone with Bennett. My mouth opens repeatedly but I can't manage the words to explain it all—to tell him everything.

"I'm sorry I didn't—"

He cuts me off with a quick shake of his head. "No, P. Don't do that."

His hands are still tucked into his pockets, brow set deeply as he watches me carefully. Neither of us move—toward or away from each other.

"You promise you'll stay here?" I hate how needy, how desperate my voice sounds, but I can't stop it.

Bennett moves, the long length of his legs taking him directly in front of me. My eyes don't move away from his sneakers. "You know you can trust me?" I nod. "You know I love you?" I nod again, swallowing against the knot in my throat, blinking away any tears threatening me. "Then let me take care of you, P. We can talk after."

He takes my face in his hands, careful as he tips my head back to look at him.

He's so beautiful.

"I'll be right here when you're done, okay?" I nod again, raising one of my hands to linger over his. "And then we're going to go home and I'm going to run you a bath and wash your hair and feed you—I'm going to take care of you, like I always do."

"Okay."

"You're so strong, Paloma."

He kisses my forehead, lips lingering, nose tilting against my hair. And then he leaves. It's only a few minutes and one hot coffee later that they bring in the detective to take my statement.

With Alessia holding my hand and Adam standing like a sentry beside me, I let the words I've held back for years spill forward.

About my mom, about the men in our house, about the cold frigid nights and my fear. I tell them about Ethan—how we met and what he did to me. I even explain that it's why I broke up with Bennett the first time.

And I spare them no detail.

Afterward, the detective leaves. Adam stands in the corner, arms crossed, anger palpable—though I know it isn't at me. It's for what has happened to me. And yet, I can't stop from saying, "I'm sorry."

Adam shakes his head and steps forward. "Don't apologize. Someone should have been protecting you. This isn't your fault—"

"It's complicated," I whisper. Alessia eyes me with a firm shake of her head.

But it's Adam who says, "You were fourteen, Paloma," in a frustrated whisper as he sits down in the chair beside me. "You didn't know any better and someone should have been watching out for you. Taking care of you."

He stands and reaches out his arms, tentative but steady. I follow suit, allowing myself to step into them this time, letting Adam Reiner hug me. Alessia pets my hair, smoothing out the tangles slowly.

"You did nothing wrong. You're okay, and you're here—alive.

And you're telling us now. Bennett won't let anything happen to you. Alessia won't let anything happened to you." He clears his throat, but it makes no difference in the garbled sound of his voice. "*I* won't let anything happen to you."

This must be what having good parents would be like.

CHAPTER 71

NOW

Paloma

We drive back to Bennett's dad's home. Bennett sits up front with his dad, while Alessia sits with me in the backseat. She holds my hand, like a mother might.

After I finished my story, telling it quickly, mostly in order, I felt . . . drained. Talking about it wasn't difficult for me, but it didn't stop the exhaustion in the aftermath.

"Have you noticed the way you talk about these things?" Dr. Sutton said once, after I'd explained my mother briefly—what growing up was like for me. *"It's like they happened to someone else."*

Maybe it was easier that way. Maybe it was safer.

And maybe I *knew* it wouldn't be like that with Bennett. With him I'm always vulnerable, my heart too soft and open because of the trust he's spent nearly four years building. Which is why I'd avoided him after we left the interrogation room, hands tight to my sides, sticking close to Alessia and as far away from the hovering goalie as possible.

The clear hurt written across his face never faltered, even as his dad settled a hand on his shoulder to direct him out. Bennett had jerked away from him, angry and confused and frustrated in a way that was almost palpable.

No one speaks for the entire drive.

When we arrive in Beacon Hill, Adam opens the door and helps Alessia out, who turns around to help me. Bennett's hand hovers by my waist when I almost fall trying to climb out—but he doesn't touch me.

Which makes me feel worse.

Alessia pulls me away from the concerned Reiner men, her palm on my shoulder as she ushers me into the house.

"Go upstairs, and take all the time you need," she commands lightly. "Do you want Bennett to come up and see you in a little while?"

I hesitate, wishing this wasn't my decision. Slipping my chin up over my shoulder, I look back at Bennett. He's standing quietly, hands in pockets, eyes on me—red and waterlogged. But there are evident traces of fury across the planes of his handsome face.

I nod.

As I step away, I can barely make out the click of Alessia's tall heels, and her voice.

"Paloma's going to shower and sleep in your room. But I think you should give her some space, just for a bit."

My steps grow quicker after that.

. . .

It feels like days go by between my shower, changing clothes, and sitting on Bennett's bed, but it's only been an hour. Seven is at my side, his paw on my thigh like he wants me to lay down so he can press his weight on top of me. He can feel my anxiety.

I feel stupid, sitting in Bennett's clothes, my usual wooden paddle brush in my hand, tangled hair creating a wet spot on the back of my shirt. But I can't do it.

A knock finally sounds at the door. I feel a hiccup caught in my chest as I wait for Bennett to enter.

"P?"

"Come in," I squeak out, eyes welling almost immediately at the disheveled sight of him.

He stands at the foot of his own bed like a stranger, eyes downcast like he can't look at me. My hand squeezes on the handle of the brush. I feel stupid, ridiculous.

"I'm sorry if I shouldn't be here," I whisper. "And I know I need to explain—"

"You don't," he cuts me off, voice gruff. "Not if . . . not if you don't want to. I don't want to ever take something from you that you didn't want to give."

My heart aches. "Bennett, I *want* to explain. To you. Because you deserve to know, but also because I want to tell you. So you can have all of me."

His eyes are blistering and sincere as he stares down at me. "Okay," he says. Bennett takes a step forward, then pauses and, voice filled with the same vulnerability I feel, asks, "Do you want me to brush your hair?"

"Please?" I ask, scooting forward on the bed.

Bennett comes around my side, settling the bulk of his body at my back. He takes the brush from my hand and starts on the ends of my tangled hair, never pulling, ever gentle.

And the almost hypnotic feeling that comes from the task allows me to speak.

This time, as I tell the story he's heard in pieces, I tell it as myself.

"Have you noticed the way you talk about these things? It's like they happened to someone else."

"I don't know what you mean," I say, hugging myself around the middle as I settle back in the chair. "It's not that—I just . . . It's fine. It happened and now it's over."

"Paloma," she says, voice soft. "It happened to you. And I think you need to remember that—"

It's hard, sometimes, to remember that the little girl with pigtails in the back of my mind, who forces me to hold on to the velveteen rabbit stuffed animal and keep a constant grip on my backpack like someone will take it, is *me*.

Bennett sits quietly, even after he finishes brushing every strand of hair, careful and tender. A solid presence against my back, firm. Unyielding—like he's always been.

I tell him everything—how Ethan found me, how he manipulated me for years. How he took my virginity at fourteen and then spent the next two years convincing me I'd asked for something I *knew* I didn't want. I explain the mind games, the times he picked me up in a police cruiser from my friends' places, keeping me isolated and terrified of leaving or telling anyone.

It takes a long time—long enough that it's three in the morning by the time I finish, voice hoarse. I'm sure there will be more stories, pieces of trauma that come out at different times throughout my life—Dr. Sutton had warned me as much, and even she hadn't gotten to talk about this with me just yet.

And there are still things I'm not ready to say, as if saying them aloud makes them more real than they already are. Or gives them more power to hurt me again.

But I've said enough.

Lastly, I explain the full story of what happened on New Year's Eve our freshman year, when I saw Ethan again. Part of me wants to downplay it, to make Bennett feel better—but lying and covering up for three years hasn't helped anyone. So, I don't.

"I'm . . . It was bad. I should've told you. But I was scared."

Bennett's arms, loose at his sides with his massive hands resting on the curve of my waist, suddenly lift and disappear. The lack of his weighted touch fills me with a rush of anxiety.

"P," he says, the singular letter nearly a gasp. "I'm—*god*. I'm so sorry. I didn't—If I'd known, I would've never—"

"I know," I say, quieting him, turning to kneel between his spread legs. "I don't blame you. I just needed you to know everything. I needed you to understand why I pushed you away that night. I'm sorry I hurt you. It hurt me, too."

A strange smile etches across my face, but it's real and warm. I feel a little lighter now as I look at Bennett—the stubble across his cheeks, his disheveled curls, the depths of blue ocean water in his eyes. He's older now, but I can see him at eighteen, eyes just as bright with wonder as I lean in to kiss his mouth slowly.

"I think for a long time I just wanted to know that someone cared if I was alive," I say. "And I was scared because I felt alone. I was worried if you knew—about Ethan, about my past—I'd lose the one person in this world who cared about me."

"You're never going to be alone again, okay?" He presses a kiss to my temple. "I care about you. My dad, Alessia, Lily, Sadie, Toren, Rhys, Freddy, Ro, Holden, Coach Harris, Seven—they all care about you. You're important to so many people." He keeps his hands on my face, pulling me forward to look into his beseeching gaze. It's desperation in his voice when he begs, "Tell me you understand."

I nod.

Bennett shakes his head, the scruff of his five-o'clock shadow scraping over my forehead. "Say it, Paloma. Tell me that you're important." His voice is all dominating seriousness.

"I'm important."

"Tell me that you are loved." He says it adamantly, with a ferociousness I can't say I've seen in him before.

"I'm loved."

"Tell me that you know how much I care about you." He gasps a breath, eyes welling. "That I couldn't do *this life* without knowing you're alive and safe and okay. That you are the greatest love I've ever known and ever will know. That your kindness, gentleness, love—it *saved* me before you even knew me. Tell me you know."

"I do," I breathe, pulling him closer, holding him tighter. He grips me the same, until I cannot tell where I end and he begins.

Time passes slowly. Bennett gathers me somehow closer, his hands in my hair starting to quiet my mind—the exhaustion I'd already felt leaving the police station renewed tenfold. My eyes feel as heavy as my body in his arms.

"I'm sorry," he whispers into my skin, leaving passionate, forceful kisses behind—as if trying to mark me. "I'm sorry. I failed you. I won't let it happen again."

He's saying something wrong—something important—but my eyes are weary now that I've found a moment of peace.

I mutter something about feeling so tired, so sleepy, to him. He quiets his own words, petting my hair and slowly maneuvering us to lay flat. I'm asleep before I can hear whatever he says next.

CHAPTER 72

NOW

Bennett

I don't sleep.

My dad is in the kitchen when I come downstairs, head bent over his phone, laptop open. I'm almost sure he never went to sleep. He's wearing his glasses, which he only wears when his eyes are irritated.

"Bennett," he says, eyes snapping up at the sound of my entrance. "You okay?"

"Fine," I slip the word out, just barely.

He nods, eyes darting back down to the papers in front of him as I ask, "Did you know? About Ethan. Is that why you never liked him?"

My dad heaves a sigh, his features sinking in exhaustion. He's always looked young and vibrant to me, but now he seems older. Serious in a way I haven't seen in a long time.

"Not exactly. I didn't know everything for sure, but I had a gut feeling about him. That—and a few of my early interactions with Paloma . . . she seemed scared of me."

Another thing I missed.

"Are those all about Paloma?" I ask, gesturing to the brown manila folders spread and stacked precariously across the countertop that he's set up as his workspace. I wonder briefly why he's not in his office.

"No. Just this one." He nods and holds up the thickest one. "The rest are from Alessia. She's been busy."

"What do you mean?"

"She's kept tabs on Ethan—at least since Paloma came to her at sixteen, through a women's shelter referral. As usual with offenders like him, where there's one victim, there's a trail. So many who came forward, only to be shut down or have their cases closed with no real help. It's . . . god, Ben. It's bad." He shuffles a few of the folders and breathes, head in his hands. "These are all the girls who agreed to come forward, testify—I'm sure there are more we don't know about and possibly never will."

My dad sounds furious, angry—never one to hide his emotions. I stay silent, nauseous and unable to think of anything to add.

"Where's Alessia?"

"She's sleeping in my room." Adam sighs. "At least, hopefully. But I doubt she's gonna sleep until she sets her eyes on Paloma again." His hands dust over the top of Paloma's file. "It's . . . it's worse than I thought. She's going to need us, Ben."

A wave of pure pain buckles my knees. My hands grip onto the counter harshly—enough that I jostle the file and a few loose items fly across the floor.

I reach down but pause and sink to my knees at the small, worn photograph between my thumb and forefinger.

Paloma—I know it's her, but she can't be more than five or six years old. She has pigtails and her favorite stuffed rabbit, though in the photo it's still bright and new, no missing threads or lopsided stuffing. She's grinning at the camera, but her eyes look almost worried. Like this was the moment things started to change.

I don't realize I'm crying until my dad's hand on my arm makes me jump, body sliding away from him with a gasping breath.

He kneels next to me, eyes wide, hands settling on my shoulders. "Breathe, Bennett. Breathe."

I try to. But I can't stop feeling it. Seeing it all, over and over again. *Her*—in her dorm room, trying to make something new. The things she let slip, the small comments that had made me look twice at her, but I'd let them all go. Because I just wanted to be *near* her. And instead, I'd only caused her more pain.

Because I wasn't paying attention, to see what was happening. What I allowed to happen.

"It's not your fault," my dad says.

My eyes slip into a glare, fury radiating off me, as I push to stand, shoving him away. "Yeah? I brought her face to face with the man who fucking abused her for years and . . . what? I'm just supposed to live with that?"

His eyes shutter, his own torrent of emotions nearly slipping through.

"You have to figure out a way past that guilt, Bennett. You couldn't have known. She didn't tell you—"

"She didn't tell me because she was *scared*. And I just let it fucking happen."

"You didn't—"

"I don't wanna talk about it right now," I grit out, almost flushed with the panicked feelings swirling through me. "Just tell me you're taking care of it."

He wrestles for a moment over what to say before brushing a hand through his hair. "Yes. Of course, Bennett. I'm doing everything I can to make sure Ethan Marks pays for everything he did. And I'm trying my hardest to keep her out of it."

My nostrils flare. "You have to. Don't—please, don't make her see him again."

My dad nods, eyes red as he rubs at them again. He looks years' worth of exhausted. "I'm trying, Bennett. Please . . ." His words trail off. "You have to trust me with this."

A long silence settles between us, heavy with tension. I nod.

"Do you want some coffee? Or I can clear out of here if you want some space to cook?"

I shake my head.

"All right," he says, a little stiff. Awkward. Words I'd never use to describe my dad. "I'll just—I'm going to shower, and I'll be right back."

Another wave of guilt rolls through me. A few years ago, it wouldn't have been like this between us, tension stretching, anxiety swirling. My dad would've hugged me already and not second-guessed his instincts when it came to what I needed from him.

But it's my fault. I did this to us, pushing him away. Making our entire situation wrong and painful.

The same way you did to Paloma, huh?

My stomach rolls again. But this time with something different—a strong emotion that has my throat clogged, my hand rubbing my eyes to hide the well of tears.

Grief. For time lost with my dad. With Paloma.

Stumbling, I step toward the stairs and back into my room, as quiet as I can be. Seven is still asleep at Paloma's side, and she's curled around him in my absence.

She's so beautiful, and so deeply sad. Each of her tears feels like ripping my fingernails out, the pain just as great as the compulsion to do something so punishing.

How did I miss it? What is so fucking wrong with me that I couldn't fix this? Couldn't take care of her?

Wrong, wrong, wrong—I should've known.

She takes in another deep, rattling breath, like a leftover sob leaking into her sleep. I clench my fist.

Everyone I've ever loved has only faced demons I can't win against—nothing physical I can lay my anger and fear into. Only things I was too late to stop. Rhys and his panic, his anxiety. My dad and his self-inflicted solitude. My mother and her self-hatred, her unsettled fear of loneliness.

Paloma.

I look at her now and I can see her as that little girl. The photo of her in the fucking case file—five years old with lopsided pigtails and mismatched bows. And the velveteen rabbit in her grip. I can see her at fifteen, confused and scared and threatened by someone who was meant to protect her. Abandoned by everyone else. I can see her at eighteen, remember her beneath my hands, wonder-eyed as we touched for the first time. Falling in love with me, so much more experienced and yet not—no one had ever held her with care.

Does she believe I abandoned her to rot in her own self-hatred? That I stood by while she hurt herself with guilt and pain, thinking that she wasn't worth the battle?

Why can't I get this fucking right? Why can't I save just one of them?

I feel like I'm drowning, only this time I don't want to come back up for air.

I feel like a failure—on the verge of a panic attack.

Breathe. I try to listen to the voice that sounds like a warbled mix of Dr. Anya and my dad. *Make a list.*

1. *I failed Paloma. I brought her worst nightmare back into her life.*
2. *Paloma is still asleep in my room, for now.*
3. *My dad noticed something was wrong. I didn't. I failed him and her.*
4. *Rhys barely came back, and I had no hand in that. He did better without me bringing him down. Is Paloma the same?*

There's only one conclusion: Everyone is hurting and I'm only making it worse.

CHAPTER 73

NOW

Paloma

Seven is in bed with me and Bennett is gone when I wake up. My head feels heavy enough that I roll over like I might just sleep for longer—before deciding that might be my worst idea.

The first time I met Alessia Baudelaire she let me stay at her apartment. I was too scared to go home or anywhere else—so she took care of it. Took care of me. And I remember feeling so sick the next morning, not wanting to leave or get out of bed. Terrified of what would happen next.

"*Take the time you need,*" she told me in that same firm but soft voice. "*But then you have to get up. That's what we do. We get up. We keep going. Women can survive anything. We're the stronger ones—remember that when someone tries to make you feel small or weak.*"

Get up. *Get up.*

I push up and grab for the water by the bed, realizing there are wrappers next to it. Goldfish and a protein bar, half eaten. I know I'm the one who ate them—but Bennett must've been in a rush if he left them here. He *never* leaves trash out.

That captures my attention.

I slide off his bed and stumble into the bathroom to brush my teeth, wash my face, and braid my hair back.

Adam is downstairs in the kitchen, still dressed as he was last night, leaning halfway over the counter as he whispers quietly to Alessia—who is wearing a sweatshirt and soft flannel pants I'm nearly positive belong to Adam Reiner. I wonder if he gave them to her, since she didn't want to leave me here. The tension between them at the police station seems to have dissolved.

"Good morning, Paloma," Adam greets first, but steps backward, giving me unneeded space.

"Good morning," I reply, quiet, eyes still searching. "Um . . . where's Bennett?"

The question seems to jolt Adam. He grabs for his phone and checks it before blowing out a heavy breath. "He went for an early morning run, I think. That's good—he needs a little movement and quiet time, yeah?"

Yeah. Except Bennett doesn't really run.

"Do you want something to eat? Coffee?" Adam asks me.

"Coffee," I say. I don't take him up on food, thinking only of Bennett. Cooking calms him and maybe feeding me will make him feel better. Maybe it will help us *both*.

Adam starts on my coffee from the expensive stainless-steel machine, while I step up next to Alessia at the counter.

"What happens now?" I finally ask, chewing on my lip.

"Everything is up to you," Adam says. The words are meant to make me more comfortable, but they have the opposite effect. "But I think most important is setting up someone for you to talk to."

"Oh, um—"

"Paloma already has a therapist she sees," Alessia butts in as Adam hands me a steaming, frothy latte. "And, as long as this guy isn't lying about how good of a lawyer he is, I think we're all set. I wish I'd gotten a hit in, though."

The memory of Bennett's fist hitting Ethan square in the nose makes me grin into my mug. It's a scene I'll be playing over again many times in my mind for sure.

Adam tries to hide a brief, amused smile toward Alessia, but I clock it.

"I'm okay," I say, taking a quick sip that burns my tongue. "But . . . I meant more that I'm not in trouble? And Sadie is okay? I just don't want to cause something—"

"Everything is taken care of on that end," Adam soothes me, sending me a quick wink. "I may not be the best father, but I'm not lying—I am a good lawyer." He says it with a slight chuckle. It makes my chest squeeze slightly because . . . I don't think he's a bad father. I don't think that Bennett thinks that either.

But trying to console him without Bennett here feels wrong.

"We can wait on everything else until you're ready and know how you want to handle it," Alessia adds. "And you have time."

I nod. I want to ask more questions: What happened to Ethan? What happens now? Will I have to talk to more people about this whole thing?

But before I can say anything else, the door opens and Seven leaves his place on my feet. I follow him, moving swiftly to the front door where Bennett now stands.

Only clad in an athletic shirt and shorts, he's pink from the icy wind and cold weather. Sweat soaks his clothes and his hair. His eyes are red rimmed.

My shoulders relax, though not fully because I can feel the tension hanging in the air, careful and almost electric.

"Are you all right?" I ask, calling his attention to me.

Bennett nods, pressing a hand through his droopy honeyed brown curls. "Yeah."

"You've got to be freezing."

"I'm fine," he says, stepping out of his shoes and standing still—not moving toward me. "Good morning, Paloma."

My heart warms at the familiar, belated greeting. "Good morning, Bennett."

It's almost like he's unsure where he wants to move, if he wants to at all. He's frozen in the hallway, muscles tense, eyes pointed at my feet.

"Are you all right?" he finally asks, the lines of his face tight, lips pressed together.

"I'm okay," I whisper. "Hungry, though."

It works like a charm, Bennett nodding and stepping past me into the kitchen. Seven is still sitting at the front door, unsure where to go. He looks at me, then down the hall, back and forth until finally he comes to my side and nudges me with his nose.

Brilliant dog.

We trek behind Bennett, both of our brown eyes filled with worry over the boy we love so much.

I nearly run into Bennett's back as he stalls out in the doorway, before stepping close to his side and grabbing him around the elbow. He clears his throat, staring awkwardly around the kitchen as Alessia and Adam stand straight from their relaxed postures.

Adam Reiner knows his son, loves him dearly, and it barely takes a second before he calls, "We were just heading to the living room to discuss a few things. We'll get out of your hair."

Bennett doesn't say anything but allows his dad to cup the back of his neck, sliding his hand to his shoulder in a tight, firm squeeze. Their eyes meet for a moment—a clash of deep ocean blues—before the eldest of them moves away, letting Alessia follow.

"Do you want me to help?"

He shakes his head, grabbing a towel and placing it over his shoulder while turning on the oven to heat.

"You can go sit with them while I do this," he says, gesturing vaguely around the room. He still won't really look at me.

"All right," I say, letting him have this time, the same way he's given me so much.

I don't pay much attention to whatever it is they're talking about, choosing to stand nearest the kitchen doors so that I can hear him if he calls for me, though I'm sure that he won't.

Alessia and Adam talk quietly. She hasn't told me much about her own story, just that she can relate, that there are similarities in our pasts. I can see her guard is up just slightly; she has a sharp tongue and witty retort to everything heart-on-his-sleeve Adam Reiner has to say.

I don't join them in their conversation, too distracted by the racing thoughts of concern over Bennett, standing steps away. Something feels off—Seven is in the kitchen, near Bennett, hovering like he can sense it, too.

A part of me is tempted to ask Adam about it, to see if Bennett's dad has picked up on anything or knows what I can do to make this better, easier for him.

Suddenly, there's a shattering, cacophonous sound, and a low curse followed by a loud *clang*. I take off to the kitchen without a glance back, hoping no one follows for now.

"Bennett?" I call, turning into the room.

My stomach drops.

Porcelain shards are scattered everywhere, a pan of biscuits is strewn across the floor, and Bennett is on his knees by the still-open oven, the top of his hands and arms bright red and darkening by the second.

"Oh my god," I breathe, stepping toward him and sinking to my knees by his side.

He grimaces, stretching one pinkened hand out.

"Don't—you'll cut yourself, P." His voice is scratchy and raw. I ignore him and scoot closer, trying to avoid shards where I can but more concerned with him.

Bennett Reiner has never broken a dish and never, *ever* burned food.

"Hey, those burns look like they hurt. Let's—come with me and let's get cleaned up, yeah?"

He doesn't argue with me. But when he does manage to stand, he hoists me up onto the kitchen counter to run his hands carefully over my bare legs and feet to check them. I grab his chin as he tries to check them a third time, shaking my head lightly.

"I'm okay. You already looked," I say, voice firm. "Now come with me upstairs."

Bennett nods, letting me down and following me upstairs.

Once we're in the bathroom, door closed, I turn on the shower. Bennett waits stationary, stiff by the door.

I nod for him to come closer, which he obliges silently, becoming a shadow at my back. I run cool water at the sink, testing with my fingers until it's just the right temperature, then reach for his arm and set it beneath the running water.

Slowly, methodically, I attempt to soothe his reddened skin on each arm, before wrapping them in soft hand towels with cool water. They're not bad burns—probably from grabbing for the pan without mittens and dropping it across his arms in pain.

After a long moment, I reach for the cold compresses, checking his skin. He watches me intently.

"Get undressed for me."

He follows the command easily before allowing me to direct him into the shower. I leave the door open as I undress, too, pulling my hair loose from the braid before stepping under the warm spray.

Bennett doesn't speak as I lather up soap and wash his body slowly. He doesn't speak as I pull at his neck, ducking his head so I can scrub my hands through his hair, washing his scalp, gentle and careful. His breath puffs more labored into my neck as I move my fingertips to the base of his scalp, massaging slightly.

A noise sounds low in his throat and he stumbles, catching himself with one hand on the tile wall behind me, the other wrapped tightly on the curve of my waist.

I gasp, feeling my skin heat under his attention.

"P?" he breathes, his voice a whisper cry.

"I'm here," I whisper back, curling my hands around his shoulder and pulling him to me. "I'm okay. Everything is okay, remember?"

He shakes his head but clutches me somehow closer. The soap lingering on his body rushes over my skin, slippery and wet as we slide against each other.

For a long time, we just stand there, water pulsing against us, only half of my body wet where he's been a wall against the spray.

"Can I wash your hair?" he pleads, his hand trailing to tuck against my hair. "Please, P."

I nod and he turns me toward the shower so he can gently, carefully wet my curls. It's impossible not to feel the hard length of him grow against me the more his fingers are in my hair.

"So beautiful." The whisper of his fingers over my low spine make me shiver and arch. "I—goddamn it, Paloma, I'm sorry—"

I try to turn, but he catches my chin. "What?"

"I want to fuck you." He shakes his head with a self-deprecating laugh. "Is that so fucked up? I can't stop thinking about it."

Normally, I'd point out that we are dating and naked in the shower together—that his desire for me is anything *but* "fucked up." That feeling desired by him right now is more healing for me than he could ever understand.

But the look on his face is filled with anxiety and self-hatred, so I shake my head almost violently.

"No, Bennett," I whisper, turning in his arms despite his attempts at resistance. "I want you. I want you to make me feel good."

CHAPTER 74

NOW

Bennett

Her permission rolls over me like a calm, lapping wave on a dry beach.

A groan works from my throat and I bury my fingers in Paloma's wet hair, pressing my mouth to her neck as I trip forward. My hands cup the back of her skull carefully to keep her from bashing it with the intensity of the kiss as I press her into the tile.

It's her in the water.

It's *her* here in my arms. Moving like I've watched her body move for more than three years. My fingers drag across her skin almost desperately. There is no exchange of power, no tip of my control; just her moving against me.

Bite down on my shoulder again and let me show you.

Like poetry in motion. Like water against skin—I tongue along her collarbone to taste her sharper edges, harder to find with the curve and softness of her skin.

The water is warm enough to give her skin the peachy flush that drives me wild, to the point that I feel like I'll break without being inside of her.

"Let me inside you," I beg into her ear, biting down on her shoulder.

She nods, head tipping back, one of her thighs tightening where she's almost climbed my body.

I take myself in hand—one hard tug—before slipping against her wet skin, into the warmth of her pussy. I'm tall, but my thighs are arguably my strongest attribute, so it's not hard to bend at the knee and rest her body against them, hoisting her up off the tile floor slightly.

It makes her entire body arch, fingers scoring into my skin with light scratches.

"Too much, love?" I breathe with a grin into her ear.

"I can take it," she whispers.

A soft kiss to her temple—so at odds with the roaring energy in my body. "I know you can. You always take it so good for me."

Another wild noise bursts from her lips as my hands dip to her hips, positioning her back against the wall so I can fuck with more power, more intensity.

Her hips move, swiveling, before rocking back and forth—enough that I pause fully seated inside her, allowing her to take from me what she so desperately wants. She grinds against me like I know she loves, the same way she always comes hard across my thigh muscles. Only now I can *feel* her as the spasms start—the inside of her gripping me.

The tightness of her is like a punch to the gut. She's so beautiful when she's put together. But here, beneath the water, droplets tracing paths across her skin, brown eyes with pupils blown wide framed by damp sticking lashes—she's otherworldly. Her skin is flushed all the way to her goddamn toes, fingers tight against the soft muscles of my arms, waist suspended in my hands, lips bitten as she comes long and hard just for me.

A goddess. A siren.

The fucking ocean herself personified and somehow *in my hands*.

"Let me come inside you," I breathe, because I *need* it. "Tell me I can. Tell me it's safe." Another near growl as I thrust into her harder. "If you don't want me to come inside you, P, you need to say it now."

"I want it," she begs. "Please—please—"

My vision nearly blacks out, eyes rolling back as I come. My thrusts grow slower, until I refuse to leave her entirely, pulling her to my body tighter, needing every piece of her skin to touch mine—like that will satisfy my need to keep her close.

And then—

My stomach drops. Guilt rages as I place a flushed Paloma back on her feet.

"I'm . . . did I . . . ?"

The words won't come. But I don't need them anyway.

"Everything is perfect," she says, hands cupping my face to angle it down toward hers. "That was fucking incredible."

She steps forward and something leaks from between her legs, making my cock pulse. I want to ask her to open her legs for me to see between them—to see the evidence of how deeply and thoroughly I've claimed her as mine.

My cheeks flush with embarrassment at my own thoughts. I shake my head as I lean down to kiss her everywhere.

"I love you," I whisper. "You're so perfect for me."

My praise continues as I wash her body, though she doesn't let me wash her hair again—*"That many times will ruin it"*—but I bask in the care of her just the same.

Later that night, we order food at my insistence, though I can see both Paloma and my father give me a look like I've grown three heads when I ask. I shrug it off and indulge in the Thai food Paloma chose, paying special attention when she says which dish is her favorite so I can learn to cook it for her.

We take it easy, watching movies in the family room. Alessia stays until it's late, and I hear my dad offer for her to stay another night, but she hugs Paloma and leaves after reassurance from my girlfriend.

I excuse myself to call Rhys and check on him and Sadie, though they seem more concerned about Paloma.

He lets the entire thing go when I say, "It's complicated." Maybe he understands because of his own situation with Sadie and her family that this story can't be mine to share. It will always be Paloma's.

"Your mother called again," my dad tells me in passing. "I know she's tried calling you, too. How do you want me to handle it?"

"Does she know?"

He shakes his head.

"Maybe you could tell her. I think she should know. And I . . ." My voice trails off. I don't think I can tell her everything without raging over Ethan again. I've avoided the monster in my mind that wants to hunt him down and *kill* him for what he's done. I have to trust my dad.

He nods and squeezes my shoulder. "I'll take care of it. Everything will be okay."

I repeat it like a mantra—as if it will make the swirling anxious thoughts that haven't quieted go away.

Everything will be okay.

You didn't notice three years ago. You didn't notice her pain once *in the last three years.*

Everything will be okay.

You let her down. You let her hurt. Just like Rhys. Just like your father. Just like—

Everything will be okay.

Nothing will ever be okay again. You did your routines and followed your rules and it still wasn't enough. You're the broken one who is damaging everything and everyone in his path.

Everything will—

You know what you've done. You let them down. You always let them down.

I don't remember how I got to bed or what I did for the hour before, but I fall asleep with Paloma curled into my side and Seven in the crook of her bent legs, his head resting up on her thigh.

And the thoughts never leave me.

CHAPTER 75

NOW

Paloma

Seven is whining.

Something is wrong—enough that I jolt awake and curse as I check the time on my phone just inches from my fingers.

Shit. It's nearly eight—Bennett's slept in.

And is *still* sleeping. Seven whines and paws at him as he rests on his back, twitching every now and then, skin flushed.

Things have seemed off for a month or so now, but more than usual in the last several days. At first, I'd blamed myself for disrupting his usual routines he so carefully follows.

Were it only the last two days, I'd put it all down to a mix of guilt, anger, and stress over everything. But it wasn't. I know—something is *wrong*.

I've developed a sixth sense when it comes to Bennett Reiner, over three years of desperately watching him in hidden moments and more public ones, letting the hockey team boys flirt with me if it meant I had even a second in his intoxicating presence.

"Bennett." I shake his shoulders until his eyes blink slowly awake. He stares at me like I'm some holy being, his hand reaching to cup my cheek.

"S'good dream," he mutters, eyes slowly closing as he tries to trap me to his chest.

"No, Bennett. You've gotta wake up. You overslept."

His body tenses beneath me. "What?"

"It's eight. You've got to be on the team bus in, like, an hour?"

He jolts up after that, leaving his side of the bed messy. I try to ask what I can do to help, but he ignores me and murmurs under his breath as he strips naked in the light of his walk-in closet.

He comes out in suit pants, a button-up, and a suit jacket, grabbing a belt off the hooks on his wall—a belt that's been wrapped around my wrists once or twice—and sliding it on as well.

For a moment, it's as if I'm not in the room, like he's forgotten I'm there entirely.

"Bennett?"

He startles. Seven sits on his feet as he straightens out the collar of the navy jacket.

"Are you all right?"

"Fine." He smiles, but it's strained and makes something in my stomach roll. "Can you—do you mind driving me? I have a bit of a headache."

The only time I've ever driven Bennett anywhere was when he was drunk—and that's rare in itself. I can't remember the last time I drove with him in the car. Still, I nod and he mimics the gesture, leaving the room just as abruptly.

Without his lucky sweatshirt.

I blanch, slipping on a bra beneath the long-sleeve Berkshire shirt I slept in, grabbing the sweatshirt and taking off after him. He's already in the garage, not bothering to eat or cook—everything is *off* and wrong.

Bennett waits for me by the door, rubbing at the bridge of his nose, across his eyebrows, a slight grimace on his features before he notices I'm there and straightens.

The drive is quiet. I play Bon Iver and Ben Howard, hoping his favorite music will lull him slightly. He keeps a hand on my thigh like an anchor. It's only then I realize I'm wearing boxers under the long-sleeve T-shirt and nothing else.

It's a thirty-minute drive to Waterfell, but I make it with ease. I took a few days off from school but kept up with my assignments online—a note from Alessia, a lawyer, and my therapist had forced them all to be quite gracious with me.

Bennett used his sick allowances and then skipped the classes he wasn't "allowed" to miss. I tried to get him to go, but he'd been antsy and shut down the conversation over and over, often suggesting a shower or rolling me into the sheets.

"Hey." I lean over the console and grab his jacket in my hand before he can open the door. "You sure you're okay? If something is wrong—"

"I'm fine, P," he says, lips tight with a smile. "I'll see you at the game."

He pops out of the car with that, and a weight settles in my chest. *Something about this is wrong. Think.*

Bennett pauses halfway to the bus area where most of the team is loading up their bags, turning back to me. He comes to the driver's side this time, opening the door and kissing me hard, pressing me back against the headrest until I'm almost breathless.

"Love you, P."

"Love you, Bennett."

And then he's gone again, slinging his bag. No sweatshirt to be seen.

Just before I'm going to back out, I spot Rhys Koteskiy getting out of his fancy BMW, fixing a gray beanie over his brown locks. Before I can second-guess myself, I throw the car back into park and hop out—wearing slippers, boxers, and Bennett's shirt—and run after him.

I thank my earlier self for slipping on a bra.

"Hey—Rhys," I call, not too loud, but enough to get his attention. His brow furrows as he heads for me.

"God, Paloma, aren't you freezing?"

I nod. "Yeah, I'm gonna get back in the car and go get ready, I just . . . I need you to keep an eye on Bennett. I don't think he's okay."

"What do you mean?"

"He's . . . everything is off. He overslept, didn't eat, didn't want to drive here." I huff out a breath and raise the fabric in my hand. "He didn't take his sweatshirt."

Rhys's eyes widen and he grabs it from my hands. "Got it." There's a more tense set to his shoulders as his eyes dart toward the bus like he'll take off. I start to turn away before he grabs my shoulder carefully.

"Hey, you're all right though, yeah?" he asks.

It might be strange, but there's no awkward feeling between us. No part of me feels strange around him. We've dated. Kissed. I've seen him fully naked. But . . . it just seems so unimportant and forgettable compared to my time with Bennett. And while Rhys was nothing but kind to me, I'm sure he feels the same way about our time together.

I've seen him around Sadie. It's like a thread loops between their fingers, tying them together. He worships the ground she walks on. He loves her. And she loves him.

And Rhys and I only have one shared interest now: Bennett Reiner.

Rhys's hand fiddles with the loose hairs sticking out of the back of his beanie. "I tried to call Bennett to make sure. Sadie's been worried sick—I just . . . he didn't say much. And I want to make sure you're okay."

"I'm . . . no, I'm not okay. But I will be."

He nods with a smile, as if that answer means more than if I'd brushed it off with an *I'm fine.*

"Great. Can you do me a favor and call Sadie?"

"Yes, as long as you watch out for Bennett."

"Deal." He laughs, reaching his hand out to dramatically shake mine.

CHAPTER 76

NOW

Bennett

Breathe. Breathe. Breathe.

It's not working—nothing is working. I can't get a goddamn breath into my lungs, only staccato huffs that play at breath but give me no relief.

Just one more time—

It doesn't help. The thoughts only intensify as I take off all my pads and start to resecure them—

Knee guards—left, then right.

Toe ties—over and under my skate blade until the knot is secured at the edge. Then the same exact pattern on my right foot.

Check it again. One is off and it's going to move. It's not secure.

I check again, redoing the back-and-forth under my blade until it's fastened. Again.

I secure my leg pads—left then right, readjusting the Velcro three times before my hands are willing to let it go—but I'm shaking, fingers numb as I reach for my chest pad. Sliding it over my body feels like tightening the noose around my neck.

Wrong. It's wrong. Do it again.

It's just my pads. I've done everything right. I've done this a thousand times. Relax.

Check it again.

My stomach rolls, sweat dripping from my hair. I want to grab my phone and call my dad. Or Paloma. I want Rhys to walk in and see me and *help*—

Selfish. Don't bring them down. Stay focused. Check it again.

Hands shaking, I rip off the half-hanging chest pad and toss it to the floor of the unfamiliar locker room. I try to stand, like I might go for my bag, before my skates slip under my uneven weight as I trip backward, my naked back slamming hard into the unforgiving wooden lines of the cubby.

Breathe. Stop doing this. Breathe—

I can't, I can't, I can't.

The pieces of myself I hate the most shattered
Discarded across the hard carpet, unforgiving, unreflective
I'm unbound then, all the pieces of myself spilling around me,
    papers in a book I've ripped to shreds. Memories scattered
    and I still. Can't—

Think of the water. Her voice is like silk in my ears, and I don't even think it's something she said, not a memory I can remember. But it's something. And I'll cling to it. *Think of the water. Try it.*

Nothing helps. Not even the idea of attempting to redo my pads, like securing them around me will make me into some strawman version of myself, enough to prop up in the goal and pretend. Just for a few minutes longer. Just for one more game.

The reminder of the game presses down on my shoulders, just adding weight to my fear and anxiety. I sink into a seated position. I'm back to square fucking one, the place I was seemingly always destined for—drowning quietly in the distance.

Panicked breaths saw out of me; my chest is heaving, skin flushed. It's a full-blown panic attack—and I'm not silent anymore.

There are desperate panting sob-like sounds bellowing from my mouth.

"Holy shit."

I can barely look up to see who it is, just lift my chin to see Toren Kane stepping back, fully dressed, skates and all. He pulls off his cage, tossing it down as he darts across the space to me, no hesitation, sinking to his knees.

"Fuck, Reiner, breathe," he begs. "Are you okay if I touch you?"

I can just barely manage a nod. Toren wraps his arms around my shoulders, his jersey to my naked chest, and squeezes tight. There's a strange relief to it before he pulls back and moves his hands across my arms to squeeze there, down to my hands where I've gone numb.

For a moment it's like pins and needles—but it fades into something better, warmth.

"Can you breathe with me? Like this?" He takes in an overexaggerated breath, and I match him, over and over, slowly, until my erratic too-quick huffs are back to normal. "There ya go. All good."

Someone comes in, but I don't look up to see. I can't. Not yet.

"What—"

"Shut up and come here, Koteskiy," Toren says, no bite to his voice. He squeezes my hands again. "You're his best friend. He needs you, not me."

I can't speak, throat dry. Toren lets go of my hands and steps back, letting my best friend take his place. Rhys is decked in our navy blue Waterfell classic jerseys, dark brown hair already messy from his helmet, brown eyes wide and terrified as he stares at me.

Rhys kneels in front of me, gaze meeting mine—soothing me with his steadying presence alone. The person I've had by my side since I can remember.

"Bennett?" he asks.

"Just . . . a panic . . . attack—"

Rhys's eyes widen, but he nods. "Okay. Okay." He stands, almost stumbling over his own skates to head to his bag, rummaging around.

"How'd you know?" I ask Toren, a little breathless still.

Toren shrugs, arms crossed. "I . . . um—My best friend used to have them a lot. Not like panic attacks exactly, but something similar. I've—I saw you needed help." He shrugs again, eyes darting away. "I'm gonna just—"

His thumb darts over his shoulder and he excuses himself. I wonder if he has any clue that we watch him go with different eyes, that this might be the moment he became part of our team completely, especially for Rhys. I can see it in his gaze, flickering over where the defenseman was standing.

"Here," Rhys says, handing me his phone with corded headphones already plugged in. "Music helps me. Maybe it'll help you, too."

The words seem weighted, so I put in a headphone and press play, letting the lull of music take over in my right ear.

"What's going on?" Coach Harris asks, stepping into the room. Rhys stands almost protectively beside me. "Reiner—are you hurt?"

"No—I'm . . ." I shake my head. I'm not hurt, but I'm hesitant to say *I'm fine* either. "I just had an episode. I need a second."

Harris nods, crossing his arms over his broad chest. He checks his watch before looking down the hallway toward the tunnel and gesturing. Toren reappears, Paloma and my dad both behind him.

My dad rushes to me, something like fear on his face, before I wave him off and stand.

"I'm fine. I can play—"

"Like hell you can," my dad snaps. "We're going home."

It's a strange mix of relief and anger that swirls inside me—desperate to leave the arena, to close my eyes for a moment, to rest. But also desperate *not* to let my team down. Especially Rhys.

He's worked his whole life for this. He hauled himself back from the dark without your help. And you would abandon him—

I shake my head to clear it, only to make my headache worse. Enough that I stumble to the side—just a hair.

Arms wrap around my torso: Rhys on my left. Paloma on my right, brown eyes looking up at me from beneath a messy pile of blond curls.

"Hey, P," I whisper.

She smiles, though it's minuscule. "Hey, Bennett." My hand slides up her back and into the ends of her hair, twirling it between my fingers. "You okay?"

I shake my head with a soft, sad smile of my own. Harris and my dad's voices fade into the background. Rhys is an unmoving pillar of strength at my side, his arm still around me—holding me up, like he has since I was a kid.

Paloma nods and huddles into my body tighter. "That's okay. You don't need to be okay right now." She turns her head to kiss my sweaty chest. "I love you."

I close my eyes and breathe.

CHAPTER 77

NOW

Bennett

They don't let me play.

It's a collective decision, but I'm not upset about it. Maybe I should be, considering it's the final game of my final Frozen Four as the Waterfell Wolves' goalie. But I'm more than that. My team knows that, and they can do this. Besides, Connor Mercer, my tandem, is an incredible goalie. A little more confidence and he'd be far better than me. Still, I know I can trust him. I know my *team* trusts him.

Paloma didn't offer her opinion, but I swear I could feel her relief when I succumbed to their insistence.

She did, however, insist on us riding back to Beacon Hill with my dad.

"I think you should tell him," she said as we stood outside the arena near my dad's SUV. Her hands adjusted my beanie again, fussing over me whether she realized it or not. "About how you feel. About hockey."

"Yeah, maybe."

So now I'm sprawled in the passenger's seat of my dad's black G-Wagon, headache slowly subsiding, silent as he drives. Paloma is seated in the center behind us, quiet and calm. Steady.

Adam Reiner wears every emotion on his sleeve. I don't know if he was always that way or if it developed when I was younger, to help me read him. For a long time, I felt safest with him because I *could* understand his every word and emotion. When I was little, I thought it was just a bond we shared. Now, I think maybe he made it that way.

Or, maybe, it's a bit of both.

My eyes flicker to the rearview mirror, where Paloma nods and smiles at me, her hands lifting to give me two thumbs-up in silent encouragement. She looks so relaxed and happy, a sheen of pride over her eyes as she looks at me.

She doesn't look like I just finished a meltdown and bailed on my team before our biggest game of the season—which she should be there for, too. Instead, Paloma looks at me the same way she did all those years ago, like something strong. Solid and impenetrable.

I wonder if she knows that she's the one who helped me become strong in the first place.

Still, talking to my dad like this again feels difficult, like a creaky unused door that needs to be forced open. I cough a little and clear my throat, trying to speak through the tight feeling of it. "I don't . . . I don't want to play hockey anymore."

My dad pulls into the driveway slowly, his jaw tight, cheeks wet, I realize with a start. He's crying. He puts the car in park and wipes harshly at his eyes.

No. Not just crying. Openly sobbing.

"I love you," he chokes out, turning to me over the console. His eyes are mirrors of my own, deep and fathomless blue. His hand grasps the back of my neck, pulling me in. "I love you, Bennett. More than anything on this fucking earth. You are one of the only good things in my life—the only thing I've done worth shit is being your father. And I am so goddamn proud of you. And . . ." His voice shakes. "And I'm so fucking sorry, for all of it."

I shake my head, pulling back. His hand sinks to my shoulder and squeezes, like he doesn't want to break the connection.

"You didn't—why are you apologizing?"

"Because you have never loved hockey. And I knew that."

"You did?" I ask, eyes glancing to Paloma and her gentle smile.

He laughs, but it's wet and half a cough. "I'm your dad, Ben. I pay attention to you. But you always wanted to play. And I was so fucking selfish to just . . . let you do it. Because it gave me something of you that was also mine, that was a piece of me and the dreams I had. And—" He cuts himself off and turns away, staring down at the steering wheel. "And I've been a shit father. I haven't . . . I've done something wrong or let something happen and you've grown to resent me for it, and I keep trying to figure out what it was.

"And then tonight? Seeing you panicked and hurting? And I did nothing? I'm so sorry, Bennett. I love you so much, do you know that?"

"I do," I say, because my entire system feels frozen and I can't think of anything else to say.

He nods, wiping at his eyes. "Good." Another shaky exhale leaves him. "I don't know what I did to hurt you, but if you just tell me, I'll fix it. I can't—" His voice breaks off. "I can't stand being so distant from you, Ben. You're my entire world."

My chest aches enough that I rub at it, feeling raw and open, but also exhausted from my earlier panic.

"I . . . maybe we can go inside and talk," I say, quiet and soft. "And I can make food. I'm . . . really hungry."

There's a light tilt to his lips before he nods.

. . .

Paloma and Seven are upstairs in my room. I told her to shower and handed her snacks until her arms were full, leaving her with a quick kiss on the corner of her mouth. She hummed and turned on her heel, my dog only following her after nudging at my hand to check on me.

It's nice to have her in my space again, especially in the house in Beacon Hill. It's nice to just be so openly in love with her again.

So, at peace with the knowledge that she's here, showering in *my* room, relaxing in *my* clothes, in *my* bed with *my* dog—I start cooking.

It's an uncomfortable thing, to tell your own father that you're quite sure he's been in love with his best friend's wife for years. And that watching him hurt himself that way had grown from sympathy to resentment. Every thought that makes sense in my own head feels ridiculous as I try to explain it, but my dad just listens, sitting at the bar top, never interrupting. Just nodding lightly.

I know it takes some effort. Adam Reiner wears his heart on his sleeve, so I know he's deliberate in keeping the stoic face, the calm features.

The end of my explanation coincides perfectly with plating our food—lemon Parmesan grilled chicken, roasted potatoes, and vegetables. A side of Italian pasta salad that I made earlier in the week.

I shrug, eyes darting away from his face. "I didn't mean to cut you out. But I was already struggling and seeing you with them— I don't know. It was difficult."

And then my dad laughs, head tilted back before grinning at me broadly.

"Max would kick my ass—maybe *kill* me—if he thought I wanted Anna for myself, Ben." He shakes his head. "You have to remember— we were twenty when we met, then only a few years later Max found Anna. We were inseparable. They were . . . mine. My family. And I love them. I always will. And sure, the three of us did some wild shit together back then." He laughs, eyes glazing with a memory.

"But Max and Anna are soulmates. And I love them together. If you saw me *longing* for something, it was . . . affection. Love. Adoration. I'd never . . . To be honest, for a long time I just thought it wasn't for me. That I wouldn't be good enough for it."

A stone lodges in my throat.

"But then, Helen had you—my *son*. My own person to love and care for and who would love me. And god, Bennett, I love you so much." His voice grows tight with strain. "And that was all I needed, okay?"

"It's not all you need," I say. "You can want more. I want you to be happy."

He nods. "I'm working on it." His eyes glint, the mischievous, almost goofy aspect of my dad returning through the heaviness. "I've always been Boston's most eligible bachelor anyways. Maybe it's time to *date* again."

"Yeah?" I laugh.

He nods. "If Alessia lets me get within five feet of her ever again, I'm going for it."

It's almost self-deprecating, but it's something other than tears and frustration.

"Sounds good." I nod, eyes ducking where my fingers draw words on the countertop. "And I promise, I won't . . . I'm not going to miss therapy again, okay? And maybe we could do our post-therapy dinners again . . . if you wanted to."

A layer of peace rolls over his features and he closes his eyes.

"Nothing I want more, Ben," he says. His hand reaches to squeeze my shoulder.

"Now go feed your girlfriend and watch your friends play," Adam says, ruffling my hair before ducking out of the kitchen. "I'm gonna head out."

"All right," I nod, plating the rest of the food on the third plate my dad had already laid out.

"She seems better. Paloma, I mean." He looks at me, eyes wide. "I hope she knows how much she's loved by us all."

My chest squeezes. "Yeah. I think it'll take some time, but"—I shrug with a brighter, content smile—"I'm willing to wait."

"Me too, Ben."

. . .

Paloma's eyes are wide pools of brown, brow dipped in concern where she stays comfortably seated on my bed, Seven curled up next to her, the Frozen Four game already streaming on my laptop. She's showered but redressed in *my* hockey sweater, which sends another wave of possessive thrill through me. Her blond hair is damp but unbrushed.

Smiling, I spot the paddle brush next to her.

"You don't have to—"

"Nothing I'd rather do, P," I say, walking over and pressing a kiss to her forehead. "Let me shower real quick first, okay?"

She nods and hums as she scoops a handful of cheese crackers into her mouth, before I grab the bag and replace it with her actual meal.

"Eat. I'll be right back."

"Yes, sir," she says. It's mocking, but I can't help the easy effect it has on me, heat reddening my face and the back of my neck. I shake myself out of it and head in to shower and redress quickly so that I can spend my time brushing Paloma Blake's hair.

"Are you okay?" she asks as I comb gently through the strands. They are drier now, the snarls and tangles a little tougher, but I take my time.

"I'm okay, P," I say, "Did I freak you out?"

She huffs a breath and rolls her eyes, leaning back into my chest. I put the brush down in favor of holding her closer, my hand massaging the peachy skin of her bare thigh.

"God, no. You just worried me. And I didn't—" Her throat works with a hard swallow. "I want to be there for you. I was worried I did a bad job." A puff of laughter, and then, "I'm still working on it."

I kiss her, just because I can. "You've been more constant than you know, love. Thank you for being there tonight, supporting me with my dad. You're the only one who knew how I felt about everything, who understood me from the first day we met and never asked me to change. Never wanted me to." I kiss her again, along her soft cheek, turning her just slightly in my arms so I can see the devotion in her warm brown eyes that mimics mine.

She's perfect. So strong and beautiful and smart. And I will happily spend the rest of my life making sure every single day that she knows she's loved and worth it all.

I don't ever want to return to a time when she wasn't like this, soft in my arms, but I'd go through all the pain again if this was the outcome.

"You know that's how I feel about you, right?" she says, her brow furrowing slightly as she peeks up at me. "You loved me through everything. Even when I was away or hurting or—anything, I never felt alone because I knew I had you, even if I didn't allow myself to have you."

My chest aches, but I nod. She raises her hand over my heart, as if she *knows* where it's most painful for me.

"Rhys and his panic attacks, your mother's difficulty with accepting you, your dad being lonely? None of that is on your shoulders, you know?"

"I know." I don't, but I'm trying to remind myself.

"What Ethan did to me isn't something you could have stopped. Now or before you knew me." She smiles despite her words. "Though I know that big brain and big heart in your big body have tried to come up with endless reasons you could have—somehow."

I shake my head at her, but it's true. The thought spirals have been extraordinarily brutal since finding out what Ethan did to her. What I allowed to—

"If you blame yourself," she says quieter now, "then I have no choice but to blame myself. Because I didn't tell you."

"No, P—"

Her harsh look shuts me up and I nod.

"You can't skip out on therapy anymore, Bennett." Paloma reaches up and holds my jaw in her hand, thumb dusting across the stubble of my beard. "Your beautiful big brain and heart are too important. You have to take care of them."

I cover her hand with my own, rubbing gently over her skin. "All right, P. I will."

"I love you," she breathes, and it's like she's pressing the words into the muscle of my heart.

"Let me touch your hair," I whisper, reciting the poem I wrote for her months ago as I tangle my hand into her hair. "Wrap it around my fingers, tightening the farther from my grasp you wander. Let me inside you."

Paloma lets me push her into the mattress, rolling easily beneath me, the game half-forgotten on the laptop as I push it away from us. I feel more than see Seven get up at the movement, opting for his real bed in the corner of my room here.

I kiss her mouth, her hair, her neck, leaning in to her ear once more.

"Let me sew my soul to yours like some great patchwork quilt across a sandless beach," I whisper, tugging at the shoulder of my hockey sweater, sinking my mouth into her shoulder. "Just you and me. And the water between us."

CHAPTER 78

NOW: Two Months Later

Bennett

The shouts are deafening. Paloma whistles loudly enough from the second row that I blush and shake my head at her.

Her eyes gleam—but she's not the only one cheering, backed up by a chorus of my team and my family: Rhys and Sadie, Freddy and Ro, Holden and even Toren Kane, alongside Coach Harris, like they came together. On Paloma's right is Lily, while on her other side are Alessia and Adam, the former cheering at a more respectful volume while my dad shouts, hands cupped.

The only other people in the scarcely populated auditorium either look annoyed or are laughing with genuine surprise at the display. It makes sense. They're treating a poetry reading like it's the Stanley Cup finals.

They're patient and slightly less enthused through the rest of the programming—but I'm thankful I went last in the reading, so my personal band of cheerleaders couldn't dull the shine of my few classmates also reading.

Dr. Britton steps forward, smirking and shaking his head at me, before turning to give his closing remarks.

Everyone disperses. I step toward the front of the stage, maneuvering to sit on the lip while my family and friends all move forward to congratulate me. Rhys and Sadie arrive first, with Freddy next to them, arm locked around Ro.

"It was very beautiful," Ro says, smiling sweetly. "You read it very well."

Freddy groans. "He's taller than both of us, cooks, and now he writes poetry?" His head tilts to Rhys's shoulder. "He must be stopped."

My best friend just smiles almost blindingly as he smacks his hand on my knee. "It was awesome, Ben. Seriously."

"Your dad was crying," Sadie mutters, smirking as she points with her chin to where my dad is drying his eyes and stepping forward to our circle. Behind him is Paloma Blake with a simple bouquet of white roses, peonies, and eucalyptus wrapped in newspaper.

She's beautiful in a cream linen dress and denim jacket, with multicolored embroidery along the pockets. All of it is thrifted, I know, because Paloma had been too excited about the find. She'd taken her roommate on her first thrifting journey, but Lily was *not* a fan of wearing "other people's clothes."

"Pretty words," she says, stepping up in-between my legs, heeled brown boots clacking on the linoleum. I slide off the edge of the stage to stand in front of her, grabbing her in a tight hug, pressing a kiss to her cheek.

"Pretty hair," I say, tangling my hand into the strands. "Are these for me?"

Paloma nods, pulling back and handing me the flowers. "For your first performance."

"It's a reading."

She shrugs, a glint in her chocolate eyes. "It went perfect, you know? I'm . . . really proud of you."

Like champagne bubbling through me, I grow brighter. "Yeah?"

"Yeah."

I tuck her back to my chest, an arm around her to keep her

body close. Our friends laugh and make plans. My dad squeezes my shoulder and nods; there are still tears in his eyes, but his smile is almost blinding.

"It was for you," I whisper, leaning down to Paloma's ear. "It always is."

Her body relaxes further in my grip. "I know."

• • •

"If I had made a wager on who would be crying today, I would *not* have said Sadie Brown," my dad mutters to me, stepping beside me with a short stack of boxes in his grip.

I stop my own movements to look, seeing Sadie, arms crossed, eyes squeezed closed as she almost hides next to my car. Like she's desperately trying to keep it together before she sees Rhys.

"Hey," I say, stepping up beside her.

"I know," she snaps, but it's half-hearted. "New York is only like four hours away and I can take the train. And it's not that bad, I can visit whenever—"

I raise my hands, trying to quiet her growing volume.

"I wasn't going to say anything like that."

She looks at me then, cat-like eyes of gray reddened and sad. "I don't want him to see that I'm upset—"

"You don't have to have it together, you know, to be with him. To deserve him." I run a hand through my hair. "You know that, right? Rhys was a mess when you found each other, and you fell in love with him anyway."

Sadie chews on her lip, eyes darting toward the door where Rhys and Max both stand. My best friend locks his eyes on Sadie immediately, like a magnet, brow furrowing as he reads the distress she's so desperately trying to hide.

"Besides," I drop my voice as he heads across the lawn toward us.

"I think crying because you're going to miss your boyfriend is very normal behavior."

"Hey. Everyone okay?"

Rhys eyes us both and I smile and step away, but not before giving him a quick nod—because I *am* okay.

Freddy steps up beside me as I head back into the house, flicking the brim of my backward hat playfully.

"So, I spoke to Paloma again," Freddy says, nodding lightly at me. He mostly avoids my eyes, tapping his foot a little intensely. "I just wanted you to know. It was . . . good. Nice, to talk about it, I guess."

He didn't share the details, and neither did Paloma, but he'd asked to speak with her the other morning after family breakfast. The way Ro explained it to me, in her soft, gentle voice, Freddy and Paloma had something in common with their pasts. Something that might allow them to find comfort in each other, at least somewhat. I'd hugged Freddy when they returned to the table, which was something we'd never really done before.

"I'm glad you both have each other," I say. He grins, all genuine and warm. He squeezes my shoulder and asks the same question Rhys asked mere moments ago.

"You good, Reiny?"

"Yeah." I nod. "I'm good."

My therapist and I spend a lot of time talking about my thought spirals—though they still plague me at times, they have become more manageable. I have a pathway or steps I can take to calm myself, which gives me the feeling of preparedness.

Last session, however, we'd discussed the upcoming changes: my friends all graduating and moving on, while I stayed at Waterfell for an extra semester to finish after changing my major.

But with Rhys and Freddy both leaving—one to play for the Rangers and one for Dallas—I decided to move out, too, to stay with my dad for the time being. Beacon Hill is a half hour from campus with *no* traffic, but I don't mind dealing with it for the couple of months I have left.

And then . . . who knows what's next? The thought would have filled me with pure anxiety four years ago. Now, I see my future and it's bright; I just haven't figured out the specifics. And that, I'm learning, is okay.

No one has to know who they are and what they want from life at twenty-one. It's *normal* that I don't.

CHAPTER 79

NOW

Paloma

"We can take it slowly, and if you want to stop, we will. You're in control, Paloma."

Dr. Sutton's voice is calm and smooth. If she'd asked me this months ago, I think I might have snapped. Or never attended another session.

But I feel different now. Not better necessarily, when it comes to this topic. But at least stronger. Something about fighting back that day instilled a new mantra in my head: *He can't hurt me. And I can hurt him.*

It might not be healthy, but it's working for now.

In the past five months of therapy, we've talked circles around my mother, my trauma, and Ethan, but never specifics. And this time, I want to go through it all. Unpack it. Learn something and feel better about it—if that's possible.

Maybe the timing is everything. Ethan's trial won't be for several months, but to see the line of young girls and women that have agreed to stand beside me and give their testimony has given me something I didn't expect: Hope. The sense of not being alone.

For a long time, I blamed my younger self for being foolish and idealistic. For getting herself into that entire mess. For degrading herself and stooping so low, as if that would earn some kind of affection.

I blamed myself for believing I'd asked for something I *knew* I never did.

It's a process, to come to terms with it all. To love and care for myself again. But I'm working on it.

"Are you ready?" Dr. Sutton asks.

I nod.

• • •

Bennett is sitting in the car, idling on the street outside when I finish. There's an overly sugary coffee in the cupholder, a pillow in my seat, and Seven in the back—the same way he always prepares to pick me up from therapy.

Sometimes Alessia does it and we do a hair and nail day afterward, if I'm not exhausted. But on the days where it feels heaviest, I like when Bennett is there.

My warm comfort. My steady shore.

"Hey, P," he says, leaning over the console to kiss me. His hand pets along my hairline, tucking strands behind my ear as he examines my face closer. "All right?"

Seven sets his snout on my shoulder, nudging my cheek, and I give him a kiss.

I smile. "I'm good. Today was good." I reach for my coffee and take a long, soothing sip. Hot even on a warm spring day. "I think I want to go swimming today, actually."

Bennett's ocean-blue eyes glimmer. "Yeah? I'll drop Seven off and we can go."

He slips his sunglasses back on and maneuvers us onto the road, turning up the music and rolling down the windows so I can bask in the sun a bit more.

Bennett swims with me now, though I could lap him easily with my speed compared to his bulk. He finds it therapeutic in some ways, too. But he enjoys swimming in the ocean more.

Instead of our usual lap pool, we go to the outdoor area. It's moderately filled with other students enjoying the last few days before graduation, suntanning and splashing one another. Bennett and I sink into the water at the deep end, his feet easily touching while I swim circles around him, caressing him freely, splashing him every now and then until his curls are damp and tamed.

"Are you excited for tonight?" he asks, catching me around the waist to hold me up.

Tonight is the Sleepover—hosted by Ro Shariff and entirely her idea. She invited Sadie, me, and Lily to the half-cleared-out Hockey House while the guys spend the evening playing video games with Oliver and Liam at the Koteskiys'.

I nod. "It's Lily's first every slumber party. Mine too."

"I know." Bennett nods, curling a finger in my wet lock of hair. "It's going to be amazing. Just—don't do anything insane."

My lips quirk. "But I already ordered a male stripper."

He dunks me under the water, hoisting me back up as I sputter and laugh, shaking my hair out like a dog against him. "Ha, ha—very funny." He leans down and kisses me on the mouth, stealing my breath and any other jokes I planned to make.

"Can I wash your hair? Before you go?"

Cheeks flushed, I readily agree, before climbing out of the pool and tugging him behind me. I'm always borderline desperate in my want of him—especially now, skin dripping, hair wet, eyes sparkling in the sun.

The thing between us, the string that's tied us together, pulls tight. Years of pain, heartache, and frustration—I wouldn't do it that way again. But if it meant this at the end—him, happy and smiling and relaxed—then maybe it was worth it.

Bennett bites my shoulder playfully as he passes me, but the words he often whispers beneath the sheets as we grasp each other linger in the air as if he said them aloud.

Bite down on my shoulder again and let me show you.

A poet in his own right, and he treats my one attempt at writing like a gospel. *It's my favorite*, he says before reciting my own words that I barely remember back to me.

Slip me into your brain, I think, looking at him as we walk back to the car. *Keep me forever.*

EPILOGUE

TEN YEARS LATER

Paloma

"Nice shot, Gabby!"

Gabrielle Huston smiles, front teeth missing as she trips forward on her skates toward me. She's seven and the best one on the team, popular with the other girls and always smiling.

"Thanks, Coach P."

I tap her helmet as she zooms over to the bench for water.

Coach P. I grin, still a little overwhelmed by exactly how much I love my job coaching the local girls club hockey team. I started it myself, with the help of Adam Reiner and the First Line Foundation—Max Koteskiy's skating charity. I've been the head coach for two years now, after training under one appointed to start the team.

I love these girls. I love this game.

I'm *happy.*

"Huddle up," I call, before handing my clipboard to one of my teenage assistant coaches, letting her take the lead today since I'm no longer allowed to skate—doctor's orders. And if she hadn't ordered it, I'm sure my beautiful, intense husband, currently seated on the steel bleachers, would have.

Bennett doesn't like to be far away from me, pregnant or not. However, now he's got an assistant worrier.

Annie, two perfect braids down her back beneath a beanie, sits in the stands right next to her dad. She'd been nervous about me leaving today—mostly due to how much time we spend together regularly—but sticking close to Bennett seems to have relaxed her somewhat.

She's always been like that with her dad—finding him the soothing presence he's always been for me.

"Hey," a deep, low voice speaks. "Shhh, you're okay."

Hiding around the corner, I peek carefully into the living room, still half asleep. A baby cries, but the previous wailing fades off into little chuffs and sniffles as she settles against the mass of her father's warm chest.

Because she knows she's safe in Bennett's arms. Just like I've always been.

He recites Mary Oliver's "The Summer Day" quietly, voice low as she slowly falls back asleep. He's read the same poem to her since before she left my belly.

This is their morning routine—though it's the middle of the night now, unusual because Annie is good at sleeping through the night.

My sleepy girl. I'm usually always awake before her.

In the mornings, Bennett wakes up first. He makes the coffee and then leaves a poem for me on the fridge with our word magnets.

Sometimes it's romantic and beautiful. Sometimes it's witty and clever.

Sometimes I write one back.

He wants me to read it when I'm alone, always blushing as he walks into the kitchen to see me standing in front of the fridge and gazing at his words. I like to be awake to see him leave for his job as a professor of poetry and literature. Mostly because he's dressed near to pornographic—brown pressed trousers, collared shirt, and tweed jacket.

One day, he'd worn a sweater vest over his button-down and I'd tackled him in the kitchen, making him take me as the sun rose over the oak wood table, his hands in my hair. It might have been the day he got me pregnant, but who knows.

At night, he's always softer. We shower together—so often that he's had a bigger one made during the remodel. But now when he washes my hair, I can feel his wedding band snag on my curls. Because he refuses to take it off.

Every tug from it is a comfort.

"Hey, P," he breathes, quiet as I settle onto the couch next to him. I tuck in close, temple pressed to his shoulder as I look down at our daughter.

"She's really perfect, huh?"

Bennett nods with a glimmering smile. "She looks just like you."

He's said it before; a phrase that haunted me as a kid into adulthood now feels warm and soothing. I'd talked with my therapist about it the first time he innocently muttered it and I'd locked myself in the bathroom to cry.

Now, I let it fill me with pride to chase away any lingering fears.

But I do worry. About being a good mom. We hadn't intended to get pregnant. I wasn't sure I wanted children. So it had been a decision I needed to make faster than I planned. Bennett had supported me no matter my choice.

Now, with the moonlight streaming in through the massive floor-to-ceiling windows of Speyside, the sound of the water outside, I couldn't be more grateful for the life I've managed to achieve. The family that I have.

It's the same now as I rest my hand on my low stomach where I've just started to show. Deep gratefulness for this family we've created. I'm on the bench—not even in skates. Still, my two little worriers watch over me.

Something warm that lives permanently in my chest with the two of them around me flares brightly, illuminated by their care.

A life and love I've fought for.

I graduated with flying colors. I testified against Ethan and helped to lengthen his sentence by appearing to read my victim impact statement alongside the other girls he'd hurt.

And then I continued to take the power of my life back.

I'd gotten offers for four different internships, but stayed relatively local for my first year so I could spend time in the Reiner house with Bennett and Adam.

And Alessia, who I'd seen next to Adam more often than not.

She'd blushed when I first asked her about it, but I knew she had her own issues, things that made her the way that she was. I also knew Adam was one of the most patient men in existence, second only to his son.

They'd been on their own timeline. But she's living with him now, slowly healing each day.

I'd worked for two ECHL teams as the first woman assistant coach for both, before I started working for all women's hockey teams. Then youth—where I really felt passionate.

And now, in our small, cold coastal town, I've found my place.

I let my assistant coach know I'm headed out for the day, calling toward the girls to rest up for their games this weekend before heading through the tunnel exit where I know my husband and daughter will meet me.

Annie runs right for me, grasping me in her little arms, while Bennett stands behind her in a beautiful blue peacoat and fancy slacks, a pleased smile across his bearded face. He gets more handsome with every year together.

"Ready to go home, loves?"

I grin and so does Annie. And for a moment, I can see it touch the light in Bennett's eyes, our faces side by side. My little mini-me I love more than life itself.

"Ready," we say in unison, stepping closer so he can cover us both in his arms.

Every breath. Every moment. He's been here through every moment. And he'll never leave me.

The shore to my rolling, calmed tide.

Bennett

"Daddy?"

I'm working a little later than usual tonight—which means I didn't get to shower with or bathe my wife, which means my mood is irritated at best. But the sound of our daughter's little voice is enough to make my frustrations completely disappear.

My face breaks into a gentle smile and I turn, spotting Annie with a messy blond braid that tells me she just woke up. She sleeps like her mom—rough, tossing around, but deep. In her hands, I spot a familiar stuffed rabbit.

Seven slowly trails behind her, the gray around his ears and muzzle growing by the day. Just like me, my loyal dog always sticks close to my girls.

"Hey, seashell," I say, opening my arms for her to come to me. She climbs up onto my lap. I reach around her and scratch Seven's ears as he sits by my thigh. "Did you have a nightmare?"

"No." She rubs her eyes again. "Mommy's sick again."

My stomach hollows a little and I have to clamp down on the anxiety.

Paloma being pregnant is . . . a lot for me. Mostly because it plays with every single one of my emotions—joy, at having another child with her. But also fear at knowing exactly how many things can go wrong. Her pregnancy with Annie was smooth sailing, but she was pregnant at the same time as Sadie, who had one of the hardest pregnancies I've seen.

I was worried Rhys would chain himself to her arm and quit hockey after that. Or never have sex with her for fear of ever getting her pregnant again. I'd reminded him that a vasectomy was much easier.

"Okay, seashell. Why don't I get you back in bed and I'll take care of Mommy." I stand, hoisting her easily into one arm. "Did you two fall asleep in Mommy and Daddy's room?"

She nods and yawns again. "We made a fort."

I grin, shaking my head as I carry my daughter to her bright-pink princess room, tucking her in—though she's already half-asleep, eyes closed. After shutting the door carefully, I head to the master bedroom, nearly tripping over the remnants of said "fort."

Paloma Blake is an incredible mother. And a far better parent that I am, though she'll never admit it.

She'd been terrified when we decided to have Annie. We'd fought endlessly, angry and tired and constantly frustrated. Her, because motherhood terrified her, convinced she'd somehow ruin our baby, even with her want of a child. For me, the frustration was that she couldn't see herself properly. But healing is never linear. And that's okay.

My love for her will never falter, never cage—it can only grow.

I'd started attending therapy sessions with Paloma so I could figure out how to help her through her fear of motherhood.

Mostly, we'd worked through it. But even now, Paloma doesn't understand the way Annie looks at her with stars in her eyes. Ask my daughter her favorite person, princess, or magical creature—"My mom" will be her answer for them all.

Seven stands in front of the bathroom, pacing anxiously, moving quicker than he usually does these days. He whines a bit and pushes his nose against the door.

"I know, bud," I whisper, petting his head.

"P?" I call, knocking lightly on the door before letting myself into our large bathroom. She's sitting by the toilet, back against the wall, face damp as she looks up at me.

"Hey."

"Damn it, love," I mutter, running a cloth under the water with shaking hands. I bring the cool damp towel to her, resting it beneath the tangled mess of her hair. "I told you to call me if you felt sick."

"It came on real fast," she mutters. "Do you think Speyside is too isolated?"

I step over to the shower, turning it to a bearable warmth for her. "What?"

"Speyside? Do you think it's too isolated for Annie and Benjamin?"

I shake my head, cheeks coloring as she calls our baby that *again*. "*We'll call him Ben, after you*," she'd told me weeks ago, when we first discovered we were pregnant again—we'd been trying this time.

"I told you, we don't even know if it's a boy."

"I can feel it," she mumbles, letting me pull her to standing and slowly undress her. "But that wasn't my question."

"What do you mean isolated?"

"For Annie and Ben to grow up here?"

My brow furrows. "Sadie and Rhys bought the house next door." Though it's miles away because of the secluded nature of the area. "They'll be here for the summers and offseason."

Paloma nods but puts her hands on my biceps before I can usher her into the shower. "I know but . . ." She trails off and pauses.

"What is it, love?" I ask, cupping her face in my palms. "Tell me what's really going on."

"I don't want Annie to feel alone. I don't want them to not have friends."

Stomach caving, I pull her naked body fully into mine, kissing her temple, her hair, anything I can touch. *My beautiful wife. My soulmate.*

"Never, P. I promise. Besides, Annie starts school soon, yeah? So we can figure it out. If it's too small here, we can always move, right?"

"And we'll always keep the beach house?"

This house is where I fell in love with Paloma Blake fully—over and over. It was her safe haven, and mine. We spent birthdays here. I lost my virginity to the girl I love here. Pieces of our souls are scattered across every inch of this house.

"You were meant to be near the water," I breathe, pressing a kiss to her neck as I dip my head down. "We'll always have this place."

And we'll always have each other.

"Take me wave by wave," I whisper, watching as she steps into the water, like the ocean coming alive. "Curl your currents into my body. Love me, love me, love me."

I always knew it would be this way.

The love of my goddamn life.

The constant shore to her tumbling, lovely, alive and vibrant sea.

ACKNOWLEDGMENTS

First and foremost, this one is for Sissy. Isabella, my one and only sister, I can still feel the same joy I felt at three years old getting to meet you for the first time. Watching you grow up feels like watching the brightest sunrise. You are, to me, so much stronger than you even know. Never doubt that.

To Austin, my dearest love—thank you for holding me up through this one. It was emotionally draining, and like my own constant shore, you never waver. To my mom and family, thank you all for being my number one supporters.

Caitlin—I would literally not do this without you. I am endlessly grateful for you, my warrior princess, my champion, and a true friend. Here's to years more of French food, fun drinks, and talking about books. You make me a better writer.

To my entire team at Atria & Hodder—thank you! Melanie, Elizabeth, Holly, Dayna, Lucy—you all make my entire world go round! Suzy, my UK queen, thank you for keeping me sane through it all and taking care of me always.

To Bal, my dearest friend—you have been by my side this entire journey. I love holding hands with you and watching you shine. Your gift for phrasing and craftsmanship in romance makes me a better author every day. PS—let's go shopping.

To Jo—you know these characters as well as, if not better than, I do. Thankful for your friendship, talking me out of a corner, and listening to me crash out over Bennett Reiner a million times. My world would not spin properly without you at my side.

To Sam—Adam Reiner is for you. Officially.

To Monica—thank you for your work on every book, but especially this one. You handle these characters with such care. I'm so grateful.

To say this book is important to me would be an understatement. Paloma Blake and Bennett Reiner have been on my mind since book one. *Unsteady* came to me quickly, written in three months flat; *Unloved* was the story I knew the least about going in, and writing it was a roller coaster (which I'm so grateful for); but *Unbound* was a different beast.

I knew this story the moment I wrote the cafeteria scene in *Unsteady*—where Bennett gets irritated with Paloma's false demeanor and clear mask but then leaves behind a colorful yogurt for her to eat. It was the base of their connection for me, and it only built from there.

I'm so grateful to every person who shared their own personal experiences with me and helped me with making sure these characters came to life properly on the page. And thank you to you, the readers, who continue to go on each of these journeys with me. I am forever, eternally grateful for each and every one of you.

I've made a habit of thanking myself each book, and—wow, I'm not sure why I'm crying typing this, but this one is for me, too. The pieces of myself carefully tucked into these pages, the words I pulled from my brain and put to paper. This one hits different.

Lastly, to my dad, the poet. As a "poetry hater" in my teen years, I apologize. I get it now. I hope you're proud of me.